THE
WIND
WEAVER

THE
WIND
WEAVER

JULIE JOHNSON

Ace
New York

ACE
Published by Berkley
An imprint of Penguin Random House LLC
penguinrandomhouse.com

Copyright © 2025 by Julie Johnson
Penguin Random House supports copyright. Copyright fuels creativity, encourages
diverse voices, promotes free speech, and creates a vibrant culture. Thank you for buying an
authorized edition of this book and for complying with copyright laws by not reproducing,
scanning, or distributing any part of it in any form without permission. You are supporting
writers and allowing Penguin Random House to continue to publish books for every reader.

ACE is a registered trademark and the A colophon is a trademark of
Penguin Random House LLC.

<<TEXT AND PHOTO CREDITS>>

ISBN: 9780593817865

An application to register this book for cataloging has been submitted to the
Library of Congress.

First Edition: April 2025

Printed in the United States of America
$PrintCode

Book design by [INFORMATION TO COME IN 1ST PASS]

To Stevie Nicks, for writing the song "Rhiannon."
Without its inspiration, Rhya Fleetwood—this
book's main character—would not exist.

THE WIND WEAVER

<~?~[MAP TK]>

PROLOGUE

THE CULL
ANWYVNIAN SONG OF THE UPRISING

The age of mortal men began
When iron armies
March'd north

A reign of faery turned to ash
With maegic blood
Spill'd forth

Hark!

An end to wicked trickery
Corroding the land
Of kings

A farewell to the evil wind
Whispering through
The trees

Hark!

The rule of sword and fist
Man's power
Undisputed

The hunt for halflings now begins
Foul bloodlines
Executed

CHAPTER
ONE

The noose chafes, a necklace of death.

I feel my pulse—steady, staccato—thudding away beneath the fragile skin at my throat. There's no fear. Not anymore. That came earlier, with the bruising hands and snarling hounds that tracked me through the wild marshland. And it fled with the sun, slipping over the horizon into crushing darkness.

What is it Eli always said?

Fear only means you have something left to lose.

I have nothing left now. Nothing but my life, and that isn't worth much of anything to anyone.

Certainly not my captors.

"Wily little bitch, isn't she?" A gruff voice barks out a laugh somewhere to my left. "Took half our unit to track her down. A dozen men. Three days we spent in that damned bog with wasps and snakes and spiders. Knee-deep in mud and moss and all manner of shit. She nearly slipped our net when we lost the light yesterday." A gob of spit lands on my cheek. "*Faery scum.*"

Another voice answers—this one younger, and slightly wavering. A new recruit, perhaps, not yet worn-out by this endless, bloody game of war the mortal men seem intent on playing. "She's just—she's so young."

"Don't let your eyes fool you, boy. Faery trickery, that is. They mask their true nature with pretty faces and sweet smiles, same as a poisonous flower. In the olden days, they say some of them cast such a glamour, could make you see anything they wanted. March you straight off a cliff, thinking you were skipping through a field of daisies."

The younger soldier sucks in an audible breath. His terror is palpable even through my blindfold.

"Don't worry, son. Maegic like that hasn't been seen in these parts in nigh on two centuries." The gruff voice chuckles. "The ones we hunt down, like this runt here, are halflings mostly. Leftovers from before the Cull, back when bloodline mixing wasn't outlawed. They're no more enchanted than you or me."

There's a marked pause. A cave of silence yawning wide between the two men.

"'Course, that don't make 'em helpless," the older soldier tacks on, almost defensively. "She'd gut us in our sleep given half the chance. Never doubt that."

"How did you finally catch her?"

"Ran her to ground by the Red Chasm. The ore in those rocks is enough to confuse 'em. Clouds their sense of direction, muddies their minds." He exhales a sharp breath. "No foe is invincible—not even a damned *point*."

I tense at the slur, binds going tight across my chest despite my attempts to keep still. *Point*. The soldiers who've taken me prisoner use the insult often, hissing it at me under their breath when they change watches, tossing it around in casual campfire conversation. As if reducing an entire race to our most notable physical trait—the pointed tip of an ear—somehow makes their barbarity easier to stomach. Every time I hear it, something within me snarls in silent rage. A broken beast, itching for retribution that will never be mine.

Gods above, grant me vengeance in my next life.

"Ain't so hard to kill 'em, actually. Just a matter of finding the right weapon," the older soldier boasts, brimming with sage wisdom. "Iron's best, of course. But, gods' truth, stick 'em with anything sharp and the job's done. Points bleed, same as any other beast in the forest. Didn't your pa take you hunting, son? Haven't you ever gutted a doe?"

"No . . . I . . . We . . ." The young solider shifts from foot to foot, boots crunching dead leaves. "We're crofters, sir."

"Crofters?"

"Yes, sir. We tithe a tract by the coast. Iceberries, mostly."

The older soldier scoffs. "Well, you'll need ice in your berries for this deployment, I'll tell you that. Cold as all fuck, this close to the Cimmerians."

Behind my blindfold, I imagine the scene. An encampment of soldiers, weather-beaten from weeks on the road. A crackling fire to ward off the chill—and the wolves. A simple dinner cooking over the coals.

The smell of meat carries to me on the wind, and my stomach rumbles a contemptuous response. Hare, most likely, or a steer. Maybe a wild boar, if one of them is skilled enough with a bow. For surely there are hunters among their number. Men capable of tracking down some prey besides me and my kind. Though if we were edible, they might eat us, too.

It's been an unforgiving winter.

I wonder to which kingdom they belong, to which of the warring kings they've pledged their fealty. Perhaps the very one who sent his armies into Seahaven and set the Starlight Wood aflame—and the only home I've ever known along with it.

A hand tugs at the shackles around my raw wrists. I hear the hiss an instant before the pain bolts through me. The smell of charred skin hits my nostrils.

My own flesh, burning.

It takes all my self-possession not to cry out—but I will not give these soldiers the satisfaction. Breathing deeply, I press my spine harder against the bark of the tree to which I'm lashed, trying not to lose consciousness.

Gods above, it hurts.

"See how she blisters?" the older soldier asks. "You'd think I'd taken a blazing log to her!"

"Y-yes," the youth stammers. "I see."

The irons stir a ceaseless tide of agony that never recedes—even now, after my wrists are scorched nearly to bone and sinew. Each shift of my chains sets off a fresh flow of anguish.

"When . . ." The young recruit clears his throat. "When will they . . ."

"String her up? Won't be long now. Commander Scythe will be here by midnight. Captain says we can't touch her till he signs off."

"Why?"

"Likes to be sure they're really dead, I suppose. Kick around the ashes a bit, make certain nothing stirs. Seems overboard to me, but it's on order of King Eld, so I do as I'm told. Hang 'em up, burn 'em down." There's the sound of a cork being unstoppered. A throat working to swallow the contents of a flask. A steadying breath. "Folks tend to get a touch superstitious when it comes to faery executions. You'll see, lad."

"Right . . ." The young man sounds unconvinced. "When I enlisted, I didn't think we'd be hunting halflings. I didn't know there were any left."

"Not many, these days. 'Specially this far up in the Midlands. The Southlanders have some . . . different practices. You should thank the skies you aren't stationed at the border to the

Reaches. Hard to stomach, from what I've heard. And I ain't heard much."

My heart lurches. I've not been spared the rumors of what happens to halflings in the Southlands. Not in full. Eli gave me the briefest of glimpses at that darkness one night over a stiff dram of whiskey.

They might not kill you right away, Rhya, but the things they'll do to you will make you wish they had . . .

I force my thoughts from that dark path. It leads nowhere good.

"Son, just keep your head down, your hands steady, and your questions to yourself. You'll be fine. It's a job like any other—no matter what the rabble around here tells you." The older man's voice drops lower. "Swear, some men's breeches get stiff watching faeries squirm on the end of a rope. Different sort of bloodlust, you understand?"

"That's foul!"

"Aye. Don't make it any less true." He takes another deep pull from his flask. "Long while back, when I was no more than a young buck like you, points were a bit more common in these parts. My unit stumbled across a whole family one day, hidden away in the caves beneath a waterfall. Greenish skin and hair like river grass . . ."

Greenish skin?

Hair like river grass?

Wherever do they think up these ridiculous stories? From children's bedtime tales? Besides our ears, halflings are nearly indistinguishable from humankind. But then . . . I suppose it's easier to justify killing a mythological monster than a living being. Some*thing*, not someone.

The soldier's voice drops almost to a whisper. "We'd lost so many in the Avian Strait. Bloodiest battle in a hundred years.

And Soren's men just kept coming. Driving us back, over and over and over. Morale was low. Our army—we needed a win. So when those faeries fell into our path . . ."

A chill of foreboding sweeps through me despite the burning agony at my wrists. I close my eyes behind the blindfold, wishing I could shut my ears as easily. I don't want to hear about the slaughter of an innocent family. I can't bear the details of a mother, a father, and their children torn apart by battle-addled soldiers. Not with my own imminent death pressing so hard against my windpipe.

A boot scuffs against the earth, and the man coughs. "Safe to say, the things I saw that day . . . well, it's the kind of scene you don't forget. Even after ten years."

There's another beat of quiet. The younger man says nothing, perhaps shocked silent by the gruesome picture his companion has painted. I'm not foolish enough to think his reticence is born of sympathy for me. More likely, he's merely doing as he's been tasked—keeping his opinions to himself.

He'll make a good soldier.

The quiet is broken by the thud of a hand slapping against a shoulder. "You're pale as a ghost, son. Go get yourself a bit of venison before it's all gone. And bring me back some, will you? I'll keep watch over the prisoner."

There's the sound of retreating footsteps, then the sigh of a body settling against a tree. In the distance, the murmur of conversation—other soldiers, wolfing down their dinner around the fire. After a moment, I pick out the faint flick of a knife against a block of wood. I allow myself to wonder what my remaining guard is carving.

A sigil for whichever god he worships? A token for the wife left behind in the land he calls home? A toy for his small daughter to play with when he finally returns from conquest?

Ten years, he said. Ten years of battles. Ten years of soldiering. Ten years of bleeding and fighting and killing.

Surely there is a life outside all this. Surely this man has a family waiting for him somewhere. Will he tell them of the faery girl he slaughtered to keep them safe? Regale them with details of the monster's mottled face and sagging tongue as she swung from the boughs, a grotesque mask illuminated by torchlight?

The gallant hero who slew the beast.

Huzzah!

After the way he spoke to his young companion, I think not. He'll take no joy in his task—but he will complete it all the same, carrying out his captain's orders without question.

The branches creak overhead, a death knell.

I'm glad they plan to kill me at night, under the stars. It would somehow be worse to die with the sun shining down and a light breeze stirring the grass at my feet. Shadows paint a more fitting final scene for the snapping of my neck.

The last breath of Rhya Fleetwood.

Ward of the renowned Eli Fleetwood.

Orphan.

Faery.

Halfling.

Fugitive.

Point.

In some ways, it will be a relief. To finally rest after all these months on the run. Since they executed Eli, since they burned the Starlight Wood to ash along with our cottage, there is no refuge left for me on this earth. No strong, protective arms to rush toward when my hair snags on the brambles or my ankle twists on a rock in the riverbed. No warm bed to crawl into at the end of a crisp autumn day.

I have no idea where I am. Before they hunted me down, I'd

been lost for weeks, wandering in search of solace that no longer exists, surviving on rubbery mushrooms dug from the packed earth and cold trout fished from icy streams. When I came across a village five days ago, the smell of fresh bread sitting on a stone windowsill proved too tempting to ignore.

I could curse my own stupidity. I know what Eli would say if he were here. *The heart makes you soft. The stomach makes you weak. Ignore their fleeting impulses. It is your mind you must mind.*

But in a moment of weakness, I abandoned his teachings. Gnawing hunger made me careless, dulled the sharpness of my senses beyond reason. I'm quick by nature, but that day I was not quick enough. As I darted from the tree line to the dilapidated house at the edge of the wood, I did not hear the click of a boot-heel on the stone floor inside, nor the nocking of an arrow in the bow, until it whizzed a whisper above my head. And by then, it was too late.

Far too late.

From that moment on, life was headlong flight. Running until the breath was gone from my lungs, until the strength was stripped from my bones, until my bare feet left a trail of bloody footprints on rocks and riverbanks alike. They tracked me—first the villagers themselves, later the soldiers they had summoned. Through a forest, across a field, and finally into a boggy marshland. I nearly lost them there in that hissing, burping mire, where the air was thick as syrup and swarms of insects blacked out the midday sun.

Nearly.

I had no way of knowing I was being herded toward a deep ravine. The Red Chasm, the soldiers call it, so named for the rusty color of its plunging depths. For there, the stone runs thick with iron deposits. Thick enough to drain me on a good day— and a good day, this was not.

I felt the ore sapping my strength with each step as the men closed in. My legs buckled, threatening to give out beneath me. Even if they hadn't, there was nowhere left to run once I reached the cliff side. Not unless I fancied hurling myself over the edge, plummeting to my death in the void.

In hindsight, tied to a tree with the fiery grip of iron shackling my wrists, a thick noose looped around my neck, and a pyre in my immediate future . . . I might prefer that sharp fall. At least then, my death would be at my own hands. My own choice.

My last choice.

Gods, I'm tired. The noose is so heavy I can no longer hold my head upright. I sag limply against my bindings, glad Eli is not here to see me. He raised me to fight. To be fierce. Steady of will, strong of mind, sound of heart.

I've failed him.

I've failed myself.

The thought makes me want to cry, but I have no strength left for tears. I can't recall the last time I had a bite of food, a sip of water. My tongue is dry as sand, the memory of a warm meal as foreign to me as the land in which I've been captured.

I try to focus through the pain and exhaustion crippling my body.

What did the soldier say?

King Eld.

The Avian Strait.

Bloodiest battle in a hundred years.

In my pain-hazed mind, there is a map, full of many kingdoms. Ever-shifting feudal lands with ever-changing paper kings. *Paper kings.* That's what Eli always calls them—*called* them. Their dominion not a divine right, but self-appointed by ink and quill; their hold on their titles as thin as the parchment upon which they are scrawled, one sovereign easily scratched out and exchanged for another.

Hardly worth memorizing, Eli grumbled once, his wizened hands splayed on his vast collection of unfurled charts. *The bloody boundaries shift with every major battle...*

I must've studied those maps a hundred times, but in this moment my memories feel gossamer thin, impossible to bring into focus. Kingdoms, fractured like pieces from a shattered shield, fall away before I can cobble them properly back together.

Carvage.

Eastwood.

Lordale.

Nythia.

Dymmeria.

The Reaches.

The names blur, the inky letters smearing. Indecipherable. Ultimately, meaningless. My spirit will return to the skies regardless of where my body burns. It's not much consolation, but I cling to it anyway.

I'm far from home, I know that much. Wherever they've brought me is a barren land. Not just cold—devoid of life. I can feel no pulse of power from the ground beneath my feet, hear no ancient whispers among this grove of half-dead trees. And even if I could . . . I'm so weak after days of frantic flight—hounds nipping at my heels, arrows whizzing past my head, torches cornering me like a wild thing—I'm not certain it would do me any good.

Sunlight cannot fix a flower on the cusp of death.

It doesn't matter anyway, I tell myself, leaning harder against my hanging tree. The nick of the guard's blade against his wood block is a steady metronome, ticking down the seconds until my execution. *Nothing matters anymore, Rhya. By morning, you'll be a pile of ash.*

CHAPTER TWO

I must nod off at some point, because I wake with a start to the rumble of hooves. A lone rider, moving through the trees with speed.

The commander has finally arrived.

The ground beneath my bare feet shakes as the newcomer thunders into the encampment. Chain mail clanks, boots thud, as he dismounts. I can see nothing with the damned blindfold over my eyes, darkening an already black night to pure pitch. Straining my ears, I struggle to pick up snippets of conversation.

"Commander Scythe. It's an honor to have you here, sir. An honor."

"Burrows." The response is curt.

"Sir, if I may say, your tactics at the Battle of Ygri last spring were simply inspired. Those Nythian scum fell like stalks of corn at harvest! I've never seen anything like it in all my years as—"

"Captain, if I wanted my ass kissed I'd be in a brothel. Take me to the prisoner. Now."

"Y-yes, sir," Burrows stammers. "Right away."

The footsteps grow louder as they approach. I take a deep

breath, bracing myself. Still, my heart gives a great lurch when a hand snakes out and rips the covering from my face.

Torchlight flares, searing after so many hours spent in darkness. I blink to clear the bright spots, but it does little good. Stars are bursting inside my eyes. Strong fingers fist in my dirty hair, dragging my lolling head upright with one rough jerk. His other hand curls around the noose and pulls tight, compressing my windpipe. Breath becomes an impossibility.

I thought I was past this—past the fear.

I was wrong.

The face that slowly swims into view makes my heart fail. What I can see of it, anyway, under the heavy black helmet. A metal nose bridge bisects his features into two unforgiving halves. On either side, the thick slashes of his brows are furrowed inward and, just beneath them, a set of eyes so dark, they seem two bottomless pits glaring out at me. In the flickering torchlight, he appears more daemon than man.

"Where did you find this one, a graveyard?" His grip tightens in my hair until my scalp burns. "She reeks like a week-old carcass."

"Frogmyre Bog," the heavily bearded man standing to the commander's left offers. Captain Burrows. I recognize him instantly—he's the one who put the rope around my neck when they caught me on the cliffside. He tied the other end to his saddle as they led me back to their camp, forcing me to run behind him or else be dragged. When, after almost an hour, my bleeding feet finally failed and I collapsed into the dirt, he'd rubbed my face in his horse's shit, laughing with unbridled glee.

My hair is still clumped with it, the pale strands stained the dull brown shade of dry manure. The odor is enough to make a steel-clad stomach curdle. Beneath his nose guard, the commander's nostrils flare. Lips pressed into a stern line, his dark gaze sweeps from my face to my feet, seeming to commit every detail to memory—skin caked in bog, skirts stiff with filth, eyes wide with terror.

"In rather rough shape, isn't she?"

"Point bitch kept us in pursuit for three days," Burrows hisses, glaring at me with unleashed disdain. "She's lucky we didn't do worse."

Several of the gathered soldiers make sounds of agreement. Their resentment is tangible—as is their impatience. They're eager to see me swing.

Scythe does not comment. Nor does his attention shift to his subordinates. Instead, it seems fixed on my wrists, where the irons have reduced my skin to a raw, unrecognizable mess of charred flesh. The agony of it is making me lightheaded. Or perhaps it's the lack of air; his hold on the noose does not relent for even an instant.

Burrows grins, a flash of stubby teeth stained brown from chewing tybeae leaf. "Iron is a beautiful thing, isn't it?"

"In the future, keep in mind, Burrows . . . Executions are my jurisdiction, not yours. You bring me a halfling in this condition again, I'll make certain you can't sit properly in your saddle for a fortnight."

A hush falls over the men. It is no idle threat, made all the more menacing by the tone in which it's delivered: so carefully bland, he might be discussing seasonal weather patterns. His expression—what little I can see of it beneath the helm—is as empty as his tone and equally chilling.

The soldiers are scarcely able to look in the commander's direction without cowering. Only my binds keep me from doing likewise. With the rope held so tight around my neck, I can't move—not even when he brings his face a hairsbreadth from mine, regarding me as a wolf would its supper.

If I had the strength, I might head-butt him. Spit at him. Even summon a glare. As it is, just remaining conscious is becoming difficult. My lungs scream for breath. The starbursts have returned to my eyes, fragmenting the world around me into air-starved delirium.

If Scythe notices my discomfort, he doesn't much care. "You said there was something . . ." he murmurs, "*odd* . . . about this one."

"Yes, sir." Burrows swallows nervously, sidling closer. "There's some unnatural symbol inked into her skin. A mark of evil, you ask me. Never seen anything like it in all my time hunting points."

At this, Scythe, already immobile, seems to still down to his soul. "What mark?"

"We thought it was a slave brand at first. It's raised like scar tissue, but blacker than the devil's cock." Some of the men chuckle, but there's a nervous edge to their amusement. "Could be a tattoo, I suppose," Burrows continues. "But even the best ink-mavens in Carvage don't have that sort of skill. See for yourself. There, beneath her dress, right between her—" Burrows chokes into silence when the commander's head swivels in his direction.

"*Beneath* her dress?" He pauses and the very air holds its breath, as in the moment before a guillotine blade plummets. "I had no idea your prisoner inspection process was so thorough, Captain."

"It wasn't— We weren't—" Burrows's shoulders stiffen at the implication. He's gone pale under the force of Scythe's stare. "Saw it while we were putting the noose around her neck, that's all. But when one of my men made the mistake of touching it . . ."

Burrows shakes his head, as if he still cannot quite fathom what happened when his second-in-command ripped open the front of my dress at the edge of that cliff and shoved down the thin shift beneath it, leaving me perilously exposed for the viewing pleasure of an entire company of soldiers.

Whatever that man intended to do to me—and I could plainly guess, from the leering gleam in his eyes—was rendered impossible as soon as his fingers grazed my strange birthmark.

"What's this?" he muttered, his foul breath fanning over my face as he leaned in and ran two fingertips down my breastbone, which rose and fell rapidly beneath gulps of panicked breath. Before I could so much as flinch away, something within me—I don't know *what*, only that it is there, and has been there for a very long time, waiting like a snake poised to strike for just such an opportunity—uncoiled itself from the center of my chest and lashed outward. The soldier reeled back as if scalded, clutching his hand with a moan that echoed through the Red Chasm, rebounding back in a sickening chorus of agony.

I was so stunned, watching him writhe in the dirt before me, it took a moment to tug my shift back into place, covering the whorled design once more. I touched it gingerly as I refastened the front laces of my dress with shaking fingers, half-afraid I'd find it white-hot. And yet, it was cool as ever to the touch—a shade colder than the rest of my flesh, just like always, no matter how feverish I become or how I exert myself.

The party of soldiers had stared from me to their injured comrade and back again, their eyes brimming with apprehension. As though I'd attacked the man on purpose. As if I might turn on them next.

If only.

Such power would come in especially handy at a time like the present. Yet, in truth, I'd done nothing to sear the skin from the man's fingertips. Not intentionally, anyway. Nor could I seem to replicate such an effect after his comrades clapped me in irons—albeit with considerably more wariness about their hand placement—and led me back to this camp.

"Here," Burrows says abruptly, reaching a hand toward my bodice. "I'll show you."

Scythe's formidable frame shifts directly into the captain's path, blocking him before so much as a finger grazes me. "You will not touch her."

"I'm just trying to help! If you'd seen what it did to my second-in-command—"

"You will not touch her."

Surprise blooms on Burrows's face, then quickly sours into seething resentment. He does not enjoy being scolded. He even less enjoys being outranked in his own camp. But he'd be a fool to question Scythe's authority. Clenching his stubby teeth, he swallows his objections and steps back a pace.

Still held painfully tight by my bindings, I cannot shy away as Scythe tugs one-handed at the neckline of my dress, undoing the laces with methodical movements. The weight of many eyes from the gathered crowd presses in, though his mammoth form shields me mostly from view. My heart hammers so loud against my rib cage, he must be able to hear it.

Cold air brushes the top swell of my breasts as the commander pulls my shift down—no more than strictly necessary, merely an inch or so—to expose the top half of the triangular birthmark. Mortification and terror mingle within me. I'd gasp if I were able to summon enough breath, but the noose is still held tight by the hand that remains above my head, preventing all but the most narrow slivers of air from entering my lungs.

I watch his face as he examines the strange design, trying to read his expression. There is no expression to read. He is blank, his intentions as inscrutable as the interlocking whorls and spirals he stares at with such intent focus.

I will the mark to strike out at him, as it did the man on the cliffside; wish for that snake of unpredictable power to come uncoiled once more and maim this new enemy standing before me. It does not comply. It sits cold and still within my breast, its fangs sheathed and silent, its existence as much a mystery as its origin.

According to Eli, I've had it since the day he first found me—a newborn babe with a crop of white hair, strange eyes, and a mysterious brand on her breast of such dark tint, it seemed infused with night itself.

Best keep it covered, Rhya, he told me again and again, so many times I grew weary of hearing it before my fifth naming day. *There are those who might think it a cursed mark, child.*

After the events on the cliffside, I fear they may be right.

Scythe doesn't touch me, wise enough to heed Burrows's warnings. But his gaze is so heavy, I can almost feel it scoring into my flesh as he slowly sets my dress to rights, his dexterous fingers making easy work of the ties. I'm not certain why he bothers—in a few moments, I'll be a pile of embers—but I'm oddly relieved I'll not spend my last moments on this earth with my body exposed for the amusement of strangers.

"The torch," Scythe barks suddenly, his free hand extended blindly to his left. "Bring it here. I need the light."

A young recruit steps forward, arm shaking as he extends the torch. I try to struggle as Scythe brings it close to my face, but my bindings hold fast. The flame is unbearably bright and scorching hot. My skin prickles with the promise of pain and, for a moment, my mind blanks with panic.

He's going to set me aflame, right here, right now.

My eyes close involuntarily, shutting out my enemy's face, my inescapable fate. Yet the torch never moves closer. Instead, there is a low growl of exasperation as Scythe finally releases the noose at my neck. Air floods down my throat, bursting into my screaming lungs. My ragged gasps are met with chuckles from the watching soldiers.

"Hardly worth hanging her," Burrows remarks. "She's half-dead already. Waste of perfectly good rope, in my opinion." A gob of spit shoots in my direction. I do not bother to look and see where it lands. I'm too busy trying to catch my breath.

I've barely had time to pull in a full gulp of air before a large hand clamps down on my left shoulder and shakes. Scythe's impatience is evident in every snap of his wrist. My bones rattle with the force of it.

"Your eyes. Open them."

His command hardly registers over the roar of my pulse between my ears. The grip on my shoulder tightens to the point of pain. I'll have more bruises by dawn—if I am still alive at dawn.

"*Open them.*"

I do as I'm told, peering at him through narrow slits. Torch held aloft, the commander glares down at me, frightening in his intensity. He's massive—barrel-chested and so tall, he blocks my view of the rest of the world. A nightmarish figure. It takes every bit of my faltering courage to hold his gaze as it burns into mine.

Does he want to look me in the eyes as he strikes me down? Watch the light leave them as his blade slides between my ribs?

I refuse to blink. If this is my last moment, I should live it eyes wide open. I brace for the pain, but then—

Scythe's stern-pressed mouth goes slack, just for a moment, a slip he covers so fast, I wouldn't have seen it at all if he weren't standing so near. However fleeting, I see . . . something that looks almost like shock.

Can it be shock?

"Impossible," he whispers with a bleakness that sends a chill skittering down my spine.

"What was that, sir?" Burrows asks from a few paces back. "Couldn't quite hear you."

"Nothing." Scythe's voice is back to its normal brusqueness, but he does not turn to face the captain. He's still looking into my eyes, searching for some hidden revelations encoded in their depths. His own eyes are unreadable. Two dark pools, reflecting nothing but flickers from the flaming torch in his hand. It would be easier to guess the thoughts of a statue.

Our gazes hold for a prolonged beat. His fingers, still gripping the torch, tighten infinitesimally. In the stillness, I feel, rather than see, him take a bracing breath.

"Shall we string her up, then?" Burrows asks tiredly. "It's nearly midnight and we're off to the southern front at first light. King Eld has called for reinforcements. Seems some Nythian rabble at the borderlands are making troub—"

The captain never finishes his sentence. The word *trouble* is halfway out his throat when the commander's sword enters it, severing his windpipe in one clean stroke. I had not even seen Scythe reach for the weapon sheathed across his back. Nor, it seemed, had any of his comrades. The sheep are wholly unprepared for the wolf unleashed in their midst.

Burrows's head has not yet hit the ground when Scythe whirls around—torch in one hand, sword in the other—and drives his blade through the two nearest soldiers with no more effort than a pair of shears snipping flower stalks in a garden. Another spin and two more men hit the dirt, their limbs crumpled petals.

Five dead in a single heartbeat.

By the time the remaining soldiers realize what is happening and begin to scramble for their own weaponry, it's too late. Scythe is a blur, moving so fast it's hard to track his movements, let alone block them.

One soldier takes the blazing torch to the face, his harrowing screams keening into the night. Six more take small, precisely thrown daggers to the neck, dropping like stones as their life-blood pours into the earth. The others, who turn and flee into the cover of the dark wood as fast as their legs can carry them, he hunts down and eliminates with the practiced ease of a natural killer.

As Scythe stalks his doomed prey, for the first time since my capture, I find myself alone. Still lashed to the tree, the ground around me littered with the bodies of the men who made me their prisoner, I'm too terrified to be relieved. In the sudden quiet, I think my heart will beat right out of my chest, cracking through my ribs and falling to my feet.

My gaze sweeps the shadowy encampment, wide with horror. The corpse closest to me is barely more than a boy. His eyes are open, fixed sightlessly at a night sky he can no longer see. Was he the young recruit I overheard asking for advice, mere hours ago? I suppose it doesn't matter. Though I can't help the pang of un-warranted sympathy that squeezes my heart.

He would've happily watched you hang, Rhya, I scold myself harshly. *When did you become so weak?*

I do not have time for foolish sympathies—even for the col-lateral damage of an innocent. Bigger problems are looming. For though Scythe has killed my captors, he is no savior. Of that, I'm certain.

I count less than five minutes before he stalks back into the clearing, his cloak billowing behind him like a reaper from the old tales, helmet gleaming dark silver in the midnight moon. With grim efficiency, he retrieves his daggers from the jugulars of the fallen soldiers, returning them one by one to their slots in the bandolier strapped across his chest.

He isn't even winded.

The broadsword in his hand is stained black with blood. In the dim light of the dying fire, I watch him wipe it clean on Burrows's decapitated body. When it once again shines, he rises to full height and takes a deep breath that broadens his whole frame.

Slowly, his head swings in my direction. The breath snags in my throat as his eyes lock on mine, pinning me in place more effectively than the binds around my waist. In two strides, he's standing before me. I try not to scream as he raises his sword, but I cannot contain the faint bleat of terror that escapes my lips.

At the sound, he goes still. One eyebrow arches upward, as if in surprise, though his mouth remains a severe line. We regard each other for a moment, neither seeming to breathe in the quiet of the night.

Do it. I glare at him with what flimsy courage I can muster. *Get it over with already.*

As if hearing my challenge, his sword hand jerks and in one smooth stroke his blade makes its cut. Not across my neck, but through the noose that binds it. The rope falls to the ground as his sword flicks again, this time ridding me of the binds around my torso.

Free at last, I topple forward into the dirt. My deadened legs are incapable of supporting my weight, and my wrists, still clapped in irons, can do precious little to shield my fall. Pain explodes in my temple as my head cracks against the hard earth. The wind evacuates my lungs in a great whoosh, leaving me gasping in a heap.

When I manage to peel my eyes open, I find myself face-to-face with a familiar bushy beard and two pockmarked cheeks.

Burrows's severed head is close enough to kiss. I shriek and roll over, pushing up on my chained hands, my motions clumsy in my desperation. The earth beneath me is saturated with soldiers' blood. I try not to notice as I drag myself along in jerky spurts, fingers clumping in dirt and fallen leaves, passing body parts and tree roots as I go. Each inch of progress is agony on my damaged wrists.

"Get up."

The voice from above is cold. I decide to ignore it.

I think I hear a sigh, but I can't be certain. I'm too focused on my rather pathetic escape attempt. I make it approximately two more handspans before Scythe reaches down, grabs me by the hair, and yanks me forcibly to my feet. I cry out in pain, but he does not yield—merely tows me along like a disobedient hound.

We cross the clearing in seconds, leaving behind the massacred men and their orderly camp. The fire has nearly gone out; there is no one left alive to tend it. At the edge of the clearing, a pack of horses graze beneath a tree. Amid the sea of dappled gray coats and soft white muzzles, one steed stands apart—a glossy black stallion, his color perfect camouflage for riding through the night without detection. He's several hands taller than the others and wears an armored saddle fit for battlefields. A plate of chain mail covers his broad nose.

There is little doubt as to which rider he belongs.

Scythe releases my hair, but only so he can toss me roughly across the rump of the great horse—face down, my legs dangling over one side, my manacled hands on the other. Seconds later, a leather saddlebag strap cinches efficiently across my middle, holding me in place.

I'm too worn-out to protest the indignity of my position.

The commander's menacing presence recedes momentarily as he sets loose the tethered horses. I hear the low cluck of his tongue, the firm slap of his palm against a series of rumps. Eager hoofbeats fade into the night as the cavalry leaves the camp—and their dead masters—behind. I hope they find peace in their early retirement, somewhere in the wild. No longer forced to ferry anyone into battle, no longer beholden to the whims of blood-thirsty kings. Just days full of sun and wind and endless grassy fields for grazing.

I fear my own fate will not be half so tranquil.

With a low grunt, the commander swings up into the saddle and, clicking his bootheels against his horse's sides, spurs us off, into the dark.

CHAPTER THREE

It's impossible to fall asleep slung across the stallion's back, each pound of his hooves against the earth jolting through my bones like a blacksmith's hammer on an anvil. And yet, my exhaustion must exceed my discomfort, for when my eyes open, dawn is breaking, its pink fingers creeping across the sky.

Gods, I ache everywhere.

My body feels more wrung out than a damp washcloth. Limp and lifeless. With the strap so tight around my middle, it's difficult to draw breath. I can see little except the lathered flank of the horse beneath me, the heel of my captor's boot in a muddy stirrup, the ground below us a rush of color.

We are riding hard. Northwest, judging by the sun's position in the ashen-gray sky. Away from the boglands, out of the forest—though I have no idea where. I rack my brain for any meaningful details the soldiers let slip last night. What was it Burrows said?

We're off to the southern front at first light. King Eld has called for reinforcements.

King Eld of . . .

The Narrows?

No.

Dymmeria?

No.

Westlake?

No.

Curse my blasted memory. Curse myself for not being a better student. Curse Eli for not beating the knowledge into me with a stick instead of encouraging me with mild-mannered expectations.

My eyes threaten to well up at the thought of Eli. For two decades, he was my protector. If he were here—if he were still alive—it would kill him to see me thus. A filthy, broken doll in the hands of the very enemy he dedicated his life to shielding me from. I'm thankful I do not possess the energy to weep.

The sun slants higher in the sky as we ride, the stallion's hooves a steady clop. I've not the slightest inkling what part of the world we're in. Anwyvn is a vast land, and until the past few weeks, I've seen precious little of it. The isolated peninsula of Seahaven was my home from the day Eli found me swaddled in a basket on the white shores until the night the invading armies arrived with their flaming torches.

We've left the deepest part of the forest behind. Absent are the towering maples, the soaring ashwoods, that sheltered me for the past month. The trees here are set farther apart—a copse of sparse pines with pale copper needles that blanket the arid ground.

It's nearly midday when we finally come to a halt. I'm so exhausted, I cannot even lift my head to take in our surroundings. I feel Scythe shift in his saddle, then listen to the dull thud of his boots hitting the earth. They step into view as he reaches up to undo the strap holding me in place, and I study their simple craftsmanship.

No spurs, no steel tips. A thick caking of dust on his laces. Leather well-worn from several seasons. That's a surprise. I figure

a soldier of his standing can snap his fingers and summon fresh
gear whenever he likes.

"Get down."

His deep voice is hoarse from lack of use and holds no kindness. I try to force my limbs into motion, but they're too stiff to
cooperate. I remain slung pathetically across the stallion's rump,
my spine an unnatural arch. I fear it will never straighten properly again.

Scythe sighs and, without an ounce of gentleness, gives my
midsection a shove. A squawk of alarm escapes my lips as I slide
toward the horse's tail and, powerless to catch myself, tumble to
the ground. I land flat on my back, sending a plume of pollen into
the air. The impact is cushioned slightly by a bed of pine needles
but still manages to knock the wind out of me. For quite a long
time I lie there, unable to do anything except blink up at the anemic sky, moaning occasionally in pain.

Scythe leads the horse to a nearby crick. I listen to them both
drinking deeply and my own parched tongue rasps against my
lips in envy. A part of me—a small one, but a part nonetheless—
wishes he'd killed me back in the camp. I'm not sure what he's
waiting for. Perhaps he plans to drag me along with him until the
dehydration withers me down to a skeleton.

It will be a slow death.

A shadow looms suddenly over me, blocking out the sun. My
captor has returned. My eyes flicker open and fix on his. They're
black, even in the bright midday light. He still wears his heavy
helmet, concealing most of his features from view. The metal
nose bridge tapers into a sharp point at the bottom, lending him
an almost serpentine look—a dragon roaming loose in the countryside. As he stares down at me, his mouth curls at one side in
either disgust or disdain.

Gods, I hate him.

A leather waterskin hits the ground beside my head.

"Drink."

I don't reach for it. I don't move a single muscle. I'd rather die of thirst than follow his bidding. Foolish as it is, that tiny resistance is the only sliver of autonomy I have left.

"Suit yourself." With a shrug, he turns on his heel and walks away. His next words drift back on the wind, almost an afterthought. "We won't stop again until nightfall."

It takes three distinct tries to sit upright, my strained limbs screaming in protest the entire time. I'm woozy from pain and lack of food, but somehow I manage to pull the waterskin onto my lap. My shackles clank, the iron biting into my ravaged skin as I lift it to my lips and take a deep pull.

It tastes like heaven.

I drain the skin in an embarrassingly short amount of time. My long-empty stomach protests at the foreign sensation of fullness, but I am still desperately thirsty. Eyeing the nearby stream as it gurgles over a bed of mossy rocks, I contemplate dragging myself to the edge for a few more restorative gulps. Properly hydrated, my head might stop spinning. If my head isn't spinning, I might actually figure out where Scythe is taking me . . . and how to get away before we arrive . . . and . . .

Without warning, I'm yanked to my feet, the empty waterskin snatched out of my hands in a flash. My squeak of protest morphs into a hiss of fear as a large hand clamps down on my shoulder, tight as a vise.

"Time to go," Scythe mutters, towing me back toward his horse. I dig my bare heels into the dirt, but it's no use. He swats away my resistance like a bothersome insect buzzing at his ear. I don't even have a chance to object before he lifts me off my feet and throws me back onto the stallion. The water sloshes uncomfortably in my stomach as he lashes me down with the same rote disinterest he might use in securing a sack of grain.

Once back in the saddle, he clucks his tongue. The horse responds instantly, breaking into a jarring canter I feel in every corner of my battered body.

Just hang on until nightfall, I tell myself, trying to ward off the despair. *You can manage that, Rhya.*

But nightfall is a long way off.

AT SOME POINT, I become aware of the fact that I am quite ill. The fever has snuck in on the heels of thirst and exhaustion, disguising itself among the myriad other aches and pains plaguing my body. But as the afternoon wanes, there is no denying the heat that burns within my veins despite the cool northern clime through which we ride. My skin flashes hot, then cold, then hot once more. I find myself thankful for the strap securing me in place; the sheer force of my trembles would knock me to the ground otherwise.

I see no point in telling my captor of my condition. What would his response be?

Let's make camp. I'll bring you hot soup and stroke your hair until you're well again, as Eli use to do when you were a child.

Somehow, I doubt it.

It is not quite twilight when we draw to an abrupt halt at the edge of the forest, where the trees yield to a wide dirt roadway. I wonder if we're making camp early, but Scythe does not dismount—nor does he explain our sudden stop after the bruising pace he's maintained all day.

I shift as best I can, lifting my head to get a better look, and in a fever-dazed voice mumble an incoherent, "Hnumph?"

Scythe whips around in his saddle. "*Quiet.*"

The order is delivered in a menacing whisper that makes my throat close up. I have no doubt that if I do not comply, he'll have no qualms about knocking me unconscious. The reason for his severity soon becomes clear. Not thirty seconds later, my ears pick up the sound of voices on the wind. Another thirty, and the road before us is filled with a company of men marching in neat rows, shields held aloft, swords sheathed across their backs. Twenty-five, maybe more. Their uniforms are not green, like those of Captain Burrows and his unit, but bloodred. Their pennants bear the sigil of two interlocking torcs, scarlet stitches waving in the breeze.

They do not see us, concealed as we are by the camouflage of leaves and branches. Clearly, that is Scythe's intention. For whatever reason, he does not want to make our presence known.

Perhaps...

A faint spark of hope flares within my breast but quickly sputters out. The fact that they are Scythe's enemy does not make them friend to me. There is no guarantee they will not drive a sword through my heart the moment I call out to them for aid. And there is nothing to assure me Scythe cannot slaughter a full score of men as easily as he slew a dozen last night.

I watch the soldiers file past, my heart sinking as they disappear around a bend. We wait until their boots become a distant rumble, then fade altogether. When the world is quiet—only the sounds of Scythe's steady breaths, the occasional twitching of the stallion's tail, the low wail of the wind in the trees—and he is certain the soldiers are long gone, he spurs us across the road, out of the forest, and into the tall grass on the other side.

We have reached the plains.

On the flat-stretched fields, without the need to dodge tree roots and fallen debris, our pace increases from a cantor to nearly a gallop. Each clap of the stallion's hooves reverberates in my aching skull. Though he gives no verbal indication of it, I sense a new tension in my captor, an urgency that was not there this morning.

If my head were clearer, I might remember where I've seen that company sigil—those red interlocking torcs on black fabric. I might realize just how closely pursuit nips at our heels. But I do not. My thoughts are fuzzy-edged. I am looking at the world through a bank of fog, my body on one side, my mind on the other. I cannot connect the two through the haze.

The plainlands seem to go on forever, an endless expanse of unsown pastures. Like the rest of the Midlands, this particular stretch is war ravaged. A veritable wasteland after two centuries of bloodshed. Fields where crops once grew are now mass graves, the men who once tended them long buried beneath barren soil.

We see no more soldiers. We see no one at all. Most travelers stick to the road, I suppose—taking advantage of a wayside inn at nightfall, sipping ale by a hearth with a warm bowl of stew, swapping out their tired mounts for fresh ones. With Scythe's horse, there is no need for such measures. The great beast who carries us never seems to tire, no matter how many leagues he runs, no matter the terrain. In my delirium, I wonder if he might be descended from the great Paexyri steeds. Legend says they could run flat out for days, ferrying faery riders from one side of Anwyvn to the other without so much as a water break. Some believe they had great wings, for their speed was something closer to flight.

Such thoughts are absurd indeed, even to my feverish mind. If the Paexyri actually existed, they had all been slain along with their riders during the Cull. That bloody uprising spared none of elemental origin, from the all-powerful emperor down to the faintest fyrewisps. They, like all other maegical creatures, were eradicated with the same brutal efficiency the mortal men now wield against one another in their endless wars. Shortsighted paper kings, usurping and undermining, slaughtering and savaging, until there is hardly any land left fit to rule. Until they've reduced everything to ash, stripped away any beauty Anwyvn once possessed.

The only creatures we encounter on our way are undoubtedly ordinary—shaggy-haired cows and unshorn sheep, grazing in the sun. Though even those become few and far between as the terrain changes from flat fields to rolling hills and finally to a sharp incline. Rock and stone soon replace grass and sod. As we climb, I suck sharp slivers of air into my lungs, unsure if my breathlessness is due to the progressing illness or our ever-increasing elevation.

My fever worsens as the sun sinks in the sky. By the time we stop for the night, I'm drifting in and out of awareness. I cannot recall sliding down from the horse and yet here I am, on my feet, the ground roiling beneath me. Or is that my legs, finally giving out? I can't quite tell.

A steely grip catches me as the world tips sideways. Scythe's stern face swims before my eyes. He's glaring again.

"Gods, you're burning up."

Am I floating?

Is he carrying me?

Will he ever stop frowning?

A delirious giggle presses against the inside of my lips, poised to escape. I cling desperately to consciousness, but it grows more difficult with each passing moment. Darkness is closing in again—blacker than the night sky overhead, pulling me into its clutches.

"Stubborn fool," Scythe hisses lowly, laying me down on a bed of stone. It feels blessedly cool against my skin. "You're no good to me dead."

Someone is giggling. It might be me.

"Hey." His hand slaps my cheek. "Stay with me. *Stay with me.*"

I blink hard, trying to keep him in focus. Perhaps it is the fever muddling my mind, but I'd swear I see something in his narrowed eyes that was not there before—a flash of worry, gone so fast it's easy to convince myself it was no more than a delusion conjured up by febrile fog.

Those black eyes are the last thing I see as the clammy grip of illness closes its hand around my neck and squeezes until the light of the world peters out.

CHAPTER
FOUR

I awaken alone.

My eyelids fight me as I peel them open, heavy with exhaustion. I am in a cave of some sort, propped against a mossy boulder wall. The earth under me is hard-packed gravel. The sky overhead is blocked completely by a ceiling of stone, excepting a narrow crevice where a weak shaft of sunlight slants in.

I have no recollection of this place.

The night comes back in fragments. Moments of clarity amid the delirium. The gleam of a metal helmet in moonlight. A large hand pressed to my forehead, checking my temperature. A flash of rock against flint, sparking a fire. Bottomless eyes, peering into mine. And a voice, an imploring rasp in the swimming dark.

Stay with me.

My captor is not in the cave, but there are traces of him all around. A thick black cloak has been spread beneath me. A few paces away, a fire burns low and smokeless, casting a faint glow in the musty space. Something is baking in the embers—a rabbit, I think, though it smells so good I would eat it even if it were a river rat. My stomach protests loudly with hunger.

As I press a hand against my midsection to quell its rumbles, the freedom of the gesture catches me off guard. Sometime in the night, my shackles were removed. I've been wearing them for so many days, my arms feel oddly light in their absence. Gone is the steady undercurrent of pain from the poisonous iron, though the traces of it on my skin will never fully heal. Staring at the raw, weeping flesh of my wrists, I try not to think about the scars I will bear for the rest of my life. Vanity is a useless pursuit, pale in comparison to more pressing concerns. The infection has gone nearly to the bone; I'll be lucky if I regain enough function to ever again draw a bow or stitch up a wound.

Some unseen vermin skitters in the corner, and I bolt to my feet. The sudden movement makes me sway off-balance. The fever has fled, but a hollow ache lingers inside my skull. I push aside the pain and focus on my next steps.

Water.

To drink, firstly, but also to bathe. If I was filthy before I was captured, from bog slime and horse shit and three weeks on the run without a bath, I'm abominable now. The scent of sweat and blood and bodily fluids is a noxious perfume in the enclosed space, assaulting my nostrils.

Following the light, I move through the cave until I find its mouth, one hand on the lichen-laced wall to guide my way. When I step out, I'm startled to find the sun already high in the afternoon sky.

A few paces bring me out into a rocky clearing. The cave, tucked cleverly in a craggy hillside of mammoth boulders, makes for a perfect hideout. A handful more steps and I'll no longer be able to see the entrance at all amid the thorny bushes.

"You're still alive, then," a detached voice remarks from behind me.

I flinch but do not turn to face him. I can't bear to.

"Since it seems you will live . . . there's a freshwater pool just through the brush. Clean yourself up." Scythe does not sound particularly invested in my well-being now, in the light of day, but I have not forgotten the look in his eyes last night when I was in the throes of fever. Nor have I forgotten his admission.

You're no good to me dead.

He needs me alive. If he didn't, he would've killed me already—or else simply let the fever run its deadly course. Still, that does not mean I can trust him.

"Get moving," he orders gruffly. "Wolves hunt in these hills at night, and the stench on you is strong enough to make every pack in the area come calling."

Embarrassment cuts through me, sharp as a blade. I'm happy he cannot see my face, for my cheeks are aflame beneath the grime. I manage a few halting steps before he speaks again.

"And don't try to run." He heaves a tired sigh. "I'll only have to hunt you down, which will put me in a foul mood."

Frankly, if this is him in a good mood, I am not altogether eager to experience what he deems a foul one. Without another moment's hesitation, I bolt from the clearing as fast as my wobbly legs can carry me. I follow the sound of running water until I find the bathing pool, fed by a gentle fall. The sun-dappled surface is so clear, I can see straight to the bottom, where tiny fish dart between the reeds. Round stones press upward against my heels, smoother than silk. A simple bar of soap sits on a flat rock by the bank, atop a thin pile of white cloth. Upon closer inspection, I find it's a woolen tunic. A man's, judging by the sheer size of it—on my short frame, it will serve more as a gown than a shirt—as well as the scent, a heady, masculine mix of sweat and smoke and spice.

It is an oddly considerate gesture from my fearsome captor, but I do not allow myself to dwell on that overmuch as I strip off my gown and underthings. The fabric is shockingly soiled, its original hue—a pretty, pale green—turned brown with mud, blood, and all manner of unmentionables.

I toss my clothes into the shallows and, grabbing the soap, wade in after them. It is frigid. Goose bumps break out across my arms as I submerge myself, but I don't care. It feels good to sate my thirst, even better to rinse off the thick coat of grime on my body. Spatters of dried blood—both mine and the slaughtered soldiers'—stain my skin. Mud pours from my hair in rivulets. It takes three separate lathers to reveal its platinum luster beneath the filth. I scrub my skin until it is red, soaping more thoroughly than I've ever done in my life.

After, I set to work on my clothing. First my shift and small-clothes, then the gown itself. By the time I'm done, the garment is nearly green again—though I know some of the worst stains will never lift out. Back home, I would've deemed the dress unsalvageable and tossed it into the fire, or perhaps turned it into scraps for cleaning. Here, stained or not, it will have to suffice.

Tempting as it is to stretch out on a sunny rock while my gown dries, I'm not certain how long my captor will allow before he comes looking for me. I certainly do not want to be caught in nothing but my skin if he does. I wring out my underthings the best I can before stepping into them. Despite my efforts, the cotton's clammy chill sets off a series of bone-deep shivers. I hesitate before dressing in my gown and shift, eyeing the white woolen tunic on the rock for a long moment.

I have no desire to pull it on. The thought of Scythe's shirt against my bare skin is too unpleasant to contemplate. Yet, the healer in me knows better than to turn my nose up at any source of warmth. I am woefully unprepared for survival in the wild. My own attire was made for sultry days in Seahaven, not these cold conditions.

I force myself to pull it on, trying not to breathe too deeply as I am enveloped by the musky scent of man. The tunic's hem falls nearly to my knees; the sleeves hang well beyond my wrists. But it is blessedly dry. Irritating as it may be to admit, I find myself glad for the additional layer of insulation as the damp weight of my gown and shift settle over it.

I glance back toward the cave, apprehension simmering in my veins. Notions of fleeing in the opposite direction taunt me, but I know better than to indulge them. If I run, Scythe will hunt me down as easily as he did the soldiers who imprisoned me. Escape is a fool's errand. Especially in my condition—hungry and hurt. I'll not make it far on these bloody feet.

Grimacing, I examine them. Now that they are clean of dirt and debris, the damage is far more apparent. Blisters cover the battered soles. Several deep gouges—a vestige of my flight through the forest—are painful to the touch. The skin around them pulses angrily, red with traces of infection.

That is not a good sign. If they are left untreated, I have no doubt my fever will return. I need medicine, badly. Or, at the very least, shoes to stave off additional injury. Unfortunately, I think my odds of stumbling across a cobbler's shop rather slim out here in the wilderness. I tear a thin strip of cotton off the hem of my shift and wrap my feet as best I can, wincing as I pull the knots tight. Not a perfect solution, but better than nothing.

Besides the bread incident that led to my capture, it was my most foolish mistake—not grabbing my boots from their spot by the door that dreadful night, when the armies laid siege to the Seahaven peninsula. But there had been no time. Not for a cloak, or a store of food, or a pack of medicinal herbs that might've helped heal my injuries. The fire was swift, and the flaming torches from which it spread were held by cruel hands, itching for violence.

I close my mind to the memory of creeping flame, of roiling

smoke. Of clashing metal, of tormented wails. And of Eli's voice, ringing out as he shoved me to safety.

Run, Rhya. Run like the wind.

I had.

Straight into the arms of the enemy.

⁓

SCYTHE SITS BY the mouth of the cave, sharpening his sword on a whetstone. He does not look up from his task when I limp into the clearing. He does not acknowledge my presence at all save to jerk his head toward a nearby tree stump, where a coal-roasted rabbit sits atop a large linden leaf.

"Eat. Before you fall over."

I tense at his curtness. My mouth opens to retort, but I swallow the urge. Fighting with him will do me no good and, in truth, I am hungry. Starving might be more accurate, really. During my bath, I'd run my fingers across my ribs, each protrusion a testament to how sparse my meals have been these past weeks.

The steady tanging of his blade on the stone never ceases as I walk over to the stump and pry off a piece of rabbit with my fingertips. It smells heavenly, and as I pop it into my mouth, I find it tastes even better. Any sense of hesitancy flees the moment the first bite hits my hollow stomach. Within the span of a minute, I devour it all—gnawing down to the bone like a stray hound would the scraps from a rich man's dinner table. I might've sucked the marrow, if I did not have an audience. When it's gone, I feel near to bursting, yet somehow still ravenous.

The hair on the back of my neck prickles under the weight of someone's gaze. Mustering the thin remains of my dignity, I set down the bone I'm still clutching and wipe my fingers clean on the linden leaf. I turn slowly to find Scythe watching me across the clearing. The sword in his hands has gone still.

If my newly bathed appearance startles him, he does not remark on it. Beneath the helm, his dark eyes are moving over my face with an intensity that makes me shiver. For a long moment, we regard each other in silent stalemate. I will not thank him for feeding me; a bird in a cage does not sing for the man who put her there. Nor will he reveal where he is taking me, or what he plans when we get there; a hunter does not explain his motives to the creature in his snare.

The air goes stale as the quiet drags on. My chin jerks higher in defiance. Finally, Scythe clears his throat.

"I suggest you get some rest. We ride at daybreak, fever or no. You have already delayed us long enough."

I bristle, filled instantly with blind rage. "Oh, forgive me, I'd hate to delay my own kidnapping." My arm swings up to point accusingly at him, the movement sending a spasm of pain through my ravaged wrist. "Need I remind you, I wouldn't be ill at all if not for you dragging me across the countryside to gods only know where?"

His dark brows quirk upward, though the rest of his face remains impassive. When he speaks, his tone is infuriatingly level. "I was beginning to think you were a mute."

"You *wish*," I bite back before I can stop myself. "I was managing just fine before you hunted me down like some . . . some . . . some wild deer to stuff and mount upon your wall."

He studies me for a long beat. "Is that how you recall it? Perhaps the fever addled your mind. Because, from my view, I saved your ungrateful ass from certain death at the hands of the Eldians."

"No doubt only for your own nefarious purposes."

He has the gall to snort.

"You . . ." My teeth clench. "You say we ride at daybreak—to where? Where is it you are taking me? What king commands you? Not King Eld, for you slew his men without blinking, though they seemed to take you for one of their own."

He gives no answer.

"Tell me, damn you!"

But he merely stares at me, totally unaffected—a man carved from marble. I want to throttle him. I bite my lip to stop myself from asking anything more, though a thousand other questions lay heavy on my tongue. Fury swirls in my chest, a maelstrom beneath my rib cage. The leash I hold over my temper is thin indeed. Eli always said my moods were like a summer storm, arising in an instant and capable of inflicting great damage if one was not careful.

Unfortunately, the commander does not seem to fear me much. With an annoying amount of nonchalance, he sheathes his sword and rises to his feet. Pine needles cling to his breeches; he does not bother to brush them off. Even here, in this most hidden of places, he is battle ready. The leather chest strap across his tunic is replete with throwing knives. A dagger is strapped to his left thigh; another peeks out the top of his boot. At full height, his helmet brushes the branches of a nearby tree. I think it must be permanently fused to his head, for I have never seen him remove it.

What kind of life is this? Armed to the teeth at all times, fully prepared to fight at any given moment? Constantly on guard against invisible enemies?

"Daybreak," Scythe says, his hard voice shattering the silence. "Be ready to ride. I don't care if you're half-dead."

"I'd rather be full dead than spend another day in your company," I snap, tossing my hair over my shoulder as I stalk into the cave, ignoring the pain in my soles. My damp skirts swish around my ankles, a slap of fabric against bare skin.

It will be a cold night, sleeping thus. The low fire inside the cave offers only the slightest warmth in the face of winter's encroaching chill. I make it a scant few steps inside before I hear Scythe mutter something under his breath.

"I think I preferred her mute."

I t's still dark when Scythe shakes me awake. Kicks, actually, the tip of his boot nudging my sore shoulder blade. Sleeping on a bed of rocks leaves something to be desired.

"Get up," he says lowly. "It's time to move."

I curse him under my breath as I scramble to my feet. It is freezing inside the cave. He's already doused the fire I fell asleep curled beside, my enemy's cloak spread beneath me. I'd shivered for what felt like hours before I finally tumbled over the edge of consciousness. Through some small miracle, my fever did not return in the night.

Scythe bends to retrieve his cloak, shaking off the gravel in one rough jerk. Without another word, he stalks from the cave, leaving me alone in the dark. I limp after him, trembling with cold as I step into the predawn morning. Snowflakes drift down, blanketing the world like a thin coat of sugar on an apple tart. They catch in my eyelashes, cling to my hair, stick to the thin fabric of my gown sleeves.

The horse is already saddled, waiting patiently beneath the boughs of a squat tree. At Scythe's whistle, he trots closer. I tense when the commander turns for me.

"Don't even think about it," I hiss, backpedaling out of his reach.

He freezes, brows raised.

"I am not a saddlebag to be lashed to your horse, nor a sack of barley to be tossed about without care."

"True," he mutters. "Barley would make for far more tolerable company."

I glare at him. "If you wish for me to go along with you without putting up a fight, you will start treating me with respect."

"Is that so?"

My cheeks flush with anger. "You can start by telling me where you are taking me. I think I have a right to know what fate awaits me at the end of this ride."

He closes the space between us in one step, looming over me. It takes all my strength not to cower.

"My respect is something earned—not given away to sheltered little girls consumed by delusional naiveties about our world and those who inhabit it."

"*Sheltered?*" I scoff. "You base your assessment on what? My age? My appearance? The handful of words we have exchanged over these past few days of silent flight?"

"I base it on the fact that you believe you are in any position to negotiate with me."

I would negotiate with the God of Death himself if it meant getting out of the underworld unscathed, but I doubt I'll garner any favors by openly comparing him to evil incarnate. I suck in a calming breath. "I merely wish to ride—upright, without shackles or rope. I will not run. I give you my word."

"Your word?"

I nod.

His expression is flat, but I see a flicker of curiosity in the depths of his eyes. There are snowflakes on his eyelashes. "And what, exactly, is the word of a halfling worth?" he asks, his voice dangerously soft.

"More than the word of a murderer, to be sure."

His flinch is almost imperceptible, but I'm near enough to see it. His eyes glint like dark flame as he leans in. The breath in my lungs seizes at his proximity.

"It seems you are mistaken about something. You exist by my leave alone. Your heart continues to beat because I have seen fit to make it so. That means you have no say in where we are heading, or the manner in which I choose to take you there. It also means you are entitled to nothing—not information, not kindness, certainly not a nursemaid to soothe a fever you brought upon yourself through sheer stubbornness."

My mouth gapes. "You make it sound as if I asked for sickness!"

"You might as well have! Out here, in the wild, one careless mistake can mean a death sentence. An injury left to fester will kill you quicker than any enemies who stalk these hills."

"Shocking as you may find it, I did not get sick merely to annoy you. I assure you, the ride would have been much more pleasant if I were feeling well."

"I'm not overly invested in what you find pleasant."

"Yes, you've made that quite clear." I grit my teeth. "I suppose this means riding upright is not open to discussion."

"Are you willfully obtuse or simply slow-minded?" His pause is rife with tightly leashed fury. "Or perhaps you mean to provoke me with your obstinance?"

I purse my lips sweetly. "Whatever gave you such an idea?"

"Do not push me, little girl. And do not ever forget who holds the power between us." His eyes narrow on mine. "Perhaps I should put your shackles back on. You seemed so very fond of the iron."

My stomach somersaults.

"Or perhaps I'll fashion another noose and tow you behind my horse as we ride. You've seen how fast he can run. Surely you won't have a difficult time keeping up?"

My face goes pale as he speaks. He notices, judging by the cruel smile that twists his lips.

"What? No more objections?" He steps back, out of my space, and I resume breathing. "Good. Get on the godsforsaken horse. Face down, like a proper sack of grain."

I do.

WE MAKE CAMP thrice more on our journey, each time in musky caves or shallow outcroppings of stone, taking momentary shelter from the elements by the warmth of a low fire. On each occasion, Scythe disappears for a short span, returning with a rabbit or some other prey lying limp in his large, bloodied hands. I eat without comment, knowing I need to build up my strength despite how much I hate taking aid from my enemy.

He is a strange travel-fellow. He does not say much of anything to me, besides the occasional gruff order. But he does not harm me. In fact, despite his claims to the contrary, he seems rather invested in my well-being.

When the fever finally clears from my head, I begin to take sharper notice of his actions. The cloak he spreads over me as we ride, to shield me from the worst of the snow. The pair of thick wool socks left beside my head as I sleep—a poor substitute for shoes, but better than nothing at all. The jar of healing salve, shoved wordlessly into my hands. The way he watches me across the light of the campfire as I apply it to my wounds and rewrap my wrists with strips from my shift, a strange gravity in his eyes.

I never see him rest. He remains constantly on guard for

unseen enemies, monitoring our surroundings with a vigilance that makes me uneasy. I think often of the marching soldiers with their red and black sigils. Are they the ones hunting us? Or is it Scythe's own men—comrades of those he slaughtered—who track us through the ever-deepening snowdrifts?

He gives no answers.

There is also the matter of the helmet. I have still never seen him remove it. I sometimes catch myself curious about what color hair is tucked beneath, or whether the absence of metal might soften his angular features in the slightest . . . but those thoughts are quickly banished to the back of my mind. What does it matter whether my captor is fair-headed or raven-haired? Such superfluous details will not change my circumstance.

I steal sleep when I can. Despite my earlier show of bravado, I am still exhausted beyond measure. I learn to rest even on horseback, lulled into a jerking sort of slumber by the metronomic patter of the stallion's hooves. But my dreams are full of dark visions—clashing swords and dripping blood and dark clouds rolling across a land of ice; carrion birds circling the smoke-streaked skies over a swallowing sea of sand. Past and future horrors swirl through my mind in the most violent of tempests.

For three days, we ride through the hills. Ever upward, ever northward, our altitude rising as the temperature plummets. Craggy hills morph into precipitous peaks, spearing into the dark sky. The air grows colder with each passing hour, the snow on the trees thick enough to strain the branches of the low-slung pines native to this mountainous region.

Face down on the rump of the horse, I watch the ground pass, a constant blur of white, and shiver so hard my bones rattle. To stave off the cold, I fill my mind with warm memories. Reading by the hearth, a thick blanket draped across my lap. Whiskers, the stray cat Eli rescued from the bramble, snoozing in a sunbeam. A cup of cider clasped in the circle of my hand. Tomas, the baker's apprentice, sneaking me honey cakes on lush summer nights. Strong arms wrapped around my shoulders, reminding me I am safe.

The indignity of my riding position chafes at my pride, but there is little I can do about it. Protesting got me nowhere. I try to focus on the positives. My shackles have been removed. With the help of the salve, my wrists are beginning to heal—more rapidly than I'd thought possible. My fever remains at bay, at least momentarily. My stomach is full, my thirst sated. And my time with my captor is almost over.

It has to be.

My knowledge of Anwyvn's geography is admittedly lacking, but I know eventually we will hit the Cimmerian Mountains. And no one travels beyond there. Not if they ever plan on returning. There is but one pass that leads through the jagged, snowy peaks. The Avian Strait—a narrow gauntlet, wide enough for only a few men marching side by side. Over the past two centuries, countless armies have fallen there, picked off by northern arrows or buried in unexpected avalanches, their corpses never to be recovered. Folks say the earth beneath the deep snow is stained red—the aftermath of many vain attempts to conquer the Northlands.

Not much is known with certainty about the kingdoms beyond the mountains. If the legends are to be believed, they're icy, inhospitable places where disfigured monsters roamed freely in the age of maegic. Since the Cull, the only confirmed monster who still calls the north home is a man. A king. For even the most common of peasants has heard talk of King Soren of Llŷr, whose barbarity rivals that of the southern warlords.

It is his kingdom that sits on the other side of the Avian

Strait—one he defends mercilessly from the Midlanders. It is his face that young children conjure up in their most horrific nightmares. Wives pray their husbands will never face him in combat. Hardened soldiers speak of his battle tactics in fear-strangled voices.

I have no desire to learn firsthand if their terror is warranted. I assure myself even Scythe is not reckless enough to view Llŷr as a viable hideout from the enemies on our heels. Yet the farther northward we travel, the less confident my assurances become . . . and the tighter the knot in the pit of my stomach twists.

WHEN WE STOP again, the skies are dark. I cannot tell the hour. The world is dim in the shadow of the mountains even at midday. The promise of impending snow presses down on us, infusing each breath with damp heaviness.

The stallion slows in a thin copse of pine trees that cling to a jutting cliff side. Craning my neck, I see it is a precipitous drop. Bottomless, to my eyes. The depths of the ravine are entrenched in inky shadow. Across that deep abyss, the Cimmerians loom, their frosted peaks blocking out the sun.

Scythe puts two fingers into his mouth and lets out a whistle that reminds me of a hawk's shrill caw. I flinch as the sound reverberates off the stone canyon, echoing far out of range.

We wait.

The world falls quiet once the echoes fade, only the stallion's occasional shuffles from hoof to hoof and the muffled plops of snow falling from overladen tree boughs to break the silence. I do not know what we are waiting for until, a few moments later, an answering caw carries back to us on the wind—hawkish and unmistakable.

Someone is on the other side of the gulch. Someone who has been awaiting Scythe's signal.

A signal . . . for what? From whom?

I don't have time to wonder long. No sooner has he heard the caw than Scythe spurs the horse back into motion, riding along the rim of the ravine with renewed energy. Face down as I am, it is difficult to make out much of anything, but my heart fails when I see how near we are to the edge. One false step, and we'll plummet to our deaths.

There is no path, so far as I can tell. Thankfully, the horse seems to know the way. After a short ride, we stop again. This time, Scythe dismounts and undoes my bindings. Before he has a chance to shove me to the ground, as has become our ghastly custom whenever I move too slowly for his liking, I slide backward and find my feet of my own accord. I have to grasp the stirrup to keep my legs from buckling, but at least I'm standing. My soul smarts with defiance as I turn to Scythe.

He's not even looking at me. His focus is on the gulch.

"We'll cross here," he says. "Slow. Single file. You'll lead the horse. I'll take the rear."

My eyes widen as I step forward and get my first glimpse at his intentions. Across the wide gap of rock and shadow, a rickety bridge has been rigged up. The thick ropes suspending it from either side of the ravine look frayed with age. Its wood slats are spaced far too sparsely for my liking—some appear to be missing altogether. It swings in the breeze, creaking perilously.

"You cannot be serious," I breathe, horrified.

"I'm not known for my sense of humor."

"There's no chance that will hold our weight!"

"It will. It must." Scythe's voice is low. "It's the only way across—unless you plan to sprout wings and fly."

"I don't plan to cross at all! I'd rather fall to my death than head into those godsforsaken mountains."

"That can be arranged."

Crossing my arms over my chest, I glare at him. "We both know you need me alive."

His eyes cut to mine. "Do I?"

"If you didn't, I'd be dead ten times over already."

A grunt is all I get in response.

I glance at the mountains. Even with my head tipped all the way back, I cannot make out the summit through the dense cloud cover. "Whatever enemies pursue us, surely they cannot be more terrifying than the monsters that await us there."

Scythe's dark scoff makes me jolt. "You know little of monsters, girl." He pauses. A halting note—could it be trepidation?—threads into his tone. "Still, we cannot stay here. The men chasing us are not far behind. We've a half day's lead on them, at best. If they catch up . . . let's just say, you will be begging for an ice giant."

"Ice giant? Did you say *ice giant*?"

"Come." His hand clamps down on my arm and he begins to tow me toward the bridge. Terror springs to life within my breast. I dig in my heels, not above begging for a stay of execution.

"Wait! Wait," I plead, trying uselessly to pry his fingers off my arm. "If we truly must go north, there has to be another route we can take!"

"None we would survive."

Eyes wide, I look across the approaching void to the mountains looming on the other side. Up close, they are even more foreboding. "You mean the Avian Strait, don't you?"

Scythe glances sharply at me but does not contradict my suspicions. "What does a Midlands peasant girl know of the strait?"

"Only that those who attempt to pass through it are equally

likely to catch an arrow in the chest or find themselves buried beneath an avalanche." My features contort into a scowl. "Though I should think an icy grave better than death at the hands of that barbarian the Northlings call king."

There is a measured pause. "You've heard of Soren, then."

"That surprises you? His bloodthirsty exploits are whispered about in every corner of this land, from the sand caravans of Carvage to the white shores of Seahaven. Anwyvn's warring kings possess little common ground, but on this one front, they seem in complete accordance: King Soren is a scourge in need of execution."

When Scythe says nothing in return, I glance over at him. His eyes seem to glitter in the darkness, full of thoughts I cannot decipher. His face is set in what, on any other man, might be annoyance.

I clear my throat and change topics. "I was told the Avian Strait was the only way through the mountains." I look to the rope bridge. "Apparently, my tutor was mistaken."

"There are other ways. Older ways. Not many know of them anymore."

"But you do." My mind is spinning. "How? How can a soldier—even one of your rank—from a Midland campaign know of such things? Unless . . ."

Unless he is not of the Midlands at all.

He does not answer me. But I have learned to read him during our time together. The stiffness of his mouth confirms what I have suspected for days. Whoever he is—whoever he has been pretending to be—he is no middling soldier from the woods, no average fighter from the plains. No paper king calls him subject.

He is of the Northlands.

Of that I am now certain.

I open my mouth to question him again, but he is done

talking. He tugs me along until we reach the start of the bridge, where two mammoth stone pillars stand like sentinels, tethering the ropes—each thicker than the span of my waist—in place. We come to a stop between them.

My stomach plummets to my feet as I look across the swaying path before me. It is wide enough for only one to cross at a time. Up close, it appears even more unsound, sagging deeply at the center-most point, stretching on seemingly forever before it reaches the other side. The entire apparatus moans like a dying man each time a gust of wind whips through the ravine.

"Go on, then."

I glare up at Scythe. What I can see of his expression beneath the helmet is uncompromising. "I think I'd rather take my chances in the Avian Strait."

"It isn't up to you." He jerks his chin. "*Go.*"

"I . . ." I swallow harshly. "I am not a fan of heights."

"Of course you aren't. Gods, I should've left you to those men in the woods, for all the trouble you've caused me."

"Why didn't you, then?" I snap back. "I don't recall asking you to save me."

His grip tightens painfully on my arm. I must make some sub-dued sound of distress, because he releases me instantly with a grunt of exasperation. His chest expands as he pulls in a steady-ing breath. "Surely, such a headstrong child cannot be . . ."

My brows rise as he trails off. I open my mouth to ask what he means, but Scythe takes a stride, using his not-inconsiderable frame to herd me forward. When I fail to step onto the bridge willingly, he shoves at the small of my back. I whimper as my sock hits the first slat. The splintered wood lets out a fresh creak under my weight, and I freeze as fear commandeers my heart.

"*Go,*" Scythe hisses from behind me.

But I cannot move. I am paralyzed, staring down through the

gap between the first two slats into the pitch-black abyss below. There seems no end to the darkness.

It will be a bleak fall.

He pushes me again, and I grab the rope railings to keep from tripping.

"You will be the death of me," he mutters.

My retort is overshadowed by a metallic clang. My head whips around in time to see an arrow bounce off the stone pillar scant inches to our left, then clatter to the ground. Its feathered fletching is black and red.

Scythe's eyes meet mine for a frozen moment. His nostrils flare. His words, when they come, are razor-sharp, cutting into me with their intensity.

"They're here."

Another arrows sings through the air, whizzing close enough to stir the hair around my face. The prospect of plummeting to my death in the ravine is suddenly not so scary; not with the alternative so blazingly apparent. Death glows in the eyes of the red-clad soldiers who pour from the tree line not fifty paces away, some holding torches, others bearing swords and shields. They are close enough that I can see the interlocked torcs emblazoned on their tunics.

"For the love of gods, *go!*" Scythe barks, shoving me forward with impatient hands. "Run!"

There is no time for uncertainty, for hesitation. I bolt across the slats, my socked feet pounding the groaning wood, hands grasping for purchase on the rope railings. The bridge rocks beneath us. It's a bit like standing up in a rowboat—one faulty shift of weight will spell disaster. I do my best not to look down at the precipice below, nor behind at the soldiers who are rapidly closing in on us. Their voices carry on the night air—a captain calling out orders, his men answering. All too soon, they will reach the bridge.

I do not allow myself to wonder if it will hold beneath the weight of an entire company of men.

The stallion's hooves are a steady clip at my heels. Most horses would balk at such a crossing, but he is a surefooted beast—even under the constant siege of arrows that rain down around us from archers on the cliff side, finding marks far too close for comfort.

"Any slower, we'll be skewered!" Scythe calls gruffly from the rear.

"Any faster, we'll flip over!" I yell back.

"Better a sharp fall than a shaft through the heart!"

Pulse pounding twice its normal rate, I increase my speed. We are not yet to the middle of the bridge, where it pitches downward—still a long way to go before we reach solid ground. If I squint in the dark, I can just make out the twin stone pillars on the opposing bank.

Running headlong, my eyes fixed on the other side, I am so focused—on the arrows whizzing ever closer, on leaping over the occasional missing step—I do not see the broken slat until it is too late. My foot goes through it like a fist through paper and, as it crumbles to dust and falls into the gulch, I feel myself falling after it.

I scream as my legs pedal the air, scrambling uselessly for something solid to hold on to. My momentum works against me, propelling my whole body through the hole. I sink like a stone, powerless to stop my fate. My mind blanks, only one thought prevailing over the white noise of panic.

I am going to die.

My legs are already through the gap when my palms slam against a slat. I clutch at it desperately, fingernails clawing into the surface. The wood is splintered and rough and far too flimsy. As its edges gouge my palms, I think it, too, will give way, but I hold fast. My heart thuds so hard within my chest, it is a struggle to breathe.

The horse pulls up short with a whinny of distress, narrowly avoiding a collision. I hear Scythe shout something over the clatter of hooves, but my mind is too full of fear to process his words, plagued by images of plummeting death, of swallowing shadow, of painful splatter. For though I've halted my descent, that is only half the battle. Pulling myself up will prove far more difficult.

Fear pulses potent as an elixir in my veins. My muscles strain more with each passing moment as I dangle, lethal calculations whirring within my skull.

How much longer can I hold on?

How much longer until the slat gives way?

Scythe's voice brings me back to reality. "Are you hurt?"

"No," I call. The word cracks in my throat. "But the step—it shattered. I slipped through."

There is a marked pause before he responds. "I can't reach you from here. Can you pull yourself up?"

"Y-yes," I gasp. "I think so."

"Then you'd better do it fast." I hear a low curse. "We're out of arrow range for the moment, but they won't wait on the other side forever. They will risk the crossing eventually—and they will come with swords." Another pause. "Even if I could fight them off one by one, I doubt—"

My eyes press closed. He does not need to finish his sentence; I already know what he'll say. The bridge will not hold long enough for him to battle them. We will all be dead at the bottom of the chasm long before the first soldier reaches us at the center, a tangle of splintered bone and snapped rope.

Aware we are rapidly running out of time, I try twice to pull myself up—to no avail. Perhaps six months ago, six weeks ago, even six days ago I might've been strong enough. But I am weak, my muscles atrophied from too few meals and too many sleepless nights. My damaged wrists are not yet healed enough to do much besides hang here, awaiting the moment my well of fortitude runs dry.

Gravity presses down, growing heavier and heavier, urging me toward descent. The skirts around my legs tangle as my feet kick uselessly at empty air, seeking purchase where there is none to be found.

Come on, Rhya, I urge, ignoring the agony that ripples up my straining arms. *You did not come this far, and survive so much, only to die here at the hands of a faulty step.*

A cry catches in my throat as I try again. *Fail* again. The sound is barely audible over the growing roar of wind through the ravine. For as I struggle, whether by misfortune or something else entirely, the wind swells from a whisper to a shriek—a change so abrupt, it seems to defy the laws of nature. Quite suddenly, currents of air are swirling around us in an unpredictable vortex, tossing the bridge from left to right with such force, I think we truly might turn over. The ropes groan, the wood creaks, tested to their limits as we swing and twist.

Any attempts to heave myself up cease instantly. It is all I can do to cling for dear life as we whip back and forth. My mind is awhirl with blind terror, a crushing force that echoes inside my skull. Spasms overtake my body as it is pushed beyond its capabilities.

Hold on, hold on, hold on.

The force of the gusts is so strong, tears stream from my eyes and my hair whips violently around my face. My skirts are a deadly sail. I try to take a breath and find I cannot. My lungs feel frozen solid. The birthmark on my breastbone is so cold it burns.

Behind me, the horse brays loudly, the sound full of equine fear. Scythe is shouting again, but I cannot make out his words over the squall's howl. I cannot do anything at all, for in the face of the sudden storm, my strength has finally reached a breaking point.

I am failing.

Falling.

My grip gives out, hands slipping against the splintered wood as I slide backward through the gap. My stomach flies upward into my throat. All around, the wind wails like a wild thing. Or is that me, wailing?

The rest of the world dims to blunt sensations. Darkness, wind, defeat. My eyes press closed, not wanting to witness my own moment of surrender.

I will see you soon, Eli.

Is it that final plea that saves me? Is some guardian spirit looking down on me from the skies to extend a hand of aid? I suppose I will never know for sure. But whether godly miracle or a lucky trick of fate, at the exact moment I begin to plummet, the bridge pitches forward in a great gust. Instead of empty air, I feel my body collide with something solid.

When I find the strength to peel my eyes open, I am lying on the bridge with only my feet hanging through the gap. I gasp for breath, mind reeling, arms aching, heart pounding with relief and fright in equal measure.

"What in the skies . . ." Scythe's words drift to me. His voice is bleak in the sudden quiet—for the roaring has ceased completely.

The wind is gone.

It flees as suddenly as it arrived, disappearing in the space between one heartbeat and the next. The wood slats beneath me are still, swaying gently in a light breeze.

Did I imagine it?

"Are—are you all right?" Scythe asks, sounding as rattled as I feel.

All right? No.

Alive? Yes.

"I'm fine."

I can scarcely wrap my thoughts around how—but this is not the time for questions. Not with the enemy so close. I push to my feet, knees shaking as I rise, hands gripping the rope railings for dear life. My lungs ache. In fact, my entire chest aches, a frigid flame that intensifies with each inhale.

When I look back, the horse's liquid eyes are locked on me. They shine with an awareness that seems almost human as his velvety muzzle butts toward my hand. Around his hulking girth, I can see the metal flash of Scythe's helmet and, beyond, torches flaming in the darkness by the edge of the cliff.

They are moving closer.

The ropes groan under fresh weight as the soldiers pile onto the bridge.

Scythe curses again. "Time's up. They're coming. We need to move. Now." He sucks in a sharp breath. "Be more careful going forward, will you?"

Biting back a retort, I grab the stallion's bridle and lead him over the missing slat as quickly as I can. I move gingerly, keeping my steps light before placing my full weight upon them. I'll gladly sacrifice a bit of speed if it means surviving this swinging death trap.

With each passing moment, tension mounts in the air until the very sky seems to crackle with it. The bridge bounces beneath heavy boots as the men follow us across, slowly but steadily gaining ground. How many they've sent, I'm not certain. I can only hope the bridge holds long enough for us to make it to the other side.

Forty steps.

Just forty steps to solid ground.

Twice the width of Eli's cottage.

A distance you've walked ten thousand times.

My heart is in my throat with each perilous stride, but I keep moving—even when arrows once again begin to sail through the sky around us.

They are catching up.

Twenty steps.

Half the span of the meadow where you and Tomas spent so many stolen evenings.

You can do this, Rhya.

Footfalls echo in the air. Voices stir the wind, jeering taunts that promise pain. The sizzle of their torches is alive in my ears.

They are close.

Ten steps.

"Hurry," Scythe urges needlessly.

My eyes are locked on the twin stone pillars, where the ropes meet their end. I focus on the dull green moss clinging to them as I jog the final distance. When an arrow whizzes by and lodges in the grass, missing me by mere inches, I barely flinch; I am so relieved to feel the earth beneath my feet, there is no space left over for fear. I could kiss the ground, I'm so happy to be standing upon it.

The stallion follows me off the bridge, the whites of his eyes rolling as arrows fall like rain. The second his hooves are clear, he trots smartly out of the archers' range, heading for the nearby shelter of a rocky outcropping. I make to follow him, but a pained roar stills my movements.

Turning, I see Scythe has caught an arrow in his shoulder. The tip protrudes just above his heart—not a lethal blow, but nearly. His mouth twists in agony as he lurches forward, catching himself on the final slats of the bridge.

He does not get back up.

For a moment, he does not move at all.

I still, frozen with indecision, torn between the urge to abandon my captor and the strange guilt that accompanies it.

Run, Rhya.

You owe him nothing.

There's little time to weigh my options. Crossing the center of the bridge—not far from the spot I nearly met my end—a small contingent of men is advancing, torches illuminating their features in the darkness. They are moving rapidly now, so close I can make out the red of their tunics. In a matter of moments, they will be upon us.

Scythe's groan draws my attention back to him. In clear pain, he drags himself upright, leaning heavily on the rope railing. His left arm hangs limply at his side. Dark blood drips from his fingertips, a steady torrent. When his eyes lift to mine, he flinches as though surprised to see me standing there. As though he expected me to abandon him.

Why haven't I abandoned him?

"You should've run, you idiot," he growls, stumbling forward, his gait unsteady. He grips the rope with his good hand, grunting in pain as he hauls himself along. In truth, he's right—I am an idiot—because I do not run as he's bid me, but dart forward, back onto the bridge, directly toward the approaching danger. Before he can say anything, I loop his uninjured arm over my shoulder.

"What are you doing?"

"What does it look like?" I snap as we hobble sideways across the final slats. Gods, he's heavy.

As soon as we step onto solid ground, he shrugs off my help. His face is a mask of pain and anger as he shoves me into the shelter of one of the pillars. He leans his own frame against its twin, panting heavily. I suck in a steadying breath as my back hits the stone, grateful for a reprieve—however fleeting.

Arrows sail all around us. I listen to them clatter as they strike the other side of the pillars, then ricochet into the gulch. If

I make a dash for the tree line now, Scythe won't be the only one with a hole pierced through his body.

"You should've run when you had the chance," he seethes, each word laced with pain. His mouth is pressed into a stern line. He looks paler than usual; he's lost a lot of blood.

"Forgive me for trying to save your life, you ungrateful lug!"

"I did not require saving."

"Could've fooled me." I jerk my chin at his shoulder wound. "How far do you think you'll get with that arrow inside you? There's no way you can outrun those archers."

"I'm not planning to outrun them."

My brows lift. I open my mouth to ask what he means by that but never get the chance—he's already stepped out from behind the shelter of his pillar.

Is he mad?

He must be. There's no way he can fight all of them. Certainly not injured.

I soon realize that is not his intention. With his good arm, Scythe reaches up, unsheathes the sword strapped across his back, and swings. He severs the left side of the bridge in one clean strike, cutting through the thick suspension ropes with a low grunt.

The soldiers scream as the bridge pitches, scrambling to hold on to the side that remains intact. Their torches and bows fall into the ravine, devoured quickly by the dark. They are close enough for me to see their white-knuckled grips, their pinwheeling legs. Close enough to hear the terror in their calls for aid. Close enough to read the fear on their faces as they look frantically in our direction.

I know that fear. I felt it myself, as my own legs dangled over shadows that threatened to swallow me whole. But these soldiers are stronger than me—battle-hardened men. They will last longer than I did. When we are long gone from here, they can climb their way back to safety.

Scythe's sword arm rises again.

"Wait!" I yell, starting forward.

But he does not. His sword slashes downward, severing the right side. In horror, I watch the bridge fall, twisting like a ribbon in the wind. The soldiers' screams carry back to us long after they disappear from view.

In the jarring silence that follows, I look across the chasm to where the tatters of the bridge hang against the opposite cliff. Above it, the remaining soldiers stand at the edge. I cannot make out their features in detail, but I know they are there from the flames that dance atop their torches.

I wonder if they are staring back at me across that void with vengeance in their hearts. If they, like me, will carry the sound of those plummeting screams from this day until their souls meet the skies.

CHAPTER
SEVEN

L et's go," Scythe says lowly.

There is no remorse in his voice. No guilt or grief over the fact that he has just executed an entire company of men—for the second time in our short acquaintance.

I stare at him, swallowing down the lump of horror lodged in my throat. My thoughts feel far removed from reality. My words, when I manage to speak, ring hollow in the quietude of dawn.

"All those men . . . you killed them."

"If I hadn't, they would've killed us. Or worse." There is a terse pause. "You think me callous?"

"I think a man who can take so many lives in trade for his own, easily as coin bartered at market, is no man at all but something else entirely." I shake my head, unable to dispel the horrific images. "Something more akin to a monster."

If he is offended by my brash assessment, he does not show it. He merely sheathes his sword and sighs heavily. "Better the monster than the quarry it devours."

"We could've gotten away without . . . without . . ." I gesture to the chasm. "You did not have to kill them."

"They would've hunted us into the mountains. Even now, with the bridge felled, we are not safe. Not for long. They will find another way across eventually." His nostrils flare on a sharp exhale and his voice drops, almost as though he is speaking to himself. "Perhaps before, when they were chasing naught but whispers, they wouldn't have bothered. They would have let us slip away, sought other bounty to fill their master's bottomless cup. But now . . . Now, they will never stop. Now that they have seen . . ." He looks at me sharply. "They will not stop until we have been captured. He will not let them."

"*He?* He who?"

Scythe narrows his eyes at me. "Can you truly be so sheltered?"

"Can you truly not give a straight answer to a single one of my questions?"

"You try my patience, girl."

"I wasn't aware you had any to try."

"Trust me, ten minutes in your maddening presence would strain the stoicism of a druid."

"Amusing, coming from the most vexing man I've ever met."

"Save your amusement. Try some appreciation instead."

"*Appreciation?* For what, exactly? Kidnapping me? Making me party to not one, but two massacres? Leading me into a mountain range few men ever return from intact?"

"Would you rather I'd left you to die?"

"Perhaps!" I fire back. "For what kind of life is one lived with so much blood on one's hands?"

"I have neither the time nor the inclination to listen to your twisted idealisms."

In my fury, I forget to be afraid of him. I take two strides closer, my eyes fixed on his. "Those men were soldiers, acting on the commands of a king they likely never even met. They had lives outside of this endless killing. Crops to tend. Homes to protect. Wives to take into their arms. Children to . . . to . . ." Biting

my lip, I blink back infuriating tears. Emotions will get me nowhere. Not with him. I could sooner move a stone wall than the
heart inside this man by weeping.

"It's curious," he says flatly. His stare is cold as it lingers on the
wetness of my cheeks. "You freely lament the fate of your enemy . . .
and yet you walk for days on bloodied soles without shedding so
much as a tear for your own misfortune. I cannot tell if that is a
mark of self-discipline or childlike delusion." His eyes narrow on
mine. "The latter, surely. If you had even the loosest understanding of the dire nature of your situation, you would be wailing for
your parents like a babe torn too soon from the breast."

"The fact that you cannot fathom my resolve does not indicate its absence. Do not speak of things you know nothing about.
My parentage, for instance." I suck in a steadying breath as I glare
at him across the thin divide between us. "And as for our situation, is it any wonder I cannot fully appreciate its shadowy nature
when you have failed to offer even a single ray of illumination at
every given opportunity?"

His scoff is nearly a snarl. "Did it never occur to you these
past few days, as we rode at a breakneck gallop, that we might be
doing so for a reason beyond enjoying the feel of the wind in our
hair? Did you never once contemplate the possibility that we
were sleeping in the wild instead of at inns, traversing fields
rather than roads, for a purpose outside appreciating the soli-
tudes of nature?"

I blink, startled.

Until this point, I assumed I was the root cause of Scythe's
outright hostility. Perhaps I've been mistaken. Perhaps his hostility is a symptom of something else. Something bigger. I still
don't know the full scope of what is going on here, but clearly,
this is more than mere retribution for what he did to Burrows's
unit. More than the hunt for an escaped halfling.

I want to ask about the men in red—who they are, why they are so dogged in their pursuit—but, as usual, he doesn't give me an opportunity.

"No. Of course not." His jaw tightens. "You, with your useless, bleeding heart. Incapable of contempt. More concerned with crying for your enemy than coming to grips with the harsher realities of your circumstance."

"It may come as a surprise to an emotionally stunted creature such as yourself to learn that evolved beings are more than capable of holding two contradictory beliefs at once. My *useless, bleeding heart* can feel both compassion and contempt for those men." I jerk my chin up, a haughty move. "And, for the record, being raised with tenderness is not a fatal flaw."

"Just because it hasn't killed you yet does not mean it won't in the future." He sighs and shakes his head, exasperated. "Misplaced empathy will earn you no favors in this world. Any empathy, in fact. You would do well to harden yourself against it."

"Why? So I can be more like you? No, thank you." I scrub my tears away with the back of my sleeve. "I wouldn't expect you to understand why I behave as I do. A man like you cannot feel anything—anything except cold-blooded calculation."

"Don't forget annoyance," he mutters pointedly. "I've felt plenty of that, these past few days. In fact, one could say I did those soldiers a favor by sending them over that cliff. Now they are forever absolved of the distinct frustration of your company."

I reel backward. "How can you jest about such things? Have you no conscience at all?"

"You think me some unfeeling villain—that's fine by me." He shrugs, wincing when the arrow in his shoulder shifts. "I don't care much about your opinion. I have one objective: to keep you alive until we reach the other side of these mountains."

"And when we get there? What then?"

On that front, however, I will get no clarity. He has already turned from me, whistling for his horse. The stallion trots obediently from the shadows, seeming no worse for wear despite our rather dramatic crossing of the bridge.

"Onyx," Scythe murmurs with surprising softness, stroking his hand along the stallion's glossy flank. "My steady boy."

I look away, not wanting to see him act thus. Not wanting to know he is capable of kindness, of connection—even if it is only with his horse. It is far easier to think him a definitive brute, with no nuanced shades of humanity creeping in at the edges.

Scythe removes something from one of the saddlebags, then walks over to a flat-topped boulder. A low groan of pain slips from his mouth as he sits down.

"Come here, girl."

Unmoving, I cross my arms over my chest. When I fail to comply with his order, he looks up. "Are you deaf now? *Come.*"

"I am not a hound."

"Mmm. More like a rabid terrier, with the way you snap back."

"Do you find insulting someone is your best strategy when preparing to ask for their assistance?"

A muscle in his jaw ticks as he attempts to lock down his temper. "I need . . ."

I know what he needs, but in this moment, I am petty enough to wait for the words it so chafes him to utter. "*Yes?*"

"The arrow." He grimaces. "I can't ride with it like this."

"And?"

"I can't pull it out myself, as you well know." His expression darkens into a scowl. "I . . . I need your help."

From the look on his face, admitting that aloud is more painful for him than the shaft embedded in his shoulder. My lips twist. "Were you not just lecturing me on the perils of empathy for one's enemy?"

"I am not your enemy."

I startle, surprised by the quiet conviction in his voice. "Well. What are you, then?"

"Are you going to help me or not?" he asks in lieu of a real answer. In the gathering daylight, his face looks quite drawn; the pain must be significant. I decide not to goad him further. With a resigned sigh, I take a few hesitant steps forward, my socks crunching on the snowy earth.

It's strange. I called him a monster. I saw him do monstrous things. And yet, as I close the gap between us, I feel no fear that he will harm me. Somewhere along the way, I lost my wariness of him. It's not trust, exactly—for who could ever trust such a man?—but rather a grudging realization that, for all his questionable methods, for whatever dark end awaits me in the Northlands . . . he will do whatever it takes to keep me alive. In that, I find a twisted semblance of solace—much like a pig, I suppose, fat and happy in the care of the same farmer who will eventually lead it to the slaughter.

Scythe holds a short dagger, its point lethally sharp, the handle etched with indecipherable glyphs. It glints in the pale dawn light.

"Are you certain it's wise to arm me?" I ask, holding his stare. "As we have ascertained already, I'm not overly fond of you."

"I find it amusing you believe you are any threat to me. Even with a blade in your hand."

"If you want my assistance, I suggest you stop insulting me."

Wordlessly, he extends the dagger in my direction, hilt first. I take it from him without comment and, after a beat of hesitation, bend to examine his wound. It is the closest I've ever been to him. His every exhale stirs the fine hair at my temples.

My mouth goes dry as a dizzying mix of apprehension and adrenaline sizzles through my veins. It's the same sensation I experienced last autumn, when I came across a juvenile lynx tangled in one of my snares. I'd worked to set him free, all the while excruciatingly aware that the moment I succeeded, he might turn and rip out my throat in thanks.

In the end, the lynx had simply limped away to lick his wounds.

Scythe is far less predictable.

Though I focus all my attention on the blood-soaked arrowhead, it takes effort to ignore the details in my peripherals. Dark stubble growing along a sharp jawline. Serpentine silver over the bridge of a nose. The smell of sweat and horse and spice—the same heady scent I breathed from his tunic at the reflective pool three days past.

Was that only three days past?

It seems an eternity.

"You'll have to saw through the shaft," Scythe says, the low timbre of his voice vibrating in the air around me. "Keep your hands steady. Go slow. And try not to pass out. There will be blood—enough that you'll need to apply pressure."

"With what?"

"Your hand will do fine."

"My hand will *not* do fine," I say crossly. "Not unless you'd like to bleed out in the snow."

"I should think that would make you happy."

My eyes roll skyward. "Despite what you think of me, I'm not a fool. I know I would not last long alone in these mountains with avalanches and enemy soldiers and gods only know what else."

I have not forgotten his earlier comment about the ice giants. Nor can I overlook the fact that, even if I do find my way south, I have no home to return to, no allies awaiting me. My life, for all intents and purposes, burned to ashes along with the Starlight Wood. There is no choice but to help Scythe now, in the hope that another opportunity to escape will arise later.

I clear my throat. "With the bridge down, I have no earthly idea how to get back to the Midlands. So, it appears I'm stuck here. Stuck with you."

"No need to sound so overjoyed about it."

The retort dies on my tongue as my eyes flicker up to meet his. They are startlingly close. For the first time, I notice their true color—a deep bronze, almost metallic shade, like embers of a dying fire. At the edges of each iris, lighter striations of reddish gold make a stark contrast. Strangest of all, his pupils are not perfectly round, but slightly elongated in a way that is . . . not entirely human.

Those eyes belong in the skull of a wolf, not a man, I think, dropping my gaze from his. Even focusing on the ground, I can feel the weight of his stare on my face. It burns like a hot brand—a feverish contrast to the pervasive chill that pulses from the center of my chest.

Gods, will my birthmark ever stop aching?

"Do you have a spare cloth?" I ask, my voice oddly thick. "Anything I can use to staunch the wound?"

"Check the saddlebags. There should be something."

I stalk toward the stallion without another word, suddenly very eager for some breathing room. He dances a bit as I begin rooting through the leather compartments. Sparsely packed as they are, it does not take me long to inventory the contents: a store of wrinkled apples, two bars of coarse soap, a hatchet, a length of coiled rope. Nothing useful until, finally, I locate a large cotton handkerchief wrapped around some stale bannocks. It's not exactly clean, but it'll do in a pinch.

As I pull it free, my eye catches on something silver at the very bottom of the bag—a thin flask with a cork stopper. I sniff its contents, nose scrunching as the strong fumes of alcohol invade my senses. A potent brew. Recorking it, I carry the flask back to

Scythe along with the handkerchief, the dagger, and the jar of salve I've been using on my wrists. It is nearly empty now.

His mouth tugs up at one side as he spots the spirits. "In need of a bit of liquid courage?"

"Not quite." I tear a strip off the kerchief and douse it with a generous pour. Before he can question me further, I press the saturated fabric to the edge of his wound, where the arrow shaft protrudes from his skin.

"*Gods!*" A hiss of pain escapes his lips. "You might've warned me."

"It may sting, but it will prevent infection."

There is a marked pause. His voice, when he speaks next, holds a hint of surprise. "You know something of healing, then?"

"Enough to set a bone, mix a salve, steep a fever-reducing tea . . ." I meet his gaze again. "And enough to remove this arrow if you'll stop distracting me."

His brows are so high, they have disappeared beneath the rim of his helm. I am not sure whether to be flattered or insulted by his astonishment in learning I am not entirely without skills. Not that it matters. I don't care what he thinks of me.

The dagger is lightweight. It fits well in the palm of my hand, not so different from the one I used back home to tend the garden Eli and I planted beside our cottage many seasons ago. Since I was old enough to memorize their names, my mentor had taught me about the different plants and their wide array of healing properties. I can tell goldenrod from ragwort in a deep forest, discern feverfew from chamomile beneath a canopy of branches, pick out allheal from nettle in a field of wildflowers. I know which mushroom caps will make you see daemons, which ones will taste particularly savory in a stew, and which ones will stop your heart cold in your chest. It is one of the skills that kept me alive, all those weeks alone in the woods.

I wish I had access to some of those herbs now, but even a cursory glance at our environment reveals it to be a bleak, barren place. The only things that grow with any sort of regularity are the piles of snow and ice weighing down the tree boughs.

I sigh.

No herbs. No boiling water. No fresh bandages. No brew of oak to temper the pain. No calming advice from Eli. If he were here, he'd fix me with those steadfast eyes and speak words of wisdom into my ear.

Breathe, Rhya. You have the skills you require; do not allow your nerves to overcome them.

Sucking in a sharp breath, I brace one hand on Scythe's shoulder to hold him steady. His muscles are hard as granite beneath my fingertips.

"This is going to hurt," I warn pointlessly. I know without asking that this man has withstood worse than an arrow through the shoulder in his lifetime.

"Just get it over with," he says, teeth clenched.

I saw through the shaft as quickly as I can, doing my best to keep it from shifting. Thankfully, the dagger is quite sharp; after only a few short strokes back and forth, the arrowhead falls into the dirt, leaving behind a blunted wooden edge protruding from his chest.

"Halfway there," I murmur.

Moving behind Scythe, I grab the back end of the arrow by its fletching. The red and black feathers are ticklish against my palm. Bracing my other hand around the margin of the wound, I chew my bottom lip.

"Ready?" I ask.

He grunts.

Taking that as confirmation, I yank the arrow straight back in one clean tug. It must hurt, but Scythe barely even flinches.

Except for a sharp intake of air, he does not react at all. Dropping
the shaft into the dirt, I apply pressure to the wound with a fresh
strip of kerchief. When it is soaked through with blood, I toss the
rag aside and exchange it for a new one. The bleeding is considerable, but not so much that his life is in danger. I'm relieved
when, after a few moments, it slows to a trickle.

Slathering the puncture with the last bit of healing salve in the
jar, I then wrap his shoulder as best I can—weaving a strip of fabric below his collarbone, knotting it tightly so it will not shift
when he moves. He is a model patient, holding himself perfectly
still. I don't even think he's breathing as my fingers skate across
his shoulder, smoothing the fabric flat. Then again, I seem to be
breathing rapidly enough for the both of us.

I struggle to keep my mind clear, relying on muscle memory
to complete my task. *He is no one of consequence*, I tell myself as
I bend close, my nose nearly brushing his neck, my pulse roaring
between my ears. *Just another patient in need of tending. You'd
do the same for any sickly villager in Seahaven who called upon
Eli for healing.*

"You won't have full use of your arm for a few days," I inform
the back side of his helmet when I am finished. The metal is dull
gray in the faint light.

"I heal quickly," is all he says in response.

Stepping away, I kneel to clean my hands in the snow. The
blood leaves a glaring stain of red against the white mound.
When I rise back to full height, I find Scythe on his feet with his
hand held out in my direction.

"The dagger."

Damn. I'd thought he missed my slipping it into the pocket of
my gown. My chin jerks stubbornly. "I'm keeping it."

"No."

"Yes," I snap, knowing full well he can easily take it from

me—even with one arm incapacitated. "Consider it payment for my aid."

He stares at me for a beat, then sighs and turns away, as though deciding it isn't worth the energy to argue. "We should get moving. The sun doesn't penetrate the mountain mist much beyond midday. It'll be dark again in a few hours, and we have a lot of ground to cover."

I follow him over to the horse. Despite my best efforts to conceal my surprise, I'm certain he sees the dumbfounded look on my face when instead of throwing me over the rump, his good arm hooks around my waist and he boosts me up onto the saddle. It is not designed for a gowned rider, but I plant myself as best I can with my legs draped over one side and my hands on the pommel.

Before I can question the sudden change in riding arrangements, Scythe swings up behind me. His chest presses flush against the planes of my back. His hands hang by my hips, effectively caging me in.

I suck in a sharp breath.

Perhaps being lashed to the back like cargo is preferable, after all.

"Take the reins," he orders, his breath gusting warm on my nape. "Onyx knows the way."

Leaving the fallen bridge behind, I ride into the mist-shrouded mountains—reins in my hand, enemy at my back, heart lodged firmly in my throat.

CHAPTER
EIGHT

The path is steep—a narrow switchback of icy stone, nearly vertical in pitch. A thick cover of clouds clings to the mountains like cologne on a courtier's neck. Ascending into it, I can see no more than ten paces ahead of us. Though I suppose any view at all is an improvement on that afforded by my previous riding position.

I hold the reins but I do not steer, for Scythe did not exaggerate—Onyx knows the way. His hooves never falter as he navigates around boulders and fallen tree limbs, over snowbanks and ice sheets, an ever-upward march. Far below, the ravine is a constant presence, growing all the more bottomless as we climb. It runs the length of the range, a dark vein of demarcation dividing civilization from barbarity.

The Northlands.

Of all the places I thought my path would lead, it was not here. Not to this hellscape. Sure as I know my own name, I am certain I'll meet my end in these mountains. As good a place to perish as any, I suppose. If my bones bleach beneath the cold Cimmerian sun for all eternity . . . Well, there is no one left to mourn me anyway.

The air in my lungs is thin, each breath tinged with the scent of pine sap. I pull in shallow gulps, trying not to shiver as the wind whips at my face. Feeling my poorly subdued shakes, Scythe presses closer to my back and adjusts his cloak more firmly around both of us. I can feel the hard planes of his chest even through the fabric of my dress, so warm it's a bit like leaning against the wall of a furnace. The leather straps of his bandolier are a pointed reminder of the peril that chases us up the mountain.

"I'm f-f-fine," I say through chattering teeth.

"Stubborn is what you are." I can practically hear his scowl. "Rather freeze to death than admit weakness."

"Honestly, of all the ways I thought I'd d-d-die these past f-f-few days, freezing to d-d-death sounds almost pleasant."

He does not dignify my snide remark with a response. And I cease my protests, for, though it pains me to admit it, the journey is undeniably more tolerable riding thus. Pressed close to Scythe's chest as I am, a slow heat begins to radiate through my body, starting at my spine and ebbing outward until I can once again wiggle my frozen fingers. After a few moments, my shivers slow, then stop altogether.

For a while, we ride onward in silence, the horse plucking a careful track on the slippery slope. Questions gnaw at me. I tell myself not to put words to them, but eventually I am overpowered by my own insufferable curiosity.

"Have you traveled this way many times before?"

"Enough to know the way." Succinct as ever.

"Which makes you—what, exactly? A spy, sent down to the Midlands by some northern king pondering invasion?"

"I'm not certain why you suddenly feel entitled to ask."

"Of course." I drop my voice to imitate his low rasp. *"Prisoners are not privy to information."*

This, he ignores outright.

I sigh heavily. "What difference does telling me a few measly details make? I'm going to find out where your allegiance lies as soon as we arrive at our destination. I'll learn the name of the liege whose boots you lick when you throw me at his feet."

Still, Scythe remains stubbornly silent.

Gods, the man is insufferable.

With one hand, I tighten my grip on the reins, wishing I could as easily rein in my temper. With the other, I finger the slim blade buried deep in the pocket of my gown. For both our sakes, I hope we haven't much farther to go before journey's end. Any more time spent at each other's throats might result in one of them getting slit open.

SEVERAL HOURS LATER, it is a vast relief when the switch-back path veers away from the summit and into a natural valley between two adjoining peaks. As the endless climb flattens to a solid plane of earth, I summon the energy to open my eyes. My lids feel stiff. As for the rest of me, I've long since gone numb. A girl carved from ice, chilled to the very bone. Even my captor's furnace-like heat isn't enough to stave off the relentless cold at this altitude.

At some point during the ascent, my stubborn nature faltered in the battle against arctic air. I now find myself slumped fully against Scythe, as much for warmth as to keep from losing my seat on the precarious incline. He is irritatingly warm. Warmer than he has any right to be, frankly, when I'm teetering on the edge of frostbite. The indignity of it—*needing him*—leeches through me like poison. Forcing my frozen limbs into motion, I grab the pommel and straighten in the saddle to create a bit of space between us.

Regret blasts through me instantly. Parted from his body heat, I feel the frigid air bite with hungry teeth. I do my best to suppress the shivers racking my body, but it's a futile effort. My very bones are rattling.

If Scythe notices my sudden repositioning, he does not remark upon it. As that would require his voluntarily speaking to me, I can't say I'm entirely surprised by that fact.

Overhead, a weak winter sun burns, dissipating the thick mountain mist as it rises higher in the sky. Beams of light refract off the peaks, a blinding white. I squint, trying to make out our surroundings. Before us lies an expanse of snow that seems to stretch on forever. Save for a few green trees, the landscape is entirely colorless. Wind stirs the drifts into vortexes that dance across the valley's surface.

Onyx draws to a halt without warning, his chain mail tackle chiming. Behind me, Scythe shifts in the saddle, grunting lowly in discomfort as he lifts his wounded arm. With his fingers at his lips, he looses a sharp, birdlike whistle.

The sound itself should not surprise me—I've heard it before, back at the bridge. Yet, in the chaotic aftermath of the attack, I somehow forgot to ask him about it. I've also failed to inquire who, exactly, sent the answering whistle that echoed at us from the other side of the canyon.

Not that he'll tell me.

This time, when it comes, the returning signal sounds much closer. Whoever awaits us is not far away. I can't help wondering where they were earlier, when we were under enemy fire. With a cluck of his tongue, my captor spurs Onyx to a canter. I'm thankful my hands already grip the pommel; it is all I can do to hold on as we race along in a thunder of hooves, snow kicking up in a cloud.

Our pounding pace does not break until we reach the other side of the valley. There, the unending tract of white earth cracks open astride a formation of fallen rock from some long-ago avalanche. As we near, I see a gap of shadow amid the boulders. The mouth of a cave—one tall enough that we do not even need to dismount as Onyx carries us under the stony canopy. I hold my breath as we pass beneath icicles long as my legs, their spear-like points spelling instant death should they break free at the wrong moment.

My eyes strain to acclimate to the sudden shift from blinding white to pitch black as earth encompasses us from all sides. The space is dim but cavernous. Shadows loom large on every side. Onyx's slowing hoofbeats clatter far out of earshot, deep underground. I am so grateful to be shielded from the wind, I do not notice the figure stepping forward to greet us until a voice shatters the darkness.

"*Oi!*"

I start violently at the sound, nearly losing my seat in the process. Scythe steadies me instantly with a steely grip on my side. His touch does not linger a second longer than strictly necessary.

"About time you showed up," the same wry voice calls, stepping forward as Onyx draws to a halt. "Been waiting all day. My bollocks are nearly frozen off."

"Brothel bells across the land will ring, rejoicing at the news," Scythe fires back without missing a beat.

The man laughs—a boisterous sound that fills the cavern, rebounding off the walls in a chorus. My eyes, slowly adjusting to the dark, widen in surprise. Until this moment, I had not known my captor capable of humor. I sit frozen, stunned at the revelation, as he swings down from the saddle. The men clasp arms with a familiarity that speaks of long acquaintance.

"What are you doing here, Jac? Last time I saw you, you were drunk off your ass in a Holywell tavern, freshly released from your last campaign. Claimed to anyone who'd listen you were done with soldiering and planned to marry a wench named Beatrice."

"I'd say I remember that conversation, but that would be a lie based on the amount of pints I consumed that night." The stranger pauses. "Turns out, Beatrice wasn't half as handsome in the sober light of day. Signed up for another stint as soon as the ale was out of my system. I figured another tour was better than waiting around for you to return home with proper marching orders, twiddling my thumbs. Though if I'd known Yale was going to stick me with the Cimmerian Division, I might've stayed with Beatrice, monobrow and all. Would've been preferable to ten months patrolling mountain passes and driving off bloody frost-fiends, praying my manhood doesn't turn to ice."

"Might be for the best, given the state of your love life."

"There's that sense of empathy I've missed so much." Jac snorts. "Anyway, thanks to my glorious new position, I happened to be nearby when one of my scouts heard your signal at the pass. Figured it might be you."

"Figured right."

"You weren't due back for two months. Run into trouble?"

Scythe grunts. "You could say that."

"I see you brought some excess baggage back with you."

Both men turn to look at me. Even in the dim light, I can make out identical expressions of solemn contemplation.

"She the one, then?"

Another grunt from Scythe.

"Must be, if you were willing to leave ahead of schedule. Not like you to deviate from a plan."

"No other choice," Scythe admits lowly. "Extracting her was . . . complicated."

Jac looses a low oath. "Is your cover blown, then?"

"Assuming the Eastwood generals have heard one of their commanders took out an entire company of men, I'd say so."

"You never were one for subtlety." Jac elbows Scythe, jostling his wound. His only indication of pain is a sharp breath, but it does not go unnoticed. "You're hurt."

"I'm fine."

"Bloody bandage says otherwise."

"It's nothing. Arrow caught me in the shoulder. Half-healed already."

"Courtesy of Eld's troops?" Jac asks. His question is met with a long beat of silence. In it, he seems to read unspoken answers, for his voice adopts a shade of stunned disbelief. "Not Efnysien's men?"

Efnysien?

The strange name tugs at my psyche, somehow familiar though I'm certain I've never heard it before. Is he the one to whom Scythe referred earlier? The mysterious "he" who will not stop until we are captured?

Scythe grunts a confirmation.

"This far north?" Jac's mouth gapes. "What in the skies are they doing all the way up here?"

Scythe again says nothing, but his gaze seems to sharpen on me. In the dark, his eyes glow like embers.

"*Her?*"

If I had any real concept of what they're talking about, I might take offense at the sheer disbelief saturating Jac's tone. As it is, I can only stare back at Scythe, trapped by his gaze of dark fire. Questions race through my mind, unchecked.

Me?

Why would anyone be looking for me?

I'm no one.

"We'll discuss it later," Scythe tells his companion.

Of course. He'd never discuss anything meaningful in front of a paltry prisoner. I nearly roll my eyes at the predictability of it all. Instead, I force my gaze to break from his and dismount with a thud that jars my bones. The mountain earth is frozen solid. Even here in the shelter of the cave, each breath fogs the air in front of my face.

When I turn to face the men, both are watching me carefully—Scythe with his typical unreadable mask, Jac with a broad grin of welcome so unexpected, it makes me stagger back a step. My shoulder blades slam into Onyx, who whinnies softly in response.

The newcomer watches my retreat, brows high on his handsome face. He wears simple but well-made mountain garb designed to blend in with the snow—thick gray fabric with a leather vest layered over the top and sturdy boots to the knee. A wolf pelt lines his cloak collar. No banners or insignias anywhere to declare his loyalties, no easily identifiable sovereign colors on display. Whoever he is, whatever business he concerns himself with, he conducts in stealth.

There are dual sheaths strapped to his back—one holding a sword, the other a double-headed battle-axe with an ornate wooden handle and wickedly sharp blades. He has a crop of dark-blond hair that falls nearly to his shoulders and a rangy, athletic form that makes him seem more youthful than his twenty-odd years. His ears are rounded—human, not halfling.

"You expect me to believe," he says, head tilting sideways as he examines me in turn, a small smile still playing at his lips, "this half-starved slip of a thing is the answer to all our prayers?"

More questions spring to life, crowding my already cluttered mind.

Me?

An answer to prayers?

Absurd.

"Jac," Scythe warns.

"Perhaps you've been praying to the wrong gods, if I'm the answer you've received." It's a struggle to keep my voice even. "I assure you, I'm not . . . whoever it is you think I am."

"No?" Jac asks, smile widening farther.

I nod.

"Who are you, then?"

"No one of importance," I say instantly. "Just an ordinary girl from an ordinary househo—"

"She bears a Remnant mark." Scythe's blunt comment cuts through the cave like . . . well, like a scythe.

My mouth snaps shut.

Remnant?

I've never heard the term before. But clearly Jac has—his head swivels to examine his friend, all playfulness extinguished. "Are you certain?"

"Would I have risked my position with Eld's men otherwise?"

"You're certain," Jac mutters.

"The Eastwood captain who captured her said it damn near seared off one of his men's hands when he tried to . . ." Scythe's own hands clench into fists. "Tried to touch her."

"Gods." Jac looks at me again. "*No one of importance*, my ass."

"Listen," I interject, attempting to sound placating. In truth, I am beginning to panic. It is bad enough to find myself here, a prisoner in the Northlands of all places, at the mercy of the scariest man I've ever laid eyes on and his slightly less scary, but nonetheless worrisome, compatriot. To then hear those men discussing me like I am some sort of strange, mythical creature about to be placed in a menagerie against my will—or worse, stuffed and mounted upon a wall—is more than I can stomach.

"Whatever you think you know about me, whoever you think I am . . . you are grossly mistaken. *Remnant?* I don't even know what that is. I certainly don't possess one." I laugh, but the sound is laced with panic. "You're mad if you've dragged me all the way up here because of a simple birthmark . . ."

The men trade a glance.

"*Simple birthmark*," Scythe mutters. "Skies above."

"Could she truly be ignorant of it?" Jac sounds baffled.

"The Midlands kingdoms were forged on blood and ignorance." Scythe shrugs. "It's possible she was so sheltered, she never had occasion to put it to use until now."

Jac's brow furrows in thought. "Perhaps someone sheltered her on purpose. To keep her safe. Undetected. Dangerous times to be a halfling with a madman like Eld on the throne."

Both of them are staring at me again. Unconsciously, I reach up and lay a hand over the fabric of my bodice, where the triangle of inky whorls is etched between my breasts. It's begun to tingle, a cold pricking of the skin. As if it knows they are discussing it. As if it truly is imbued with some dormant ability.

The thought makes me itchy with discomfort. My fingers press harder, wishing to quell its icy ache. Unwilling to be soothed, the mark seems to press back at me, pushing upward, the slightly raised surface pulsing with the unsettling energy I've spent a lifetime trying to ignore. Something deeper than the cold. Something older. Something . . . alive.

Awake, it seems to whisper. *Finally awake.*

I shiver, unnerved. I do not particularly enjoy the idea that there is something sentient lurking there, under my skin. My body invaded by something I cannot control.

For all my life, the mark has been a source of secret shame. Never to be discussed openly. Not even with Eli. Some of my earliest memories in life are of my mentor, eyes grave as his tone, tasking me to keep it covered at all times. No exceptions.

Why is it so dangerous if they see? I'd asked him once, when I was eight years old and wanted more than anything to go swimming with the other children from our village. It was rare enough that they'd invited me—the friendless halfling runt—to play; it was unfathomable that I would not accept such an offer. And yet, he'd shaken his head, an unequivocal *no.*

There'd been no stopping the flow of tears. *Am I cursed, Eli? Am I . . . bad?*

No, Rhya. Not bad. Just . . . different, he'd explained in that solemn way of his. *Humankind fears the unfamiliar above all else. You must always remember—the things that make you unique are the first weapons they will use against you. Best not give them the advantage. Best blend in, whenever you can. You cannot hide your ears, but you* must *hide your birthmark. Understand?*

I had nodded. But truthfully, I had not understood that day, sitting in my favorite tree on the riverbank, watching the human children splash and frolic in the waves, their laughter a painful underscore to my loneliness.

I understand now.

Different is dangerous.

The way Jac and Scythe are looking at me . . . I feel as though I am about to be flayed open, my insides examined for some proof of mutation. I want to reject everything they are saying, insist that I am just as Eli always assured me I was: a normal girl— despite all evidence to the contrary. But even as I stand there, my mind flashes back to the Red Chasm, the moment I was captured.

The soldier tears open my dress . . . He's reaching for me with ill intent . . . And I feel it—an outward lash of power. A snake of self-defense, uncoiling from deep within me, striking out before I can be harmed . . .

Not something I controlled, not something I conjured. Something instinctual. Inherent. Natural as breathing. Unconscious as blinking.

Awake.

Alive.

I wish, with a fierce rush of longing, that I could talk to Eli about all this. He would know exactly what to say. He would launch into action, poring over old texts from his collection until he found some reference to the term *Remnant*, some confirmation of these strange claims . . .

Belatedly, I realize both Scythe and Jac are staring at my hand as it presses against my bodice, as though if they look hard enough they might see through the fabric to the strange symbol beneath. I quickly drop my arm back to my side.

"She's not from Eastwood."

I jolt at Scythe's frank assessment.

"She's not?" Jac asks, brows arching. "I thought . . ."

"I found her there. But look at her clothes. The fabric—it's thin. Made for warmer climes."

Jac's eyes scan me head to toe. Aware of my disheveled, dirty state, it is all I can do to keep my shoulders from caving inward in diffidence.

"You're right," he agrees, nodding. "She's not wearing that gods-awful high-necked fashion they've adopted in recent years down there."

"Who are you, girl?" Scythe asks bluntly, ignoring his friend. He phrases it like a question, but his unyielding tone informs me I have no choice but to answer.

My chin jerks higher. "I told you already. I'm nobody. You made a mistake in bringing me here."

"Where are you from?"

"The Midlands."

"The Midlands are vast," he notes, eyes glittering. "Specify."

I grind my teeth together. I do not want to tell him a godsdamned thing. Certainly not about where I come from. Whom I come from. Eli may have returned to the skies, but I will not betray his memory by divulging a single detail about him to an unknown enemy. I will not put Seahaven—whatever remains of it, after the invasion—into the sights of any more hunters.

"My patience is dwindling," Scythe informs me.

"Westlake," I lie, picking the sprawling forested kingdom to the south of Seahaven, neighbor to King Eld's territory. I've never been there, have only ever seen it on maps. I rack my brain for a random town name, trying to recall the words stamped across fading parchment in my memory. With time running short I blurt, "A village near Narbeth."

Scythe stares at me, then echoes, "Narbeth."

"Yes. It's a trade-post town on the border of Westlake and Eastwood." At least, I think it is.

"And how does a girl from Narbeth end up in the hands of someone like Burrows?"

My mind rushes to conjure details that will flesh out my skeletal fabrications. I am not a good liar. I decide to weave in threads from a story I already know—one I heard firsthand from a refugee girl Eli and I treated last spring. Her family had arrived in Seahaven sick and starving, like so many others who fled the Midlands, desperately seeking a reprieve from war and blight and famine.

We'd tried our best . . . but there is only so much damage even the best medicines can reverse. A few days after her arrival, the girl died in my arms, her frail lungs full of fluid. Her parents quickly followed suit, one after the other. We burned all three together in a driftwood pyre on the beach, then scattered their ashes in the sea.

Wherever the girl is now, I hope she does not mind my borrowing fragments of her story.

"My father is a farmer. My mother makes soaps and balms to sell in the market once a month—half a day's journey from the farm in our cart." I swallow hard, trying to sound like I'm not lying through my teeth. "My mother fell ill a fortnight past, so I went to market without her to sell our wares. We needed the money, and it's always been safe in the past. I thought it worth the risk. Even people who don't strictly approve of halflings trading are at least tolerant, assuming we stay mostly out of their way and keep our heads down. But this time . . . things were different."

Scythe waits, impassive.

I stitch fear into my voice. "There were soldiers there, Eldian ones, posted throughout the market. And culling priests, preaching on the dangers of blood mixing, warning of repercussions for anyone caught harboring halflings. They must've spotted me. Or maybe someone reported me. I don't know. All I do know is, when I tried to get away, the guards chased me. My cart overturned. My horse bolted. I ran for three days, trying to get home. But I didn't make it. I was captured by Burrows and his men." I pause. "You . . . well, you know the rest."

There is a long silence.

I hope my lies are enough to convince him. I keep my face clear and my eyes wide, trying for an innocent, trustworthy expression.

"A farm girl," Scythe says eventually, eyes scanning me up and down. "From Narbeth."

I swallow again. "That's right."

He takes a sudden step forward, closing some of the distance between us, and I feel my heart trip over itself. He is dangerous enough at five paces; at four, he is lethal. I press back against Onyx's flank, wishing I had more room to retreat—somewhere far, far away from those burning-ember eyes fixed so intently on my face.

"Firstly," he murmurs, voice soft as a blade sliding between two ribs. "Farm girls do not use phrases like *grossly mistaken* or *cold-blooded calculation* or *evidently*. They certainly do not lecture on the merits of morality after witnessing a massacre. Not when they spend their days routinely butchering animals."

My temper flares. "I suppose you've met many farm girls?"

"Enough to know you aren't one. Next time you pretend to spend your days churning soap from tallow and lye, make sure you've got the calluses to back it up. You've the hands of a healer, not those of a washerwoman."

I stiffen. "That's not—"

"Secondly." He takes another step, bringing him so close I can almost feel the heat radiating off his body. So close, it makes my breath catch and my airway close up, like a noose has once again been looped around it. "Narbeth is no border town. It's nowhere near Eastwood, nor is it anywhere close to the woods where you were discovered."

I press my eyes closed at this news. *Maybe the girl had said Naxton, not Narbeth...*

"And lastly," Scythe says, taking one last step, delivering the death stroke as his body stops just short of mine. "You'd been on the run for quite some time when Burrows and his men found you. Not three days. A full month, I'd guess, judging by the state of your dress."

"Burrows didn't exactly pour me a hot bath and allow for pampering." Anger rises sharply within me. "Seeing as he planned to execute me, it didn't much matter how I looked."

"I wasn't talking about the stench. You're skin and bones.

That dress hangs off your frame, no match for the body beneath it."

"Times are tough," I retort haughtily, clinging to my rapidly fraying lies.

"No shoes, no proper cloak." His eyes flicker down my form. "You ran, and you did it quickly. Without warning."

I clench my teeth to keep silent.

"What were you running from?"

Flashes of that terrible night—torches and flames, the Starlight Wood burning. The baker, the cobbler, the tailor, incinerated inside their shops before they could flee. My favorite meadow reduced to ash. Children calling out for mothers who could not save them, their pleas piercing a smoke-hazed sky.

I bite my tongue to keep the memories locked within.

"You will tell me." A declaration. A vow. His words as unshakable as his gaze. "Today, tomorrow. Perhaps in a week. You will tell me your story, girl. All of it."

"I won't tell you a godsdamned thing," I hiss.

Behind us, Jac laughs softly.

Scythe does not. "Stubborn. So stubborn. No wonder you managed to evade them for so long." He shakes his head, frustration written plainly on his face. "A trained contingent of soldiers, some of King Eld's best men. Gods."

If I didn't know better, I'd swear there is a note of grudging respect buried somewhere beneath all his exasperation.

"You were trained," he says decidedly. "Someone taught you survival skills. How to move through the woods in silence, how to stay alive in the elements." He pauses. "Not to mention, how to slow the bleeding of an arrow puncture and wrap a wound with quick efficiency."

I keep silent, focused on breathing steadily. Quite a feat, given his proximity.

"You are no ordinary halfling, Remnant aside. And you are certainly no farmer's daughter from Westlake. So, I'll ask you one last time . . ." Scythe leans a handspan closer and the world around us seems to still, the howling wind outside the mouth of the cave cutting off abruptly, leaving behind a pervasive silence. "Who the hell are you?"

NINE

The back of the cave narrows into a low-ceilinged passageway that leads deep into the belly of the mountain. We walk in silence, Jac at the front, me in the middle, Scythe close on my heels. Two horses bring up the rear—first Onyx, then Jac's mount, a dapple-gray mare I had not seen tucked in the depths of the cave during the tense standoff between Scythe and me.

I had not answered his questions, had not told him who I am or where I come from, remaining stubbornly silent even in the face of his gathering vexation. Eventually, he'd seemed to decide it was not worth his effort, stalking away in disgust and barking that it was time to depart.

Jac shot me an amused wink before whistling for his mare and leading us to the passageway.

I don't want to like the man, but there is something undeniably charming about his easygoing nature—especially in contrast to Scythe's brooding malice. I also cannot deny my relief at his presence. Traveling alone with Scythe feels a bit like being locked in a cage with a feral wolf. One who hasn't eaten in weeks and will not hesitate to consume you the moment you stop serving his purposes.

The passageway grows narrower as we walk, the stone path

descending in a gradual slant. It's cold beneath my socked feet, but I do not protest. I am afraid if I open my mouth for any reason, I will encourage further interrogation from my captors. Best to keep still and silent for the time being. The less they know about me, the harder it will be for them to track me down when I eventually escape their clutches.

The flickering glow of Jac's torch dances across the walls, casting strange shadows on the pointed salt deposits hanging from the roof like canine fangs in the mouth of a beast. Here, in the deep, the world seems devoid of life. A realm of utter stillness. Except for the intermittent drip, drip, dripping of water droplets, echoing back at us as they plummet, nothing stirs in the dark.

We walk for a long time, a single-file parade moving ever deeper, ever downward. We walk for so long, I grow convinced I will never again feel the sunlight on my face or the kiss of wind upon my skin. A sort of panic begins to churn within me, brought on by the tight-pressed claustrophobia of our entombment. The musty air moves in and out of my lungs, tasting of dust and decay, staleness and stagnation, and I struggle for calm.

For someone like me—raised on the wild, windy shores of Seahaven, with the crashing waves and churning surf, running amid the sun-dappled shallows with salt on my skin and sea-foam in my hair, skirts a tangle of sand, heart alight with the tang of the tides—this sort of earthly confinement feels like walking through a crypt. One I will never escape. Not only my body, but my soul itself, trapped ever more beneath the mountain, unable to find its way to the skies.

Just when I think my nerves will crack, just when I think I cannot take another moment of this cloistered death march and will beg Jac—or even, gods help me, Scythe—for a reprieve from the torment . . . the passage widens once more. We step through a roughhewn archway into another cave and are immediately greeted by a chorus of voices: male, hushed, resounding from all sides so their origin is difficult to pinpoint.

I haul a breath of marginally less musty air into my lungs as we round a bend and find ourselves at a campsite of sorts. There is a low, smokeless fire burning merrily. Three men sit around it, armed to the teeth—swords lashed to backs, daggers tucked into boots. A bow and quiver lean against a bundled bedroll. A massive wooden crossbow rests beside a canvas pack, accompanied by dozens of heavy bolts. A trio of dark brown horses stand by the far wall, tacked to ride.

"*Oi!*" Jac calls, his grin back in place. "You lot could at least pretend to patrol. I trained you better than to be caught with your pants down. Or do you let just anyone waltz into your camp unawares?"

"You walk like a lout after last call," the closest of the men retorts. "Heard you coming a league away."

"True," the red-haired man across from him agrees. "Jac, you tread with all the deftness of an avalanche."

"Is that any way to speak to your battalion leader?" Jac asks with faux anger.

Chuckling, the men rise and, one by one, clasp forearms with Jac, fingers to elbows, holding for the length of two heartbeats. Once the greetings conclude, the red-haired man turns his attention my way. His mouth parts in curiosity at my unexpected presence, but when he catches sight of Scythe coming to a halt close beside me, he disregards me completely. His eyes go wide and his face splits into a grin.

"As I live and breathe! Penn! What in the skies are you doing here?"

Penn?

My eyes flash over to Scythe. I find him already staring back at me, resignation etched across his features beneath the helm. He doesn't want to share his true identity with me any more than I want to share mine with him. I arch a questioning brow and his mouth flattens into an even sterner line.

"Farley," Scythe says in greeting, stepping forward to clasp the redhead's forearm. "Been a long time. "

"Too long. I can't believe you're here! Thought we wouldn't see you again until the first melt of spring."

"Plans change."

Farley's light-green gaze slides to me. "I can see that."

"Hungry?" Another of the men—with longish graying hair and steady eyes of the same hue—interjects. "We've got a bit of dried venison. Not much in the way of hunting, this high up in the range, but we had a spot of luck last week." His chin jerks toward the redhead. "Farley is a damned good shot, on the rare occasions he stops chattering long enough to stop scaring off supper."

The redhead responds with a vulgar hand gesture.

My stomach gives an audible grumble. Scythe glances at me for a heartbeat before his head shakes, rejecting the offer of a meal. "We need to make for the Apex Portal. I want to be in Caeldera by nightfall."

Jac and his men nod at once.

"We'll accompany you as far as the crossing, but we can't go through with you." Jac sighs. "Four more months on this frigid icicle before we earn a reprieve, I'm afraid."

"It'll fly." Scythe—or is it Penn?—assures him. "You get cold up here, think of Beatrice and her lovely monobrow, awaiting you in warm tavern sheets."

There is a riot of laughter from the rest of the men. It cuts off abruptly when the ground beneath our feet begins to shake and shift. The trembles are so great, I think the mountain must be coming down around us, an avalanche of stone and ice that will bury us alive.

I have endured earthquakes before, of course. They've grown more and more common in recent years; sharp, unpredictable shudders that make me think Anwyvn might be situated atop the back of a great slumbering beast who is shaking awake after a long hibernation. Usually they last no more than a moment or two, rattling cups in their saucers and jostling books off shelves.

This is nothing like that.

These tremors are far more concentrated and come far faster than anything I have previously experienced. It is so intense, I fear the cavern floor will crack open directly beneath our feet, a deadly vein dropping us straight into the bowels of the earth. The three brown mounts by the far wall bolt before their riders can catch them.

Without thinking, I reach out a blind hand toward Scythe, grasping his arm to keep myself upright. Such is my fear, I do not realize that I'm clutching just below his still-fresh wound. If my grip causes him pain, he does not seem to notice. He is already in motion, jerking the sword from the scabbard across his back with his opposite hand, shoving me closer to the fire and shifting his body to block mine.

I peer around the broad planes of his shoulders and see the rest of the men have taken up similar positions—backs to the fire, swords at the ready, a practiced formation for an incoming assault. Their knees are bent slightly to absorb the continuous shock waves. I mimic the stance, instantly steadier on my feet.

They are silent, but their expressions speak plainly. Whatever is coming—whatever is causing the cave floor to pitch and heave like water in a bucket—will not be a welcome addition to their company.

"What is it?" I dare whisper in the turbulent dimness, hearing the fear in my own voice and hating it. "Is it . . . ice giants?"

Scythe's head twists—not enough to meet my eyes, but enough for me to see the severe lines of his profile beneath the heavy nose bridge. Frowning, he mutters, "Worse."

Worse?

I open my mouth to ask what could possibly be worse than an ice giant, but I never get the chance. Because at that moment, the incoming enemies make themselves known. And I find, as I take in the sight of them—their scurrying legs and clacking pincers and beady eyes—Scythe is correct.

Whatever horrors an ice giant might unleash . . .

This is far, far worse.

They do not come from the cave mouth, as I'd expected. They burst up from the ground all around us in a violent explosion of stone and dirt. Two dozen of them, perhaps more. There's no time to count once the melee begins.

Centipedes.

Not the small, screech-inducing bugs I'd glimpsed scurrying across the floors of the storage closet back at Eli's cottage. These are a giant variety I've never seen, never even fathomed, except perhaps in legends of old. Each as long as a horse and as wide as a barrel, with hundreds of legs jutting from either side of their armored insectile bodies. A pale, putrid white hue, they remind me of maggots. And they reek—an acidic stench that stings my nostrils and makes my eyes water.

The first of them erupts from the earthen floor just beside Farley. I watch in horror as its serrated mandible closes around his shin and, with the ease of snapping a twig, cleaves the bone in two. Even as he falls, screaming in agony, he swings down with his sword and beheads the beast in one clean strike. Green goo spurts from its decapitated body, a flood of venomous fluid. Its legs continue to squirm and clack against the ground long after it is dead.

"Stay by the fire," Scythe barks, gutting another of the centipedes as it rears up before him, jerking his blade free before I can so much as blink. "Cyntroedi can't stand the flame."

I try to respond but my throat feels fused shut. I can only watch as the men take on the vile creatures. One after another after another. Jac's double-headed axe neatly shears half the legs off one as it plummets from an outcropping of rock overhead, leaving it limping in wobbly circles. The gray-eyed man whose name I have not learned battles two at once on the far side of the fire. On his knees, Farley continues to fight—slashing out against anything that comes within range of his sword. The final man, bald and stocky, with midnight skin, stays close to his fallen friend, firing bolt after bolt from the mammoth crossbow.

For all the bloodshed, it is Scythe I cannot tear my eyes from. I have seen him kill men before, saw his grim efficiency as he slaughtered Burrows and the other troops who lashed me to that hanging tree. But now, as I watch him whirl and slash, skewer and thrust, I realize I have not seen even a glimpse of his skill before this moment. The man who takes on a half dozen massive insects at once, monsters sent straight from the realm of nightmares, appears inhuman. Impossibly fast, his motions a blur, his helm a dark gleam in the firelight.

With a wounded shoulder, no less.

He moves like a man possessed, caught in the throes of battle fury. Occasionally, between kills, his eyes dart across the cave to find mine. They seem lit from within, that fire in their depths burning bright despite the darkness, no longer an ember but a flame. His blade, too, appears to blaze red-hot, as though it has been left to heat in the coals for hours on end.

Surely a trick of the light, I tell myself, shaken by the sight.

The men, for a time at least, seem to have the upper hand. Until the earth begins to shake once more, fresh shock waves announcing the arrival of a second cluster of cyntroedi. It is at this moment that I finally come unstuck from the paralyzing grip of terror that stills my limbs. My gaze sweeps the space around me, landing on the bow. It is larger than the one I used back home—a man's bow, crafted for killing worse prey than I was accustomed to hunting in Seahaven's tranquil woods—but I grab it anyway, slinging the quiver across my back and nocking an arrow with familiar ease.

Mere days ago, when I saw the state of my iron-ravaged wrists, I wondered if I'd ever again be able to draw a bow. But Scythe's salve has healing properties I've never seen in all my years mixing tonics and brewing teas with Eli. My skin is practically mended, the gaping wounds scabbed over in a way that should not be possible—not for weeks.

Not for a lifetime.

Yet, there is no more than a twinge of residual pain, a faint ache of protest in the tendons as I set my stance, lift the bow, and anchor it against my body. I'm breathing rapidly, the rise and fall of my chest making it difficult to take aim as I pull back the bowstring. With a steadying gulp, I hold the air inside my lungs. My eyes narrow on a centipede that has just burst from the earth behind Scythe. It skitters toward him, intent on striking him unawares.

I let the arrow fly.

I've always been a good shot. Since I was no more than a child, when Eli placed a novice bow in my hands, I excelled—first at the stationary targets he set up for me in the gardens, later with the distant marks hidden deep in the foliage, designed to challenge me. By the time I reached my fifteenth year, I did all our hunting, bringing home a steady supply of game to fill our table. Our coffers, too. I sold a fair bit of meat to villagers who were too hungry to be picky about buying from a halfling.

Thus, even with the large bow, even with my aching wrists, my shot makes impact—not precisely where I aim, not straight through the head, but in the center of the armored body. The creature gives a pained screech, its pincers clacking at empty air as it whirls around. The beady eyes fix on me, glittering, and my whole body trembles.

Faster than I ever imagined possible, the creature comes my way, carried across the cave on a hundred spindly legs. Locking my knees against the trembles of fear, I barely have time to notch another arrow and fire before it reaches me.

This time, my aim is true. The arrow slams home directly between the creature's beady eyes. It falls to the cave floor with a thud, pincers clacking one final time as its vile fluids leak out around it in a viridescent puddle. I catch myself grinning as I reach for another arrow in my quiver.

The smile freezes on my face when my eyes turn to locate new prey and instead lock with Scythe's. He is on the opposite side of the cave, in the process of dispatching two especially mammoth cyntroedi. He does not look pleased with me. If prisoners are not privy to information, I'm guessing they aren't privy to weaponry, either.

Ah, well. He can brood at me later. Preferably when we aren't under attack by stallion-sized insects.

"Jac!" the gray-haired man yells, voice tense. "Need another blade over here!"

I watch a blur of dark-blond hair race by, taking down monsters as he goes. My eyes trail him, picking off the creatures who give chase, covering him as he moves. Two, four, six. I lose count, firing without hesitation. Without thought.

The acidic smell of venom thickens in the air as the armored bodies pile up, filling the pitted floor of the cave until all I can see are legs. Legs and pincers and putrid white carcasses, an invertebrate graveyard.

A sharp whinny of distress has my head whipping in the opposite direction. My heart seizes as Jac's gentle gray mare is taken down by three cyntroedi, no more than a dozen paces away from me. Onyx rears back and slams his hooves down on one of them, crushing it instantly. I fire two arrows in quick succession, taking down the others. But it is too late for the mare. She is beyond saving, deep scores in her hide gushing irreparably. The venom is already working its way through her system, causing damage the best healers in Anwyvn could not undo.

Deep down, I know it's pointless, but my irrational heart refuses to admit as much. I make my way toward her, tears glossing my eyes. If I can get there, maybe I can do something. I have to at least try . . .

I make it no more than a few steps. Scythe's sharp whistle sounds from across the cave. At first, I think it's to get my attention.

I'm mistaken.

He is calling his horse.

Onyx responds instantly to his master's signal. He trots to my side and, with an intelligence far surpassing that of a normal horse, herds my body back toward the safety of the fire. His glossy eyes are rolling with white, infused with the same fear that churns though my veins. I let my hand stroke his flank just once to soothe him before I turn back to the battle with my bow aloft.

"Need some help over here!"

It's the stocky, bald soldier this time—the one fighting beside Farley. Alarm fills me when I see he's been drawn away from his post, pulled deeper into the crush. Leaving Farley on his knees, wholly unprotected. The cyntroedi are encroaching on his hard-fought patch of territory, enticed by a meal so close to the ground.

Sidestepping Onyx, I rush around the fire to his side. I'm running low on arrows, but I don't think about that as I reach into my near-empty quiver and fire. Once, twice. A third time. My arms are aching fiercely, the exertion catching up with me. It's been too long since I used my body for anything except running, hiding, and cowering. I've withered away to nothing.

Skin and bones, Scythe's voice whispers inside my head.

He's right. Even if I had unlimited ammunition, I'd still be useless, unable to lift my arms to fire. That grim realization haunts me as I reach for my final arrow.

"The lads say I'm a handy shot," a hoarse voice says from beside me. "But I'm nothing next to you, Ace."

I glance down into light-green eyes. They are hazy with pain. Farley's face is pallid, his breaths coming in rapid pants. His left leg is bent at an unnatural angle and I know the bone is in pieces below the knee. A difficult break to set. Even with the best treatment, he'll likely walk with a limp for the rest of his days. The fact that he's still upright—still swinging his sword—instead of curled into a ball of limbs, sobbing freely, is a measure of his self-discipline.

It is a miracle that he killed the beast so swiftly when it attacked. Had he not, it might've taken his leg clean off. Or worse, punctured the skin with life-sapping venom that would've stopped his heart in seconds. By comparison, a break is a blessing.

"If we live through this, Penn should recruit you for the Ember Guild." He grins through his agony. "Might be worth living with a bum leg, just to see that play out."

I don't know what he's blabbing on about, but I grin back at him nonetheless as I nock my arrow.

"It's my last," I tell him, drawing back the bowstring with a shrug.

"Use it well," he murmurs, lifting his sword as another centi-pede bursts from the earth five paces away and comes at us. We take it down together—my arrow through its left flank, Farley's sword through its right. When the creature lies twitching, I set down my useless bow and slip the empty quiver off my shoulder. Farley watches it clatter to the ground, then looks up at me.

"You should run."

My mouth gapes. "What?"

"No need for you to die here with us." He jerks his chin to-ward the center of the cave, where the soldiers rage on—Scythe, Jac, and the two others still in death grips with what seems to be a never-ending onslaught of colossal, carnivorous predators. "They'll keep coming. Wave after wave." His eyes hold mine, steady despite the suffering in their depths. I strain to hear his words over the constant clash of swordplay. "You stayed. Helped. Did what you could. That's good. Doesn't make you cowardly if you save yourself now."

"But I don't even know where—"

"There's a passage just behind us. It's not far from the fire. A dozen paces at most, tucked in behind a boulder." His chest heaves and I know his injury is draining every bit of energy he has left. "Run. Don't stop. When you come to a fork, go left. There's a set of rock steps, straight up into the mountains. Once you make it there, you're safe. These things"—another chin jerk, the time toward the pile of twitching, skeletal bodies—"stay down here in the dark."

I hesitate. I don't know why. He's just handed me a chance at freedom. A chance I should snatch as soon as it is offered. I owe no allegiance here—not to the injured man at my feet, certainly not to the fearsome one across the cave who fights like a general trained by the God of War himself.

Scythe is not my friend.

Not my protector.

Not my savior.

But...

He gave you socks.

He brought you salve.

He kept you warm and fed and safe.

He saved your life on more than one occasion.

I silence the unwelcome voice of conscience in the back of my mind with a swift shake of my head. Scythe only did those things for his own benefit. He needs me—for what purpose, I'm not certain, but I doubt it is anything good. He believes the mark on my chest is some kind of sigil, a power source to be tapped. For all I know, he plans to sacrifice me on an altar of blood as soon as we reach our destination.

"For the love of gods, girl, *go!*" Farley snaps weakly. "Take a torch and get out of here."

I look into his pain-hazed eyes for another long beat.

And then, I do as he's bid me.

CHAPTER
TEN

I'm running.

Running on my useless, half-healed stocking feet. Running for my life. I do not look back. I cannot bear to see how close on my heels I'll find my demise, how near I am to being skewered on a set of razor-sharp mandibles. I keep my gaze fixed forward as I race down the pitch-black passage, only the dying torch to light my way. But my mind is back at the encampment, back at the bloody scene I left behind when I fled into the dark . . .

Coward.

I push aside the guilt and focus on the passage. I found it exactly where Farley described, tucked behind a boulder ten paces from the campfire. It had taken some swift maneuvering to get around Onyx, who seemed determined not to let me pass. In the end, only fidelity to his master stayed him from following me from the cave.

His stalwart loyalty underscores my lack of it. I had not even spared a glance at Scythe as I slipped out of view.

He is your enemy, I tell myself over and over.

So why do I feel like the worst sort of traitor?

Shouts and sword tings chase me down the narrow tunnel, away from the bloodbath. I clutch the torch, wishing I had a better weapon. For while it may ward off the creeping shadows, if a single cyntroedi follows me, I will be no better off than poor Farley. Worse, actually—he, at least, has a sword to swing.

After a stretch, I come to the split he described. The right tunnel veers off into darkness. The left offers salvation in the form of a set of stairs. I race headlong toward it, ignoring the pain stitching through my ribs, hauling air into my lungs in ragged gulps. So focused on escape, I do not feel the telltale shock waves until it is too late to reverse course.

The centipede that erupts from the ground in front of me is bigger than any I saw back in the camp. Beside it, Onyx would appear a miniature pony. It slithers from its hole, white maw clacking, the froth of venom already coating each sawlike pincer in a toxic sheen. Its body is more bulbous than the others, its legs thicker and covered in fibers that look sharp enough to pierce through flesh and bone.

If this hive of creatures has an alpha . . . here he is, in all his vile glory.

I backpedal rapidly, trying to create some distance, the torch extended in front of me like a shield. It is, I cannot help but notice, burning dangerously low.

When the creature makes to lunge at me, I brandish the flame with a menacing swipe. It pauses, as if reconsidering its plan of attack. I dare not turn my back to it. I know better than to try to run. Despite its size, it's faster than I could ever hope to be, and as it rears up to full height, its myriad multijointed legs swiping at the air, screeching with what I can only describe as unearthly anticipation for the moment my torch flickers out . . . all I can pray for is a swift, clean death.

I have no desire to perish like the mare.

My free hand clenches at my side, pressing firmly against my thigh as I watch the creature eyeing me. My fist meets unexpected resistance—something hard presses back at me through the pocket of my skirts.

The dagger.

The one I confiscated from Scythe this morning. I'd forgotten it entirely. Not that it will do me much good—what damage can a slim blade do against such a gargantuan creature?—but it is better than nothing at all. In a flash, I've pulled it free. I hold it out along with the torch, one weapon per hand, my grip white-knuckled as I back away.

The creature hisses and lunges again.

"Back!" I scream at it, waving my torch. "Stay back!"

The creature pauses. Its angular head tilts to and fro as my voice ricochets down the tunnel. Its eyes are not like those of its smaller brethren, back in the cave. They are clouded, pearly with age. Reminiscent of the blind beggars at market with their hands extended sightlessly for alms.

Can it see me? I wonder suddenly, breath catching in my throat. *Or have all these years in the darkness left it blind?*

If so, it is tracking my voice, my pounding pulse, my shredded breaths. Pinpointing my position from the vibrations of my feet against the earth each time I move.

Clamping my mouth shut against any more foolish declarations of bravado that will betray my position, I make an effort to slow my breathing and creep backward as softly as I can manage, thankful—for the first time in weeks—for my lack of shoes. The creature stills, as if it truly is listening for me. Hope flares in my chest. A fool's hope, but hope nonetheless.

Perhaps I can get away. Not past it, not to the stairs, not to freedom . . . but back to the campsite. Perhaps, against all odds, the men survived. Perhaps—

My foot hits a loose stone.

It tumbles across the floor, a thunderous cacophony in the

otherwise noiseless passage. The moment it does, the centipede lunges straight for my throat.

I see it coming. See my death in its milky, murderous eyes. See my fate closing in like the snap of its serrated pincers around my throat.

I see it coming and I do not scream. I do not run. I hold my ground, torch extended along with my pitiful dagger. Because if I am going to die, there is no way I'm going alone. I will be this monster's final kill.

And it will be mine.

My weapons are still outstretched when its head is parted from its body. There is a flash of heat—a glowing blade, swinging down from my periphery—and then it hits the ground at my feet. A second later, the squirming body follows suit.

Dead.

Definitively, unquestionably dead.

Green goo sprays all over me, coating the front of my dress, burning my skin like lye. I scramble backward, eyes squeezed shut as I wipe frantically at my face, praying none of the foul venom got into my mouth. I'm still wiping when a large hand peels my fingers away from my cheeks, grips me roughly by the chin, and jerks my head back. I find myself staring upward into a set of burning eyes. The hand at my jaw flexes, anger thrumming through every digit.

"When I say to stay by the fire," Scythe grits, face dark with fury. "*Stay by the bloody fire.*"

⌒〰

MIRACULOUSLY, ALL THE men survive.

Back in the cave, Uther and Mabon—the tall gray-haired fellow and his stocky bald counterpart, I learn after brief introductions—are packing up the camp. Jac is cleaning weapons, a disgusted grimace on his typically cheerful face as he wipes green goo from blade after blade.

The pile of dead cyntroedi is massive. It nearly reaches the ceiling. There must be a hundred of them. I shiver at the sight and swiftly look away.

"The archer returns!" Farley greets me with a wan smile. He's sitting by the fire, propped up against his daypack. His leg is strapped into a makeshift splint of wood and rope. It looks like he fashioned it himself. "Glad you're still breathing, Ace. You don't mind if I call you Ace, do you? Seeing as I don't know your real name . . ."

"It's R—" I catch myself just in time, swallowing down the slipup. "Call me whatever you'd like."

"How about *fool* or *idiot* or *insufferable bane of my existence*," Scythe mutters from beside me.

I shoot him a dark look. He is still seething mad, that's plain to see. He was furious to find I'd wandered off, disobeying his direct order to stay by the fire. That fury had heightened to a blind rage when he found me in the passage, going head-to-head with what I later found out was not an alpha male, but rather the queen of the cyntroedi hive, her bulbous body laden with eggs.

Thankfully, now that she's dead, there is little chance of another strike. According to Jac, the remaining creatures will retreat and regroup until a new queen is born to lead them. This news should be comforting. But, amid the carnage, all I can think about is getting out of here. Back to the light, back to the air, away from the astringent rot of dead insects.

"Did you see her?" Farley asks Mabon, pointing at me with undisguised mirth. "Sharpshooter! Bullseye! She must've taken down twenty of 'em. Grabbed the bow and started firing. Never even blinked."

"I saw," the bald man grumbles, looking in any direction but mine. He is smart enough to realize any praise heaped on me will only further incite the pillar of wrath towering beside me.

"Of course you saw!" Farley is undeterred. "Only a blind man could miss her. She saved our asses!"

"Your ass was the only one in need of saving," Uther chimes in, but his gray eyes hold a teasing light. "Seeing as you spent most of the battle sitting on it."

Mabon snorts.

"I took down just as many as you did!" Farley yells, incensed. "Even sitting on my ass!"

Uther glances at me, grimaces, and shakes his head. I clamp my lips shut to keep my smile at bay.

"Can we get the hell out of here?" Scythe growls. "Before you call whatever other monsters reside in this mountain down upon our heads?"

Everyone falls silent and makes quick work of grabbing the rest of their belongings. In mere moments, the whole camp is cleared out. With the other horses gone, Onyx's saddlebags are double-stuffed with gear. I hope the three that bolted fared better than the poor mare. My eyes linger on her prone form for a moment before we file out of the cave, Uther and Mabon carrying Farley between them like he weighs no more than a feather, Onyx following with a jangle of tackle. Scythe lingers behind, waiting to take up the rear as usual.

Jac stops beside me near the boulder, chucking me lightly beneath the chin with his fist. My eyes move to his.

"No one of importance," he murmurs, echoing my earlier description of myself. "Right. *Ace*."

With a quick grin and a shake of his head, he ushers me out of the cave. It takes effort to keep from glancing back, looking for Scythe as we make our way to the fork at the end of the passage. It seems so much shorter now that I'm not running for my life.

"He'll be along in a minute," Jac informs me quietly. "He's clearing out the cave for the next unfortunate travelers who take this route."

"You think the creatures will come back?"

He shrugs. "Hopefully, we did enough to deter a new den of them from taking up residence in that particular tunnel. But monsters thrive in the dark. So long as there are shadows, there'll be things to stalk around in them."

The heat of the fire blasts down the passage at our backs. It must be a massive blaze. I wonder how he's managed it. Except for the sparse pile of kindling beside the campfire, there was no extra wood in the cave anywhere I'd seen. No accelerant to spread flames so quickly—unless the vile green venom is highly flammable.

I could ask Jac. There's a chance he might even tell me. But I'm too tired to indulge my curiosity with more questions. I stay silent, focused on keeping my steps measured all the way down the passage. Lifting one foot after the other, my gaze pointedly averted from the decapitated body of the queen when we reach the fork. I need no more memories of her burned into my mind. The ones I already possess will haunt me well enough.

Waves of exhaustion flood my system as the surge of adrenaline subsides. In the aftermath of the fight, my entire body aches. My arm muscles scream in protest at the simplest of movements. I am covered in grime and dried goo, my skirts stiff with it. Just lifting them to climb the steps takes monumental effort. Only the promise of fresh air and freedom keeps me from collapsing in a heap.

Jac soon outpaces me, climbing steadily after his unit, seeming no worse for wear despite the battle he's just fought. I have to stop periodically to catch my breath. I might lean against one of the walls for support if I weren't so scared something will burst through it at any given moment and devour me.

Who can say what else nests down here?

My progress upward is so slow, Scythe eventually catches up to me. He smells of ashes and smoke and the acidic afterburn of insectile corpses. I can hear him breathing, one step behind, his body heat immense enough to warm the air between us.

"Any slower, we'll be going backward," comes his wry greeting after a few moments.

I glower. "I do wish the centipedes had eaten you."

He barks out a laugh. It sounds rusty coming from his throat, like he hasn't found occasion to use it in quite some time. I am so startled by the sound, I trip over my skirts and nearly face-plant. But he moves like lightning, grabbing me before I can fall and hauling me back upright.

"Almost there." His voice is low. I can feel the strength of his chest against my back. The bandolier of blades presses tight to my spine. "Ten more steps and this place is a memory."

I nod, not trusting myself to speak, and he releases me. Somehow, I manage to ascend the final stretch without falling again. When I step into the light, squinting at the blinding flare of the sun, I could weep for joy. If I never again find myself back in the bowels of the earth, it will be too soon. I have never been so thrilled to see the barren tundra of the Cimmerian Mountains; have never been so deliriously happy to feel the sharp lash of arctic wind on my cheeks. I resist the urge to spin in circles like a child, acutely aware of five sets of male eyes resting heavily upon me.

They've somehow gotten Farley up into Onyx's saddle. He looks even paler than he did down in the caves, his complexion peaked. His shattered leg is lashed to the stirrup. Someone has removed his boots. Despite his obvious pain, he attempts a smile when our gazes meet.

"Don't look at me like that, Ace. I'm not dead yet. You'll wound my ego."

"He needs a healer," I say bluntly, looking at Scythe.

"I thought you were one," he returns.

"I have some skills, but not out here." I sweep an arm around the sparse landscape. "Not without proper tools, not without herbs. That bone needs to be set, and all weight kept off it for at least two months."

Farley looks aghast at this news. "Two *months*? Did she say two bloody months?"

"If you ever expect to walk again." I plant my hands on my hips—a move I regret instantly, seeing as the fabric is coated with all manner of foul fluids. "Where is the nearest town? There must be an inn somewhere on this summit. Even those crazy enough to travel at this altitude need a place to sleep and suck down ale."

Scythe and Jac look at each other for a long moment, a wordless exchange unfolding between them. When their gazes break, there is an unhappy tightness to Scythe's jaw. But his voice is level as ever.

"We'll make for Vintare. It's not far—just on the other side of this valley. We can spend the night at the inn, set off in the morning."

"Penn . . ." Jac shakes his head, frowning. "We can't delay your journey. The Apex Portal is in the opposite direction."

"And?"

"*Go*. You'll be in Caeldera by nightfall. Leave us. We'll manage."

"The rest of your unit is more than a day's ride from here.

How do you expect to rejoin them with no mounts? And what of Farley?"

"Don't worry about me," the redhead interjects. "I'll not be a burden."

Scythe shakes his head, the metal of his helmet catching the weak, mist-shrouded sun. "It'll be dark in an hour. You plan to carry an injured man across this ice plain?"

There is a heavy pause.

"I thought not," Scythe mutters.

Jac runs a hand through his dark-blond hair, blowing out a sharp breath. "We'll owe you a debt, old friend."

"I'll add it to the tally."

"There's a tally?"

"Mmm. Long one."

"Damn." Jac shakes his head, chuckling. His eyes drift to me but his words are for Scythe. "Come to think of it, it might not be the worst idea to clean up a bit before you go traipsing into the throne room. Your excess baggage is looking rather rough around the edges. And while you may not care what anyone else thinks . . . a bath would go a long way before you throw her to the court wolves."

Court wolves?

That sounds ominous—far more than any wild variety I might encounter in the woods. I jerk my chin higher, covering my unease with my most withering glare. I am fully aware of my dreadful appearance without his reminders.

"*Apologies.* There wasn't much time to pretty myself for your viewing pleasure," I seethe. "I've been a bit busy trying not to be lynched or gutted or eaten alive. Next time I'm kidnapped and dragged to the Northlands, I'll bring a lady's maid along with me to keep my countenance fresh as a daisy in spring. Unless you'd like to volunteer for the role. How are you with plaiting hair?" My eyes narrow on his long blond mane. "Seeing as your own looks like it hasn't seen a brush since you left civilization, I'm guessing not so great."

Farley cackles so loud, Onyx prances his front hooves against the snow in protest. Mabon and Uther both seem to be choking down laughter. Jac merely grins at me, not at all offended, and turns back to Scythe.

"Best do what you can to make her presentable. Her charming disposition isn't going to win any favors at court."

Scythe's lips twist. "You're not wrong."

"Plus, it's time you ditched the Eldian getup. You look like Midland swine. I know you were trying to blend in but, gods, if this shoddy shit is what they dress their commanders in, what do the foot soldiers wear?"

"Typically whatever they can steal, salvage, or strip from the corpses on the battlefield before the stiffness sets in," Scythe says darkly.

"Foul place." Jac grimaces. "Glad you're done there. Your homecoming is long overdue. Shame we won't be around for Fyremas, but we'll have a proper celebration when this mountain stint finally ends and the whole guild is back together in Caeldera. Start ordering ale as soon as you arrive; you only have a few months to import the good stuff. None of that flavorless Frostlander swill, either. I want Titan gin from Prydain."

My mind struggles to sort through the terms he's rattling off, rapid-fire. *Caeldera. Frostlander. Prydain.* None of them sound remotely familiar to me. That's not exactly surprising. Not one of Eli's many maps had covered the Northlands. When I'd once asked him why, he told me they'd all been burned.

The Cull spared few fae records. Even the maps were de-

stroyed when the empire fell. The mortal kings were resolved to erase all lingering traces of maegic. Not only those who could wield it, but every aspect of their—your—very culture, Rhya.

It had seemed like an unnecessary step. An overreaction. I'd told Eli as much, but he'd fixed me with one of his wise looks and gently disagreed.

To annihilate a race, you must do more than kill its people. You must kill its music, its artwork, its architecture. Its customs, its traditions, its religions. You must eradicate the beauty, so only horror remains in the memories of those who live on in the aftermath. So no one attempts to rebuild—or even remembers why they might ever want to.

"Oh, is that all?" Scythe mutters, jolting me out of my thoughts.

Blithely ignoring his sarcasm, Jac adds, "A cask of Dagger-point lager wouldn't go amiss, either."

"By all means . . ." Scythe's amused snort puffs visibly in the chill air. "Use me as your next excuse to get falling-down drunk."

"Don't be absurd. When have I ever needed an excuse?"

"Fair enough."

They grin at each other. The sight of that ultra-bright smile on Scythe's face is so startling, I have to look away. Thankfully, there is little time to dwell. We are soon on our way—me wearing a laughably large pair of boots borrowed from Farley, who'd declared, with considerable vehemence, that he wasn't using them so I should put them on my godsdamned feet and keep my godsdamned mouth shut about it. The laces are pulled as tight as they can go, but they still rattle loose around my calves with every step we take across the stretch of crunching snow.

Mabon and Uther lead the way, Onyx plodding after them with his hefty load of gear and the additional weight of a grumpy Farley on his back. I stick close to the horse's side as we make the journey, steadfastly ignoring the moment Scythe drops his cloak around my shoulders as he walks past me to join Jac at the rear of our ragtag band.

It's deliciously warm, and it smells like flame.

Like him.

To keep Farley company, I chat with him as we cross the valley. He seems to crave the distraction from his injury, firing question after question until I have no choice but to answer.

"Where'd you learn to shoot like that?"

"Hunting."

"What sort of game?"

"Doe, mostly. Sometimes a boar or two, but only if they were disturbing the gardens." I pause, shoulders lifting in a shallow shrug. "I may be a decent shot, but I didn't often hunt with my bow back at home."

"Why not?"

"I never liked to take too much from the forest. The herds get thinner every year." The last few springs, game was so sparse I could go days without seeing a single deer. "Besides, it always felt wasteful to kill a large animal when I could get by with just my snares. Sometimes, I could sell the extra meat, but . . ." I chew my bottom lip. "Lots of folks won't buy from a halfling."

Farley looses a low, unhappy grunt. "Ignorant fucks."

I say nothing, rather startled by his strong reaction. Sure, he and the others have treated me better than the last company of male soldiers I found myself caught up with . . . but I doubt the Northlanders as a whole are beacons of tolerance. The Cull affected all of Anwyvn, a unified extermination from the ice-capped North Sea to the desert depths of Carvage. Forgetting that would be beyond foolish.

"Anyway . . ." Farley steers us past the awkward silence. "You said you used snares? For what kind of quarry?"

"Foxes. Hares. Sometimes squirrels, if things got desperate."

"Things get desperate often?"

I smile wryly. "I take it you haven't spent much time in the Midlands, if you feel the need to ask."

"Mmm. Doesn't sound like paradise on earth, that's for certain."

A bitter exhale shoots from my mouth. "Paradise burned a long time ago. All that's left are the ashes."

He's silent for a moment, absorbing that. "So, Ace, are you ever going to tell us your real name?"

"Why would I?"

"Why wouldn't you?" he counters playfully. "We're all friends here."

"*Friends?*"

"We've done battle together. Fought side by side. If that doesn't make us friends, nothing will."

"Farley," I say with emphatic enunciation, as though he's a bit slow in the wits. "You do realize I'm a prisoner here, don't you?"

At that, he barks out a laugh. He only sobers when he sees I'm not laughing with him. Twisting in his saddle, his eyes shoot to the back of our group. I don't turn to see, but I know he is looking at Scythe.

"Penn!" There's that name again. "Why does Ace here think she's a prisoner?"

"Farley," comes the terse reply. "Keep talking and your leg won't be the worst of your injuries."

"Testy, testy." The redhead returns his attention to me. "Trust me, Ace. You don't need to be so closed off. We're not going to hurt you. Well, Penn might, but his bark is worse than his bite. Most of the time."

"How comforting."

"Oh, don't be like that. He's fresh off a campaign. Can't really blame him for nursing a grouchy disposition, after spending all that time in the Midlands. Enough to drive a fyre priestess to drink, I'll tell you. It's going to take him some time to adjust to normal life again. Give it a week or so; we'll get him laughing." He pauses, mouth twisting. "A fortnight at most."

I contemplate the idea of a different version of Scythe than the one I've come to know. One who makes his comrades' faces light up with joy. One who laughs with his friends. One who does anything besides brood and scowl and insult me.

Frankly, it seems incomprehensible.

Farley must read the doubt in my expression. "Despite what you think, Ace . . . you're safe with us. I promise."

I give him a halfhearted smile. It feels like a lie on my lips.

Safe?

I am not safe. I haven't been safe in so long, I barely remember the feeling. And after all I've endured these past weeks at the hands of human males, I doubt I'll ever allow myself to actually trust another one.

I don't tell Farley this. Because I like Farley. Hell, I even like Jac and Mabon and Uther. But my feelings toward the man who made me his captive are decidedly less clear-cut.

There is absolutely nothing *safe* about Commander Scythe.

Penn.

Whoever he is.

Nice as it is to entertain the notion of genuine companionship again after so long on my own . . . there is no chance in hell I'm about to let my guard down around these men.

Not today.

Not ever.

My hands slip into the deep pockets of my gown as we continue to walk, gripping the dagger concealed there. Though I know my actions are hidden from his vantage, I cannot shake the feeling that the helmed man trailing a dozen paces behind me can somehow see straight through the folds of his cloak on my shoulders, to my hand as it curls around the hilt.

My grip is so tight, my fingers are numb from far more than the cold by the time we reach the outskirts of Vintare.

CHAPTER
ELEVEN

Vintare isn't so much a town as it is an outpost for frostbitten travelers. Tucked deep in the dip between two misshapen peaks, the scattered collection of buildings—some no more than shacks to shield from the wind—rings a central square of hard-packed snow. Large barreled firepits pepper the area, bastions of welcome beckoning us in from the elements.

It is barely midafternoon and already dusk is pressing down upon us, the meager day yielding to greedy night. At this elevation, the sky feels so close you might reach out and run your fingers along the underside of a cloud, snatch a handful of mist straight from the heavens. As I take in the settlement sprawling before me, a tiny oasis of warmth against the endless chill, I cannot deny there is something starkly beautiful about it. Despite the biting cold, despite the unfortunate circumstances that led me here, I find my eyes widening to drink in every detail.

People are bustling about in shapeless mountain garb. They eye us warily as we limp inside the town limits—covered in dried venom, filthy from long days on the road, the men strapped with more weapons than an armory. None of them greet us. Most keep their eyes firmly averted.

I don't blame them for their surreptitious glances any more

than for their scurrying out of our path. We are a hair-raising lot. We look like trouble at best, and we smell even worse.

The inn is instantly recognizable, seeing as it is the only structure taller than a single story. Several horses are tied to posts in front—mountain stock with blond hair feathering their hooves and thick, furry coats, bred to withstand the plummeting temperatures. Beside them, to my unexpected delight, I see two teams of black-and-white sled dogs lashed to a pair of sleek carved sleighs, awaiting their masters' return. They are so large, I almost mistake them for wolves . . . until I spot their lolling tongues and wagging tails.

With Onyx hooked to a post outside, happily munching from the communal hay trough, and Farley once again slung between Uther and Mabon, we step onto the porch and approach the front door. The building is constructed in a stacked-log style, with frosted windows gouged at uneven intervals. Through the thick glass panes, light and laughter trickle into the night—the latter of which ceases the moment we step over the threshold, the snow caking our boots melting onto the planked wood flooring.

Every head whips to the door with undisguised curiosity. Conversations halt mid-word. The fiddle player's note falls off with a tuneless screech of strings. For a long while, there is only silence as they examine us, and we them. Vintare may be a mountain outpost, accustomed to travelers of all kinds, but our appearance is such that it could shake the unshakable.

The innkeeper, bless her, recovers first. With nary a word to us, she snaps her fingers at the two male servants standing behind the bar and points at Farley. "Bring him back into the healer's chambers. Get him settled, best you can manage."

The manservants do not hesitate before lurching into motion. Her word is law, her authority absolute. As Farley is transferred into their care, the innkeeper turns her attention to the rest of us.

She sees me, the sole female figure amid a collection of savage warriors, and bustles my way in a swish of brown skirts.

Scythe and Jac both tense at my sides, but she does not even spare them a glance. Her rounded frame pushes directly to me, and as she gets an up-close glance at my face, she gasps.

"Heavens, my lady! Whatever happened to you?"

"Would you believe me if I told you I was kidnapped mid-execution, nearly died of a raging fever, narrowly escaped demise on a decrepit rope bridge, and battled a den of carnivorous cyntroedi?"

She blinks at me, eyes like saucers.

Scythe's elbow digs sharply into my side, a clear warning to shut my mouth. His voice is tense. "We'll need two rooms. Adjacent, if possible."

The innkeeper doesn't even look at him. Her gaze is locked on my face, the picture of motherly concern. Or what I imagine to be motherly concern, as I've never had a mother of my own. "She'll be getting a bath, first and foremost. I don't know where you heathens hail from, but in my inn—"

"Madame," Jac interrupts, his tone infused with ill-concealed amusement. "You might want to look at whom you're speaking to before you start tossing insults."

Her light brown eyes move first to Jac, then to Scythe, at which point she pales and immediately begins spewing apologies. "Oh! Pende—I mean, Prince Penn! Your Highness—" A blush steals up her cheeks as she struggles to recall his proper title. Her hands fist nervously in front of her apron. "*Prince Pendefyre*," she settles on, taking a trembling breath. "I did not recognize you beneath the helm. I should have. I beg your deepest pardon for the mistake. It will never happen again, I assure you." She dips into a belated curtsy, her movements out of practice.

My body stills, every muscle turning to stone as her words process.

Prince.

She said *prince*.

Prince Pendefyre.

I guess that explains his men's calling him Penn.

Because he isn't Scythe at all.

I knew already. Of course I knew. As soon as I realized he bore no true allegiance to King Eld's army, I'd assumed his name itself was likely a fabrication. Still, suspecting a thing and hearing it officially confirmed are two entirely separate realities. My mind rearranges all I've seen and heard these past few days, since he thundered into my life. I struggle to reconcile the beast of a man beside me with royalty.

Royalty.

He is a prince of a bloody Northlands kingdom.

But which one?

I can picture the northern territories on the map—a stretch of glacial tundra spanning beyond the Cimmerian Mountains—but at the moment, I can recall only the name of the most famous. The most barbaric.

Llŷr.

King Soren rules that frozen iceberg beyond the Avian Strait, his brutality as far-reaching as his archers' arrows in battle. I can be grateful at least that I have not fallen into *his* hands . . . though, for all I know, Prince Pendefyre is a direct relative of that notorious brute.

A brother, perhaps?

A cousin?

A son?

"Don't trouble yourself," Scythe—*Penn*—is saying from beside me. "We mean to pass through without any fanfare, not advertise our presence here. Ridiculous royal protocols only draw unnecessary attention. Better if you treat us like any of your other guests. I trust you understand?"

She is already pale but somehow seems to pale even further as she rises from her hasty curtsy. "Of course. I'm sorry, Your Hi—I mean, my lord." Her throat works as she swallows down her nerves. "I'll see to your rooms right away." Her eyes move once more to me. "I assume the lady will have her own chambers?"

"Your assumption is unwarranted."

My heart quails at his flat contradiction. The innkeeper must see my horrified look because, prince or no, she pins Penn with a steely glance that suggests she is not to be trifled with.

"The lady is barely able to stand upright. She needs a proper bath and fresh clothes and, more than likely, a moment of peace judging by her haggard appearance." With that, she steps firmly forward, slides an arm around my shoulders, and pulls me from the huddle of warriors who've ensconced me from all sides. "Come, lass. We'll get you cleaned up and tucked into bed. Nothing like a warm meal and clean sheets after an ordeal."

I hear Penn sigh, a deep rattle of resignation, but he does not object. I'm too tired to protest as the kindhearted woman leads me across the tavern to a creaky set of stairs tucked behind the bar.

I do not look back at the men.

But I know they watch me go—along with every other set of curious eyes in the inn.

I GAPE AT the girl staring back at me from the mirror's age-fogged surface. My reflection is unrecognizable. If I passed myself on the street at market, I wouldn't pause. I look like a skeletal stranger. A shadow of my former self—cheeks hollowed, bones jutting. Beneath the layer of filth, there are rings of exhaustion bruising my eyes and a gaunt, guarded look in their silvery depths that makes me flinch.

"Come, my lady."

I turn to look at the innkeeper. While I used the chamber pot tucked discreetly behind a trifold privacy screen—a luxury, after weeks of crouching in the shrubbery to relieve myself—and examined my ghastly reflection, she and two scullery maids have been busy filling a deep tub with steaming water, one bucket at a time. Their efficiency makes the arduous task look easy when I know it to be anything but.

"You don't need to call me that," I half whisper, feeling heat steal across my cheeks.

"Call you what?"

"My lady."

"Oh?" Her brows arch. "And why is that? You're my guest here, are you not?"

"It's just . . ." I gesture lamely at my ears, their pointed tips poking through the matted pale mane tangled around my head. "I'm no lady. I'm just . . . a halfling."

She stiffens. "And whyever should a thing like that matter?"

I blink at her, not sure what to say. For that very thing has mattered a great deal to a great many people, ever since I learned the ways of the world.

She takes a purposeful step toward me and, in a precise move I cannot fail to miss, tucks her orderly, gray-streaked bob behind an ear. An ear with a tapered point at the tip.

An ear just like mine.

"You're in the Northlands now, child," she says simply, ignoring my startled gasp. As if that explains everything. As if the Northlands aren't just as treacherous as anywhere else in Anwyvn—if not more so.

I decide not to push for an explanation as her hands clasp mine and she tugs me gently toward the bath.

"Come now. Let's see what's under all this dirt and dust, shall we?" She snaps her fingers at the two girls hovering by the tub. "Marta, Inga—help me get her out of this dress. While you wash her, I'll find something suitable for her to wear. She's not so far off my niece's size, I should think . . . And this . . ." She grimaces as she eyes my formerly mint-green, now many-hued garment, its fabric streaked with a multitude of putrid stains. "This must be burned without delay."

I might be insulted if it weren't the gods' honest truth. The dress isn't even fit for cleaning scraps, at this point. I don't put up a fuss as Marta and Inga whip it off me along with the woolen tunic and my tattered shift, clucking under their breath when they see how my ribs poke through my skin, how my hips and stomach have gone concave after the bitter months of flight stripped my former curves, day after day. They stare for a long moment at the strange triangular pattern between my breasts but curb their curiosity—for which I am eternally grateful. I have no answers when it comes to the supposed Remnant mark I bear.

They are gentle as they pull off my boots and socks, unraveling the cloth-strip bandages I'd applied last time we made camp. Before the bridge, before the mountain, before the cyntroedi. Before Jac or Farley or Mabon or Uther. Before I learned Scythe was Penn, and a prince at that.

Was that only last night?

It doesn't seem possible.

Tears fill my eyes as I sink into the warm tub. It takes all my strength to keep them from spilling down my cheeks as the girls begin to wash me—dousing my head with scoops of water, lathering my hair with coarse soap that smells of evergreens. No one has touched me with anything resembling kindness in so very long.

Physical contact is something I took for granted in all the years of my youth. There was never a time growing up when I was farther than a few steps from strong arms, from a steeling embrace. Eli may not have shared my blood or my race, but he showered me with all the affection of a father nonetheless. Most of my neighbors were good, kind folk, who accepted me without protest, for all that I was different. While halflings on the mainland were being executed in mass numbers, the peninsula remained a tolerant sanctuary.

And then, last summer, came Tomas. The baker's apprentice with the quick smile and the flour-dusted hands. He may never have entertained a serious future with the healer's halfling ward—not when he could have his pick of any perfect girl in our secluded hamlet—but he had touched my body with reverence and called me beautiful in the dark, when there was no one else around to hear.

It was not meant to last. Not for long, not for more than a handful of stolen nights in a summer meadow. But in his embrace, I got my first glimpse at a different sort of comfort, the kind that makes your heart ache and your skin burn. The kind that lights a fire inside your veins warm enough to ward off the chill of loneliness.

I've needed every scrap of warmth I could conjure since I left Seahaven behind. The real world is colder. Crueler. It is a rare person who offers another comfort instead of seeking to satisfy their own; who gives freely instead of taking. I had begun to wonder if I'd ever again feel the touch of another's hands in any form other than violence. And so, as fingers work through the many snarls and tangles of my hair, as my nails are brushed clean of dirt and my tired limbs are wiped with perfumed washcloths, I allow myself to float outside my body for a time, my mind completely disconnected from everything except the sensation of water around me, lulling me like a warm embrace.

It takes two full drainings and refillings before the bathwater runs clear and I am deemed, at last, suitably clean. My skin is red from their scrubbing and has long since gone clammy. My fingers are pruned at the tips. Marta and Inga wrap me up in a warm towel and pat my body dry before I catch cold.

Edwynna, the innkeeper, returns briefly to the bathing chamber with a bundle of clothing in her arms. I don't ask where she found the undergarments and dress, merely thank her for doing so. They are too big for me but blessedly clean, the thick muslin fabric smelling of soap and dyed a faded reddish color that brings out the golden strands in my white-blond hair. They loop a braided bronze sash low on my waist, belting the fabric close to my frame. Its tassels hang almost to my feet, which are shoved into maroon slippers a half size too large.

Once I am dressed, Inga sits me down on a padded bench in front of the vanity mirror and brushes out my damp mane in luxurious strokes that make me want to purr like a cat. It has grown quite long since my last trim, falling well past my waist. Her deft fingers work quickly, braiding the top half into a thick circlet of tendrils around my crown, leaving the rest free to fall down my back in a cascade of loose curls.

"There." She smiles at me, catching my eyes in the reflection. "You look quite lovely, miss."

Lovely is a stretch. Though I do look significantly better than before. I am definitely still haggard, my eyes shadowed from unchecked exhaustion . . . but I am clean, clothed in a freshly laundered dress, and have been combed and clucked over with more kindness than at any other time in recent memory. I feel like a new woman.

"Thank you," I murmur, trying out a smile. It does not quite reach my silver-blue eyes as they slide to Marta, who holds an armful of wet towels. "Both of you."

"It's our pleasure, my lady."

I'd hoped I could simply go to bed after my bath, but I'm promptly ushered out of the bathing chamber, down the stairs, and into the tavern. In my hours of absence, a boisterous energy has infused the barroom. The tables are packed with patrons standing shoulder to shoulder, metal mugs of mead and ale frothing over the rims as they clank them together with cheers to good health. The fiddler is in high spirits, a lively jig spilling from his strings as the bow ebbs back and forth like a wave kissing doggedly at the shore.

Inga keeps one hand at the small of my back as she steers me through the crowd. Besides Edwynna and her girls, I note only one other woman in the whole room—a fearsome-looking fur trader with a cloak made from a white bear pelt, watching the door like she expects danger to step through it at any given moment. Her cold eyes shift toward me and I immediately drop my gaze to the floorboards.

She is not my only observer. I feel the weight of many stares as Inga propels me forward. When I see where we are headed, relief and dread war for dominance within me. Jac and his men—minus one redhead with a shattered leg and an easy laugh—are gathered around a large oak table against the far wall, a position of honor beside the roaring fireplace. They all look freshly bathed, their hair still damp, their skin ruddy from scrubbing with coarse soap.

In the shadows closest to the wall, I can make out only the

vaguest outline of another man. The breadth of his shoulders, the firm line of his torso. His face is hidden by darkness, his features disguised by the helm he wears, even now.

I halt a few paces away, digging my slippered heels into the hardwood when Inga tries to urge me onward. Jac is the first to spot me. His gaze, ever watchful, scans across the sea of revelry for potential threats. It skims right over me at first, passing by only to jerk back with a snap of his head. He sits up straighter in his chair as his eyes drink me in, a head-to-toe sweep.

"Skies!" He whistles so wolfishly, heat rises to my cheeks despite my best efforts. "Almost didn't recognize you without goo in your hair, Ace!"

It seems my nickname is catching.

Mabon and Uther both pivot on their stools to get a look at me. Inga puts more pressure on my spine, forcing my feet into motion, and I smile wanly as I yield, walking toward the unoccupied stool beside Uther. I tell myself it is because his gray eyes are kind. Not at all because it is the farthest possible position from the shadowy corner where His Highness himself is holding court.

"Bloody hell, you look almost . . . female."

"*Almost?*" I roll my eyes. "What an overwhelming compliment. Thanks so much, Jac."

Mabon snorts into his ale.

I hop up on the stool, slippers swinging in the air, and give Inga a goodbye wave as she disappears back to her duties. Jac watches her go, his eyes fixed on her buxom behind with blatant interest.

"She's married," I tell him, relaying information I learned while she brushed out my hair. "Five years now. Her husband is a whale oil trader in the Frostlands. Happy as can be. They're expecting their first child by midsummer."

Uther chuckles and elbows Jac, who is scowling at me.

My smile widens as Mabon pushes an untouched pint of ale in front of me. My hands shake slightly as I lift it to my lips and take a deep pull, foam coating my upper lip. "Thank you, Mabon."

"Least I can do, lass." He scratches at his bald head, looking sheepish. "After your help in the cave, I mean."

"I didn't do much."

"You could've done far less," Uther notes, his gray eyes steady as ever as they hold mine. "Most hardened soldiers would've fainted on the spot or run screaming for their mothers."

"I never had a mother," I say unthinkingly. "And I have no one left alive to run to, screaming or otherwise."

Quiet descends on our table, an island of solemnity in a sea of laughter and music.

"How is Farley?" I ask after a long sip, thinking a swift change of subject is in order.

"Putting up an awful fuss, per usual." Jac drains his own ale. "The display of melodrama is astounding. When he gets back to Caeldera, he should audition for a troupe of traveling players. Try out his act onstage."

"His leg is broken," I feel compelled to point out. "He's got to be in considerable pain."

Mabon grunts in soft acknowledgment.

"Did the healer give him something to dull his senses?" I ask, looking from one man to the other. "Or put him to sleep while the bone was set?"

"Small hiccup with the healer." Jac sighs. "Turns out, he's not here."

"What?"

"He was called away to another outpost on the other side of the range. Blacksmith found himself on the wrong end of a hot forge yesterday. Grisly scene, by all accounts."

My eyes widen—not at the imagery, but at the realization that there is no healer here. Which means Farley . . .

I'm off my stool and around the table before any of the men have time to react. I make it three paces past the fireplace when a hand shoots out from the shadows, hooks me by the braided belt at my hips, and hauls me backward. An *oof* of air escapes my lungs as I stumble on my slippers and collide with something granite hard. A chest, I realize, when a low voice rumbles from it, directly into my ear.

"And where do you think you're going?"

"To set Farley's leg," I say instantly, ignoring the shiver that moves down my spine. "Even if the healer isn't here, I'm sure there's a stockroom of herbs and supplies. I'll—"

"Eat."

Shaking off his hold, I spin around to fix him with a glare. In the shadows, Penn's eyes are two glowing embers. "Excuse me?"

"You'll eat."

My spine stiffens. "I told you—"

"You can tell me whatever you wish. But before you do, you're going to sit and you're going to get a warm meal in your stomach."

"You can't force me—"

"I'll spoon-feed you if necessary," he returns bluntly. "But I shouldn't have to. If you're clever enough to set a broken bone, you should also be clever enough to realize you need a clear mind to do it. Not to mention a fair bit of strength. You claim you want to help Farley? Then you'll help without your head spinning from hunger."

My mouth snaps closed.

Gods damn it.

He's right. A meal will do me good, clear some of the cobwebs from my overtaxed mind. Much as I hate to admit it, I'm of little use to Farley in my current state.

Penn sees on my face the moment I cave to his logic. He doesn't say another word—merely jerks his chin at the stool on the other side of the table and, with a broad hand at my middle, gives me a gentle push out of his shadowy corner. I keep my gaze downcast, unable to meet anyone's eyes as I stumble back to my seat in my too-large slippers. My stomach roils as I swallow my pride.

It tastes bitter.

Thankfully, the stew Marta delivers a few moments later is anything but. Thick, tasty broth swims with soft carrots and chunks of tender meat. The spoon in my hand trembles as I tamp down the urge to shovel the contents of my bowl into my mouth at embarrassing speed.

As we eat, the men—mostly Jac and Uther—chat about their campaign, describing a skirmish they faced last week against a clan of Reavers from the ice shelf on the western coast, who are encroaching a bit too close to sovereign borders. The Cimmerian Mountains, I learn, are considered neutral territory. Too vast to be ruled by any one king and far too wild, they are shared by all Northlanders from the three kingdoms— Llŷr, the Frostlands, and Dyved.

The names pop back onto the mental map of Anwyvn in my head like they've always been there, merely obscured for a time. Dyved sprawls to the west. Llŷr dominates the east. The far smaller Frostlands occupy the sliver of glacier between them at the northernmost tip of Anwyvn.

Each kingdom protects its main trade routes through the mountains but otherwise leaves the range to govern itself. As such, it is a lawless place, home to as many exiles and fugitives as monsters and snow beasts. The men grin as they tell me this, as though it is an amusing anecdote instead of a terrifying fact that will cause me to lose sleep at night.

For the past ten months, their unit has been assigned to clear out a particular stretch of snowy passes that lead in and out of the kingdom they call home.

Dyved.

"Can't let just any monsters wander down into Caeldera." Jac swallows his last sip of ale and immediately waves a hand at the barkeep, requesting another. "The only beast permitted to prowl those streets goes by the name of Pendefyre."

"Jac," a deep voice warns from the corner.

Jac's grin is lopsided from drink, but he manages to muffle his voice. "Right. *Low profile*. Got it."

Penn is keeping to the shadows. Given Edwynna's reaction earlier, when she realized her inn was hosting royalty, I think that is a wise choice. No wonder he never takes off the helm. Even this high in the mountains, a prince of Dyved would be recognizable. Not to mention a potential target for the nefarious Reavers I've heard so much about.

My eyes drift across the tavern, examining the men at the surrounding tables. A mishmash of hair colors, races, and body types, with grizzled beards and wind-burned cheeks. Their cloaks are lined with fur, their shoulders draped with animal pelts. Most have double-bit battle-axes leaning beside their stools as they play rounds of a card game I don't recognize. A fair few of them glance our way as fresh hands are dealt and new bets placed. I pray it is in curiosity, rather than ill intent. We have enough to deal with already without adding more enemies to our list of concerns.

I drink the last sip of my tea—I'd pushed away the ale as soon as I realized there was a need for my healing skills—and hop off my stool. My eyes cut to the shadowy corner where I know Penn is staring back at me.

"Farley," I say simply.

I turn and walk away from the table. This time, no hand reaches out to stop me. After a moment, I hear the distinct jolt of several pairs of boots hitting the floorboards, following in my wake.

CHAPTER TWELVE

The break is not as bad as I'd feared.

For this, I am grateful. It's been some time since I last set a bone, especially without Eli's watchful guidance. I kneel beside the pallet where Farley lies, conscious of Mabon, Uther, and Penn watching my every move like hawks circling a field of carrion.

Just as I had two summers ago, when our neighbor's youngest child fell from an ashwood and splintered his arm at the wrist, I run my fingers along the exposed limb, keeping my touch light as I explore the extent of the fractures. Beneath the mottled bloom of bruises, I feel two distinct sections of bone. No fragments, no punctures in the skin. A single crack along his shin.

"No shards," I tell Farley.

"That's good news, right?"

I smile into his pallid face. "Very. It's a clean break. We'll have you on your way to healing in no time at all."

His returning smile is thin but relieved. In his eyes, I see the drugging tincture I'd found in the healer's storeroom doing its fine work. His lids are drooping as the pain is banished to the farthest reaches of his mind, no match for the effects of valerian root and verbena extract.

"Rest now," I tell him. "When you wake, you'll feel much better."

He doesn't respond. He is already unconscious.

The door swings inward. Jac stands there, the shoulders of his cloak dusted with fresh snow, his hands holding the ice I'd requested he fetch from outside.

"Cold as an ice giant's cock out there," he declares, plunking down beside me by the pallet. "Where do you want this?"

I take the block of hard-packed snow from him, my palms tingling at the frigidness, and gently apply it around the break.

"What are you doing?"

"Numbing the wound," I murmur, focused on my task. "The ice will make it less inflamed when I realign the bones. And less painful when the herbs wear off in a few hours."

"Can't you just give him more?"

"Too much medicine can kill a man quicker than any battle wound. More than one dose a day, he may never rouse from the stupor."

Jac blows out a sharp breath but asks no more questions as he rejoins the other men by the door. I continue to ice the break, sopping up the runoff with a spare sheet as the snow melts in watery trickles. Only when I feel the leg is thoroughly numb do I glance up. My gaze snags immediately on Penn's. I swallow hard and look into Uther's steady gray eyes instead.

"I'll need someone to hold his shoulders. The tonic I gave him should keep him sedated, but there's a chance he'll wake and, if that happens, the last thing I need is him thrashing about, causing himself more damage."

There is a beat of silence as the men look at one another.

"I'm half-drunk," Jac announces happily. "So I'm out of contention."

"Mabon is the strongest," Uther offers, looking at the stocky man beside him.

Mabon shifts uneasily, scratching at his neck like there are bugs crawling beneath his midnight skin. "Suppose I could . . ."

"I'll do it."

I don't look at Penn when he speaks. I'd somehow known it would be him who helped me even before I asked for assistance. I merely nod and turn my attention back to the task at hand.

Beside me, a pile of materials pilfered from the healer's orderly shelves sit at the ready—firm slats of wood and a roll of cloth for splinting. Thin leather straps to secure it. A dowel to twist the knots tight once the cast is in place.

I can do this.

I *will* do this.

Just as soon as my hands stop shaking.

I look up into Penn's eyes. He is crouched by Farley's head, his grip planted firmly on the sleeping man's shoulders. Ready to hold him down if necessary.

"I'll start now," I tell him needlessly.

He nods.

I chew my bottom lip. "Have you ever done something like this before?"

He shakes his head.

Of course he hasn't. He's a *prince*, for gods' sake. There is probably a team of royal healers at the ready whenever he catches a case of the sniffles.

"It's rather straightforward," I say, as much for his benefit as my own. "The bones are out of alignment. I'll need to pull down until they separate, then slide them back into their proper place. Once that's done, I'll set the leg with a splint so it doesn't shift as it heals."

He arches a dark brow. "Are you asking me or telling me?"

"I'm telling you," I snap, abruptly annoyed.

"Good."

His dark-flame eyes are unwavering on mine. I cannot read the emotion in them. I do not know him well enough to decode the way he's watching me in this moment. But I do know, for whatever reason, snapping at him calms me. Brings me back to myself. Slows my racing heart and stills my shaking hands.

I'm ready.

I look down at Farley's bruised leg, exposed from the knee down. I take firm hold of his ankle. And, with a deep breath, I begin the meticulous process of bonesetting.

THE DOOR CRACKS open.

So do my eyes.

I stare up at the log ceiling, instantly alert. I've been asleep only minutes, judging by the exhaustion still infusing my limbs with lead. After the ordeal with Farley, I made it up the stairs and into the sparsely decorated chamber on the top floor with Marta's aid. She said little as she helped me into a loose-fitting white nightgown and tucked me into bed, dousing the candles and stoking the fire with a fresh log before she shut the door. I'd barely heard the latch catch when I tumbled into unconsciousness.

Heavy boots pound on the floorboards, crossing toward me. I sit up in a flurry of blankets. The dagger on my nightstand— which I'd retrieved from Edwynna before she confiscated my old dress for burning—is in my hand in a heartbeat.

The footfalls stop.

"Planning to stab me?"

Penn.

I blink into the dark. "Maybe."

"Maybe?" His voice is amused as I've ever heard it. "What's

holding you back? That intractable sense of morality you tote around like a war medal?"

"I'm surprised you can even recognize morality in others, seeing as you possess none of your own."

"Trust me, I can recognize a great many shortcomings I my-self am not afflicted with—naivety, for instance."

"Did you come here to hurl insults?"

There is a marked pause. "No."

"Then what are you doing in my room?" I grumble grouchily. "I was sleeping."

And I was. In a bed, no less. The first one I've been lucky enough to utilize since I fled my own in the cover of night. Sure, it's lumpy and smells faintly of mildew. But it is a bed. One that, until his rude interruption, I'd been thoroughly enjoying.

"By all means, carry on," he mutters, crossing to the dressing table by the window, where a shaft of moonlight slants through the pane.

As my sight adjusts to the darkness, I'm able to make out the finer details of his tall form. He is dressed in black, as usual, but not his Commander Scythe garb. These are a Northlander's clothes—the fabric thicker, sturdier, built to cut the wind and blunt the chill. There is nothing fancy or frilly about his attire, but it is clearly well made, crafted with care by a skilled seam-stress. The shirt has a row of black buttons down the front. His heavy leather boots are to the knee, and recently polished. As I watch, his hands reach down to undo the laces.

I jolt. "What are you doing?"

"I thought you were sleeping."

"I can't sleep with you in here!"

"Then you're in for a long night."

He pulls off his boots. They hit the floor one by one. Each thump makes me flinch.

"But— You— I—" My voice is hoarse with panic. "I cannot believe this!"

"Believe it."

The weariness of those two words makes me overlook their inherent arrogance. He sounds tired. Exhausted, in fact. Maybe even more so than me. And, though it shouldn't, it catches me by surprise. Because until this point, he's seemed so tireless. So inexhaustible. The formidable Commander Scythe. Never sleeping, never at ease. Never succumbing to mortal failings like hunger or fatigue.

I'd been with him nearly a week now and had never once seen him rest—not even when we made camp at night. If he wasn't nursing me back to health from the throes of fever, he was hunting to keep us fed or chopping wood to keep our fires burning. Riding hard through each day, holding watch through each night. Battling men and monsters alike in his unflagging determination to get us north.

To get us safe.

My protests dry up as I stare at him, my hand a death grip on the dagger. He stands in the shaft of moonlight, facing away from me, the broad planes of his back stiff with tension. There is a prolonged beat of silence. Then, reaching up, he does something that makes my heart seize within my chest. Something, I realize, I've been waiting for. For days. For a week. Since the very first moment I saw him, in fact, standing in front of my hanging tree, staring at me like my existence was the worst thing to ever befall him.

He takes off his helm.

There is a dull metal clank as it strikes the table. He braces his hands on either side of it, fingers splayed out along the wooden surface, and takes a deep, shuddering breath. I watch the muscles in his back ripple beneath his shirt as he exhales in slow degrees, releasing what seems to be a torrent of pent-up energy. His head is turned away. His hair falls around it, a shaggy curtain.

I catch myself wondering what expression he wears in that fraught moment; what he might look like with those shafts of moonlight painting him in shades of silver. By the time he turns to me, he's schooled his face into the mask of cool indifference I've come to know so well. Still, I feel my tongue parch, my mouth going completely dry at the sight of him without the severe lines of his helm, without the serpentine nose guard to bisect his undeniably handsome features.

I swallow hard.

It is not the boyish beauty of a stage player, nor the flashy appeal of the male courtesans I'd seen loitering outside the brothels in Bellmere, Seahaven's main port, on the rare occasion Eli allowed me to accompany him to the city. Penn's is a sharp, symmetrical face with clean lines, a strong brow, and a straight nose.

It is, I decide, even better than I allowed myself to envision, all those nights I'd lain awake beside our campfire, wondering if I'd ever get a chance to see him unobscured. His hair, like the brows I've seen furrowed at me so often in frustration, is a lush, darkish brown. Neither long nor short but somewhere in between. I wonder if he wears it cropped when he isn't undercover in the Midlands. The ends curl just past his ears—

His ears!

My breaths cease. My eyes widen. Because those ears . . .

They're pointed.

He's fae.

The dagger in my hand is clutched so tight, I think my knuckles might shatter. My heart begins to pound, my pulse increasing its tempo from a thrum to a roar in an instant.

"You," I whisper, unable to say anything else. Unable to think anything else. Unable to even breathe properly. "You're . . ."

A halfling.

Like me.

He does not move. Does not speak. Does not do a thing but stand there in that shaft of moonlight, staring at me.

"You're fae." I shake my head, rejecting the words even as I say them. "That's . . . That's not . . . You *can't* be."

His dark brows arch. "Can't I?"

"But . . . you're a prince!" I blurt stupidly.

"And?"

"How can a halfling hold such a position?" I must still be dreaming. "How can anyone with a drop of fae blood be so . . . *visible* . . . without being hunted down for daring to exist?"

"Things are different in the Northlands." His shoulders lift in a brief shrug. "We do not hold with the more primitive customs of our southern neighbors."

At this, I blink. Stupefied. "Then, in Dyved . . . There are more like me? Like . . . us?"

"Nearly all who live beyond the mountains are at least partly fae. It's rare to see a full-blooded human past the range."

"Your men aren't fae," I point out.

"They are."

I shake my head rapidly. "But their ears—"

"There are glyphs stitched into their uniforms. Enchantments. Nothing powerful, but enough to cast a faint glamour that allows the wearer to pass as human. If you honed your senses, you could pierce through the illusions easily." He pauses. "Try it next time you look at one of them. You'll see for yourself."

"I can't see through glamours."

"You can." His voice is growing irritated. "You simply have neglected that ability—along with all your others."

My spine stiffens at the implication. "You seem to believe I possess some kind of power because of . . . *what*, exactly? An odd birthmark on my chest? Surely, you realize how absurd that sounds. There hasn't been maegic in Anwyvn since the Cull. It was extinguished when they slaughtered all the high fae. Everyone knows it."

He is quiet for a beat. His question, when it comes, is delivered with terrifying softness. "Then what happened on that cliff side? To that man who tried to rape you?"

I flinch. "I don't know."

"You do."

"No, I don't!" I gnaw my bottom lip, trying to quell the surge of rising panic. "All I know is, one minute he was tearing at my dress and the next he was on the ground writhing in pain. Whatever happened to him wasn't something I did."

Not consciously, anyway.

His voice is still soft. Soft in a way that makes me nervous. Soft like a snake, just before the kill strike. "And what's your explanation for the bridge? Hmm? How have you rearranged reality to suit your safe little delusions when it comes to that?"

"The bridge?"

"When you fell through that splintered slat. What happened?"

"I . . ." I shake my head again, a swift jerk of confusion. "I got lucky, I guess. The bridge pitched in the wind . . . I was tossed up onto it."

"*Lucky*," he mutters. "Skies above."

"Yes, *lucky*!" I snap. "What else would it be?"

"You're serious."

I nearly bite through my lips trying to hold in my more furious retorts, instead uttering a bald, "*Yes.*"

"Fine. Let's talk for a moment about that lucky wind." Penn sidles a step closer to the bed, putting me instantly on alert. He stops just short of the carved post at the foot—not close enough to touch me, but still too close for my liking. "Wind that came up out of nowhere, so quickly it defied the laws of nature. Wind that moved not from one direction, in a current, but whirled in a curious vortex that centered around *you*. Wind that pitched your dangling body in such a way that you were delivered, in one piece, from almost certain death. Wind that dissipated in a single blink as soon as you were safely back on solid footing." He pauses, letting his words penetrate the thick fog of denial and confusion wrapped around me like a blanket. "I have seen some strange things in my time on this earth. Inexplicable things. Monstrous things, even. But I have never, in all my years, seen anything like that wind."

If my pulse was a drumbeat before, it is now a roar. The blood rushing between my ears is so loud, I can barely hear my own thoughts.

"It was a squall," I say weakly, not believing the words but somehow still needing to voice them. "A freak windstorm . . ."

"It was no squall and you know it. You know the truth. You just don't want to believe it."

"And what truth is that?"

He takes another step toward me. His eyes never leave mine as his left hand rises to grip the bedpost. "You *called* that wind. Conjured it from thin air."

"That's . . . That's not possible."

"It is."

"What does . . ." I suck in a sharp breath. Inside my head, my thoughts are a jumble. Each question spawns two more, until my mind swarms in increasing disquiet. "What are you saying?"

Penn's patience has all but evaporated. "I'm saying that mark on your chest is no birthmark. It is a Remnant mark. A sign of elemental power. I recognized it the moment I saw it."

Memories slam into me, hurling me back a week's time—to

my hanging tree. Noose around my neck, iron at my wrists. And two burning eyes fixed upon me with such intensity, it seemed to singe my skin as he pulled loose the laces of my dress to examine the whorls and spirals etched between my breasts.

He'd known even then.

What that mark means.

What I am.

It seems wrong, somehow, that he knew so long before I did. That I *still* don't know. Not really. Even now, I feel frustratingly in the dark about my own identity.

"What am I?" I whisper in horror, mostly to myself.

To my surprise, Penn answers. "When I found you, I suspected but wasn't certain which of the four elements you controlled. After the bridge, I knew for sure." He stares at me, eyes glittering. "You are a wind weaver. You are Air. Air, awoken."

Something deep within me thrums, like the deep strike of a mallet on a drum, reverberating through every nerve ending in a silent current.

Air.

Air, awoken.

The mark on my chest prickles, a familiar ache of cold.

Awake, now.

Finally awake.

A breathy, borderline hysterical edge creeps into my voice. My last gasp of denial. "Don't you think if I could call the wind, I would've used it to my advantage these past few days? Against, let's say . . . *you*?"

"I think if you'd bothered to learn to control your maegic instead of allowing it to lash out unpredictably whenever your life is endangered," Penn says on a murmur, "yes. You might well have wielded it against me. But as things stand, you seem entirely ignorant of the birthright you carry. Of the untapped power within you."

"Power," I echo, my lips struggling to form the word as my mind struggles to come to terms with all he is saying. Impossible as it seems, there is a part of me—a very small part, speaking from the darkest recesses of my mind—that feels acute relief in hearing someone confirm what I've long suspected.

There is something wrong with me.

Something that sets me ever so slightly apart from others. More than just the mark on my flesh or the points of my ears. An innate strangeness, a peculiarity in the very marrow of my bones that whispers in the dark of the night that I will never lead a normal life. That I am destined for something else. Something far from the sunny shores of Seahaven. Something beyond a pleasant, predictable marriage to a soft-spoken man like Tomas.

Something greater.

That voice has been silenced for so long—first, at Eli's urging.

Best keep it covered, Rhya.

Best not allow anyone too close, Rhya.

Best try to blend in, Rhya.

And, later, at my own.

Be good.

Be normal.

Be ordinary.

I had tried. Oh, how I'd tried. Day after day, year after year. I had pushed down my disquiet, forced out the voice that taunted that I was different. Wrong. Cursed. I had buried it over and over, every time it resurfaced, until I forgot it existed in the first place.

But now that voice is screaming out, each word strengthening from a whisper to a shout I cannot ignore. Cannot bury.

Wind weaver, the mark seems to mock, its murmur ancient as time itself, its cold sting so acute I actually shiver. *Sylph of the skies... No more hiding...*

I press my free hand against it through the fabric of my borrowed nightgown, trying to quiet the unwelcome voice. My heart is a mad tattoo in my veins as my eyes rise to Penn where he stands a handful of paces away. His grip is tight on the bedpost, his knuckles stark white in the darkness.

"And what if I don't want it?" I ask, the words barely audible. "This... *Remnant.* This... power."

The smirk that twists his lips has a cruel edge. His eyes are flinty with tightly leashed rage. "Then I should've let you swing and saved myself a week of wasted effort."

My lips part on a shocked gasp.

"Now," he says, pushing off the bedpost, "I'm exhausted. First light is four hours away. I don't plan to use that time talking in circles."

He rounds the bed, approaching in unhurried strides. I scramble backward, trying to maintain some distance, but there is nowhere to go—my shoulder blades hit the headboard. I press my spine flat against it as Penn sits, his weight depressing the mattress, and slowly unfurls his long limbs into a reposed position atop the blankets. His head dents the pillow beside mine as his lids slide shut.

For a moment, it is silent. I sit there, pressed against the headboard, staring at the man lying inches away. His bare feet are crossed at the ankles. The back of his arm is thrown across his eyes to shield them from the moonlight.

"Either stab me with that dagger or put it on the nightstand," he mutters. "At this point, I really don't care which."

I jolt in surprise, staring down at my hand. I'd completely forgotten about the dagger, but sure enough, its hilt is still clutched in my grip, my fingertips pale from lack of circulation.

Throat working to swallow the lump of nerves lodged there, I reach over and set the weapon down with a light metallic clink. My fingers tingle as blood begins flowing once more. When I look back at Penn, he is in the same position—ankles crossed, arm over his eyes—as if completely unconcerned that I could gut him in his sleep. His breathing is level, chest rising and falling in even beats. His mouth is slack, slightly parted. His lips seem fuller in the absence of the stern frown he wears most often when looking my way.

Can he be asleep already?

A faint crease mars his forehead, furrowing his brows together. I wonder whether he is in a great amount of pain from the wound in his shoulder but do not ask, loath to let such an opportunity slip away. To study him without his knowledge is perilously rare. He is always on his guard, his gaze seeing everything at once, no detail too minute to escape his notice. Even now, with his eyes closed, there is a part of me that feels he is watching somehow, his perception so sharp he does not need to look at me to see me.

I force my eyes away from his face.

Despite my deep exhaustion, I doubt I'll be able to sleep. Not after everything he's told me. Certainly not with him lying next to me.

It is not a large bed, and he is a very large man.

Heart in my throat, I slide as far to my side of the mattress as I can manage without tumbling to the floor, turn my back firmly in his direction, and curl into a ball—knees to my chest, arms looped around them. I hug myself tight as I stare into the dark, my thoughts chasing one another across my mind like a dog after its own tail.

I think about birthrights and strange winds, Remnant marks and metal helms. About fallen bridges and screaming soldiers,

red-plumed arrows and bleeding wounds. About milky eyes and
serrated mandibles, viridescent goo and snapped bones. About
the Northlands and what awaits me there. Most of all, I think
about the strange bedfellow beside me, his breaths a steady harmony to the melody of worries clanging around inside my head.

Somehow, lulled by that strange song, I drift off to sleep.

CHAPTER
THIRTEEN

The next time the door opens, it does so with a crash instead of a creak. Jac's broad shoulders fill the frame, silhouetted by the light of the candles flickering in the hallway sconces.

"Reavers," he clips, urgency bursting from the word's every syllable.

"Fuck!" is Penn's only reply.

He rolls me off his chest and unwinds my arm from where it is wrapped around his waist—for, to my utter horror, in sleep I have pressed my body tight along the length of his side, seeking out warmth like a cat curled up before a winter hearth. There's no time to be properly mortified by my unconscious actions. Penn is already out of bed, pulling on his boots before I've even worked my way out from beneath the blankets.

Cheeks aflame, I vault from the mattress, stumbling over the long fabric of the nightgown in my haste. I'd have cracked my head open on the dressing table had Penn not materialized from the shadows in front of me. He steadies me with one hand while his other snatches my gown from the wall hook where Marta left it earlier.

"Get dressed. You have two minutes until your ass is in a saddle."

"But—"

"*Two minutes.*"

The door slams and he is gone. With no other choice, I blink away the film of sleep, slip off my nightgown, and struggle into my shift and red muslin. I've barely gotten the sash belted at my hips when the door swings inward again. I tense, expecting Penn, but it is Edwynna. Her hair is a bit wild, the gray-streaked mane frizzing beneath a sleep bonnet, but her eyes are focused as she bustles into the chamber.

"Here," she says, shoving a pair of thin calfskin boots into my hands. "Put these on."

I don't question her. I bend and jerk the boots on over my thick knitted stockings, grateful to find them a far closer fit than Farley's. The laces are scarcely tied when Edwynna tugs me up and whips a white cloak over my shoulders. It is lined with arctic fox fur at the collar and cuffs.

"This was my niece's," she tells me, her hands working at the brass neck clasps. "She left it behind when she moved to Llŷr last spring. No need for fur in Hylios, that's for sure."

"I couldn't possibly—"

"You can and you will." She grips my shoulders. "Now, go. Your men will already have their horses saddled. You make them wait much longer, they'll shout my whole inn awake."

"Thank you, Edwynna," I say, popping up onto my toes to press a quick kiss to her cheek. "For everything."

She blinks rapidly, looking a bit stunned by my unexpected affection, but says nary a word as she starts herding me toward the door. I manage to snag my dagger off the nightstand before I step into the hallway and am half shoved down the stairs into the dim, empty tavern.

There are no pockets in the red dress, but my new cloak has

several to choose from. I'm dreaming about all the potential weaponry I can stash on my person when I step out into the cold predawn morning. Jac, Mabon, and Uther are already there waiting astride long-coated draft horses.

"*Finally*, she deigns to appear." Jac's eyes narrow on me, stripped of their normal playful light. "Any longer, we'd have left you behind."

I pause, brows lifting along with my hopes. Perhaps escaping from Penn is merely a matter of dawdling in my dressing chamber until he is so annoyed, he goes on without me . . .

"Of course, without our protection, you'd be killed within the hour," Jac adds lightly.

Of course.

My stomach clenches. "What's happening?"

"Reavers," Mabon mutters bluntly, as though that single word is explanation enough.

"The same ones your unit has been clashing with?"

Jac nods distractedly. "A few of their associates were in the tavern last night while we ate. Spotted us—spotted Penn—and sent out word. Luckily Uther overheard some of their chatter, otherwise we'd have all been dead in our beds before daybreak."

My breath catches in my throat. I take two steps across the porch, suddenly wanting as little distance as possible between me and my heavily armed traveling companions. "Where are we going?"

"We'd planned to escort you to the Apex Portal and send you through to Caeldera, but there's no chance you can use it now. They'll be watching it. Expecting it. We'll have to take the long way around and hope they don't follow." Jac scowls, as though this is a grave inconvenience. "My unit is two days' ride from here. Three, if we take the Widow's Notch to avoid detection."

"Your unit . . ." I echo, struggling to follow.

"An armed escort to the border will send a message, loud and clear. A show of force. You understand?"

I don't—not remotely. But a far more important thought occurs to me. One that makes my breath catch. "What about Farley?"

"He stays here." Jac's eyes scan the abandoned square, as though on high alert. "Can't ride with that leg. We'll send a wagon in a few days."

"Oh, he'll love that." Mabon chuckles. "Jolting back to Caeldera like an expectant mother."

"But we can't just leave him," I cry. "He'll be a sitting duck!"

"Relax, Ace. He wasn't with us in the tavern last night. They don't even know to look for him."

That is a slight relief. "Still, he shouldn't be alone. Not in his condition. If the bones shift or he spikes a fever, I need to be here to treat him."

"No, you don't."

My head jerks around at the sound of Penn's voice. He appears from the shadows, helm on his head, bridle in hand, Onyx in tow. A pelt-lined cloak drapes his shoulders. His eyes are on me but he, like the other men, looks as though half his focus is monitoring our surroundings for an invisible threat.

"But—"

"The healer will be back by tomorrow." Penn plows over my objections. "And Edwynna has run this outpost for longer than you've been breathing. She's seen her fair share of battle wounds and bar scrapes. I think she can handle one cantankerous red-head for a few days on her own." He pauses, extends a hand toward me, and flicks his fingers impatiently. "Come."

Swallowing down any further objections, I hurry to his side. As soon as I'm within reach, he practically tosses me up into the saddle. I have less than a single breath to settle before he vaults up behind me. One arm snakes around my waist, hauling me back against his body. The other gathers the reins and, as he spurs Onyx into motion, steers us across the empty, snow-packed square, around the low-burning firepits, and beyond the limits of Vintare.

WE RIDE LIKE there are a hundred hungry cyntroedi on our heels, stopping only when the sun is high in the sky to give the horses a brief respite from our punishing pace. Unlike Onyx, the borrowed mounts do not have a ceaseless reserve of energy and require regular watering from crisp mountain streams.

I'm grateful to be out of the saddle, even if it is only for a few moments. My aching muscles need relief. The instant my boots hit the frozen ground, I race for the line of scraggly pines, in dire need of a different sort of relief altogether. There had been no time to use the chamber pot before our hasty departure, and I'd spent the past two hours in increasing discomfort. I pray Penn hasn't felt my thighs clenching against his as I squirmed and shifted around the saddle, battling my full bladder with each jolting hoofbeat.

My headlong rush for the woods is thwarted when a large form steps into my path. I swallow an infuriated scream as I pull up short.

"Where the hell are you going?" Penn is scowling.

"To spill secrets to your enemies, of course," I retort, scowling right back at him. I latch on to my anger to cover the deep fissure of humiliation cracking wide open within my chest. I cannot—*will not*—beg permission to relieve myself like a morose hound scratching at the door, waiting for its owner to take notice.

"It's not safe," Penn informs me flatly. "You're not to go anywhere unattended until we're well within Dyved's borders."

"Then however will I tell the Reavers where best to ambush you?"

He stares at me, unamused.

"I need . . ." I shift on my feet. The pressing urge in my abdomen has passed discomfort and reached desperate. "I need a moment of privacy." My voice goes so cold, I'm surprised the air between us doesn't frost. "If you don't mind, *Your Highness.*"

His jaw tightens, but he does not otherwise indulge my goading remark with a reply. He steps out of my path—but, before he does, he reaches into his cloak pocket and extracts a hollow shaft of wood dangling from a thin leather cord. It is no longer than my middle finger, with several small holes carved on one side to let the air escape. A rudimentary reed whistle. He presses it into the palm of my hand and closes my fingers around it.

"For emergencies." His grip tightens. "You find yourself in trouble . . . three sharp blasts, we'll come running."

"Okay," I whisper, still staring down at my hand holding the whistle, his hand holding mine.

"You take longer than five minutes, we'll come running anyway."

"Okay," I repeat.

"Don't go far."

His hand vanishes. I practically bolt into the woods. I wait until I am a good distance away, far out of sight, before I stop to slip the leather cord over my head, lifting my hair so it can lie flat against my neck. Beneath my cloak, the whistle falls down to rest directly over my Remnant mark.

Four and a half minutes later, I walk back to the waiting men. I avoid Penn's eyes as he boosts me back into the saddle. We do not speak again—not as his arm wraps around my middle, not as my back fits itself against his chest in what has become a familiar position, not as we continue our journey northward through the endless range of frosted peaks. But every so often, I reach up to hold the whistle at my neck and wonder why it feels so soothing tucked in the palm of my hand.

WE MAKE CAMP at dusk in a narrow glen where natural hot springs bubble from beneath the mountains. The air that wafts off the pools' steaming surfaces smells faintly of sulfur, but it keeps the worst of the evening chill at bay. I cast a silent call of thanks to Edwynna when I find a pair of lightweight leather gloves in one of my cloak's many pockets and pull them on, grateful for another layer of insulation.

I don't mind sleeping under the stars. Especially if the alternative is another cave. After the cyntroedi incident, I am not eager to head back into the bowels of the earth. I doubt the men are, either.

Mabon and Uther deal with the horses as Jac and I set up the camp. There isn't much to do. We retrieve the bedrolls and blankets from the saddlebags, then build a fire—low and smokeless, so as not to draw any unwanted attention.

"Never use more than two or three logs out here in the wild, Ace. Your fire gets higher than that . . . Well, you might as well send up a smoke signal to everyone within striking distance saying, 'Come murder us in our sleep,'" Jac tells me, poking at the embers with a slim branch. "We wouldn't want to make things too easy for the Reaver trash on our trail."

"Do you think they're close by?"

He shrugs. "They're not trackers so much as opportunists. They take what comes across their path. That said, this isn't their typical play. It's personal for them."

"Personal how?"

"Reavers hate the fae. Always have. As their closest neighbor,

Dyved bears the brunt of that prejudice. They don't just want us to yield our borderlands. They want us to yield in general—some deranged declaration of mortal supremacy."

There are similar factions in the Midlands. I've seen them in the port cities—the culling priests, clad in their bone-white robes, preaching on the foul sins of maegic to anyone who'll listen. They make it their life's mission to report halflings to be hunted down and hanged. Once they brought their poisonous hatred to Seahaven's shores, Eli stopped letting me tag along on his trips to Bellmere.

When I mention the priests to Jac, he merely shakes his head. "Reavers aren't unique in their hatred of us, but they are unique in the brutal way they demonstrate it. You remember what we told you last night? Our unit"—he jerks his chin toward Mabon and Uther—"has skirmished with this particular clan a few times now. They've been encroaching on Dyved's borders. Testing our resolve, seeing how far they can push us before we retaliate."

I nod as I tidy our pile of kindling.

"They pushed a bit too far about a fortnight ago and lost a handful of their men to our best archers as a result of that miscalculation. We sent back their bodies for burial—but also as a warning."

I glance up, paling at his casual admittance to killing.

He notices. His shrug is light, unbothered. "Cost of war, Ace. They knew when they started playing with fire, there was a chance they'd get burned. They're lucky we didn't do worse. Could've taken their actions as provocation for a full invasion. Snatched up that gods-awful ice shelf they call home like *that*"— he snaps his thumb sharply—"and slaughtered every last one of them."

If he's trying to comfort me, he is not succeeding.

"Needless to say," Jac carries on, "they were none too pleased to have their plans foiled and their top fighters eliminated. They still want a chunk of our land, but they can't afford to lose any more men. So, they're stuck." He pauses. His eyes are solemn as they hold mine. "That all changes if they find something to negotiate with. Something Dyved wants badly enough to yield. Say . . . the sole heir to their throne, for instance."

My heart skips a beat.

They are coming for Penn.

"The way they see it, if Queen Vanora starts getting pieces of her little brother shipped back to her encased in blocks of ice, she might just surrender that chunk of territory. You understand now?"

"I understand," I murmur.

"Good."

He rises to his feet and begins unfurling the bedrolls, arranging them in a circle around the fire. I help him in silence, trying to keep my expression blank. But my thoughts are far beyond the reach of the fire's soft glow, caught up in the ice-crusted woods Penn stalked into shortly after our arrival, a hunting bow slung over one shoulder.

If anyone should not be permitted to leave the group unattended, it's him. Yet, he's received no lecture. He's not been chased down and given an emergency whistle in case enemies come upon him unexpectedly,

"Don't worry your pretty little head about Penn," Jac says, catching my eyes across the flames. "If the Reavers do find him, it'll be their funeral pyres burning. Not his."

"*Worry?*" A strangled laugh bursts from my lips. "I'm not worried. Don't be absurd."

"You look worried. Or you did a second ago."

I ignore that. "Why on earth would I worry about him, Jac? He's my enemy."

"Ace—"

"The sooner he gets taken by Reavers or eaten by monsters, the sooner I can get off this blasted mountain and back where I belong!"

"And where's that, huh? The Midlands?" He shakes his head. "Doesn't seem like there's much worth going back to in that miserable place. Or have you forgotten they almost hanged you?"

"It doesn't matter where I go, just so long as I'm not *here*!" I hiss, heart thundering with fury and something that might be fear. "I don't want anything to do with whatever is waiting for me in Dyved. I don't want anything to do with *any of this*. All I want—all I have ever wanted—is a simple life. No more talk of Remnants. No more running from Reavers. No more sleepless nights." I'm breathing hard, practically panting. "But I'll never get what I want so long as your precious princeling is getting what *he* wants. The specifics of which, I might add, he hasn't bothered to share with me."

"He's been a bit busy keeping you alive."

I narrow my eyes. "And why is that, Jac? What's his endgame here? Why does he need me in the first place?"

"I don't know, Ace. That's above my pay grade. All I know is, you're mighty worked up for someone who claims to be indifferent to his existence."

"For the last bloody time, I am not bloody worried about bloody Prince Pendefyre!" I seethe, holding tight to my anger. "As far as I'm concerned, if he dies, I'm *free*."

Jac's expression flashes with disappointment. I don't like seeing that look in his eyes as they behold me. I like even less that seeing it bothers me so much; that the thought of him holding me in poor regard is enough to shake my resolve.

I care what he thinks of me, I realize, aghast.

Even worse . . .

He's right: I *am* concerned about Penn. And my sudden surge of hostility has as much to do with my own conflicted feelings as it does with Jac's pointed insight. No matter how my mind insists that it is absurd to worry about the well-being of the man who hauled me, kicking and screaming, into the Northlands . . . my heart stubbornly rebuffs every bit of sound logic I present to it.

Horrifying as it might be, my gruff, monosyllabic, borderline savage captor . . .

Matters to me.

I would care if he were killed.

I would care a great deal.

Jac is still looking at me like I've let him down. I open my mouth to smooth things over just as a dull thud sounds in the night. A dead doe hits the snow not two paces away. My gaze moves from her white-tufted chest to her sightless eyes to a set of black boots planted on the ground beside her.

The instant I look up into Penn's carefully blank expression, I know he's heard every word I said. All the blood drains from my face in one great whoosh. My throat works to swallow the knot of emotion lodged in it, but it is no use. The tangle of regret and shame is firmly stuck, blocking my airway.

If he dies, I'm free.

"Trust me," Penn says, his voice completely devoid of feeling. He stares at me like I am a clump of dung clinging to the bottom of his horse's shoe. "The feeling is entirely mutual."

~

THE FOLLOWING DAY is, in a word, frigid. Not only the temperatures, but the attitudes of the men.

Penn is outright ignoring me. Jac is avoiding my eyes. Even Mabon and Uther seem to go out of their way to dodge my presence on the one occasion we stop to rest the horses and eat strips of roasted venison on slices of the thick, crusty bread Edwynna packed into our saddlebags.

Their silence speaks volumes.

My harsh words last night will not pass over the bow unchallenged. My lack of loyalty is a direct affront to their own.

To pass the time, I study the barren landscape. There isn't much in the way of variation. No vegetation sprouts from the icy ground, no birds circle in the thin air. Mist-shrouded peaks jut into the clouds. The valleys between them are blinding-white stretches of snow, without a lick of color to break up the monotony.

I wonder if the main passes are any less dull. We've taken what the men refer to as the Widow's Notch—a seldom-used route that snakes through the peaks at a higher elevation than most travelers dare venture, where the snows are thick and the trees are sparse. We follow no road that I can discern and see no more settlements like Vintare. My questions concerning when we might reach our destination are firmly rebuffed. I am given only the vaguest details—that we are going to rejoin Jac's men, who will provide escort to Dyved, and taking the long way to get there thanks to the Reavers.

"Not much farther now," Uther tells me when I corner him during our midday break. His gray eyes evade mine. "Another day, if the weather holds."

By the time the sun begins to droop in the sky, I am bone weary and bored out of my mind with nothing to watch except the occasional swishing of a horse tail. I've all but memorized the back of Jac's head. I consider counting the individual strands of his hair, just to give myself a task.

My eyes are glazed over, unfocused on anything in particular, when it happens. The air around Jac's dark-blond mane seems to ripple, shimmering opaquely in the waning sunlight, like a mirage dancing across the horizon's edge on a hot summer day. Certain my eyes are playing tricks on me, I blink—hard—to clear the haze.

Yet, when I do, instead of returning to normal, my vision somehow . . . *sharpens*. As though my eyes have sprung blades. Blades that tear straight through an invisible blindfold—one I had not even realized I was wearing.

Another blink, and the shimmers are torn to filmy tatters. One more, and they are gone completely. I suddenly find myself staring at a pair of pointed fae ears instead of the rounded human ones I've come to know these past few days.

His glamour.

I've seen through his glamour.

Just like Penn said I could.

I flinch back into his chest with a sharp inhale. He grunts softly at the impact. I'm so startled by the sudden clarity I am experiencing, I shift around, craning my neck to catch his eyes. Whatever expression I'm wearing makes his brows arch in question.

"What is it?"

My mouth opens, then shuts again at the cold look on his face. "Nothing," I murmur. "Never mind."

I twist back around, my heart racing at double time. Jac's glamour is back in place, his ears benignly mortal once more. I've no sooner narrowed my eyes when I feel a faint pulse of power from my Remnant mark. The enchantment vanishes instantly, its telltale shimmer dissolving between one blink and the next.

Dazed by my own success, I look past Jac to Uther and Mabon, riding at the front of our party. Both of them have similar shimmers in the space around their heads. Now that I've seen them, I can't believe I never noticed them before.

My eyes narrow. The Remnant prickles. I manage to pierce both shimmers at the same time—so easily, I nearly cheer aloud.

I can see through glamours.

It's unbelievable. A rush like I've never felt before. Along with that rush, however, comes a flurry of questions.

Have I always possessed this ability?

Have I simply repressed it?

And, if so . . . what other abilities are lying in wait beneath the dark whorls of ink embedded in my chest?

CHAPTER
FOURTEEN

W e are nearly there.

This is evident for several reasons. Firstly, because our path through the peaks begins to slant downward, our elevation yielding more with each passing hour. Secondly, because Jac had said it was a two-day ride and, as we've twice made camp under the stars, I dare to hope. And finally, because our pace increases from a plodding clop to a steady canter as we descend into a valley peppered with pines. Amid them, trails of smoke from what must be at least three campfires ribbon into the sky.

My heart leaps at the sight.

The passage widens at the entrance to the valley, the slope flattening out as we round an icy bend and ride through the copse of trees. It is warmer here, shielded from the wind. Not that I am ever cold riding with Penn. His body radiates heat, an internal furnace blasting beneath his skin. If he were anyone else, I would've ordered him to lie down and shoved a brew of feverfew into his hands, thinking him ill.

"Not far now," Jac calls, turning in his saddle to grin at us. "There's a clearing up ahead where we set up camp last week. Let's hope there's something tasty in the cook pot."

His spirits are high. He even shoots me a playful wink to

prove he's done punishing me for my outburst two nights ago. But Uther's face holds no such playfulness as he slows his mount, falling back to ride alongside Onyx. His voice is grim as he meets Penn's gaze.

"No scouts," he says on a whisper.

Penn stiffens, his chest turning to a slab of stone. "None?"

"Not at the last two posts we passed."

"Fuck." Penn's curse is a low rumble. He pauses for a beat, then mutters, "Eyes open, blades close. We go in slow."

Uther nods and presses his heels to his horse's flanks, urging it slightly ahead. He has one hand on his reins; the other is reaching for his sword. Beside him, Mabon already has his heavy crossbow at the ready.

"It's just an oversight," Jac insists, though his face is pale with sudden dread in the late-morning light. His hand fiddles with the carved wooden hilt of his battle-axe. "I'm sure all's well . . ."

But all is not well.

This is abundantly clear the moment our horses nose out of the forest, into the clearing where the men made camp. The tents are still pitched, the fires still burning low beneath the cook pots where thick porridge bubbles. The soldiers had been in the middle of breakfast.

Now, every last one of them is dead.

Carnage.

That is the only word I can think of—the only word that encompasses what I am seeing. The horror of it. The barbarity. An entire unit of men, their blood staining the snow in a river of red. A pile of butchered corpses, reaching toward the sun.

Jac's roar of agony rends the sky.

Vomit rushes into my mouth, bile burning at the back of my throat. I swallow it down, gasping for breath. There is no time to fall apart. No time to do anything at all. Because, in that moment, they come—running out of the trees on the other side of the clearing, their battle-axes swinging with lethal promise as they charge headlong in our direction, their faces streaked with black war paint as they fix us in their sights.

Reavers.

⌒〜

PENN DISMOUNTS BEFORE I can blink, grabbing the reins and jerking his horse back behind the shelter of the tree line. On instinct, I bend low over Onyx's neck, my cheek pressed to his coat, my hands clutching his mane. I try to glance back—to keep track of Mabon and Uther and Jac as they spur their own steeds straight toward the crush of barbarians—but I never get the chance.

Penn's face appears before mine. I flinch at the savageness darkening his expression. There is death in his eyes, a vow flaring in their fiery depths—for vengeance, for retribution. For the blood of his enemies. His hands are itching for his hilt.

"Take this," he barks, voice rife with impatience as he shoves the hunting bow and a quiver of fresh arrows into my fumbling hands. I had not even seen him retrieve them from their strappings. "Ride back up the pass to where we made camp last night. You should be safe there. If anyone follows you, shoot them through the heart."

"I'll stay," I say, slinging the quiver over my shoulder. "I'll fight—"

He is beyond listening. "Wait for me there. I will come for you."

"Penn—"

"*I need you to go.*" His voice cracks—a desperate sound that makes my heart stutter and my words fail. His eyes never leave mine, and I swear I see a promise of a different nature burning there as well. One that has nothing to do with bloodshed or battlefields. "I need you to stay safe. Stay alive. Even if you have to kill to do it. Even if it offends your damn morality."

"Penn—"

His hand reaches up, and before I can react, his fingers thread behind my neck, fisting in the thick fall of hair at my nape. He hauls me closer, so our faces are a hairsbreadth apart. His eyes move to my lips and seem to get stuck there.

I stop breathing.

For a split second, I think he's going to do something insane, something inconceivable—like crash his mouth down on mine and kiss me. I'm not sure if I'm more relieved or disappointed when he doesn't. His gaze jerks back up to meet mine, and the look of exquisite torment simmering beneath his battle fury shakes the foundation of everything I've come to believe about our relationship.

"If you run out of arrows," he whispers, his face so close each word tingles across my lips. "Don't forget you have another weapon at your disposal." His other hand rises, pressing through the fabric of my cloak, directly over my Remnant. "*Use it.*"

At that, his hands disappear, he steps away, and with the crack of his palm against Onyx's rump, he sends us flying back the way we came. Over the thunder of hooves and the distant echo of pained male screams, I hear the sound of his sword sliding from its sheath. The crunch of his boots on snow, carrying him into the clearing.

By the time I get the reins under control, find a firm seat in the saddle, and whip around to look for him . . .

He is already gone.

I DO AS Penn bids, riding back through the woods to the passage that leads up toward the summit. I don't want to, but I do. Because he asked. Because . . . he pleaded.

I need you to go.

I need you to stay safe.

And so, I go. But I leave my heart behind. Back in that blood-drenched camp. Back with Jac and Mabon and Uther, the soldiers who have forced themselves inside its chambers, becoming friends despite all odds. Back with Penn, the man who has saved me again and again, even when I've punished him for it.

With each of Onyx's hoofbeats, my conscience screams out that I am a coward for running, for leaving them behind when they are so vastly outnumbered. There were so many Reavers. A never-ending wave pouring from those trees.

What can four men possibly do against forty?

The odds are too grim to dwell on. The outcomes too painful to contemplate.

I hear the screams of pain before Onyx carries me out of earshot and wonder from which side they come. There are other sounds as well. The clash of steel, the twang of crossbow bolts. Strangest of all, a dull, distant roar that carries on the wind, the origin of which I cannot pinpoint. Perhaps my ears are playing tricks, fear conjuring phantom sounds as I flee into the forest.

I do not make it to the ridge.

When Penn sent me barreling through the trees, he did not know a second contingent of Reavers had closed ranks from behind, blocking the pass to prevent us from backtracking up the mountains. I spot them only a moment before they spot me—a group of men clad in leather and fur, their skin decorated with a familiar dark metal. Iron. Bolts and rings of it, piercing through lobes and brows, puncturing nostrils and nipples and lips. Their bare chests and pale faces are streaked with black paint, which gives them an otherworldly look, despite the rounded human ears that jut from their skulls.

The Reavers' outer appearance is a visceral representation of the inner hatred they harbor for halflings. For all maegical beings. Jac said they choose to carve out an existence in the wild reaches of the Cimmerians rather than pledge loyalty to a fae kingdom like Dyved. Their ancestors not only participated in the Cull but reveled in the bloodshed, hunting down halflings and high fae alike purely for the sport of it.

There is little doubt about what they will do if they catch me. Penn, they will perhaps keep alive to use for negotiation, for torture, for things too gruesome to imagine. But the rest of us are marked for a much swifter end.

When I see the blockaded pass, I do not even consider trying to fight. I do not reach for the bow slung across my back. For though this company is smaller than the one back at the camp, there are still far too many of them to take on. More men than I have arrows for in my quiver. More than I can ever hope to survive on my own.

I tug the reins sharply right. Onyx responds straightaway, changing directions without so much as a stumble, but no amount of haste can save us. I hear the guttural cries—"There! Get the point bitch!"—as they spot me in the trees, their words a clipped, distorted dialect of the common tongue. The alarm rises. Booted feet thunder in pursuit.

They aren't on horseback, but they are fast and they know these woods in a way I do not. I ride blindly through the thick pines, picking directions at random, searching for a place to hide, if not escape. The wind begins to howl as I am brought up short again and again—by a sharp crevasse in the earth too wide to jump, by a sheer rock face too tall to scale, by a half-frozen river too deep to ford. My hair whips across my cheeks. At my chest the Remnant burns, the cold bite of fear tingeing every breath I haul in and out of my lungs.

Above the building gale, I hear the Reavers closing in, narrowing some of the distance between us each time I hit another dead end. Their feet snapping twigs, their yells an urgent volley. My panic rises sharply and the wind with it, wailing like a wild beast caught in a snare. Onyx whinnies, eye whites rolling. I stroke his neck to soothe him, though my own nerves are fraying.

Is this my doing? Have I called this screaming gale down from the skies somehow, as Penn insisted I could?

Even if I have, there is no opportunity to wonder how. Not with the painted warriors closing in on me. Even now, I can hear them thrashing through the underbrush.

Not far.

Not far at all.

I press my heels inward, guiding Onyx away from the ice-jammed river. We gallop along the bank, looking for a place to cross, but it only widens as we follow it down the mountain, the surface half-solid with flows of pulpy water. Every hoofbeat carries us farther from the Widow's Notch, where we were supposed to find solace. Farther from the clearing, where my companions battle for their lives.

If they are still alive to battle.

I banish the thought as soon as it occurs.

We ride on, following the water down the summit. A light snow begins to fall. Or so I think at first. I soon realize they are not snowflakes drifting down upon us but ashes, carried on the air currents I've stoked into a frenzy with my panic. Confusion flares briefly, but as I stare at the falling embers, awareness dawns with breath-snatching swiftness.

That roar I'd heard as I left the battle had been no trick of the senses. It was the all-consuming crackle of a great, blazing fire. Even now, half a league away, I can hear it if I strain my ears—a steady bass note beneath the wind's caterwaul.

I chance a glance back over my shoulder and my eyes widen. When we first arrived in the valley less than an hour ago, it looked idyllic—a snowy stretch of pines and firs illuminated in weak sunshine. A rare cloudless day on the range.

How quickly the world has changed. The sky is now dark—not with storm clouds, but with smoke. Black billows up from between the trees at the center of the sloping woods that stretch above me, where the inferno burns brightest.

The campsite.

It has to be.

I shiver at the sight, praying no one I care about is caught on the wrong end of that unnatural blaze. For this is no normal fire. It is massive. A wall of flame that sweeps a path through the valley, moving with incalculable speed, devouring everything in its wake. Fueled by the whipping wind. Pulled by it, feeding on it, chasing it . . .

Straight toward me, I realize, thunderstruck.

If I were at the ridge, if I were where I was supposed to be, I'd be far from its reach. Safe and secure, high above its fiery clutches. Instead, I find myself standing directly in its path.

"Go!" I spur Onyx faster, turning my back on the blaze. "Come on, boy!"

The fire surges down the valley, razing through the copse of pines, pursuing us through the foliage with greedy, grasping hands. So swift, so bright, it seems the infernal fires of the underworld have been loosed upon the land.

I hear the cries of panic from the Reavers who've followed me down the slope as the smoke and flame overtake them. I hear them call out for aid, hear their agony ring into the skies. And then I hear nothing at all. Nothing but the bellowing roar of fire, the answering wail of wind.

No matter how fast I ride, the inferno is faster. The smell of fumes thickens the air until my eyes water and my throat is hoarse. The smoke is choking me, pressing inward in a noxious cloud I can barely see through. I cough and gasp for air, blinking away tears as I clutch the reins.

With a distressed whinny, Onyx slows, struggling to maintain his pace in the gathering darkness. I urge him forward, feeling death circle close, but we make it only a few more strides before his back legs lock and he rears up, front hooves punching the air. I'm nearly tossed from the saddle. My fingernails score the pommel in my effort to keep my seat.

"Whoa, boy," I croak, voice an ashen rasp. My shaking hand strokes his neck. "I know you're scared. I'm scared, too."

He snorts his displeasure, head tossing. He will go no farther.

My body is tight as a bowstring. If we do not put distance between ourselves and the flame . . . if we do not find a way forward . . .

But how?

I am out of options. Out of time. Out of hope.

Unless . . .

Use it, Penn had said.

Could it be so simple?

The Remnant at my chest is silent. Deathly still. As if it is waiting to see what I will do. Waiting to see if, after all this time, I will finally reach deep inside and test what awaits me there.

Weaver of wind . . . Something stirs in my bones. A whisper. An answer. *Summoner of skies* . . .

To call upon the air itself—I must be mad. Utterly mad, even to consider it. The wind has always seemed a wild thing. Alive, intangible. A force that cannot be tamed or controlled. But as I choke on the deadly smoke, I do not have the luxury of weighing pros and cons. There is no opportunity to debate.

Only to act.

To trust that Penn is not mistaken about me or my abilities.

In desperation, I close my eyes and seek out that strange pulse of energy I felt when I pierced through Jac's glamour for the first time. The surge I felt on that cliff side with Burrows's men. On the bridge as I dangled, close to death. On the night I fled the scorched earth of Seahaven. And, if I'm honest with myself, a dozen other times before that day. Times I'd pushed away, brushed aside, clinging to the safety of being . . .

Nothing.

No one.

Nameless orphan.

Powerless halfling.

Worthless point.

Cold prickles at my chest, an icy kiss.

Wind weaver . . . A whisper within. *No more hiding . . .*

I grasp hold of that voice like a loose thread, winding it round my finger and pulling, pulling, pulling until a spool unravels deep inside me. Somewhere out of sight. In my marrow. In the fabric of my being. In the stitching of my very soul. Somewhere so far down it will never be detected, even if they hack me apart with blades and peer into my bleeding chest cavity.

The prickle of power becomes a pulse; the pulse becomes a surge. It flows within me, a flood of cold that washes through my body in a great tide, then crests on a wave of recognition.

I am no stranger to this sensation.

I have felt it many times before.

On the sandy shores, whipping at my skirts, spraying salt and brine across my skin as I peer out to sea. On the mountain's summit, the icy chill crystallizing each breath in my lungs, freezing each inch of exposed skin. In the dead of night, whistling through the trees, carrying an electrical storm on its wings. In the pink-stained dawn, stirring the fragile new blooms of spring flowers.

Wind.

Air.

Sky.

It thrums inside my skin, a live current. I cannot control it—I do not try. But as it surges through me, instead of trying to push it down, to keep it in, to contain it as I always have before . . . I reverse course. I push outward. I let it loose from the hold I've maintained for twenty years. And as I do, I cast out a desperate plea to whatever gods are listening.

Let me breathe.

Wind erupts from me in a shock wave, a violent vortex blasting out from beneath my skin. The sky itself screams with the force of it, loud enough to shatter my eardrums.

Or is that me, screaming?

I can do nothing but cling to the saddle pommel as waves of wind move through me. Ripping me from the inside out. I think my skin will tear, my soul with it. The cold in my chest is so strong, I nearly lose consciousness.

Something drips down my face. Blood, I realize, tasting it on my lips. It leaks from my nose like I've taken a fist to it, spilling onto my pretty white cloak like ruby tears. With the tang of copper on my tongue, I hold on to the pommel, riding out the currents as they reverberate outward in an unchecked tempest.

I focus on my breath. In and out, out and in. Again and again and again, until the shock waves subside. Until I can breathe again.

I can breathe again.

The air is clear of smoke.

My eyes crack open. The sight that greets me is a shock to the senses. The fire blazes not twenty paces away, a wall of flame and death that pins me up against the icy riverbank . . . but it is no longer advancing. Something holds it at bay. An invisible boundary, one made of impenetrable air, pushes back against its relentless pursuit. The flames lick at it hungrily, sparks crackle at its base, fumes furl with malice . . . but the inferno comes no closer. I have blocked its path.

But for how long?

The Remnant at my chest aches like an open wound. I would not be surprised to find it bleeding through the fabric of my dress. My head spins from the nosebleed as much as the dizzying sight of my . . . I don't know what to call it, exactly.

Fence?

Barricade?

Shield comes closest, I suppose. A shield of solidified air.

I tell myself to move, but I'm too terrified to do it. Terrified that, should my focus slip for even a moment, the wall that holds my death at bay will fall. Even as I hesitate, I can feel my strength waning, my energy draining. I have no idea how to properly wield my power. It was blind luck, more than anything else, that saved me.

I pray that luck holds as I press my heels to Onyx's flanks and urge him to walk on. His head swings back and forth, his bridle jangling. He does not like this situation any better than I do. But he is nothing if not loyal. At my urging, he trots a few steps away from the fire, his back rigid with tension beneath me. As though he, too, is waiting to see if the wall will fall away or follow us.

My stomach flips when I first see the flames lurch, devouring the patch of untouched earth that appears the instant my air shield shifts forward. Hands shaking on the reins, I pull Onyx to a stop once more, testing a theory. The fire's advance halts as soon as we do.

It's holding.

Relief crashes through me. It seems safe enough to keep moving. If I were a bit less cowardly—or a bit more reckless—I might ride straight through the wildfire, back to the camp, back to the Widow's Notch, trusting my power to keep death at bay. But it is terrifying enough to see the flames pressing at me from one direction. The thought of them on all sides . . . pushing in from every angle . . .

I shudder and look away.

For now, I will get to safety. I will find shelter. And when the fire has burned itself out, I will make my way back into the smoldering ashes. I will find my friends.

Find Penn.

I ride on, following the snaking stream down the valley. Every so often, I glance back to ensure the fire is still safely on the other side of my shield, that it does not encroach closer than twenty paces.

It never does.

After a stretch, I grow bold enough to pause for a moment by a bend in the river, where the shallows run calm and clear. Dismounting, I lead Onyx to the edge. He drinks deeply as I crouch to do the same, cupping my gloved hands in the frigid water and slurping desperate gulps. My throat is raw—from my screams, from the smoke. I wash away the taste of fire and blood, drinking until my thirst is sated. Splashing my face, I scrub away all traces of the nosebleed. My white cloak, I fear, will bear the stains forever.

It is an effort to push back to my feet. I sway, off-balance, blinking away stars from my vision. The air itself feels heavier than normal. Each step is like walking waist-deep in mud. I lean against Onyx, weary down to my bones. Too weary to even climb back up into the saddle.

My Remnant thrums, a constant low-level pulse tapping every shred of strength I still possess. I will not last much longer before it is wholly depleted . . . unlike the blaze, which shows no signs of petering out. It rages on in the distance, sweeping down the valley with insatiable hunger.

My eyes shift to the river. It is gentler here, the water far less rough than near the summit. No rapids froth its surface. And it is narrow—about a dozen paces across. A distance, under normal circumstances, I could swim in seconds.

These circumstances bear little resemblance to normal.

The cold will be breath stealing, no doubt. But if we can cross, it will not matter when my shield inevitably fails. We will be safe on the other side, protected by the natural barrier of the water.

"What do you think, boy?" I ask Onyx, stroking my fingers through his long, dark mane. "Should we risk it?"

His glossy eyes hold no answers.

"I don't think we have a choice," I confide, pressing my forehead to his neck. Breathing hard as my head swims with exhaustion.

He whinnies softly in response.

"Together," I tell him. "We'll make it together."

At least, we'll try.

In a stroke of good fortune, the crossing is not as bad as I'd imagined. While the river appeared rather deep from the shoreline, I never find myself submerged higher than my waist. My skirts drag, heavy and waterlogged, but I hold fast to Onyx's bridle as we forge our way across.

It is shockingly cold. Nearly as cold as the Remnant at my

THE WIND WEAVER 183

chest. But the current is gentle, lapping lightly against my legs. At times, it almost seems to be propelling me forward. Helping me along with aqueous shoves. Even so, making it to the opposite shore saps the last bit of strength I possess. I'm gasping by the time my feet hit the bank.

I release the bridle and fall to my knees, scarcely able to keep from collapsing entirely. My leather gloves plant against the ice-crusted earth as ragged gulps of air move into and out of my lungs. I feel my power hanging by a thread, my hold on the shield growing perilously thin.

Without bothering to rise, I glance over my shoulder at the wall of flame. It's five paces from the opposite bank and appears to be pushing at the invisible barrier. As if testing my resolve. As if waiting for the moment my strength will sputter out.

I pray, when it does, the river will be enough to keep it back.

Onyx's tackle jangles as his hooves dance with nerves. His whinny is one of warning. My head swings toward him but freezes halfway when my gaze snags on something planted in the dirt before me. Close enough to touch.

A pair of boots.

How they got there, how I had not heard them approach—for I am tired, but not so tired my senses have failed completely—is an utter mystery to me. My head snaps back, my gaze shooting up a set of muscular male thighs encased in dark navy trousers, over the broad planes of a chest, and into the strangest set of eyes I've ever seen.

Fae eyes, unquestionably. The pupils are ever so slightly elongated, the irises a shade of blue so brilliant, the finest sapphires in Anwyvn would look dull by compare. They are set in a face that makes my breath cease and my fingers curl into the dirt.

As I hold them, they flicker away for the briefest of instants, looking beyond to my wavering shield of air. By the time they come back to mine, they've taken on a predatory light. His lips twist as he examines me sprawled there at his feet. His head tilts in wry contemplation.

"Well, well," the stranger murmurs in a deep, melodious voice that flows like water over river rocks. "Aren't you interesting."

That's when everything goes black.

CHAPTER
FIFTEEN

I dream of a great, dark sea.

Of the waves and the water. Of the brine and the bitter cold. A vast expanse of ocean, fathomless as time. And I, a tiny piece of flotsam, tossed by tidal whims. Drowning in slow degrees as my head slips under, never to resurface.

I should be frightened, but I have dreamed this dream before. I have swum this sea a thousand times, my slumbering mind returning again and again to the plundering depths, to the swells that crash around me with frothing whitecaps. To the currents that caress and cajole as they drag me to the bottom, whispering sweet nothings even as they kill me.

This deadly sea of dreams is not the sunny shore of Seahaven, but somewhere else—a place I've never been. A figment of sleep-fueled imagination. For if such a place exists, I've never seen it. Yet it feels so real, so vivid, sometimes I think it must be a memory left over from a past life, carried through the aether as my soul sprung into existence.

When I gasp awake, I can still taste sea salt on my lips.

It takes me a moment to shake off the residue of the dream. I glance around, eyes wide, struggling to get my bearings. Searching for threats. Finding none.

I'm alone.

Alone in an unfamiliar bed, in an unfamiliar room. No sign of my belongings anywhere. Not my bow, not my quiver, not my dagger, nor any of my clothes. The bedspread clutched in my hands is light blue; the plush feather mattress beneath me is of the highest quality. The chamber itself is the color of sand, while the floors are a luminous ivory tile.

It looks like an ordinary—if rather richly appointed—bedroom, everything finely crafted out of light-hued wood, from the carved writing desk to the nightstands to the wardrobe. Across from the bed, a large window with crisscrossed panes dominates the wall.

I throw off the thick blankets and stalk toward it on bare feet, legs wobbling like jelly with every step. I am not sure how long I've been unconscious, only that it was not long enough to counteract my exhaustion. I am spent, every ounce of strength sapped from my bones. Not only physical, but a soul-deep sort of weariness I have never before experienced. It centers at the mark embedded in my chest the same way a headache gathers at one's temples, then radiates outward.

Evidently, using my power comes at a price.

I wonder where my boots are as the tile's chill seeps into my soles; wonder who took me out of them when they put me in the flimsy nightgown I'm wearing. My heart thuds as a face jolts into my thoughts—the man I encountered on the riverbank. His bright-blue eyes are the last thing I remember before everything went dark. That predatory gleam. That self-satisfied smirk. That voice, like a deadly fall of water, ribboning the air.

Well, well. Aren't you interesting.

I do not like to think he was the one to strip me to my skin and dress me in this garment. The nightgown is borderline indecent, the fabric so gauzy and light it is almost sheer against my skin. Not silk, but something far finer. The stitching is so tiny and precise, I can barely detect a single seam. It flows around me like liquid as I stop before the window.

My mouth gapes.

While unconscious, I have undergone a vast change in altitude. The Cimmerians are spread out before me—above me, rather. Wherever I've been taken is situated at the base of the range. If I squint my eyes toward the summit of the centermost peak, I can just make out a dark scorch staining the snow-topped tract of evergreens. A smoldering wound, scarring the face of the mountain—the only remaining trace of the raging wildfire. It looks to have consumed half the slope before finally burning itself out.

Looking at it, I can hardly believe I walked away unscathed. My eyes ache with unshed tears as I think of Penn and his men, fighting for their lives. They'd been at the very heart of the blaze. Even if they'd survived the Reavers . . .

Could anyone survive such a fire?

The door swings inward with nary a knock of warning. Tears forgotten, I spin around to face the intruder. I backpedal a step when I see it is the fae man from the river, my spine pressing against the sill so hard it will undoubtedly leave a bruise.

"You're awake," he says, strolling into the room like he owns the place. Which, it occurs to me, he likely does. "Good."

He stops six paces away. We stare at each other in silence, each taking the other's measure. He is just as alarmingly attractive as I remember. A tall, powerful frame encased in tailored navy fabric. Deeply tan, almost golden, skin. Dark, lush hair framing a face that could make an artist weep. Bone structure fodder for a thousand sonnets. The crystalline eyes are balanced by a jawline so chiseled, sculptors could labor for a lifetime and still never quite capture its finer nuances.

"Did you sleep well?"

Did I sleep well?

As if I've taken a nap in a field of wildflowers, not been knocked unconscious and dragged down a mountain. Is he insane?

"What did you do to me?"

He arches a single brow at the thick accusation in my tone. "What did *I* do to you?"

"You . . ." I shake my head, trying to sort out my thoughts. "You brought me here."

"And?"

And? Is that not enough? "You . . . you knocked me unconscious! You must've drugged me or hit me or—"

"No." A muscle jumps in his cheek as his jaw tightens. "I did not lay a finger on you, except to carry you here when you so foolishly drained your powers to the point of exhaustion and collapsed at my feet in a pathetic heap. Though, if I'd known this was the kind of thanks awaiting me . . ." He shrugs with a nonchalance I do not believe, even for a second. "I might not have bothered."

There is a frigid pause.

"Oh," I whisper weakly in its aftermath.

"Yes." His eyes glitter. "*Oh.*"

"And Onyx?"

"Feasting on hay in my stables."

"Where are my clothes?"

"Being laundered by my staff. They were covered in blood and soaked from the river."

I nod, accepting this. I attempt to keep my voice level. "And I assume I also have you to thank for this"—I gesture down at myself—"garment I am wearing?"

He does not respond. He is staring at the aforementioned garment as though his eyes have followed my gesture and gotten stuck there. It is not a lascivious gaze, but one of undisguised fascination. For, in the slant of sunlight, the dark whorls of my Remnant are plainly evident beneath the gauzy fabric gathered at my breasts.

When he steps toward me, my whole body tenses with fear.

He halts instantly. His eyes flicker back to mine. "I'm not going to hurt you."

To this, I say nothing. Words are only worth as much as the actions behind them.

Lifting his hands in a gesture of surrender, he takes a purposeful stride backward. My audible exhale of relief seems to amuse him.

"You have nothing to fear from me. I merely wanted a closer look. It is not every day you see a Remnant standing before you."

So, he knows what I am. Then again, even without the mark, he would've known. He'd seen me cast an air shield on the mountain.

My shoulders stiffen as wariness tiptoes in. "And what is it you want from me?"

"Perhaps I desired a glimpse at Prince Pendefyre's new pet."

Hope and fear stir within me when he speaks Penn's name. Hope that he might still be alive and, even now, on his way here to find me; fear because this stranger, whoever he is, does not sound like he much cares for the Crown Prince of Dyved.

"If a glimpse were all you wanted," I whisper softly, "I doubt you would've brought me here."

"Historically speaking, Pendefyre isn't fond of sharing his toys." His lips twist up at one side. "I wanted us to have a chance to get to know each other. Uninterrupted."

"For what purpose?"

"Call it . . . curiosity."

"About me."

"About you," he agrees. His eyes search mine. "Your presence at the Vintare inn was noted far and wide—and not only by my scouts. For days, ravens have been busy flying to every corner of the Northlands, spreading the news from crofters to courtiers." His voice gains a mocking edge. "The long-awaited Dyved heir has finally returned to the north. He does not come alone, but with a fae girl in tow. Slip of a thing, with strange silver eyes."

My breath catches.

"Chased into the mountains together, according to the rumormongers. And by Efnysien's men, no less," he continues. His head cants to one side as he stares at me. "Normally, I am not one for idle gossip—especially where Pendefyre is concerned. But I must admit, this particular tale piqued my interest."

The men in red and black. *Efnysien's* men. I've heard that name before. I still recall Jac's shocked question to Penn back at the summit—*This far north? What in the skies are they doing all the way up here?*—but I'm hesitant to reveal as much to this stranger. Instead, I shrug with the same airy nonchalance he's adopted to counterbalance the sharpness of his gaze.

"Well, now you've seen me." I swallow hard. "I assume your interest is sated and you will send me on my way."

"To Dyved."

I say nothing.

"With Pendefyre."

The silence lingers.

"Gods help you." He looses a humorless laugh. "Gods help us all."

"Where I go next is no business of yours," I say stiffly. "Much as I appreciate you getting me to safety, what I do from this point on has nothing to do with you. So, if you wouldn't mind returning my clothing, I'll saddle Onyx and be on my way."

He speaks as though he hasn't heard me. "You don't have any idea what you are, do you?"

My teeth clench.

"Given your clumsy attempts at wielding your power, that much is obvious," he continues. His expression darkens, sudden as a summer storm. "What can that fool be thinking, putting you at risk? Leaving you exposed to all manner of dangers? Reckless. Bloody reckless. Even for him."

"He is far from a fool," I snap without thinking. "We were attacked by Reavers."

"How quickly you spring to his defense." His smile is a knife-edge—cutting and cruel. "I'm guessing that means he hasn't told you why he is so eager to bring you back to his homeland."

I try not to react. Try not to succumb to his transparent provocations. The idea that Penn has an ulterior motive is not a novel one. I've suspected as much from the moment he drove his sword through Burrows's throat and threw me on the back of his horse. Yet, for some reason, contemplating it hurts more now. For some reason . . . I had begun to believe him when he said he is not my enemy. To hope Farley had not lied when he'd called us friends.

Penn may not be a fool, but you certainly are one, Rhya Fleetwood.

"I'm guessing he hasn't told you much of anything," the blue-eyed stranger continues, each word a fresh blow. "Not very big on sharing, is he?"

"And I suppose you will?" I retort. "I don't know you, but you don't seem the forthcoming type."

His knife-blade smile sharpens. "What do you want to know?"

"For starters, who you are and what you truly want with me."

He stares at me for a long while. He says not a word as his hands lift to his shirt. It is fashioned in a timeless style, appearing at once very old and immaculately new. The fabric is such a dark blue, it looks black at first glance. The buttons down the front are polished stones carved with intricate patterns. My eyes widen as he begins to undo them, one by one.

"What the skies are you doing?" I shriek, pressing back against the windowsill in alarm, my pulse a cavalry charge within my chest.

"Not what you think." He continues to work at the buttons, his deft fingers moving quickly down the line until his shirt flutters open. With fluid grace, he shrugs it off, revealing a muscular chest that looks carved from marble. The navy material flutters to the floorboards.

And I gasp.

Not at the sight of a man's naked torso—I have seen plenty of those in my time healing sickly villagers with Eli—but at the dark whorls that mark the otherwise flawless stretch of golden flesh on the left side of his chest. A triangular pattern spirals outward from the center, across his pectoral. Darker than pitch and ever so slightly raised from the rest of his skin, almost like a blackened brand.

There is no denying what it is.

A Remnant.

It is the same as mine, yet different. Not only the placement, but the design itself. Where the whorls of my own mark are ethereal, almost gossamer, his have more substance. There is a fluidity to their wavelike coils, but also unquestionable strength in the thicker lines, the bolder curves. If my mark is a breeze on the surface of the sea, his is the riptide roaring below.

Without a thought as to what I'm about to do, I take two strides forward. My hand flies up to touch the intricate design, needing to confirm what I'm seeing is actually there. That it's real.

That *he's* real.

He sucks in a sharp breath as my fingertips make contact, but I barely notice. His skin is somewhat cool to the touch and surprisingly soft, like satin over the steel of his muscular chest. When I start to trace the waves and spirals of his Remnant, a sound rattles low in his throat—half groan, half growl. His hand flies up to manacle my wrist and jerks it away, stopping my exploration almost before it's begun.

"That," he hisses softly, "is sensitive."

Skies.

I should be embarrassed. I'm sure that will come later, but in this moment, I'm too unnerved to process my own emotional state. I glance up into the stranger's face, craning my neck all the way back to accomplish it. He's quite tall. His strong fingers still grip my wrist—not painfully, but also not gently. Though I tell myself to pull away, I'm paralyzed into stillness by the piercing weight of his eyes. Blue as the ocean and just as bottomless.

"Who am I?" The stranger's mouth twists in a half grin as he finally answers my question. "I am . . . *Water.*"

I MAKE MY way downstairs when my head stops spinning.

After revealing his Remnant mark, my enigmatic host said nothing else. He'd merely bent, extracted his shirt from the floor, and left me alone to gather myself with orders to meet him on the terrace whenever I feel ready.

Frankly, I doubt I will ever feel ready for whatever revelations await me there, but at least I am properly clothed. I'd found a gown—just as he said I would—in the wardrobe and wormed into it, contorting my arms to do up the laces at the back.

The dress is in a style I've never seen before, with belled sleeves, a fitted bodice that plunges scandalously low in the front, and long, lightweight skirts made of the same gauzy material as the nightgown, but dyed a dozen different shades of blue. Sheer, overlapping layers of navy and cerulean, turquoise and sapphire, lapis and indigo, froth around my heels as I move. The effect is such that the wearer appears to be clothed in a part of the sea itself, caught in the crest of a wave with each step.

It is exquisitely beautiful.

I hate how much I love it. I am ashamed to admit I spend a fair stretch of time examining my reflection in the mirror before I leave the chamber. I'm still far too thin, but no longer appear quite as feverish or malnourished as I did the last time I saw myself. Against my fair coloring, the gown does not look altogether too terrible. I pinch some color into my pale cheeks and run my fingers through my mussed white-gold mane. Lacking all skill with ribbons and pins, I let the locks fall freely around my shoulders and down my back.

As I turn to leave, my gaze catches on my wrists in the mirror's shiny surface. The skin that peeks from the bottom of my draped sleeves is almost completely healed. I can barely see the scars where my iron shackles scorched down to sinew. Only a hint of unevenness remains where days ago there were angry red puckers.

It is miraculous. Impossible. No one heals this fast.

No one normal.

I try not to dwell on it—when I do, my mind begins to brim with disturbing thoughts I have neither the time nor the inclination to wade into. Not at the moment, as I descend the final polished step of a steep stone staircase and find myself immediately ushered by two silent, soft-footed servants down a short hall that opens up into a sun-drenched sitting room.

Like the bedchamber decor, the furnishings are well crafted but sparse, almost utilitarian. There is no art, no adornment anywhere I can see. The wall of windows provides the only visual diversion. From this vantage the entire range is on display. The full splendor of the Cimmerians stretches out before me, an unending flow of peaks and valleys. There is a rare beauty to their snowcapped slopes, an undeniable pureness in the way they pierce the sky. The only flaw in the spectacular view is the man standing on the terrace outside—his back to me, his eyes on the horizon.

One of the servants propels me across the room to a set of double doors and practically shoves me through them. My host turns as I approach, his gaze raking me from head to toe.

"A wind weaver in my colors. That is something I never thought to see again in all my days."

His colors.

Who is this man?

A general?

A lord?

Someone powerful, clearly. But he has not given me so much as a name or an affiliation. I am not sure whether we are still within the autonomous region of the Cimmerians or if we have entered sovereign territory.

I stop a good distance from him, turning my head toward the mountains and laying my hands on the stone railing. Despite the snowy clime, the terrace itself is warm. Twin fires burn in low stone trenches that run along the perimeter of the floor to either side of us, casting a pleasant glow across the entire veranda.

"Where are we, exactly?"

"The Acrine Hold."

I keep my gaze fixed on the mountains. "Am I supposed to know where that is?"

"You would, were you from the Northlands." He pauses. "Which, obviously, you are not. Tell me—where did the princeling find you after all this time?"

I finally glance at him, brows raised. "You seem to know quite a bit about Penn's activities."

His gaze gains a cutting edge when I let slip the casual nickname. "I make it my business to know a great deal about a great many people," he says with aching slowness. "You, on the other hand, remain an enigma. Especially as you haven't answered a single one of my questions, while I have entertained several of yours."

"On the contrary, you seem to know more about me than I know of myself."

He arches one brow in silent inquiry.

I blow out a sharp breath. There is not much point in playing coy. He already knows what I am. And if anyone can offer me an explanation about my fate . . . I suppose it is someone who shares it.

"The truth is, until a few days ago, I'd never even heard the term *Remnant*," I tell him. "Besides the mark on my chest, there was never any indication I was anything but an ordinary halfling. I'd never tapped into any power. I wasn't even aware that I had power to tap into."

He shows no reaction.

"I didn't understand that the mark meant I was . . ." I shake my head. "Actually, I'm still not sure I truly understand what it means."

There is a heavy beat of silence, followed by a low, angry oath. "*Fucking Pendefyre.*"

I open my mouth to retort, but he doesn't give me a chance. He turns on a heel and crosses to the other side of the terrace, where his servants have arranged a beautiful dining table. It is big enough for six but set only for two, the surface covered with more food than I've seen in quite some time.

"Come on, then," he calls back over his shoulder, the flash of anger already smoothed over. "We'll sit. We'll eat. We'll talk."

I hesitate only a moment before I trail after him. It takes effort not to flinch when he pulls out my chair for me. I swear I hear the ghost of a chuckle in the air as he pushes me in, the picture of polite manners, and takes his own seat at the opposite end.

Our eyes meet over the platters of food and hold for a long moment. Neither of us seems to know where to begin. Or perhaps he merely does not want to. He studies me, his eyes drinking in the angles of my face, the pale waves that frame it. The dark whorls of my mark peeking from the plunging bodice of my gown.

"Wine," he mutters tightly, pouring clear golden liquid into two glass goblets. The muscle in his jaw is ticking. "Wine will help."

He slides one goblet toward me, then promptly drains his own in two gulps and refills it to the brim. "Let's begin with what happened on the mountain."

"You mean the Reavers?" I ask. "Or the wildfire?"

"I mean the display of idiocy I witnessed from you."

I stiffen. "Excuse me?"

"Tell me . . . are you so young, so untested, you cannot understand the risk you took in doing what you did?"

My brows rise at his calling me young. I may be especially lean these days, but I am not a child. Back in my village, half the girls my age were married by their sixteenth naming day; at twenty, I am on my way to spinsterhood.

Besides, he himself does not look so very ancient. When I first saw him on the mountain I'd placed him around Penn's age, in his mid- to late twenties. Looking at him now, I question my own perception. Despite his youthful appearance, there is something about him—a stillness, a sense of unflinching control—that seems unquestionably . . .

Older.

"Forcing that much raw power when you have no idea what

you're doing is not only dangerous," he says bluntly. "It is reckless beyond belief."

"I managed just fine."

His fingers tighten on his goblet stem. "The blood on your cloak painted a different picture."

"I lived, didn't I?"

"By the skin of your teeth."

"That was hardly the worst thing I've had to survive in my life," I mutter. "Not even in the past week, come to think of it."

"Mmm. And what if you had collapsed at someone else's feet? What if I had not been the one to discover you there, on the brink of exhaustion? You could've found yourself in bad company."

"I'm not so sure I haven't."

His lips twist at one side. He lifts his goblet in a salute. "Fair enough."

I watch him drink, the tanned column of his throat working rhythmically. My own wine sits untouched. I will not accept anything from his table—no matter how tempting the spread set out before me looks. Slices of cured meat, cheese, and crusty bread are stacked on platters beside marinated olives, fresh grapes, and a variety of other delectables. My eyes fix on a bowl of ruby-red strawberries and a rush of saliva fills my mouth.

It has been a long time since I've had a strawberry. Years. The past few harvests, even Eli's thriving gardens had begun to fail. Whatever ailments plague Anwyvn, whatever blight grips her growing seasons in the Midland kingdoms, blessedly spared Seahaven for most of my youth. But the peninsula's fertile stretch of soil could not remain forever immune to the spreading sickness that leaves crops to wither on the vine and farmers to go hungry at their dinner tables. By the end, all we could grow were the most hardy vegetables. Corn. Potatoes. The occasional carrot or radish.

Still . . . I have not forgotten the sweetness of a strawberry on my tongue.

"Take one," a melodious voice interjects into my thoughts.

I start, glancing up into a set of piercing blue eyes. They are fixed on me with such intensity, my pulse quickens to a patter.

"No, thank you."

"You clearly want one. Why not indulge yourself?"

My teeth clench as I lie, "I'm not hungry."

"I didn't poison it, if that's what you're thinking."

"I'm not thinking anything."

"Suit yourself."

Quick as a flash, his hand darts out and he plucks a particularly plump strawberry off the top of the pile. His eyes hold mine as he takes a bite. I tamp down an unwelcome flutter of envy as I watch him chew, his chiseled jaw working with taunting slowness. The pink tip of his tongue darts out to lick the juice from his bottom lip.

"Delicious," he murmurs, still looking at me long after the strawberry is gone.

"I'm glad one of us is enjoying themselves."

"Am I not charming you with my delightful company?" His eyes narrow. "I doubt you'd like my less charming side. Trust me."

"But I don't trust you."

"That may be the wisest decision you've made so far."

My pulse's patter becomes a pound.

He takes another sip of his wine. "Speaking of decisions . . . perhaps you could explain to me why you thought it wise to summon a power you are blatantly unprepared to wield. Do you have a death wish?"

"No, I have a survival instinct," I rebut. "I couldn't breathe. I had to push back the smoke somehow. I didn't have any other choice."

"There is always a choice."

"When the alternatives were giving myself a little nosebleed or being scorched to death . . ." I shrug. "Things seemed rather clear-cut."

"A little nosebleed? Is that all you think it was?"

He drains the final sip from his goblet and refills it once more—not with wine, but water from a sturdy stoneware pitcher. He does not drink. He slowly spins the goblet stem between two fingers. Light refracts through the glass, dappling a dozen tiny round diamonds of sunshine across the table's surface as the liquid begins to swirl.

His voice is low. "Think of every breeze that has ever stirred between every blade of grass in every corner of this world. Think of every ripping squall that has ever filled the sails of every ship in every far-off sea. Think of every soaring current that has carried every bird that dared spread its wings in every distant sky . . ."

His hand is no longer touching the goblet, yet the liquid in his glass still spins—not slowing but speeding up, faster and faster, a tiny vortex under his command. I taste the tinge of maegic in the air, the faintest whisper of it threading into every breath I take. And beneath it, deep inside my chest, the answering stir of power as my mark blinks awake after a long slumber.

Transfixed, I cannot tear my eyes away as the water rises past the rim of the goblet, stretching toward the sky like a waterspout in the center of an ocean gale. Several globules the size of fat raindrops break off and start to orbit around the glass, a delicate waltz of water and air that mesmerizes me.

I swallow a gasp and force myself to look at the man responsible. He is watching me, paying no attention at all to what is occurring in his water glass, as though the dazzling display costs him so little effort, it is beneath his notice.

"Every gust. Every gale," he continues. "From a whisper to a scream, from the lightest puff to the wildest tempest . . . All that resides within you. All that and still more."

I cannot speak. It is all I can do to keep from gaping at him as the spinning liquid abruptly drops back into his goblet. There is no splash, no messy overflow as it is released from his control. Not even a ripple disturbs the surface. The water is utterly still.

Heart pounding, I tear my eyes from it. He is still watching me. If he sees how rattled I am, he feels no urge to quell my unease. His tone is a light caress; his words are anything but.

"Left unchecked, untrained . . . you have no idea how easily your own power can break you. It will crack your mind like the shell of an egg if you are not careful. And everything that makes you who you are will spill out onto the pavestones of your skull, a useless puddle of wasted potential."

CHAPTER SIXTEEN

I pretend not to notice the way my hand shakes as I reach out, snatch my own goblet off the table, and lift the wine to my lips. It is finer than anything I've ever consumed, but as I swallow deeply, all I can taste is my own terror.

At what he said.

At what it means for me.

It will crack your mind like the shell of an egg ...

"You need a guardian," he says softly. Eyes on my throat, watching me swallow. Eyes on my fingers, white-tipped with tension. Eyes on my shoulders, cowed in with dread.

I force them straight against the back of the chair and lift my chin in frail defiance. "Perhaps I already have one."

"Who? *Pendefyre?*" His scoff is dark. "Pendefyre is no guardian. Not for someone like you."

"He has kept me alive so far."

"Oh, he can keep you safe from clearly marked enemies. From hideous monsters and hungry beasts," he acquiesces. "But can he keep you safe from yourself?"

Everything that makes you who you are will spill out onto the pavestones of your skull ...

"That's what I thought," he murmurs, reading the fear in my expression as easily as one might the page of a novel.

My mouth snaps shut with a soft click. I did not realize it had fallen open. I cannot seem to formulate a word, to corral my scattered thoughts into anything coherent.

"You need more than some fierce warrior on the battlefield. You need someone to teach you how to wield that power you carry within you. How to channel it without letting it crush you completely. The biggest threat you will ever face, the toughest battle you will ever fight, is against your own limits." He pauses. "You have only begun to scratch the surface of who you are, little wind weaver. Of what you are. Of what you will become."

"And whom do you suggest for this illustrious role of guardianship?" I ask shakily, swallowing against the emotions clogging my airway. "Let me guess: *you*."

"Mmm. Much as I'd revel in the opportunity to rile Pendefyre"—his smirk is wry—"I refuse to get involved with another doomed attempt at overturning fate. If he insists on trying to remedy the past in some vain attempt to assuage his guilt, that's his prerogative. Not mine."

"His guilt? Guilt over what?"

He laughs—actually laughs, head thrown back, the sound ringing across the terrace like the boom of a cannon. When his eyes return to mine, they hold no mirth but rather that same gleaming, predatory light I remember so well from our first encounter.

"Poor little skylark," he whispers. "Caught in a web so tangled, she'll never have a chance to test the skies. You know, you're almost better off not knowing anything. To die in ignorance might be a blessing."

"Death is never a blessing."

His lips curl. "You may yet change your mind about that."

"I have tasted death on my tongue many times already," I tell him flatly. "I did not care for its bitterness. I doubt welcoming my demise with the wool still pulled over my eyes will do a thing to sweeten such an end."

He seems to consider this, weighing my words against his own reservations. For a long time, there is only silence—so long, I think he might not speak at all. But then, with a casual shrug that belies the intensity of his gaze, he heaves a sigh and settles back into his seat.

"Don't say I didn't warn you." He plucks another strawberry from the bowl and begins chewing. "Let's begin with what you know."

"I know I bear a Remnant mark . . . I know I am . . ." I shrug helplessly. *"Air."*

"And?"

"What else is there?"

"Gods." He dashes the water in his goblet onto the terrace, then refills it with wine. Leaning back in his chair, he gazes at me through half-lidded eyes. "Do you even know what a Remnant is?"

"A sigil of elemental power." That's what Penn had said. "It marks those with dormant maegical abilities."

"That's it? That's all he told you?"

I glance away, glowering.

"Firstly, a Remnant is no common mark for just any fae who can stir a breeze or spin water in a goblet. Plenty of high fae can do parlor tricks. Some of the oldest bloodlines can do more—cast a glamour, activate a portal. But only four souls bear a Remnant mark. One for each of the elements. Water, air, fire, earth."

My body stills as the words register. Four elements. Four souls. I'd assumed—wrongly—that there were many others in the

Northlands bearing marks like mine. Many who might manipulate the elements. Or, if not many, at least . . . some.

You are a wind weaver, Penn had said.

Not you are *the* wind weaver.

The *only* wind weaver.

My face must pale, for the man sitting across from me sighs and runs a hand through his dark hair. "I see he didn't tell you that part."

"No," I breathe, shaken. "No, he didn't tell me that part."

"Mmm." He takes another sip from his goblet. "At any given time, there are four Remnants in existence. No more, no less."

"Always?"

"Always."

"What if one dies?"

"Another is sent."

"Sent? Sent from where? Sent by whom?"

"There are some questions even I do not have the answers to," he murmurs. "The gods above rarely share their motivations. The ones below are even less inclined."

I take another sip of wine to steady myself.

"What do you know of Anwyvnian history?" he asks, eyes narrowed. "Before the wars broke out. Before the blight began to sicken the land."

My nose scrunches as I cast my mind back to Eli's lessons. They seem a lifetime ago, a distant memory. I recall only basic details, but like a dutiful scholar, I recite them. "Anwyvn was once one great kingdom, ruled by a single fae emperor. During his rule, maegic was not seen as a scourge to be extinguished, but as a gift to be embraced. Humans and high fae lived in harmony, even interbred without consequence. It was supposedly an age of great peace."

I shake my head, hardly able to fathom such a time. All I

know is war. I'd been born into it. I'd spent twenty years mired in it, watching shortsighted kings fight for scraps of the wasteland they created, caring little for those of us caught in the cross fire. Any other way of life seems like some snippet from a bedtime tale.

"Go on," he urges softly.

"I don't know much more." My brows furrow. "At some point, things changed. The mortals banded together and overthrew the emperor. After the empire fell, maegic became punishable by death. Bloodline mixing was outlawed. Anyone with even a trace of power was hunted down and killed. It's been that way ever since. For two hundred years." I pause a beat. "And I don't foresee it changing anytime soon, given the dark state of the Midlands."

He digests that statement for a long while, then murmurs inscrutably, "It is not your foresight that counts."

"What?"

"The prophecy—that is what counts, far more than your imaginings of the future."

I stare at him, perplexed. "I know of no prophecy."

"Unsurprising. The mortals have a nasty habit of eradicating all mention of fae lore from their annals. Beyond the range, such things have been forgotten for generations." He sighs, as if annoyed by a group of errant children instead of Anwyvn's most powerful kings. "Alas, there is a prophecy. An old one, remembered now by few. It speaks of a fae tetrad, destined to restore the balance. Remnants, reborn over and over again, until all four elements are once again bound together."

"The . . . the *balance*?"

"The balance of power. Of maegic. Without it . . ." His head cants in reflection. "Anwyvn is sick. The land is dying. It has been for a very long time. Since long before your lifetime. It began the day the mortals killed the royal family—slaughtered the fae emperor and wiped out his bloodline."

"The Cull."

He nods. "An act so heinous, so abhorrent, it tore apart the fabric of the land. Ripped the seams that hold Anwyvn together and left it to unfurl. To fray. It has only worsened with time. A black stain, spreading like a plague across the land."

"Is it a curse, then?"

"Some certainly think so. That the emperor, with his final breath, doomed those who had betrayed him to the same death they delivered upon him."

"Is that what you believe?"

"I don't care about the origin so much as the consequences. Whether the imbalance was born of a curse or is merely a symptom of the mortal war on maegic . . . Either way, we're all forced to endure it. Some with more success than others."

"What do you mean?"

"Here in the Northlands, where the maegic has not yet fled entirely, we are somewhat sheltered from the blight. Our geography spared us the worst of the bloodline culling two hundred years ago. It continues to shield us now—from the ceaseless wars that rage on in the Midlands, from the occasional attempts at invasion when a particularly foolish king gets it in his mind to test his mettle in the Avian Strait."

I nod absently, thinking of Seahaven. Of the Starlight Wood at the farthest reaches of the shore, where the branches glowed with unearthly light and the soil hummed beneath my feet, an untapped current. Were those lingering traces of power what had kept our land fertile despite the growing blight?

After seeing more of the Midlands these past months, I'm almost certain of it.

"Beyond the mountains," he continues, "pathetic mortals

live short, miserable lives full of hunger and suffering while their false kings battle over land so poisoned, it can no longer produce crops."

My eyes jerk back to his. "You speak like they deserve such a fate."

"Do they not?" He quirks an eyebrow. "Was it not the mortal men who threw the balance out of alignment in the first place? Was it not their selfishness that spurred them to betray an emperor to whom they'd pledged fealty? Was it not their greed that brought this curse down on the whole continent?"

"Their ancestors' greed, maybe. Not theirs."

"Who are we but the legacy we leave behind? They are as culpable as their forefathers."

"A man is not his history."

"No?" His eyes are so blue, so bottomless, I think I might drown in them. "Do you think any of those mortal men—men raised on the glory of that murderous lineage—would lift a hand to help someone like you?"

I think of the noose around my neck. Of my hanging tree. Of sneering mouths and half-lidded stares and eager hands reaching for hilts.

Point bitch.

Faery scum.

"There are good people in the Midlands," I insist, pushing aside the cobwebbed memories that haunt the darkest corners of my mind. Finding bright spots.

Tomas passing me a honey cake fresh from the oven. He was mortal, and he showed me kindness.

Eli's warm face, his comforting arms. He was mortal, and he loved me. A love so strong, he'd died for it.

"There are people who are too busy trying to survive to

bother hating halflings. And, hard as you may find it to believe up here in the pampered shelter of the north . . ." I look hard at the bowl of strawberries. "There are people who would not only lift a hand to help someone like me, but would risk everything— would give their very *lives*—in exchange for mine."

His tone is dubious. "You have met such people."

"I have." I swallow hard against the emotions that claw at me. "You cannot condemn an entire region for the crimes of a few."

"I don't condemn anyone. I don't care enough to—not anymore."

"But you did once?" I find it hard to believe the caustic, cynical creature seated before me has ever genuinely cared about anything.

His jaw tightens. "A long time ago."

"What changed?"

"I thought perhaps the balance could be restored. That I could help the prophecy along. That my role in this actually mattered in some way. Now I know better." He stares deeply into his glass. "I am a mere observer in all this. I will sit back and sip wine as I watch the southern kingdoms crumble into ash and bone."

"That sounds very dramatic."

He grins, an unexpected flash of white teeth that makes my heart stutter. "Indeed."

"This prophecy you mentioned . . ." I knit my hands together beneath the table. My fingernails dig into the skin, leaving behind a row of crescent moons. "What else does it say about us?"

He sighs again, as if he does not want to tell me, but eventually relents. His tone drips derision. "Four elements. Four Remnants, reincarnated in flesh and blood. A fated tetrad, bearing the marks of the gods. Scattered across the land. Should all four come together and be bound as one, the balance will be restored. Maegic will return, the blight will end, the land will recover, all will rejoice. Bounty, glory, et cetera." He snorts into his goblet as he takes another sip. "False promises of a senile old seer who probably made the whole thing up after too long in the opium baths."

I stare at him for a long beat. "And if you're wrong? If it's true?"

"Like I said, Anwyvn's fate no longer concerns me."

"But you . . . You are . . . *Water*," I declare dumbly.

"I am a great many things. Fantastic waltzer, for instance. Superb fighter. Halfway-decent cook." His eyes sparkle with amusement. "Damn near godlike in bed."

I ignore his attempts at distraction. "Are you so jaded you'd ignore your own destiny? Or simply so selfish you'd doom the rest of the world rather than disturb your own serenity?"

"Careful." The threat is delivered with such contradictory insouciance, it sends a shiver down my spine. "You speak of things far outside your limited understanding."

"Of course this is out of my understanding! You've just told me I'm one of four keys that, together, unlock the door to the world's salvation," I cry, too angry to heed the warning in his words. "Yet, in the same breath, you expect me to blithely accept your utter apathy regarding your own role in it."

"Apathy is the wisest course, I assure you. The alternative is an exercise in frustration."

"How? How can that be, when we are already halfway there? When we've got two of the four elements sitting across from each other at a table?"

"And a third rapidly closing in, no doubt," he mutters.

"What?"

He ignores my pointed query. "I thought our history lesson over, but it seems I need to clarify some minor points for your half-developed mind to adequately grasp our current reality."

He leans in slightly, tone tightening. "The first four Remnants were born over two hundred years ago, in the wake of the uprising. Some think their souls entered this world the exact moment the emperor's fled it."

"So?"

"*So,* had the original tetrad found one another, do you think we would be sitting here having this conversation?"

"I suppose not."

"You suppose correctly. Every time a Remnant dies—and we *can* die, do not doubt that, though we heal quickly and are harder to kill than most—the element is reborn as someone else. Sent back to start again, in a new body. A new soul." His eyes scan my face. "You're, what . . . seventeen? Eighteen?"

"Twenty."

"And scrawny." His lips twitch when I make a crass hand-gesture that suggests precisely where he can shove his unwanted opinions. "That means, somewhere in this world, around twenty years ago, the last wind weaver died. Probably painfully, on the end of a noose or at the point of a sword."

I cannot disagree with that assumption, seeing how closely it aligns with my own near fate. My mind spins with curiosity, caught up in thoughts of the others who came before me. Past incarnations of Air. How many had there been? Who were they? Where did they live? What had their lives looked like before being snuffed out?

"And then came you," he drawls, drawing me back to the present. His head tilts in thought. "Yet, the last Air Remnant I can recall meeting must've been . . . oh, at least seventy years ago now. However many others lived and died in that half-century gap of time between her demise and your birth, I have no idea. It could be one; it could be one hundred. If they survived longer than infancy, born into the hands of superstitious mortal peasants . . . If they made it safely from the clutches of murderous kings . . . I never had the pleasure of meeting them."

I blink, stunned into silence. The man sitting across from me is not a day over thirty. I'd stake my life on it.

"How . . ." I swallow my surge of disbelief. "How old are you?"

"That's a very rude question, according to every woman I have ever known."

"I'm not in the mood to jest."

"Pity."

"Could you just give me a straight answer?"

"Oh . . ." He waves a hand, a noncommittal gesture. "A couple centuries, give or take a few years. Though I've been told I don't look a day over a hundred and fifty."

My eyes bug out of my head. Only the highest fae—fae royalty—are gifted preternaturally long life. Ordinary halflings are seldom afforded the luxury of growing old—at least, not in the Midlands—but the rare few who are live no longer than a hundred and fifteen years. Perhaps a hundred and twenty. And in those exceptional cases, they surely *look* their age. But there is not one wrinkle or age spot anywhere to be seen on this stranger's perfect face. His dark, lush hair has not a single strand of silver.

I can only manage to gasp a bewildered, "*What?*"

"As I've already mentioned, Remnants are difficult to wound and even harder to eliminate entirely," he says, as if I am rather slow of wit. "Long life span. Quick healing. You will soon learn." His eyes drop to my wrist as I reach again for my wine, noting the faded scars that ring the flesh there. "If you have not already."

I swallow a large sip. My head is beginning to spin—either

from the deluge of information or from drinking on an empty stomach. "So, unless someone takes pains to kill me, I will simply live . . . forever?"

"Perhaps."

"I don't want to live forever," I whisper, my voice stark.

"Most would see eternal life as a gift."

"To live on while everyone else perishes . . . To linger as all those you've come to care for are slowly whittled away by time . . ." I fight back a shudder. "That sounds more like a torment."

He says nothing. Merely stares at me—stares with such acute intensity, I fight the urge to squirm in my seat. As though he is trying to peer directly into my soul.

A thought occurs to me. "If the prophecy is fulfilled . . . If the balance is restored, I mean . . . What happens then? Do we . . . pass on?"

"I don't know. Seeing as I don't have much faith in that ever happening, I don't waste much time contemplating it."

"But—"

"We've never found the final element," he says bluntly. "Earth. Not once. Not one single trace of them. Not in all my many years. And while my current apathy may seem disappointing, I assure you . . . there was a time when I devoted significant efforts to that search."

I suck in a breath.

Never.

Never once.

Not in two hundred years of looking.

His gaze drifts over my shoulder. I turn to see one of the soft-footed servants standing there, her eyes conveying some silent missive. Whatever it is makes a scowl contort my host's face and a stiffness settle onto his shoulders.

"Our time is running short," he explains, looking back at me. "Your darling prince approaches to slay the villainous dragon who's captured his fair maiden."

I sit upright in my seat. "Penn is here?"

"Brooding by my front gates as we speak."

"Take me to him at once," I demand, lurching to my feet. "And return my things."

"Ah yes, your pretty cloak."

"You can keep the cloak. But I want my dagger back." I do not pause to wait for him as I race across the terrace on flimsy blue slippers.

"Listen to her, giving orders." The amused remark comes from just behind me—he's closed the distance between us in soundless strides. "So high-and-mighty."

I shoot a glare over my shoulder as I reach the doors. They swing inward in the hands of two uniformed servants. Both are at least partially fae, given the pointed ears I spot on their bowed heads as we pass by.

We do not speak as we make our way through the keep. Only the soft patter of my slippers against the stone breaks the pervasive quiet. He, as ever, moves in total silence. I wonder if the ability is an inherent gift of his power, the result of extensive military training, or some combination of the two.

It does not take long to reach the front gates. The property is not as large as I originally thought. Though it is clean of dust and detritus, I get the sense it is seldom used. The hallways we traverse are devoid of character. I peer into open rooms as we pass and find them empty—of art, of life, of people. Besides the soft-footed servants, I see not a soul. Not even guards. Even after we step through a set of massive wooden doors banded with metal braces and walk into a walled courtyard, I note not a single man on duty. The garden beds are barren, the grass studded with weeds. In my swishing blue skirts, I feel like the only spot of color in a world gone gray.

"I don't generally spend much time here," my enigmatic host says from beside me, noting my curious gaze as we walk.

"You don't live here, then?"

He glances with distaste at the heavy stone, the lifeless courtyard. "Gods, no. The Acrine Hold is near the strait, on neutral ground. We keep it for formal matters of state, battle strategy meetings . . ." He glances at me, lips twitching as he tacks on, "Hostage negotiations."

"So I *am* a hostage."

"I'm certain Pendefyre thinks you are."

"Are you trying to provoke him?"

"If I were trying to provoke him, I would've brought you back to Hylios." His smile vanishes. "Though it does not take much to provoke him."

Hylios.

I have heard that name before, from the innkeeper in Vintare who gave me her niece's cloak. What was it she said?

She left it behind when she moved to Llŷr last spring. No need for fur in Hylios, that's for sure.

Llŷr.

Hylios is in Llŷr.

I glance sharply at my companion as new questions about his identity bloom within me, but his blue gaze is fixed toward the stables. A groom is leading a great black stallion from them. The horse appears to be fighting every step, pulling at his bridle and baring his teeth, his head swinging as his brays echo off the keep.

"Onyx!" I call.

His head swings around at the sound of my voice. His glossy black eyes fix upon me and the braying stops. I walk to him, hand extended, and stroke his velvet nose when it butts against my palm. He is tacked to ride. My bow and quiver are right where I left them, strapped in place behind his saddle.

"It's okay, boy," I whisper, dropping my forehead against his neck. "It's over now. Penn is here. He's come for us."

A sharp cough calls my attention back to the man standing beside me. "Your belongings are in the saddlebags. Dagger and all."

I nod.

"Here—put this on."

I haven't noticed the cloak in his hands until he lifts it toward me. It is a deep shade of blue, nearly midnight. The material is a rich, warm velvet. I do not put up a fuss as he wraps it around my shoulders. It's cold in the courtyard; the ride will be even colder, especially once the sun drops below the horizon.

His hands linger for a moment at the neck clasp as he stares down into my face. With a gentleness that makes my breath catch, he reaches beneath the curtain of my hair and frees it from the heavy fabric.

"The next time you nearly kill yourself channeling power you scarcely comprehend," he murmurs, "at least the blood won't show."

I almost smile. "Fantastic."

His hands are still at my collar. "It would be a shame, you dying on me so soon." His voice drops to a murmur so low, I'm no longer sure he's speaking to me. "A few hours of conversation in exchange for seventy years of waiting? Hardly seems a fair trade. Then again, the God of Luck has always been a fickle bastard."

I have no idea what he's talking about, but I respond anyway. "Perhaps you might have better outcomes where the gods are concerned if you'd refrain from insulting them."

His eyes crinkle at the corners. "And whom would you have

me appeal to, little skylark? The God of Death?" He pauses and, as I watch, every trace of humor bleeds out of his expression. His tone grows oddly serious. "No. The Goddess of Fate, I think, is the one I owe thanks for this rather interesting turn of events."

I swallow hard against the sudden lump in my throat, trying—and failing—to formulate a clever retort. Our faces are already quite close, yet he leans in closer still, until all I can see are the perfectly symmetrical planes of his face—those cutting cheekbones, like blades beneath his golden skin. Those sardonic brows atypically furrowed. That smirking mouth momentarily sober. And those eyes—two devouring oceans, so deep they threaten to swallow me where I stand.

Every muscle in my body goes utterly still in response to his proximity. Like the hapless prey that has wandered far too near a deadly predator, I freeze when it would be smarter to flee. I feel excruciatingly aware of his nearness; searingly sensitive to the flex of his hands against my cloak collar as his fingers tighten in the fur.

My heartbeat picks up speed as the moment lingers on, neither of us saying anything. I want to shatter the strange tension, but I am too tongue-tied to speak. Our stares are locked together with a magnetism I do not even attempt to escape. I know, without trying, it will be futile. A fool's errand.

No one escapes this man, I think, pulse a deafening roar between my ears. *Not unless he wants them to.*

"What's your name?" he asks, finally releasing me—both his grip and his gaze.

I blink, caught off guard as the supercharged air abruptly clears and I can once again pull in a proper breath. My first in far too long. "I'm surprised you care enough to ask."

"I don't. It's just that calling you *Remnant of Air* seems a tad formal."

"I don't expect you'll have many more occasions to call me anything at all," I point out. "I doubt we'll ever see each other again once I depart."

A soft laugh tumbles from his lips. "Do you?"

It seems safest not to answer.

"If we're never to see one another again, why would it matter that I know your name?"

I ponder his question. And perhaps it is because I am tired. Perhaps it is because he has given me so much information without asking for anything in return. Perhaps I simply miss the sound of my name on someone's lips . . .

"Rhya," I tell him in a halting whisper. "My name is Rhya Fleetwood."

"Rhya Fleetwood." He repeats it slowly, as though tasting each syllable as it forms in his mouth. "Pleasure to meet you."

I wait, but he does not return the favor. My nose scrunches in annoyance. "Aren't you going to tell me yours?"

"No."

"*What?* Whyever not?"

"Names have power. Especially full names. Never give yours to a stranger when you don't know how they plan to use it."

"But . . . I gave you mine!"

"And?"

"And it's common courtesy to give back that which you've received!"

"Oh, I haven't dealt in anything as common as courtesy in a century." He grins, greatly enjoying my discomfort. "Your foolishness does not necessitate my own. And, anyway, I expect you'll learn my identity soon enough, with or without my telling you."

I glare at him. "Is every conversation between us to be like this? Full of trickery and verbal traps?"

"I thought we were never to see each other again."

My glare intensifies.

He does not seem to mind, or even notice. His blue eyes turn mocking as his hand sweeps toward the far end of the courtyard. "Your hero awaits."

SEVENTEEN

W e walk side by side to the metal portcullis that divides the keep from the outside world, Onyx trotting along behind us. With a groan, it rises as we approach, inching toward the sky on thick chains. My eyes widen at what waits on the other side.

A full company of uniformed soldiers is gathered. I've never seen so many fae in one place before. Thirty of them, maybe more, all clad in matching dark maroon tunics and armed with swords. Banners bearing the crest of Dyved—the flaming mountain—wave in the air.

This must be the famed Ember Guild. Farley had spoken of it—the special unit of warriors who operate directly under Penn's command whenever he is home in Caeldera. Highly skilled on the battlefield, thoroughly trained in all areas of combat.

At the front of the battalion, slightly apart from the rest, six men sit atop horses. Their uniforms are a slight deviation on the standard, the additional emblems at their chests marking their higher rank. I recognize Mabon, Uther, and Jac among them, all looking grim and guarded.

In the very center, astride a gray mount, sits Penn. He wears no helm. I've never seen him without it in the daylight, I realize, mouth suddenly parched. His hair is a rich chestnut, the ends burnished with lighter shades of coppery gold. His skin is tan from riding in the sun, his cheeks ruddy with exertion. His expression is carefully blank.

And his eyes are fixed on me.

I swallow a gasp at the heat banked in their depths. Fury and fire. They burn bright enough to scald, never shifting from my face as he dismounts and approaches the gates. My heart sails up into my throat as his long-legged strides close the distance between us. My relief is a palpable underscore to my frantic pulse.

He's here.

He's come for me.

My hand tightens on Onyx's bridle as Penn halts a dozen paces away. His eyes sweep down my body, scanning for signs of injury or traces of maltreatment. Finding none, he gives a short nod, then turns his attention to the man at my side.

"Pendefyre," my host greets with faux brightness. "What brings you here?"

"Soren," Penn returns stiffly.

The world seems to lurch under my feet. I'm surprised I keep my legs beneath me as reality shifts, then resettles with bone-shaking swiftness.

Soren.

The man beside me is King Soren. King Soren of Llŷr. A man whose name alone is enough to make grown men shake in fear, whose title is synonymous with death. A savage. A brute. The tales of his feats on the battlefield—the unparalleled viciousness that holds invaders at bay, the unmatched wrath delivered upon his foes—are borderline mythic, spreading far and wide through all of Anwyvn.

And I had sat with him. Watched him sip wine and eat strawberries. Seen his head thrown back in laughter and his eyes shining with mirth.

I cannot reconcile reality with reputation.

"It's been a long time." Soren's voice is light as a feather. "Seventy years, isn't that right?"

"Let's skip the pleasantries," Penn growls. He isn't looking at me. I get the feeling that is intentional. That, if he does, he might lose his grip on a precariously leashed temper. "This ends now. Return her to me."

"Is that any way to thank an old friend for taking such good care of the rather intriguing new possession he so carelessly misplaced?"

Penn's jaw tightens. "Enough."

"I couldn't agree more. It is enough." Soren's tone loses all hint of warmth. "Enough of you trying to meddle in matters you know are better left alone. Or didn't you learn your lesson last time?"

Penn's eyes flash hotly. "This isn't like that."

"Isn't it? All I see here are old patterns repeating. The only difference is, this time I have no intention of standing by and watching as you set fire to our best chance in a century."

Penn's teeth grind together so tightly, I think they might crack. "This isn't the same. She isn't the same."

"It's not Rhya I'm worried about."

Penn's entire body jerks at my name. Though he quickly conceals his shock, it is too late. Soren sees his near-imperceptible flinch and realizes immediately what it means. His lips twist with smug self-satisfaction as he glances at me and murmurs, *"Interesting."*

I glare at him.

"Glare all you want." He laughs. "You'll need that fighting spirit if you're to survive Vanora's wrath."

"You'd be wise not to say anything else," Penn warns tightly.

"Why? Afraid, when she learns the truth, she might not be so eager to go with you to Dyved?"

"I'm not sure why you care. Didn't you just say you have no intention of getting involved?" Penn doesn't wait for a reply. Without looking away from Soren, his hand extends blindly in my direction. "Come. We're leaving."

I hesitate only a brief moment before sliding my hand into his. In a flash, he's yanked me away from Soren and has me tucked firmly against his side. His warmth blasts into me, hot as a furnace through his thick maroon cloak.

"Fire and Air, together again," Soren says, staring back and forth from Penn to me. "If that isn't history repeating, I don't know what is."

Fire and Air.

I still in shock as reality shifts for the second time in as many moments. Penn feels it—my jolt of awareness. He must. But he does not look at me. Does not so much as address the powder keg Soren has all too happily tossed into our path.

All at once, a dozen pieces fall into place in my mind, a picture emerging from the puzzling fragments. Penn's body burning with inexplicable inner heat, as though he has a fire beneath his skin. His sword flaming red as he fights, like the blade has been left to rest for hours in the embers. The blaze incinerating the dead cyntroedi in the cave despite the lack of fuel to spark it. The wildfire raging out of control on the mountain, consuming the Reavers in a swath of unnatural flame. His words, after I pulled the arrow shaft from his shoulder.

I heal quickly.

It all makes sense. So much sense, I cannot believe I failed to put the pieces together before. Even Soren's offhand comment about the previous wind weaver—whom they knew *seventy years ago*—did not fully register until this moment. But if Penn was there as well . . . he is also gifted with preternaturally long life.

He is no halfling, but high fae.

Fae royalty.

The Fire Remnant.

I look from Pendefyre to Soren, from Fire to Water, scarcely able to catch my breath. They aren't looking at me—they are too fixated on each other, gazes locked like a pair of circling wolves about to fight for dominance.

"Use the portal at the strait if you'd like," Soren offers airily. "You have my leave. This once."

Penn shakes his head. "We'll ride."

"Dyved is a four-day journey. "

"I know how far my own bloody kingdom is," Penn seethes.

"Then you also know how many perils await you on the road there."

"Nothing my men cannot handle."

"You would risk her safety? After all this time—all these years of searching—you would put her in jeopardy just to prove a point?" Soren's voice rises, only for a moment—a single furl of temper quite at odds with his typical indifferent lightness. "I know of Thawe Bridge. I know who chased you there."

"Keeping tabs on me, Soren?"

"Keeping tabs on Efnysien, as you well know." He pauses. "Did his men see her?"

Penn is silent.

"*Did they see her?*" Soren thunders softly.

"Yes," Penn clips.

"Fuck."

There's a long beat of tension. The two men stare at each other, silently communicating something I do not understand.

"He will have suspicions, hearing of you with a fae girl,"

Soren says finally. "As did half of Vintare, I might add. You might as well have paraded her through the streets of Dymmeria shouting out snippets of the prophecy."

"That would be redundant," Penn mutters. "He already knows she's no halfling. She used her power on the bridge, in plain view of an entire company of his soldiers."

Another oath explodes from Soren's mouth. He glances at me briefly, jaw clenched tight, then looks back at Penn. "Perfect. That's just perfect. Well done, Pendefyre. He'll never rest now. Not until he has her."

My breath catches.

Penn's hand tenses around mine. "That will not happen."

"You know Efnysien. He is relentless in his pursuits. He will send more men. He will keep coming until he claims her."

"Let him try. Thawe Bridge is down. I severed the ropes myself," Penn says flatly. "And I assume you still hold the Avian Strait secure."

"There are other ways into the Northlands. It is only a matter of time before Efnysien locates one of them."

"Do not lecture me, nymph."

Soren inhales deeply, bringing his temper under control. His hands lift in a dismissive gesture. "Fine. Good luck to you, then. But if the men in red make landing in your precious Caeldera and take her from you, do not come crying to me."

There is a terse pause from Penn, then a stiff, "Goodbye, Soren."

"I'll be seeing you." Two sapphire eyes slide to mine. "Soon."

"Don't count on it," Penn growls.

"Oh, but I will. Now that you've returned to the north, your presence is expected at Arwen's wedding festivities on the summer solstice. Or have you forgotten your princely obligations to uphold our treaty?"

Fury is emanating from Penn in waves. "That is for formal matters of state. I have no intention of attending your sister's wedding."

Soren only smiles. It is a cruel, knowing grin—one that makes my stomach flutter with nerves. "I should think your queen will have something to say about that." His brows arch. "I wonder what she'll have to say about our new wind weaver. Given how close she was with Enid, I can't imagine it will be a warm reception."

"*Stop.*"

"Stop what? I'm not doing anything."

"You will not toy with her emotions like you did—" Penn breaks off, his voice strained. "For fuck's sake, Soren. This isn't a game. And she isn't Enid."

"I know she's not," Soren says carefully. "Do you?"

Penn's hand tightens on mine so hard the bones grind together. I loose a tiny whimper of protest and he instantly eases his grip. Soren's eyes cut toward me at the sound, so blue they make the sky look watered down. I try to glance away, but I can't manage to—not until Penn physically turns me around and leads me down the front walk. Onyx, ever loyal, shadows our steps.

We make it more than halfway to the waiting company of soldiers before Soren calls after us.

"One last thing, little skylark," he practically purrs in that voice that flows like water over a bed of smoothest stones. "Careful with the princeling. His temper burns hot. I'd hate to see your wings scorched before you ever get a chance to fly."

I DO NOT look back as we leave the Acrine Hold behind.

We ride in silence, Penn forgoing his other mount to sit with me on Onyx. He presses close at my back, his arm so tight around my middle it is difficult to draw breath. As though he thinks I might disappear again if he lets go for even an instant.

He had not said a word to me—except for a stiff, "Are you hurt?" and a brief murmur of assent when I assured him I was perfectly unharmed—before he boosted me up into the saddle and spurred us away.

I allow myself to melt back into his chest, the heat from his body keeping me warm along with the thick blue velvet cloak. Deep exhaustion tugs at me relentlessly. The conversation with Soren, followed by the confrontation with Penn, is proving too much for my worn-out body and mind. I need to crawl into bed and sleep for a week if I am ever going to be able to properly sort through all I've learned today.

After a few moments, we come to a fork in the road, the single route splitting into three. The first leads up into the snowy peaks, an ice-encased incline I send out a silent prayer we will not take. I've had my fill of mountains. The second diverges sharply southward, past several low-slung soldiers' barracks, to what I discern must be the infamous Avian Strait—that narrow, bloody pass where so many hopeful armies have found themselves crushed beneath the weight of Soren's bootheel. The third goes northwest, a flat, winding route that snakes along the sliver of neutral territory at the base of the range.

It's the third that we take.

The midafternoon sun is already beginning to tilt toward the horizon. We chase it as it sinks across the sky, a handspan for each hour spent on the road. Our pace is achingly slow, a plodding clop set by the men on foot, who march in orderly rows behind us. Nothing like our frantic flight across the summit.

With the full Ember Guild at our backs, there is no possibility of discretion. There is also no need for it. If the spectacle of force does not scare away any potential enemies, the swords sheathed over their shoulders surely will.

Jac keeps pace to our left, looking uncharacteristically solemn as he rides. Uther and Mabon flank our other side, riding a set of tan mounts. I wonder what happened to the feather-footed draft horses they rode into battle. I hope they made it through the wildfire.

I want to ask—about the horses, about the turn of events that led them to Soren's doorstep—but swallow my curiosity. The tense atmosphere is not conducive to idle chitchat. None of the men seem up for conversation. They are far too busy scanning our surroundings for incoming threats.

It's a shame, for I could use a distraction. The inside of my head is not a particularly comforting place to be at the moment. After weeks spent parched for even the smallest drop of information, I suddenly find myself drowning in it. My thoughts stray to Soren almost as often as they turn to the man pressed against my spine.

Two vastly different men, with vastly different temperaments. One a crackling ember of temper, the other a fathomless, mercurial undercurrent. No wonder they butt heads with such vehemence. The only thing in which they seem in total alignment is their utter dislike for each other.

There is history there—a scarred one, at that. Whatever happened between them, whatever has shredded their association into the combative rivalry they are so intent on perpetuating, seems to involve one of the previous wind weavers.

Enid.

The name echoes in the farthest recesses of my mind, prompting so many questions I have no choice but to bury them all deep, otherwise risk losing my grip on reality. I keep my attention fixed on the minutiae of the road as we trudge onward. League after league, hour after hour.

Eventually, when my exhaustion proves itself too strong to overcome, I drift mercifully into unconsciousness. I do not dream—not of the dark sea, nor of anything else.

MY EYES SNAP open when we jolt to a stop.

Full night has fallen while I dozed. Light flickers from lampposts lining the courtyard of a town house on the main street of an unfamiliar town. All around me, men are dismounting and disassembling. Hooves clatter as horses are led away to the stables; boots crunch on snowy pavestones as the large company of soldiers breaks apart into smaller clusters of two or three. The men melt into the dusky night like shadows—some slipping through the front gates, following the boisterous sounds of music that leak from the center of town; others taking up guard posts on the perimeter of the courtyard and the property beyond. I do not see Mabon, Jac, or Uther anywhere.

"Are you awake?" Penn asks hoarsely. His arm is still tight around my middle.

"I'm awake."

He slides from the saddle, then reaches up to help me down. His hands do not linger at my waist for longer than a breath. Still, I feel his touch through the gauzy layers of my gown, through every corner of my tired body. My muscles ache, stiff from the ride, but I swallow my protests as he laces his fingers with mine and pulls me up the walk.

The house is gray with black shutters, every one of which is bolted firmly—against the cold, against intruders, against curious eyes from the street, where townsfolk stroll beneath the lamplight, shopping and socializing despite the late hour.

"Where are we?"

"Coldcross," he says succinctly.

"Which is where, exactly?"

"Trade-post town. Straddles the border between Llŷr, the Frostlands, and the Cimmerians. The royal family keeps a residence here."

He leads me up three stone steps toward a heavy wooden door. It opens before we've made it within knocking distance. A male servant hovers on the threshold, bowing slightly when he sees Penn.

"Crown Prince Pendefyre. Welcome, welcome. We've made all the arrangements requested in the raven you sent this morning."

"Thank you, Gael."

Releasing my hand, Penn pushes firmly at the small of my back so I have no choice but to step through the doorway, into the house.

"See that she's settled in. I need to sort out my horse and my men."

"Certainly, sir. But, if you'd like, the stable hands are more than capable—"

Penn is already walking away.

"Never mind," Gael says brightly, shutting the door. "Come now, Miss . . ." He trails off, a question in his voice.

Soren's warning about names and their power is fresh in my mind. I offer him an apologetic smile. "The men call me Ace."

He blinks. "Very well, Miss . . . *Ace*."

"Just Ace will do."

"Erm . . . right." His composure is, thankfully, far less shakable than mine. "If you'll just head up those stairs, Miss Ace . . ."

Two minutes later, I am alone in a rather spacious bedroom on the upper floor of the town house. The shutters are latched and the curtains pulled, preventing any glimpse at the world outside. A fire burns low in the grate, warming the room.

I take off the cloak of blue velvet and hang it on a hook by the wardrobe. Resisting the urge to peek inside dresser drawers and riffle through the writing desk, I make use of the attached bathing suite tucked behind a screen in the corner. Then I sit in the brocade armchair near the fire and wait.

I do not have to wait very long.

Penn crashes through the door with such force, it rattles on its hinges. The saddlebags he's holding hit the floor with a dull thud as he strides across the chamber. His eyes rake me head to toe, a cutting sweep that slices deeper as he takes in the dress I'm wearing.

"Gods," he hisses. "You're in his bloody colors."

"I didn't have much say in it. It's not like I chose—"

The savage look he shoots at me stills my tongue. "What a fool I was for thinking you needed rescue. It appears you were enjoying Soren's company more than you ever have mine."

"I was not."

"No?" He scoffs. "It's amazing, really, how chummy you got with him after—what was it? Two days? Yet you've been in my company for nearly a fortnight and I had to hear your name from his mouth."

"Penn . . ."

When I say his name, the fire in the grate leaps higher, as though someone has thrown a cup of spirits on it. My eyes widen.

He swallows harshly, struggling to get himself in check. "I can't stand to look at you when you're branded like a piece of his property."

My spine stiffens and I rise slowly from my seat. "Are you . . . *angry* at me?"

His chuckle holds no humor. None at all. "Angry? Am I *angry*? *Angry* may be too tame a word for what I'm feeling."

"Why?

"*Why?*" The flames leap again. "The last time I saw you, you were headed for safety at the Widow's Notch. I fight my way through a godsdamned horde of Reavers, burning down half a mountain in the process, barely managing to keep my men shielded from incineration . . . only to find you're not there at all. You're nowhere to be found. Vanished, without a trace."

"The pass—" I try to interject.

He cuts me off. "Then, after two days—two bloody days of searching that summit, thinking you were dead, blaming myself for ever letting you out of my sight—I get word from the basest sort of man, a man I would not trust with my worst enemy, let alone with—" He exhales sharply. "And you're not dead at all. You're just fine. Sleeping soundly at Acrine, holding court with the devil himself."

Two days?

Had I really slept for two entire days?

Soren never mentioned that.

My eyes find Penn's. His are full of fire, practically glowing with it. As though whatever power the Remnant has bequeathed him burns perilously close to the surface.

"I didn't know," I whisper, not wanting to rile him further.

"What didn't you know?"

"Any of it. Who he was, where I was, what had happened . . ." I shake my head. "It's not like I went there willingly."

Sparks shoot from Penn's fingertips. I scramble backward, highly aware of the gauzy fabric that swooshes around my legs. He stomps them out with his boots before they scorch the wood. But his roar is loud enough to make me realize a few sparks are the least of my worries.

"He took you against your will?"

My mouth snaps shut at the absolute rage suffusing his voice as much as the fiery display of it. I consider my next words with extra care. Words that could, I realize belatedly, give the Prince of Dyved grounds for retaliation against the King of Llŷr. Words that could, intentionally or not, start a war.

Are you trying to provoke him? I'd asked Soren earlier.

If I were trying to provoke him, he'd answered, *I would've brought you back to Hylios.*

"No, not against my will. Not exactly," I quickly assure Penn, eager to douse the blazing anger inside him. "He found me on the mountain. I was exhausted. Incapable of carrying on. He . . . he helped me."

Penn takes a series of deep breaths. He seems marginally calmer when he walks over to the fireplace and lays his palms on the mantel. It must be hot, but he does not seem affected by heat any more than he is bothered by extreme cold. He does not look at me as he barks a brittle, single-worded command over his shoulder.

"Explain."

And so I do. I tell him what happened after he sent Onyx galloping from the clearing. Of the second band of Reavers, who'd cut me off at the pass. Of their pursuit through the woods. Of the wildfire pressing in.

He tenses at this news, the lines of his shoulders going rigid. But the fire in the grate does not leap and his hands on the mantel produce not a single spark, so it seems safe to continue the tale. My voice falters only as I describe the moment I decided to use my Remnant.

How does one put the sensation of being torn inside out into proper words? I will never be able to capture just how it felt, tapping into my power for the first time. How my skin had seemed too thin to contain it, my mind too feeble to comprehend the wind whipping through me. It was like taking a sip of wine from your glass and finding a full cask poured down your throat instead; inhaling a singular breath and receiving a gust strong enough to explode your lungs.

He lets me speak without interruption until I describe crossing the river with Onyx.

"You forded the river," he says flatly. I can see the frown marring his profile from six paces.

"Yes," I confirm, not sure why he's so addled. I just told him that wind had burst from within me in a tempest, nearly killing me in the process, and he barely batted an eye. Yet the simple crossing of a mountain stream gives him cause to doubt me?

"This late in the season that river is one endless, icy rapid, from the summit to the base. There's no way you could make it across without drowning. Certainly not in a waterlogged dress, stallion in tow."

"I found a narrow bend where the current was gentle," I insist.

"I rode along that entire bank searching for you. There is no such bend."

"Perhaps you didn't see it—"

"I didn't see it," he agrees. "Because it's not there."

"And yet," I rebut, annoyance stirring within me. "Here I stand."

"Then you're the luckiest girl I've ever met."

My brows shoot to my hairline. Lucky? I do not feel lucky. Then again . . . even as I reject his assertions, my mind is back in that river. Knee-deep in that frigid water, remembering the way it lapped around me as I forged my way across. Not dragging me down, not fighting my progress. At times almost propelling me forward. Helping me along.

Straight into Soren's grasp.

He was there. Standing on that opposite bank. Almost like

he'd been waiting for me. Almost like . . . the water delivered me to him.

Had he ensured my crossing? Had he held off the rushing rapids, the ripping currents, as I made my way to safety?

I shake my head, banishing the suspicions. Even if they are true, I'm not about to share them with Penn. His temper hangs by the thinnest of threads. Soren is just the knife to sever it completely.

"Call it what you'd like. Luck, obstinance, desperation . . . I did make it across," I say softly. "But doing so took my last bit of strength. I collapsed on the bank, my air shield gave out, and I lost consciousness. When I woke up this morning, I was at the Acrine Hold. Despite your belief that I was *holding court with the devil*, in truth I spent no more than an hour in his company before you arrived at the front gates."

Some of the tension bleeds out of Penn's shoulders. Removing his hands from their grip on the mantel, he turns to face me. He takes a stride in my direction and, without thinking, I scuttle backward, heart leaping into my throat.

He freezes. "You're afraid of me."

"No," I whisper. "I just . . . I've never seen you this way. You're usually so . . . controlled."

"I . . . Soren, he . . ." His throat works, swallowing roughly. "You have no idea what seeing you there, by his side, did to me. Knowing he was close enough to even breathe your air . . . The thought of what he might've done to you . . . That I might not get to you in time . . ."

"He did nothing to me. We talked; that's all."

"You cannot trust him," he tells me, eyes igniting with fresh flames. It's like staring into the depths of a forge. "There is nothing he will not say—will not do—to turn you against me."

"Why?"

"We have a—" He struggles for words. "A complicated history. I don't know what he told you about me—"

"Very little."

Penn scoffs darkly. "I doubt that, given that you're flinching at my presence when, not two days past, you reached to me for support."

I blink in surprise. I've wounded him more deeply than I realized by retreating. I'm not sure why that makes me feel so guilty.

I've wounded *him*?

He's wounded *me*!

He is the one who lied. He is the one who kept his identity hidden. He shared nothing—not of our joined fate, not of the prophecy, not of Soren. Certainly not of the mysterious Enid, and whatever happened to her seventy years ago.

I owe him nothing. No trust. No true allegiance. He may be my protector, but he is not my friend.

Then why does looking at him make your heart ache, Rhya?

I shake off the unwarranted pangs of sympathy. All that truly matters is that, for the time being, Penn is the string that tethers my kite to the earth. Until this storm passes, I have little choice but to remain by his side, under his protection.

Ignoring the thudding of my own pulse, I force my gaze to meet his and take a purposeful stride forward, to prove I'm not afraid of him.

"Penn . . ."

His whole body jolts at my whisper.

"I'm exhausted. All right? Can't you understand that?" My voice cracks on the question. "I'm so tired, I can barely stand. And every time I think I've found my footing, my feet are swept out from under me again. These past few days . . . Between using my power for the first time and hearing I'm part of a fated tetrad upon which the future of Anwyvn rests—"

"He told you, then. About the prophecy."

I nod. "Needless to say, I'm trying to sort through my thoughts. I need a little time. More than that, I need some sleep."

He stares at me for a long beat. "Of course. I'll let you rest."

"Thank you."

He turns for the door, pausing halfway over the threshold.

"I am . . ." he begins haltingly. His shoulder muscles ripple beneath the maroon fabric of his cloak. As if he is holding himself back, straining beneath the force of all the words he cannot—will not—say. "I am very relieved you're alive."

With that, he steps into the hall and shuts the door with a firm click. It isn't until I am alone in my chambers, breathing deeply to regulate the mad tattoo of my heart, that I see the matching scorch marks marring the wood mantel over the fireplace.

They are burned in the shape of two large, precise handprints.

CHAPTER
EIGHTEEN

I wake to the sound of muffled voices drifting through the floorboards. It takes me a moment to recall where I am and how I've come to be here. I blink up at the ceiling for a while, trying to get my bearings as the haze of sleep lifts.

I slept, deep and dreamless—the best night of rest I've had in ages. Rejuvenation hums through me, a buzz beneath my skin. I practically bounce from the bed to the window. Throwing the curtains wide, I unlatch the shutters and get my first glimpse of Coldcross in the light of day.

A sea of smoking chimneys and gray slate roofs greets me. The town house is set on a slight rise at the edge of town, giving me a prime view of the cobbled streets that wind, labyrinth-like, outward from a central marketplace. Crowds of people are already gathered there, perusing the many steaming food stalls, trading coin for new wares.

Sharp longing sluices through me. I want desperately to join the stream of shoppers, to lose myself for a time in the crush of browsing and bartering. I doubt I'll get the chance. We are to ride at first light.

Or . . . we were.

Peering at the morning sun already climbing high in the cloud-draped blue sky, I wonder what's forced the change in plans. Whatever it is, I'm grateful for it. The opportunity to wake fully rested, rather than being roused forcefully by the pound of a fist or the bark of an order in the dead of the night, is a rare gift.

In the saddlebags by the door, I find my clothing and—just as Soren promised—my lethally sharp little dagger. I'm also surprised to discover a store of food, a blue suede bag brimming with Llŷrian coin, a silver-handled comb, and the scandalously sheer nightgown I'd worn at the Acrine Hold. My cheeks flame at just the sight of it, but I am quickly distracted by the unfamiliar item stashed at the very bottom.

My brows furrow inward as I pull it out to examine it up close. It's a book. Quite an old one, given the state of its yellowed pages. It's no larger than my hand, with an odd symbol gouged into its leather cover. Four outward-facing triangles, each unique in design, coming together to form an intricate diamond.

The tetrad.

My fingertip slowly traces the topmost triangle. The Air Remnant. I recognize its familiar ethereal quality from the mark scored in my own flesh. Of its own accord, my hand drifts downward and slightly to the left, landing on the bolder furls that make up the Water Remnant. My teeth sink into my lip as my touch ghosts over the elegant swirls and coils. I fight an unwelcome flush as I remember the moment I did the same to Soren's chest.

His sharp intake of air. His low hiss of surprise.

That is sensitive.

My hand jerks back from the engraving as though I've been scalded. After a fleeting glance at the other two Remnant symbols, I crack open the cover and scan the first page. Blocky letters adorn the parchment in faded black ink.

THE FATED TETRAD: A HISTORY OF
ANWYVNIAN REMNANTS

Excitement blooms in my stomach. This is the best parting gift Soren could've given me. Far better than gold coin or a colorful dress.

The gift of answers.

I'm eager to devour its contents until every gnawing question has finally been put to rest, but I'm highly aware of the morning slipping by outside the window. Penn could walk in at any moment. Who knows how he'll react, seeing me with a gift from the King of Llŷr in my hands? He might confiscate it before I have a chance to read more than the title page. Given his recent combustible reactions, the whole book could go up in flames, reduced to useless ashes.

Answers will have to wait a bit longer.

I tuck the tome back into the depths of the saddlebag and cover it with the gauzy blue nightgown, promising myself I'll find an opportunity to peruse it when I'm certain I'll not be disturbed.

In a bid to avoid Dyvedi ire, I dress in my red gown and sturdy boots instead of the gossamer blue dress. As I shake out the wrinkled folds of my skirts, something falls to the floor with a clatter. The carved wood whistle. It feels a lifetime has passed since Penn gave it to me. I hold it in my hand for a long moment before I slip the leather cord over my head.

Following the sound of voices, I make my way down the stairs, toward the back of the house. The formal sitting room is empty. They've gathered in the kitchen instead, at a rustic wood table—Mabon, Uther, Penn, Jac, and two others I recognize from yesterday's ride. All conversation screeches to a halt when I appear at the threshold.

"Um . . . good morning," I say, trying not to fidget.

"Don't just stand there, Ace." Jac grins broadly at me. "Take a seat."

Smiling weakly in return, I make my way to the free stool beside Mabon. As I sit, I notice the bandage affixed to the right side of his bald head, just behind his ear. It is stark white against his midnight skin.

"Are you all right?" I gasp.

"Fit as a fiddle."

"What happened?"

"Reavers," he mutters like a curse.

Any further questions are cut off by Uther setting down a steaming bowl of oatmeal before me. I hadn't even seen him leave the table.

"Thanks, Uther."

He winks at me as he takes his seat. I still have not looked at Penn. My gaze skitters past him to the other end of the table. The men sitting there are both high-ranking members of the Ember Guild, judging by the insignias on their maroon tunics. They are also not thrilled by my presence, judging by the way they are regarding me—like a meddlesome insect that's found its way inside your home and must be exterminated at the first opportunity.

"Is there something wrong with the porridge?" I ask, scrunching my nose at them.

Both men blink in surprise.

"It's just, the way you're looking at me right now, I'm half expecting you've tipped a vial of nightshade in it. And if I'm going to die, I'd rather my last meal not be porridge." I grimace. "At least give me a rasher of bacon. An omelet. Something *edible*."

Jac, Mabon, and Uther all chuckle lowly. One of the men—the one with limp black hair and a dour disposition—gets up and leaves without a word. His counterpart, whose hair is nearly as blond as mine, leans slightly forward on his stool and eyes me warily.

I eye him back.

"Poison's a woman's weapon," he says finally. "If I decide to kill you, you'll see it coming."

"I'll be sure to keep my eyes closed around you, then." My head tilts as I examine his handsome features. "No great sacrifice, really, with a face like that."

His lips twitch. "I'm Cadogan."

"I'd say it's a pleasure to meet you, Cadogan, but I don't like to lie." With that, I pick up my spoon and tuck into my porridge.

There is a marked silence at the table. It's Cadogan who breaks it, his bark of laughter setting off a chorus of masculine amusement that takes several seconds to die down.

"She's mouthy," Cadogan notes when they've all stopped. "I like her."

"You should see her with a bow," Jac says. "You'll fall in love."

A low, unamused grunt comes from Penn's direction. I ignore it, narrowing my eyes at Jac, who is seated directly across from me. "I wasn't aware you were capable of loving anything besides your own reflection."

Mabon snorts.

Jac throws a hand over his heart. "You wound me, Ace."

I take another spoonful of porridge. It actually isn't terrible.

"By the way . . ." Uther's gray eyes are full of reassurance. "Don't mind Gower. He's an eighty-year-old curmudgeon in the body of a fighter."

"I assume Gower is the man who fled the table upon my arrival?"

Uther nods.

"He's got his nose out of joint because he wanted to be on the road already," Jac chimes in. "The man doesn't know what to do with his hands when they aren't holding his reins or his cock."

"Why the delay?" I scrape my spoon against the bottom of my bowl. "I thought we were off at first light."

Silence descends again. Everyone is suddenly avoiding my eyes.

My brows lift. "What? Why are you all so quiet?"

It's Penn who answers, his words a low rumble. "You needed to rest."

My head whips around to him. "You delayed because of *me*?"

He nods.

Gods.

A company of thirty trained soldiers, sitting around on their hands so that I could get my beauty rest. No wonder Gower loathes me. I would've loathed me, too. Mortification barrels through my chest. I jolt to my feet, spoon clattering. "I just need two minutes to grab my cloak and we can be off—"

"Sit."

My mouth snaps shut at Penn's command. "But—"

"*Sit.*"

I sit.

"Finish your breakfast. Three full days of road separate us from Dyved. You'll need your strength."

"I'm ready to ride."

"Good. But that's not why you'll need your strength. Later, we're going to talk about your time at the Acrine Hold. In detail."

His eyes are two hot coals, smoldering with intent as he rises from his seat, nods to his men, and walks out of the room without another word.

I force myself to eat the rest of my porridge as Jac, Cadogan,

Mabon, and Uther carry on a light conversation about which route we'll take to Dyved. But the once-tasty oats are like sludge in my mouth, lumpy and flavorless.

COLDCROSS IS THE last bit of civilization we see for three straight days. We wind slowly west, traveling along the base of the Cimmerians through the snow-sheathed plains that abut the Frostlands. We do not cross over into the tiny kingdom that serves as a buffer between Dyved and Llŷr. Nor do I have any desire to—from what I can tell, it is an icy, inhospitable spit of glacier. When I ask Jac how people manage to survive there without fields to sow or crops to tend, he grimaces and says, "You don't need to grow anything when you've got a fleet of raiding vessels to rape, pillage, and plunder every bit of coast across the North Sea."

I do not ask him to elaborate further.

We make camp at night in clearings just off the road, cooking dinner over campfires and sleeping on bedrolls beneath the stars. Usually, one of the men will pull out an ocarina or lute and play a tune as we eat. There is the occasional after-dinner sparring bout or arm-wrestling match, which get quite heated but always stop short of drawing blood. Otherwise, life on the road is rather dull, a slow, monotonous march without much in the way of danger. In fact, the scariest foe I encounter during our journey shares a saddle with me.

After the first day on the road passes without Penn uttering more than a grunt in my general direction, I think—hope—he has forgotten his intention to interrogate me about my time in the clutches of his enemy. By the time I sit down to dinner that first night, I've begun to drop my guard. After a full helping of rabbit, courtesy of Uther, washed down with the two cups of strong mead Mabon silently pours for me, I drop them completely.

This is a mistake.

But I do not recognize it as one, even as I steal off into the dusky night for a moment of privacy in the thick shrubbery, away from prying male eyes and sharp-tuned ears. I am careful not to stray too far or stay away too long.

Jaw cracking on a massive yawn, eyelids heavier than anvils, I meander back to camp with my attention fixed on my bedroll and the sleep that awaits me in it. I nearly jump out of my skin when a massive man-shaped form melts from the shadows not ten paces from me.

"Gods!" I press a hand to my thudding heart. "You scared me halfway to an early grave."

Penn walks to me, glowering. "You shouldn't be out here alone."

"There are some things that do not require an audience." My cheeks tinge pink. "Besides, I brought the whistle."

His eyes drop to the leather strap that hangs down over my bodice. In three short strides, he's closed the distance between us; in another, he's closed his fist over the whistle, so hard the wood creaks.

"And what good is it," he asks with low menace, "if you fail to put it to use when you're in trouble?"

"W-what?"

"This is not a godsdamned fashion accessory."

"I know that!"

"Really? Because history suggests otherwise."

"How so?"

"You should've used it that day on the mountain, the moment you realized you couldn't make it up the Widow's Notch! I'd have known you were in trouble. I'd have come for you."

"And so would every Reaver with a set of ears!"

"I would've handled them. I did handle them, in fact."

"Your fire did, you mean."

His eyes narrow at the accusatory note in my voice, but he says nothing. He is still holding the whistle, his fingers twisting in the leather cord like a leash at my throat.

"I heard them scream," I say bluntly, trying to get my pulse under control—and failing miserably. "When the blaze overtook them, I heard them die. I've heard men die before. Young men, old men. From fevers and sharp falls and all manner of illnesses. But I have never heard men scream the way those Reavers did when the inferno you unleashed caught up to them." I shudder at the memory as goose bumps bloom on my arms. "It was horrible. It was . . . unnatural. Fire does not move like that. With such *hunger*."

"You weren't supposed to be there," he says through clenched teeth.

"It still happened, whether or not I was there to witness it."

"And?" He scoffs. "Do you expect me to feel sorry for a clan of barbaric fae haters who would've done far worse to us? Cut off our ears and worn them from straps around their necks like jewelry? Pierced us full of iron until the agony was so great, we'd beg for death long before they delivered it?"

I pale. "I . . ."

"Have you already forgotten what you saw in that clearing? What they did to Jac's unit?"

I shake my head, unable to speak. I have not forgotten. I will never forget, not as long as I live.

"They like to drag it out," he continues. "The last few of our soldiers they captured . . . I'll spare you the full details, but suffice to say, there wasn't enough left of them to bring back to their families for funeral rites by the time we found them." His brow furrows. "No. I don't feel sorry. I will lose no sleep knowing that murderous horde of blood purists died writhing in pain beneath my flame. I'll sleep all the more soundly in that knowledge. I only wish I'd been close enough to hear it for myself. Their screams would be a lullaby."

I flinch as much at his grim words as at the abrasive tone in which they are delivered. My breaths are coming rapidly; my voice is thready. "Do you think by convincing me you're a monster you'll somehow scare me into submission?"

"You thought I was a monster long before you knew I could command the flame." He leans forward, bringing his face within a handspan of mine. As he does, he puts pressure on the leather cord, holding me in place so I cannot retreat from him. "Isn't that right?"

I have no rebuttal. I had indeed called him a monster after he cut Thawe Bridge and killed the men crossing it. At the time, he seemed unbothered by my assessment. Looking at him now, I realize his indifference is a mask, shielding his true emotions more effectively than the helm he so often wears to hide his identity. Beneath it, there is something else, something I am almost afraid to look too closely at. A savage sort of desperation that seizes me by the heart.

"I thought you did not care what I thought," I whisper—voice stark, eyes fixed on his, heart thundering at twice its normal speed.

There is a moment of silence. In it, I taste the same possibility I see in his gaze as it drops to my mouth; the same possibility I feel at my neck as the pressure on the cord increases a shade, urging me nearer.

Almost a challenge.

Almost a dare.

One I accept, refusing to be the one to flinch away. Not this time. I yield a few scant inches, bringing my face so close to his, our noses nearly bump. As the distance narrows, the tension mounts—a treacherous give-and-take. Our lips are so close, we share each breath. I'm dizzyingly aware of the fact that if either of us moves even the slightest bit—me rising onto the balls of my feet, him craning his face down just a little more—we will no longer be fighting, but doing something vastly different. Something I tell myself I have no business even thinking about, let alone longing for.

And yet . . . there is no denying the desire that races down my spine as the moment lingers on; no pushing aside the furl of attraction that spirals like smoke in the pit of my stomach—the first warning sign of a fire that, if allowed to catch, will undoubtedly turn to an all-consuming inferno.

My heart skips a beat when, at last, he moves, bridging that tiny divide. His lips brush mine, light as the beat of a butterfly wing.

Not a kiss.

The shadow of one.

I feel each word he whispers against my lips long before they reach my ears.

"I would give *anything* not to care."

Before I can even process it, he's gone. His mouth tears from mine, he releases the whistle, and, with a laugh of pure bitterness, he turns away. My pulse is ragged as I watch him stride five paces forward. I try to breathe, but I can't seem to fill my lungs with enough oxygen. Every inhale is shaky and shallow. My emotions are a tangled lump, lodged firmly in my throat, as contradictory as they are confusing. Regret and relief. Unfulfilled desire and undeniable disappointment.

I would give anything not to care.

That makes two of us, then.

I think he's going to disappear—to walk into the forest, leaving me alone in the dark. But he stops. He, too, appears to be breathing heavily, each exhale rattling the broad expanse of his back. I count his labored breaths—*one, two, three*—before he gets himself back under control, locking down the rare breach of emotions with the same self-possession he uses to swing his blade and steer his horse.

For a moment, we are both utterly quiet. Only the faint screech of an owl swooping overhead shatters the silent night. When I finally feel able to speak again, I ask a question that's been nagging at me since we departed the Acrine Hold.

"Why didn't you tell me you are a Remnant? That you are . . . like me?"

He does not turn to face me, speaking to the shadows. "Would it have made any difference? Would you have trusted me any more than you do now?"

"Maybe."

"I doubt that."

"Trust has to start somewhere. But you have given me nothing to go on. I learned more in one hour with your so-called enemy than I have from you in weeks."

The silence that descends is so icy, I am surprised I cannot see my breath. "So you trust Soren more than me, is that it?"

"I didn't say that—"

He spins around, pinning me with a glare. "Did he sway you to his side with an expensive dress and a few honeyed compliments? Did he win you over so easily with his practiced manners and fine wines? I thought you wiser than that."

"He did not win me; I am not a prize."

"But you put more faith in his empty words than in my actions." He scoffs. "Perhaps I should've taken the time to coddle you as we fled north, barely escaping Efnysien with our hides intact. Perhaps I should've been gentler as I ferried your half-dead corpse across plainlands and ice fields. Then you might afford me the same benefit of the doubt you've extended blindly to Soren."

I jerk my chin higher. "I don't put any faith in him, blind or otherwise. I know he is dangerous."

"You know nothing."

"I've heard the battle stories—"

"Those stories are but a fraction of his crimes." His tone is brittle. "You have no idea who he is. What he has done. The blood he has spilled. The lives he has ruined. Whatever whispers make their way to the Midlands are a weak, diluted measure of his true nature. Only sycophants and simpletons give their allegiance to such a man. Do you count yourself among those ranks?"

"No!"

"Then where does your allegiance lie?"

"With myself!" My voice rises sharply. "You say I would be a fool to trust Soren. What would I be to trust *you*, when you have given me absolutely no reason to?"

"Keeping you alive all this time counts for nothing, I suppose."

"Not when you fail to share your reasons for doing so. And do not paint yourself some gentle savior. You may have kept me alive, but you did so with palpable reluctance."

"*Gentle savior.*" He laughs bitterly. "Is that what Soren seems? Of course he would, safe behind his borders. Never risking his neck for anything that does not benefit him exclusively." His voice drops to a snarl. "It is easy to be a gentleman sitting inside a castle. I certainly did not have the benefit of such *gentleness* when I was undercover in Eld's army. I did not have the luxury of maintaining my court manners while knee-deep in corpses on the battlefield."

I flinch.

He sees it and his eyes lose some of their burning wrath. Taking a deep breath, he manages to rein in some of his anger. "What is it you require? An apology?"

"No," I declare, even though there is a part of me that would appreciate one. "Your past actions do not concern me half so much as your future ones." I narrow my eyes at him. His face is half-turned from me, one hand braced against the trunk of a tree. "What are your plans for me in Dyved?"

"You'll see for yourself soon enough."

"Am I to be a prisoner?"

"A *prisoner*?" His head shakes in disbelief. "Gods, you cannot be serious. Would I have gone through all the effort of saving you—repeatedly—only to make you my prisoner?"

"If I'm not a prisoner, what am I?"

"You are a piece in a puzzle I have been trying to solve for over a century."

I blink slowly. "So, you aim to fulfill this prophecy Soren spoke of? To restore the balance? Or is it . . ."

"Is it what?"

"He indicated that . . . That you . . . Well, that you were trying to assuage your guilt over something that happened a long time ago." Sucking in a sharp breath, I force myself to continue despite the tension ebbing from Penn in waves. "Something with the previous wind weaver. With . . . Enid."

The bark beneath Penn's fingers begins to smolder. He quickly pulls back his hand, clenching it into a tight fist at his side. I keep my eyes on the blackened tree trunk as he mutters, "This is not the time or place to discuss this."

He begins to walk away.

"*Trust.*" The word rings out, halting him in his tracks. "This is where it begins, Penn. You want me to stop questioning your motives? Give me a reason to."

It is as close as I'll allow myself to get to begging. The plea in my voice must register somewhere beneath his brimming anger, because he does not walk away. His shoulders are stiff as he turns around to face me. The ten paces between us feel at once far too vast and far too near.

"Ask, then," he says flatly. "Ask your questions."

"Who was she?"

"A Remnant of Air, as you know already."

"I didn't ask what she was. I asked *who* she was."

His expression is blank, all emotions carefully contained. "I found her seventy years ago, in a city near Lake Lumen. What is now Westlake, though it had another name then. Another king. She was born the daughter of a lord there. Her father was wise, for a mortal. He had read of Anwyvn's history, had seen the slow sickness spreading through his lands. So, when his wife gave birth to a babe bearing a strange mark on her breast . . . he did not cast the newborn out, as others would have." He takes a deep breath. "Harboring a halfling was punishable by death. But he knew she was a child of the prophecy. He named her Enid, which means *soul* or *spirit*, for she had moved his with her first breath. And for sixteen years, he did his best to keep her safe."

I have never heard him speak so much. I keep very still and very silent, afraid any interruption will break the spell of his words.

"But discontent grew in the Midlands, spurred by famine and plague. And, with it, an insatiable violence. Wars raged, kings usurping one another with such speed, it was hardly worth writing down their names in the historical annals."

Paper kings, Eli called them. *Their sovereignty easily scratched out.*

"It was a bloody time," Penn continues. "A dangerous time for everyone, but especially for the fae. Most especially for a

Remnant. Enid spent her whole life locked away in that manor house, hidden from a world that would kill her on sight. She never stepped outside, never got to laugh or play or be a child. Books were her only escape from confinement. Still, it was not enough. Servants talk. Even her father's position could not halt the whispers forever."

My stomach turns leaden with foreboding.

"Once the rumors began to spread, there was no stopping them. A changeling girl lived under the lord's roof, they said, swapped at birth for his real child. Fae trickery at work. And he, a fool for loving her. Not fit to see the truth in his own household. Not fit to rule their small fiefdom." A muscle leaps in his jaw. "I got her out as the townsfolk closed in with their torches and pitchforks, as the king's soldiers rode in to finish the job."

"Her family?"

"Butchered. Everyone in the manor, down to the scullery maids. They even killed the hounds."

My throat is thick, my words choked with horror. "And Enid?"

"I brought her north. To Dyved. Eventually, to Llŷr." Penn's voice is flat, his face expressionless. Even his eyes are banked of their normal fire, as though speaking of this requires such control, he has no choice but to contain his emotions in a vise. "There was a time when Soren and I were not at odds. We were not even mere allies. We . . ."

"You were friends," I finish. I had guessed as much. Theirs is no feud between estranged enemies, no disagreement between acquaintances. Such enduring vitriol is only possible because it feeds upon the fuel of a ruined friendship. For what is hate but love turned poison?

Penn stares at me, delaying for a long moment. I get the sense he does not particularly want to share whatever he is going to say next. "You must understand, there is a certain . . . bond . . . that exists among all the Remnants. Like it or not, we are linked."

My brows lift. "What do you mean by *linked*?"

"We share an inherent compatibility. A common energy. Think of it like a blood bond or a family tie—only deeper, for this connection cannot ever truly be severed. We are four weighted scales hung from the same beam, forever seeking a balance only the others can deliver. Independent, but irrevocably tethered."

I think of the ornate tetrad symbol etched into the leather of Soren's book—those four triangles, individual yet interlocked. "That's how it is with you and Soren?"

He nods stiffly.

"And with Enid?"

"Yes." He pauses. "And, I can only assume, so it will be with you."

I start, incredulous. "When I was with Soren, I didn't feel any . . . link."

"You have barely begun to understand your own powers. You are stumbling around in the dark, unable to tell shadow from night. In time, your sight will adjust and adapt." His eyes hold mine. "Do you feel it with me now?"

"Feel . . . what, exactly?"

"The energy. Like an invisible string, connecting us. Tethering us together."

"I don't . . ." I shake my head. My heart pounds so hard, I cannot hear myself think. "I'm not sure."

He closes some of the distance between us and orders softly, "Close your eyes."

I hesitate.

"Trust," he echoes my earlier statement back to me, gesturing from his chest to mine. "Goes both ways."

I close my eyes.

"Good." I hear him move closer. "Now, calm your breaths. In through your nose, out through your mouth. That's it. Slow and steady. Feel your pulse. Focus on each heartbeat."

I do as he says, shutting out everything except the thudding of my heart against my ribs. Eventually, it slows from a frantic, panicked patter to a uniform rhythm.

"Good," Penn says. He's even closer now, his voice only an arm's length away. "When you're ready, reach out with your senses."

"I don't know how."

"How many senses do you have?"

It is a question even a young child could answer. "Five."

"Wrong."

"Sight, smell, taste, touch, hearing. That's five."

"*You* have another," he counters. "You merely need learn how to use it."

His hand comes down on the fabric of my dress, directly over my Remnant. I suck in a breath. I can feel the heat of his fingers, his warmth a sharp contrast to the chill that always ebbs from my mark. It is an effort to keep my heartbeats steady.

"Here," he says, applying a bit more pressure. "This is the center of your power. Do you feel it?"

I nod. I feel it. That cold prickle, coiled within.

"What does it feel like?"

"It's like . . . Like there's a storm swirling inside me," I explain haltingly. "My mark is the eye of that storm. A dangerous point of stillness, surrounded by chaos."

"Focus on the stillness. Shut out the chaos. Find your center."

I try to envision the storm within me. In my mind, I see a hurricane moving fast over the water, clouds spinning round and round with increasing violence, waves cresting white with each swell. And, at the center, an eye.

Calm.

Cool.

Contained.

The surface still as a looking glass, the sky above clear blue. I concentrate on it until the clouds are a distant rumble, until the wind gentles to a breeze, then drops off completely. Until the sea around me feels like cool bathwater.

"I'm there," I breathe, floating. "I'm at the center."

"Reach out with your senses. Beneath the storm. Beyond the chaos. What else do you feel?"

"Nothing. There's nothing."

"Not nothing. Look harder."

"There's. . . ." I search the calm waters, not knowing what I am supposed to be seeking until I see it. Feel it. A faint ripple, disturbing the serenity. "Wait. There's . . . something else."

And there is. Like an invisible current, tugging me forward. Warm as an underground hot spring amid the cool waves of my mind's eye. Beckoning like the smell of burning chestnuts on an autumn wind. I glide toward it, following my senses. Pushing past the confines of my consciousness, I open my eyes and stare at the source.

"It's you," I murmur in surprise. "I feel . . . *you*."

He is startlingly close. His eyes are a living flame, burning into mine. "What do I feel like?"

"Like . . . a hot swallow of tea after a day out in the chill." I test the current between us, exploring it, running my mind across it like hands over a precious object. "Like the faint char of a bonfire in the air from somewhere far away. A hint of flame and heat."

He does not say a word. He does not move a muscle. He does not even appear to be breathing.

"Is that what I feel like to you?"

"No. You . . ." A muscle leaps in his cheek as his jaw tightens. "You are like a crisp trickle of water down the back of a sun-scorched neck. Like cold aloe on a burn."

"Oh," is all I can manage to say.

We stare at each other for a long time. Drinking each other in with this newfound sense of awareness. He's right: it is like having a sixth sense. A second sight. Just as I can see him, smell him, touch him . . . I can now actually *feel* him standing there. Even with my eyes closed, I know I would be able to pinpoint his exact location. It is akin to looking through a glamour, but instead of seeing his true likeness, I see straight to his soul.

"You will be able to sense when I'm nearby," he tells me in a gruff voice. "Even sense some of my emotions, if I do not guard against it."

My eyes are wide with sudden horror. "Can you sense mine?"

"Sometimes."

"*Sometimes?*"

"Only the very strong ones." He glances away from me. "As with any connection, the more you hone it, the stronger it becomes. The more time we spend together, the deeper the bond will grow and the keener my perception will be." His throat bobs on a swallow. "That's how it has been for me in the past, anyway."

With Soren.

With Enid.

A flash of something unpleasant flares through me. "Right. Of course."

He stares at the tree line for a long while in silence. "We should be getting back. It's dark. The men will be looking for us."

"But—"

He turns and walks away before I can ask him anything else.

Mind reeling, I wait until he is almost out of sight before I follow him back to camp.

It isn't until later, when I've burrowed into my bedroll by the fire, that I realize he did not ask me a single question about Soren or my time at the Acrine Hold.

aeldera is nothing like I imagined.

After so many days spent in the icy shadow of the mountains, perhaps my expectations are unfairly low. I pictured the capital city as a larger version of Coldcross or Vintare.

I could not be more wrong.

On our third day of riding, the frost plains come to an abrupt end when we reach a wide canyon. Stretching out of sight from the Cimmerians to the North Sea, it forms an unquestionable boundary between the glacier-bound Frostlands and the flat, snow-topped plateau upon which Dyved sits. The mesa juts against the blue sky, not nearly as tall as the range but elevated enough to make an invasion almost impossible.

No wonder the Northlands weren't conquered during the Cull. With the mountains to the south, seas to both north and west, and the canyon to the east, Penn's entire kingdom is uniquely shielded from all sides.

After crossing the border, we make our way up a winding switchback pass to the top of the plateau—a climb that takes several hours. Whatever Dyved's natural geographical protections, it is clear they take no chances when it comes to safeguarding their territory. I count at least five guard posts along the way, each stationed in a wooden tower with a unit of armed soldiers in dark brown uniforms. They stand at attention when they see our company coming, then drop into deep bows of respect as soon as they recognize Penn. At my back, he nods to return the greetings.

The top of the plateau is not sparse, as I'd envisioned, but densely forested with white-barked pine trees. A thick bed of needles blankets the frozen earth on either side of the trail as we make our way inland. I wonder if the snowdrifts here ever melt completely, even in the heat of summer.

Would I still be here in two seasons' time to see for myself?

For hours, there is nothing but forest. But then the woodland trail widens into a dirt path, and eventually into a cobbled road that branches in many different directions. Stone markers are placed at each crossroads, counting down the distance to Caeldera. As we approach, we pass settlements and villages, along with other travelers—in carts and carriages, on foot and on horseback. Everyone who sees our riding party drops into the same deep bows of deference to their returning prince.

I have never been more conscious of my riding position, seated before Penn. I feel the weight of many eyes on me, curiosity swirling in the air as we near the outer limits of the city.

Prince Pendefyre has returned.

And brought with him a girl.

I keep my spine straight, my shoulders set, and my hands fixed on the pommel as the road hooks around a sharp butte of rock, then slopes suddenly downward through a deep tunnel in the earth. In a blink, midday sun is swapped for shadows, a shift so abrupt it makes my breath catch. The clatter of our horses rebounds in every direction, an echo chamber of hoofbeats. The walls drip with fern and lichen in the low light. The stone is striated with lustrous ore, a galaxy of glittering mica, almost dazzling to the eyes.

There is a dark beauty about it, despite my innate dislike of enclosed spaces. The clawing sense of panic I typically feel whenever I lose sight of the sky is offset slightly by the soaring ceilings of the passage, as well as its width. All the same, I find myself breathless and reeling when we exit through a set of ultra-thick doors at the far end, and I catch my first proper glimpse of Caeldera.

We are at the bottom of a deep, verdant crater. Like a hollow center of a tree stump, the gorge is encircled by the sharp walls of the plateau that rise around us on all sides. Built into the cliffs, some hanging at precarious angles, are dwellings of many different shapes and sizes. They look carved from rock itself, their walls roughhewn and capped with a fuzzy coating of moss. Tidy chimneys spout from their copper-plated roofs; glass-paned windows twinkle brightly against the gathering twilight. Narrow, near-vertical roads slash their way down the snow-dusted cliffs like claw marks, funneling into the bottom of the crater, where a large lake pools in dazzling shades of teal.

The lake is fed by a great waterfall that thunders from the upper cliffs. Open-air markets line its banks, food merchants and spice traders bartering with a sea of shoppers clad in fine cloaks and fashionable gowns. Narrow streets web out in circular rings from the lakeside to the base of the cliffs.

It is all spectacular. I can scarcely take it in. But the thing that steals the breath right out of my lungs and makes my eyes widen to their limits is not the dazzling lake or the charming stone-fronted buildings that surround it or even the cascading falls, but the keep.

No.

Not a keep.

It is a palace. Built into the rock wall by the base of the waterfall—in fact, one wing looks to be nearly *within* the waterfall—the spires and ramparts shoot up toward the sky, piercing the shroud of mist. The tallest tower almost reaches the top of the crater.

"Welcome to Caeldera," Penn whispers into my ear.

We follow a wide avenue through a central marketplace to the arched bridge that spans the lake beyond. I had thought the attention we drew up on the plateau was intent, but it is nothing to the fierce scrutiny of thousands of Caelderans who line the way, their rapt eyes fixed upon us. Some throw flowers in our path; others call out in welcome.

"Prince Pendefyre!"

"Welcome home, Your Highness!"

Penn is not at all affected by this. He continues to nod sedately, occasionally lifting an arm to wave at someone he knows in the throng. I hope my expression is not as pale and shaky as I feel inside. By the time we reach the foot of the bridge, my stomach is a ball of lead.

At some unseen command, the foot soldiers break away from the contingent of us on horseback, bound for their barracks and a well-earned rest from the road. Only seven of us—me, Penn, and the highest-ranking Ember Guild—are to continue to the palace. Though the bridge itself is wide enough for at least four horses riding abreast, the other mounts drop back to let Onyx lead the way. Jac, Uther, and Mabon trail directly in our wake. Cadogan and the ever-unpleasant Gower bring up the rear.

All around us, two-seater paddleboats and angular rowing craft knife across the lake surface, carrying residents from one shore to the other. I crane my neck in an attempt to keep the tallest turret in my sights as we near the palace. There are three round towers of escalating height—shortest on the left, tallest on the right. The tallest is so mist shrouded from its proximity to the falls I wonder if anyone inside can see out the windows, if the walls within are damp and cold from constant moisture.

By the time we reach the front gates, which are at least thrice the height of the average soldier, my face is dappled in fine beads of water. It takes four brawny guards to open them for us. They swing inward with a creak of hinges, leading into a courtyard of dark flagstones, where a greeting party has gathered to receive us. A contingent of uniformed servants line the walk, all clad in the same dull brown shade, heads bowed in subservience. Standing beneath the stately threshold to the inner keep, a flock of courtiers position themselves like colorful peacocks.

Perhaps I am a girl of simple tastes, with no eye for the regalia of court, but their exaggerated finery seems ill-suited for the natural beauty of Caeldera. They drip with gemstones—rubies glitter at cravats, sapphires sparkle at cuff links, emeralds twinkle from earlobes, diamonds drape ample necklines. It is such a dazzling display of fortune, I am nearly blinded as we cross to them in a clatter of hooves.

None shine so resplendently as the silver-haired woman standing at the very center, whose gold crown is so weighted down with gems, I'm not sure how she manages to keep her neck from buckling. Even without the crown, I would know her for royalty by countenance alone. Her posture is unyielding. She seems carved from marble, more statue than flesh and blood.

Penn pulls Onyx to a halt before her. He is oddly rigid at my back, an atypical stiffness emanating from him as he dismounts, then helps me from the saddle. Behind us, I hear the sound of the other men doing the same, their boots thudding against the flagstones, but I do not look at them. I am busy brushing road dust from my cloak, running quick fingers through my tangled locks. I cannot say I have ever dreamed of being presented to a queen, but if I had, I likely would have envisioned doing so with the benefit of a recent bath.

Penn keeps one hand at the small of my back as he leads me

straight to her. His *sister*. It is jarring to see the two of them together. I know they must be of similar years, yet their appearances could not be more contrary—one ravaged by time, the other untouched by it.

Penn bows at the waist. He puts slight pressure on my spine and I drop quickly into an awkward curtsy. Considering I've never attempted one before, I don't think I do too badly. Not until I rise again and find the queen and her posse smirking at me like I am a bear trained to walk upright in the traveling circus.

"Pendefyre. You've returned to us."

Her purr is for him, but her eyes never leave me. They are the same gray shade as Uther's but hold none of his steady warmth; hers are void of anything resembling welcome. Wrinkles feather the skin around them. Not the lines of laughter, but of one who's spent most of her time on this earth with her features fixed in a discontented sneer.

"Sister." Penn's voice is carefully bland. "Thank you for greeting us. There was no need for it." His pause is artful. "Truly."

"How could I let my beloved brother return home after so long away without a proper reception?" She finally looks at him. Her lip curls in distaste. "Though, had I known you would be bringing half the filth from the Range Road with you, I might've had the servants roll out drop cloths first."

"By all means, head back inside, Vanora. I'd hate for someone of your advanced years to risk catching a chill."

The gathered courtiers titter, a ripple of unease moving through the crowd at the unmistakable insult. The queen's stare hardens, gray eyes turning to unflinching stone in her age-lined face.

She was beautiful once. Exquisite, even. You can still see it—a faded imprint of beauty that lingers beneath the burden of a century on this earth. Just as clearly, you can see that she has not weathered the loss with grace. Her vanity has bloomed into bitterness as seasons turn and her petals wilt, then wither away completely.

It is no wonder she can scarcely stand to look at her brother. Penn, the picture of youth and vitality. Penn, standing tall and broad-shouldered and very nearly immortal. Her resentment hangs thicker than the mist in the air.

"Your concern for my health is noted, brother. I must say, I was surprised when I received word of your arrival back in the Northlands. We were not expecting you until the spring thaw. I'm afraid the servants have had little time to prepare your chambers."

"I don't mind a bit of dust."

"No, I don't suppose you would. You were always most at home rolling around in the sparring pits."

"Better the sparring pits than the viper's den you call a court," Penn mutters.

"Mmm." Her lips curl in a humorless smile as she looks behind us to the Ember Guild, who've formed a line at our backs. My knees almost give way when her granite gaze shifts to me once more. "Pray tell, who is this you've brought with you? A new kitchen girl? I'm afraid our staff is quite full, but perhaps I can find her a position in the stables. They're always in need of another set of hands to muck the stalls."

Penn goes very still.

"I do hope she's not another one of your whores," Queen Vanora continues. "The last one made such a spectacle of herself when you grew tired of her charms. Such *weeping*. Even my hounds don't make such noise when they expel a litter of pups."

My cheeks flame as every set of eyes in the courtyard lands on me with keen interest. My mouth is so parched, even if I were able to think of a coherent response, it would not make it past my lips.

"This woman is my guest," Penn says with finality. "I expect her to be treated with all the respect that affords. Even from you, dear sister."

The queen's kohl-penciled brows arch. "You would command me in my own palace?"

Penn leans in a few inches, trapping her gaze with his. "You may sit on that throne, Vanora, but we both know it is only by my continued grace that you do so. I am the Remnant of Fire. My birthright outweighs all your overinflated self-perceptions. If I were to pluck the crown from your head, there is not one soul in Dyved who would move to stop me."

Vanora visibly quails.

Penn's hand reaches out and grasps mine, fingers intertwining in a bone-grinding grip. His voice lifts to address the entire courtyard, servants and courtiers alike, a commanding ring that reverberates across the flagstones.

"Our household now has the distinct honor of hosting not one but two Remnants beneath its roof. Let me be the first to formally introduce you to the long-awaited Remnant of Air. Weaver of Wind. And, until I see fit, our honored guest."

A collective gasp explodes from the courtiers. I imagine their faces are a tableau of shock and surprise, but I have no chance to see for myself. Penn drags me by the hand, sidestepping his sister and cutting a path through her stunned-silent posse, straight through the open doors of the inner sanctum. I hear the sound of boots close behind us and know Jac, Mabon, Uther, Cadogan, and Gower follow.

We pass through a majestic ballroom with soaring ceilings too fast to properly see any of the details, then rush up a grand staircase of stone that diverges in three at a landing. Penn takes the right bend without hesitation.

When I trip on my skirts, he does not even pause. Grabbing

me around the waist, he hauls me upright and carries me the rest of the way.

"Would you *stop*?" I cry, scrambling for purchase on the stone steps, feet windmilling the air uselessly. "Put me down! I can walk!"

Penn grunts as I land a kick to his shin.

He does not stop.

Up, up, up we climb, a seemingly endless stretch of steps. They steepen sharply, then narrow and begin to spiral round and round. We must be inside one of the turrets. The walls are circular, the windows water beaded. Though I would never admit as much to him, I'm grateful for Penn's strong arms supporting me. It is a long climb, and after three straight days in the saddle, I am bone weary.

I don't realize we've lost our guard detail until we finally reach the top. Penn shoves open a thick wooden door, then deposits me over the threshold inside a spherical chamber. It is dusty from disuse but otherwise not at all unpleasant. There is a stately bed pushed up against one wall, a desk of dark wood centered before a large window, and a neglected wardrobe shoved into a corner beside several heavy chests. A fireplace scales the wall directly across from the bed, its mantel one massive slab of stone. Several bookshelves brim with thick tomes. Two tall weapon racks are set up near a screened-off bathing area, fully stocked with lethal-looking blades of all shapes and sizes. Despite the dust motes, they shine like they were sharpened hours prior.

The room is not overlarge—perhaps twenty paces across in any direction. The windows at the front overlook the entirety of Caeldera, while those on the far side are misted with water. The back of the tower is built into the cliff side, natural stone forming the wall instead of slab and mortar.

"Is this your bedroom?"

Penn nods.

"When were you last here?"

"Six—no, seven months."

"So long away from home."

He pauses a beat. "This has not been my home for a long time."

I stare across the room at him. He is standing by the window, looking down at his city. From here, the lake is a teal jewel, winking in the late-afternoon sunshine. The boats gliding across its surface look like bugs on a water bowl.

"How long did you spend with King Eld's army?"

"The better part of a decade." He runs his hand through his thick hair. "Before that, I was with the king whom Eld eventually usurped. And another before him, in a territory farther south."

I'm shocked by this. So shocked, I cannot stop myself from blurting, "*Why?*"

He glances at me, brows raised. "Even with my abilities, it took time to work my way up to a high-ranking position. Glamours and mind tricks only go so far."

"No, I mean why do it at all? Why stay there? What was the purpose?"

"Do you truly not know?"

My breath catches. Surely he does not mean . . .

"I have been looking for you for a long time," he murmurs, watching me carefully. "I have lost track of the years. Of the men I have commanded. Of the enemies I have killed. I cannot begin to count the number of halfling executions I oversaw in my role as Commander Scythe."

The blood drains from my face. "You . . ."

"I could not save them. Not all of them. The mortals' fervor for killing is too strong, the appetite for violence too insatiable.

Most times, the best I could do was to offer a clean death. To hold off the more hideous inclinations of the hunting parties." His stare turns hard. "You thought I was monstrous before? You have no idea how much blood stains my skin. How many piles of fae ash I have scattered to the skies. How many lives I have snuffed out, incapable of lifting a hand to stop it."

No wonder he had not an ounce of gentleness in him when we met. It had been stripped away by the horrors of war. I think suddenly of Farley's words, back in the Cimmerians.

Can't really blame him for nursing a grouchy disposition, after spending all that time in the Midlands . . . It's going to take him some time to adjust to normal life again . . .

Did one ever truly adjust after life in a war zone?

Did one ever return to normal?

My tongue sits lamely in my mouth, refusing to form words.

Penn does not seem to require a response. His eyes have gone unfocused; his voice has softened to a whisper I am not sure I'm meant to hear. His thoughts are far away—in the blood-drenched horrors of his past.

"So much death. So much despair. It was endless. Year after year. Hanging after hanging. Pyre after pyre. I had begun to lose all hope of ever finding another Remnant. But then . . . then, *finally* . . . Word of a halfling. A girl, captured near the Red Chasm. A strange little slip of a thing with silver eyes and the devil's mark, who'd somehow seared the flesh from a man's hand without lifting a finger."

"Me," I whisper.

His eyes refocus on my face. "You."

The air goes static. Electric. Like the sky before a lightning strike. I am afraid to look at him and somehow equally afraid to look away. I force myself to turn, fixing my eyes on the natural wall at the back of the chamber. I run my hands over the rough surface. It, like the rest of the cliffs, is dark, almost black in color, and veined with deep red. I have never seen anything like it.

"What kind of rock is this?"

"It's not rock. It's petrified ash."

"Ash?"

"Caeldera is built inside the crater of a long-dormant volcano. Those walls, like most of the cliffs here, are hardened lava flows."

"We are inside a volcano," I breathe. "Right now."

"A dormant one, yes."

My eyes are round as a barn owl's. "How long has it been dormant?"

"Longer than living memory tells. A millennium or more. The city was built by my ancestors' ancestors, during the time of the empire. The Fire Court. One of Anwyvn's four maegical strongholds."

"And the others?"

"Two were destroyed after the uprising—their temples sacked by culling priests, their palaces looted by invading armies." He pauses. "The Water Court remains. Soren holds it still."

"Hylios?"

He nods. "Soren and I may not be friends, but Dyved and Llŷr are allies in war. Whatever our personal issues, we stand united against the grasping Midland kings . . . and the darker dangers brewing in the Southlands."

"The red army?"

"Yes. Efnysien's army."

"You and Soren both speak of him—Efnysien—like he is the worst sort of evil."

"Because he is."

"But who is he?"

"Once, Soren called him family. A tie of marriage, not blood, made them brothers. But jealousy left to fester can reduce even the bonds of kinship to a bitter feud. Eventually, Efnysien was banished from Soren's court. From all of Llŷr."

"What did he do to warrant such extremes?"

"To this day, I do not know all the details. Even if I did . . . it is not my story to tell, but Soren's." He sighs. "All you truly need to know about Efnysien is that he is an enemy—not merely to his former family, but to all fae."

"Like the Reavers."

He shakes his head. "No. The Reavers hate fae for possessing maegic, which they see as unnatural. Prejudice has soured into poison. Efnysien . . . He hates us not because we possess maegic, but because he himself does not. Jealousy and ego are at the heart of his crusade. He covets fae abilities and has spent a lifetime searching for ways to acquire power that will outmatch his step-brother's."

"Are there such ways?"

"Dark ones, yes. Ancient druidic arts of blood and sacrifice, from the time before the empire. Where he discovered them, whom he learned from . . . I do not know. I do not wish to know. But it is a vile practice—a perversion of all moral codes, both mortal and fae." His brows furrow in deep thought. "To steal maegic is akin to ripping a soul in two, tearing away the vital essence of one's very being. Efnysien has no scruples. He drains power from any source he can find. Any halfling he can find."

"But halflings are powerless."

"Most. Some are born with minute traces. Like a few drops at the bottom of an otherwise empty cup. Efnysien finds those drops and uses them to fill his own vessel. It does not matter that he himself was born empty, so long as he gorges himself on the gifts of others. Shoring himself up by brute force, a vile conglomeration of countless blood sacrifices."

"And he—" My voice is halting. "He can wield maegic?"

"Not natural maegic. Not elemental. It is something . . . darker. Distorted. It has given him an unnatural long life—one he has used to build a dark kingdom of his own. Dymmeria."

I remember Dymmeria from Eli's old maps. A vast territory of desert at the southeastern tip of Anwyvn, isolated from the rest of the continent by a wasteland of sand and shadow. I know nothing else about it, save what my mentor told me—namely, that any halfling in the Southlands is better off dead than captured. Based on what Penn is describing, I cannot say Eli was misguided. To tear apart a soul is an evil I can scarcely contemplate. Even the mortal Midland kings in all their endless war and senseless slaughter are not half so horrific.

My quick-churning mind strikes upon a thought that makes my throat clog with panic.

"What?" Penn asks, taking a sudden step toward me. Reading the terror plainly on my face. "What is it?"

"If he hunts halflings for mere traces of power . . . what would happen if he got his hands on a Remnant?"

Penn's eyes are hard, as is his voice. "We are never going to find out."

"But he—his men, they saw me on the bridge." I shake my head, thoughts spiraling faster than I can sort them out. "They know what I can do and you said—oh, *gods*, you said it yourself, you said it to Soren! They'll come for me. He'll come for me—"

"Rhya."

My eyes snap to his face. It is the first time he's ever said my name and hearing him say it makes my heart, which is already pounding, stumble inside my chest.

"You are safe here," he says with uncharacteristic gentleness. "You are safe with me."

"But . . ."

"Even if they made it through the Avian Strait—which they will not, not while Soren of Llŷr still breathes—they will never make it here. The whole city is warded. No one will breach Caeldera. Not even Efnysien's red army."

My brows rise. "Warded?"

"Wards. Protective shields that rebuff unwelcome guests, like an invisible net of deterrence. They surround the entire city. Those with ill intent are kept at bay."

"How? Is it a maegic spell of some kind? An enchantment?"

"No. I'm no sorcerer, I assure you."

He walks to me and lays a hand on the wall beside mine. The veins in the black ash begin to glow bloodred, responding to his touch. I snatch back my palm when the heat grows too intense. He drops his as well, and the flare instantly fades from the dark stone.

"The petrified lava that flows throughout the city walls is imbued with natural energy. That energy can be tapped. Infused, rather. Like a conduit or a crystal, absorbing a charge."

"You provide the charge?"

"Yes. A pulse of my power once or twice a year is enough to reinforce the natural defenses that shield Caeldera. Like a magnetic force field, it attracts positive energy and repels anything that poses a threat." He shrugs lightly. "It also heats the whole crater during the cold months. That's why everything here is so lush and green, even in the heart of winter. And why the castle is so warm, even up here in the tower."

I think of my paltry air shield, offering a friable bubble of protection, and almost laugh aloud. I'd been proud I could defend a handful of paces of earth. How absurd it feels now, hearing

Penn so casually describe the net of safety he casts over an entire city. The scale of his power is so immense in comparison, I find myself looking at him with fresh eyes.

Who is this man, standing before me?

This stranger who was once my enemy, this enemy who became a protector. A man with a scarred past and an inferno in his bones. For all our time together, I still do not know him. I have scarcely scratched the surface of all he's endured in his extended lifetime. But . . . a part of me wants to. Wants to with a desperation that will not relent.

That wanting shakes me to the core. My newfound curiosity is at war with every instinct of self-preservation, which screams at me to run from his blazing complexities as quickly as I fled the fires of Seahaven.

"Come," Penn says, calling me back to the present. "I'll show you to your sleeping quarters."

"Am I not . . ." I glance around, fighting a blush as my eyes skate past the bed. "I thought I was staying here."

With you.

By your side.

Where it's safe.

"In a way, you are." He leads me across the round chamber. Near the wardrobe, there is a ladder bolted to the wall, leading up into the lofted ceiling rafters that divide Penn's room from the pointed spire that sits at the very top of the tower.

"Go on, then." He jerks his chin at the ladder. "Up you go."

"You jest."

"I do not."

"Is there even space up there for someone to stand?"

"Only one way to find out." He gives me a push, his hand at the small of my back. "I don't have time to stand here arguing with you about your sleeping arrangements. I have some matters to attend to—pressing ones. I'll be back in a few hours to bring you to dinner. In the meantime, do not leave the tower. There are eyes everywhere in this palace."

"Your sister's spies?"

"Spies, courtiers. Call them what you like. Her glittering posse loves nothing more than gossip, and your arrival has stirred up a storm of it. They will be eager to corner you alone. Try not to give them an opportunity." He pauses, lips twitching up at one side. "Though it might be amusing to see you go up against them. A fledgling owl loosed among a pride of preening peacocks."

At that, he turns and leaves me alone. I wait until the door closes behind him before I heave a sigh and climb up the ladder, into the spire.

Full night has fallen by the time a fist pounds at the door to the tower. My heart skips a beat at the sound. I scurry down from the spire—which, upon exploration, is actually quite cozy despite the pitched ceilings and lack of windows—and practically fly across the chamber. But when I open the door to Penn, I instead find Jac standing there on the threshold, holding familiar saddlebags in one hand, an unfamiliar satchel in the other.

"Special delivery," he says, thrusting both bundles into my arms. "Courtesy of the royal dressmakers. You're to change into something suitable for dinner, then I'm to escort you to the Great Hall."

I glance down at my weather-beaten red muslin. Admittedly, it's seen better days.

"How long does it take to make yourself pretty?" Jac asks, a teasing lilt to his words. "I'm guessing a while . . ."

I roll my eyes. "Where's Penn?"

"Busy."

"Doing?"

"Princely things, one can only assume." He looks pointedly at the bags in my grip. "Time is ticking. Queen Vanora is unpleasant even when she's in a good mood. If we show up tardy to her table, she will *not* be in a good mood, Ace."

"Are you to watch me undress or can I have a moment of privacy?"

"I'll be right outside. Growing older by the second. Do try to hurry."

I slam the door in his grinning face.

My hair is still damp from my bath. I've already made use of the screened area, which houses a porcelain basin for bathing, a simple pull-cord toilet, and a time-warped looking glass that casts distorted reflections. The pipes had groaned in protest as I turned on the tap, but after a few moments of sputtering, warm water had streamed into the tub. It was glorious to scrub all traces of road dust from my skin with lemony soap; a luxury to comb through my hair with a serum that smelled of jasmine. I feel properly clean for the first time in ages.

In the satchel, I discover a neatly folded dress the dull shade of dung, along with a matching pair of satin slippers. With a high neckline and a boxy cut, it is not half as pretty as the gossamer blue gown still tucked in the depths of the saddlebag, but I know better than to even consider wearing the colors of Llŷr while traversing Dyved's royal palace. I quickly tug it on, tie my damp waves back with a simple ivory ribbon, slip into the toe-pinching slippers, and head for the door.

Jac is leaning back against the stone wall of the stairwell. He whistles when he sees me. "You look nice, Ace."

"You're quite dashing yourself." I tilt my head, examining his fine maroon shirt, dark fitted breeches, and stiff white collar. "You should bathe more often. You're almost tolerable to stand near."

"Don't you go falling in love with me," he warns, eyes crinkled with amusement as he extends his arm. "*Milady.*"

"Good sir."

We joke and laugh all the way to the Great Hall, which is already brimming with people. Every seat on the main floor appears full. Jac makes several inappropriate comments as we weave through clusters of tables occupied by soldiers and courtiers, distracting me from the inquisitive stares that follow my every step across the shiny marble.

My stomach flips when I realize we are headed for the raised dais that runs the length of the room. The banquet table that sits atop it is large enough to seat thirty, and already crowded with favored courtiers. The queen's inner circle. They are even more ridiculously bejeweled than they were in the courtyard this afternoon. Vanora herself is not yet in attendance; the ornate chair at the head of the table sits empty.

We aren't late.

That is a relief, as is the sight of several high-ranking members of the Ember Guild occupying seats at the opposite end. I see several faces I recognize—Penn among them. He's seated at the table's foot, looking astonishingly at ease with a cup of wine clasped in the circle of his hand. The light from the flickering candelabra in front of him plays across his sharp features. His hair is still wet from a bath and he's wearing elegantly tailored clothes I've never seen before. For the first time since we met, it is not hard to reconcile him with royalty. He looks every inch a crown prince.

He does not even spare me a glance as Jac and I squeeze onto seats next to Uther somewhere near the middle of the table, entirely absorbed in conversation with Cadogan.

I've been seated mere seconds when the queen and her posse sweep in. The entire court clambers to our feet in a show of respect as Vanora makes her way to the head of the table. She settles in a flurry of silk skirts, her ornate crown a golden halo atop her silver hair. I make to sit back down, but Jac stills me with a hand on my wrist before my knees bend more than an inch.

"Wait," he murmurs.

Evidently, we need queenly permission to sit—something she takes undue time giving, thoroughly examining each of us at the banquet table in turn, her flinty eyes moving down the line. She purses her lips in disapproval at some, nods with faint acceptance at others. Most, she gazes at with practiced apathy. Her brother, she ignores outright. But when her eyes land on me, a delighted laugh bursts from her lips.

"My word, in that brown drab I thought she was one of the servants, come to dine with us!"

The courtiers all join her laughter.

Jac and Uther both stiffen beside me.

"Enid, at least, knew how to dress," Vanora continues, looking positively delighted by the opportunity to publicly humiliate me. "But *she* was the daughter of a lord. Tell us, girl, where is it you hail from?"

Hundreds of eyes bore into me. The hall is so silent, even the flames in the hearths have ceased crackling.

I cough to clear my throat. "A small kingdom in the Midlands."

"Which one?"

When I remain silent, the air grows markedly tense. To ignore a direct inquiry from the queen is simply not done. Not in private and most certainly not in the company of the entire royal court.

Not at all.

I look fleetingly at Penn, hoping he might interject. But it seems he, too, wants to hear my answer. His face is set in a stony expression, his mouth pressed in an uncompromising line.

"Are you hard of hearing, girl?" Vanora snaps. "Answer me at once!"

"Ace," Jac prompts lowly, pressing an elbow into my side.

I clench my fists and force my tongue to form a single word. "Seahaven."

"That little spit of land that sticks out into the Westerly Sea, isn't it?" Vanora asks her closest adviser. At his nod, she laughs with abandon, prompting a chorus of sycophantic amusement from the rest of her courtiers. "My word! Can one even call such an inconsequential place a kingdom? I doubt that backwater peninsula even has running water or basic roadways."

My teeth grind together to keep from snapping back.

"No wonder you blend so well with the help." The spiteful old crone smiles. "Tell us, girl, what kind of upbringing did you have in *Seahaven?*"

I look at her, veins sizzling with defiance. I know my eyes must be blazing with it. "I was no lord's daughter, if that's what you're asking. I grew up in a cottage no longer than this table."

The jewel-draped woman across from me snickers behind her gloved hand.

"Mmm." Vanora's eyes flash with gloating triumph. "Are you quite certain she is the Remnant of Air, brother? Perhaps it was not a mark on her chest but a smear of dirt from whatever pigsty you found her in."

The flames in every taper candle in the hall leap abruptly, a sudden blaze of light. The courtiers' snickers become shrieks of fright. All laughter dies instantly, replaced with eerie silence. It is broken several moments later by the screech of a chair being dragged back.

Beneath my lashes, I risk a glance at Penn. He's taken his seat at the foot of the table despite the fact that Vanora has not given him leave to do so. The move sends a subtle yet unmistakable message to the entire court.

Queen or no, he will not bow to her authority.

"Rhya," he says without looking at me. "Take your seat."

Perhaps I'm imagining things, but I think I feel a pulse of fury through the bond, furling round the invisible thread that ties us together. I stare at the blazing candles on the table. They burn so hotly, wax is flooding down in rivulets. No one in the hall moves, no one even breathes, as I slowly pull back my chair and take my seat.

Vanora's jaw tightens with displeasure but she says nothing more, thoroughly engaged in a silent battle of wills with her brother across the span of the table. Every particle of air in the Great Hall turns stale with discomfort as the confrontation drags on.

Finally, she relents, lifting her hand to give the command for the rest of the hall to sit. Hundreds of chairs drag back in unison, the sound ear-splitting. Everyone is soon distracted by the servants who flood in from the wings, carrying with them dozens of platters and pitchers.

"Those two siblings make the air in the Cimmerians feel warm." Jac unfolds his cloth napkin with a scowl. "It's enough to make a man long for a simple campfire cook pot, I tell you . . ."

TWO HOURS LATER, I'm inclined to agree with Jac: I'd much rather be eating coal-roasted rabbit under the stars than endure another moment of Vanora's sumptuous banquet.

I stare down at my gold filigree dinner plate. There is more food on it than I could ever possibly ingest in one sitting. The banquet table is piled with so many platters and serving dishes, it is difficult to see the brocade tablecloth beneath. Roasted tenderloins and stuffed turkeys, braised chops and honey-glazed hams. Baskets of fresh breads, a dozen different shapes and sizes. Steaming piles of husked corn. Boiled potatoes topped with crumbled bits of bacon. Baked carrots and turnips. Seared asparagus sprinkled with cheese shavings. Exotic purple-hued vegetables that do not grow in the Midlands—at least, not any-more. And that is just the food in my immediate sight line.

If this is a regular meal at the palace, what must a true feast look like?

The smaller tables for those who dine on the main floor are less stocked than ours, but not by much. Most of my dinner com-panions pick absentmindedly at their plates, as though the food is just another decoration in the lavish hall. More for show than actual consumption. It is ostentatious enough to sour the delica-cies on my tongue.

So much waste.

Half the families I'd known in Seahaven were starving. The other Midland kingdoms seemed even worse off, from what little I'd seen of them.

"Hanging in there?"

I glance left at Jac's hushed question. He looks just as uncom-fortable as I am, tugging at the stiff doublet at his throat like an animal newly forced into domestication.

"Better than you, from the looks of it," I say, suppressing a laugh.

"Earlier, you said I looked quite dashing in this fancy getup!"

"Earlier, you weren't shifting around your seat like your breeches are full of fire ants."

"She's right." Uther leans around me to join our low conver-sation. "Gods, man, have you spent so long on the range you for-got how to have a proper meal?"

"It's not the meal so much as the company," Jac mutters. He lifts his goblet, signaling for one of the circulating servants to refill it with wine. "I'd have more to discuss with a block of ice than half these pompous society types."

"How long are we expected to stay?"

"Another hour at least," Uther answers me. "Though if the

opportunity arises, I may slip out sooner. Carys is home and I don't like to leave her alone after so long away. Especially in her condition."

"Carys?"

"My wife."

My mouth drops open. "You're married?"

"I am indeed." His smile lights his gray eyes from within. "Four years now."

"I had no idea."

"Well, you wouldn't, seeing as I never told you." He chuckles. "Wasn't much of an opportunity, between fending off cyntroedi and cutting down Reavers and rescuing you from Acrine and getting you back here in one piece."

"Don't let him fool you." Jac scowls playfully at his friend. "He keeps Carys all to himself on purpose. Selfish, isn't he? I think he's afraid she'll fall in love with me if he lets her get too close."

"Yes, that's exactly it." Uther's lips twitch. He looks back at me. "You'll have to come by the house and meet her. We live just beyond the barracks, on High Street. She's not able to wander very far at the moment."

"Is she well?"

"Quite well. Quite pregnant. Due in less than a month."

"Oh, Uther!" I exclaim loudly, grinning so wide it makes my cheeks ache. "Congratulations! That's fantastic!"

Conversation at the rest of the table hushes for a moment as those dining around us hear my sharp exclamation and strain to listen in. I feel curious eyes on me from both heads of the table. With effort, I keep my gaze on Uther and lower my tone.

"Your first child?"

"Yes." He smiles happily. "We're very excited. Most of all since I'll now be home for the birth. Carys is determined to thank you in person."

"Me? Whyever would she thank me?"

"We had four more months on our mountain rotation before we were due back here. If we hadn't run into you and Pendefyre on the range, we'd still be up there."

"Or worse," Jac adds, sipping his wine.

We fall quiet. None of us has forgotten the massacre we witnessed on the mountainside. Yet I had not contemplated until this very moment that it was *their* unit the Reavers killed. Men who'd fought side by side with Uther and Mabon and Jac for nearly a year. They had lost more than fellow soldiers that day. Undoubtedly, they had lost friends.

I suck in a breath. "I never got to tell you how sorry I am about what happened to your unit."

Jac grunts and takes another swallow of wine.

"It's not your fault, nor is it Pendefyre's—though he's apt to blame himself." Uther cuts a sliver of roast and forks it into his mouth. Still chewing, he murmurs, "Like Jac said, meeting you may be the only thing that spared us the same fate."

I set down my own fork. I have lost my appetite. Not that I had much of one to begin with. My stomach has been aflutter with nerves all night. I've not risked a glance at Penn since I took my seat. But I can sense his eyes on me more and more often as the night wanes, the fiery heat of his stare making all the fine, feathery hairs at the back of my neck stand on end.

"I don't think I'll survive another hour of this torture," Jac declares. "I have things to do, people to see . . ."

"Brothels to visit?" Uther guesses. "I'm surprised that wasn't your first stop this afternoon."

"Who's to say it wasn't?" Jac's dark blond brows waggle suggestively. "It was a long, lonely winter on the range. Buxom Brenda and her ample charms are worth a second visit."

"Don't you worry your fist will get jealous?"

I snort into my wineglass at Uther's sly remark.

"Careful, old man, or I'll use my fist for a less self-satisfying endeavor—one which involves your nose."

The dour-faced woman seated directly across from me makes an affronted noise, looking down her nose at Jac like he's crawled out from a swamp. She plainly does not approve of our chosen conversation topic. Still, she will not express as much to us. Since the queen's efforts to humiliate me, I have been summarily ignored by her posse for the duration of the meal. If they think I'm insulted by this, they do not know me very well. I am all too happy to fade into the woodwork.

A sudden strum of strings resounds from the main floor of the hall, drawing everyone's attention. A minstrel dressed in a voluminous striped tunic begins to pluck out a song.

"Dear gods, not the bloody lute." Jac groans. "We'll be here until the summer solstice . . ."

But Jac's heavenly pleas go unheeded. We are subjected to three jaunty tunes as the servants sweep away our dirty plates and trade dinner platters—most still heaped with food—for a myriad of desserts. Pies, tarts, cakes. Fruits dipped in chocolate. I stare at the strawberries for a long moment before plucking one from the top. Soren's voice whispers in my mind as I lift it to my lips.

Mmm. Delicious.

Shivering, I drop it back to my plate untouched.

"Thank you for your patronage, Your Majesty." The minstrel's voice booms out during a break between songs. He turns from Vanora to Penn. "And Your Royal Highness. Welcome home. It is my great honor to play for you tonight—and your esteemed guest."

When his eyes move to me, fixing upon my face with intensity, my mouth parches. He is older than I'd thought at first glance—the years are etched plainly into the wrinkles around his temples and mouth—though he carries it well; his voice is still strong and clear, his fingers still quick on his instrument.

"I wondered if I might play 'The Song of the Prophecy,' in tribute to the Remnant of Air being found at long last." His focus never shifts from me as he speaks. "Her presence brings us all hope. Hope long thought lost in these parts, in the decades since the lady Enid's soul departed."

Vanora huffs. "That is not necessary—"

"By all means," Penn cuts in smoothly. "Play on, sir."

A hush falls over the hall, all chatter quieting. The minstrel lifts his lute, and this time, when his fingers find the strings, they do not dance merrily over the chords as they had before. The tune he weaves is slower, softer—a melancholy rhythm that spins through the air in such a way, it seems to cast a spell over everyone.

I find myself utterly transfixed as I watch him perform. I am not familiar with the song, yet when he begins to sing, I feel I somehow know the words even before they leave his mouth.

"At the end of times,
The Remnants shall rise.

That which floods,
That which burns.

That which whispers,
That which turns.

Four paths divide,
Four fates entwine..."

His voice is clear, each word crisp and light as they flow in a gorgeous stream of sound. I commit them to memory.

"One alone shall perish,
Scorching flame unchecked.

Two at odds shall falter,
Drowning tide unquenched.

Three in arms shall fragment,
Piercing wind untrained.

Four as one shall triumph,
Shaking earth unrestrained."

I cannot tear my eyes away. But through the bond, I feel something strong from Penn. It might be grief. It might be worry. It might be something else entirely. I am afraid to examine it too closely.

"Bound in power,
Blessed in light.

The tetrad ascends,
To banish the blight.

When last the final,
Binds the four.

The balance reborn,
To rule evermore."

The minstrel warbles into silence. He sweeps into a bow, lute held aloft at his side, and absorbs the shock wave of applause that explodes from everyone in the Great Hall. As the clapping reaches a crescendo, I cannot help myself—I turn to glance at Penn. He is watching me, his expression carefully schooled into an apathetic mask. But the feelings I sense from him are anything but indifferent.

I wonder what he senses from me. Panic, most likely. It was one thing to hear about the prophecy secondhand from Soren. It is quite another to have it performed in full, every fateful syllable ringing out, an inescapable declaration of destiny.

Penn lifts his chin, a gesture I do not quite understand but find oddly comforting all the same. Attempting a weak smile, I shrug back at him.

"Do play something less somber," Queen Vanora calls sharply to the minstrel, cutting short the applause. "We brought you here to entertain, not to put us to sleep."

"Of course, Your Majesty."

With that, the minstrel launches into a bright, happy tune. The moment passes. But the undercurrent of panic remains pulsing through my veins, pricking at the mark on my chest. And though he sings an altogether different song, the words that loop through my mind on repeat are of piercing wind and drowning tides, shaking earth and scorching flame.

PENN AND I walk back up to the tower together after dinner finally draws to a close. He is quiet as we ascend the stairs, his demeanor so closed off I dare not risk conversation. Only when we reach his chambers does he finally acknowledge my presence.

"I'll go out on the balcony for a moment," he says stiffly. "Give you some privacy."

"You don't have to—"

My words dry up. He is already halfway across the tower, headed for the floor-to-ceiling glass window. I don't realize it is, in fact, a door until he pulls it open and steps out into the night air. The balcony is narrow, barely wide enough for two people to stand side by side. But the views of the crater are spectacular. Even from behind Penn's broad form, I can see how the houses built into the cliffs sparkle like a second constellation of stars, mirroring the dark sky overhead. The teal lake shines brightly, luminous despite the late hour. Even the mist from the falls seems to glow, a candescent haze hanging in the air.

He remains outside as I prepare for bed. After weeks of bathing in streams and squatting behind bushes on the road, real plumbing is a gift from the gods. Refreshed, I strip off the brown gown and slippers, leaving me barefoot in my thin shift.

Penn is still on the balcony when I return—back to me, hands braced on the railing. The wind reaches into the warm chamber with icy fingers. His posture clearly articulates a need for solitude. I give it to him, climbing up into the spire and crawling beneath the blankets without so much as a murmur of good night.

It seems hours later when I hear the balcony door click closed. I strain my ears, listening to the muffled noises of him kicking off his boots, stripping out of his clothes, running the water tap with a metallic groan of pipes. The creak of his bed frame as he climbs into it. The sound of his breathing, deep and even, as he falls asleep.

It is a long time until I do the same.

My bed in the spire has no frame to speak of—it is little more than a pallet laid upon the creaky wood rafter boards—but it is topped with a plush mattress of down and layered with warm wool blankets to drive off the chill. The distant roar of the falls far below makes for a strange lullaby. As the night ticks on, the wind begins to whip around the turret in a ceaseless wail that mirrors my own screaming emotions.

For hours, I toss and turn, my thoughts caught up in the lavish wastefulness of Vanora's banquet, in the words of the prophecy, and—undeniably—in the man sleeping one floor below me.

It's strange. I know more about Penn now than I ever have before. Yet, since arriving in Caeldera, he feels more a stranger than ever. As though he's dropped a wall but instead of gaining admittance, I've merely found myself confronted with more stone, more mortar. Another wall, twice as thick as the last, and half as likely to yield.

⁓

AT SOME POINT I must nod off, because I awaken with a start, nestled in the spire like a bird in a roost. An absentminded feminine whistle drifts up through the rafters, accompanied by a rustle of skirts. I discover the source as I descend the ladder. Two maids in dull brown uniforms are tidying the room, removing all traces of dust and grime. They both stop when they spot me, bobbing into half curtsies.

"Good morning, miss." One of the women bustles toward me. Her golden-brown eyes are a shade lighter than the halo of unruly curls escaping her kerchief. "I'm Teagan; this is Keda." She gestures to the other maid, a tall beauty a few years her junior with dark skin and bright eyes. "We've been assigned to sort out the prince's chambers while he's in residence, and to see after your needs. Anything you require, just let us know and we'll do our best to arrange it for you."

"Oh, I don't need anything. Really."

"Nonsense, miss. We've hung up your clothing in the spare wardrobe over there." Keda points across the room. "And we laid out a gown for you to wear. When you're ready, we'll help you dress for the day."

"Where . . ." I trail off, feeling foolish. "Did Penn . . . the prince . . . Did Prince Pendefyre say where he was going?"

"No, miss. I'm afraid not."

"And did he happen to mention how I'm meant to spend my day?"

"No, miss. But . . ." The maids trade a worried glance. "We believe it's his wish that you remain here. There are plenty of books and we've brought up a tray with your breakfast . . ."

So, I'm to pass my time locked away in this tower?

My lips press into a line of displeasure. But I say not a word as I eat my breakfast. Nor do I utter a single protest as Keda and Teagan help me dress for the day—something, I might add, I've been doing perfectly well on my own for twenty years. The gown they've selected is a creamy beige. Thick white woolen tights are smoothed over my legs. My hair is brushed until it shines, then arranged in artful braids that drape heavily over one shoulder. As they work, they chat to each other about the unseasonably sunny weather and upcoming Fyremas Festival, which will mark the official start of the spring thaw.

I sip my tea, only partly listening. Most of my focus is fixed inward, floating in a quiet sea at the center of a storm. Homing in on that link that connects me to Penn. At first, I cannot sense him at all. He is too far away. But I wade there, letting my power wash over me, through me. Reaching out with my senses until, at last, I feel a faint ripple from somewhere far below. A fissure of warmth, nearly undetectable. A hint of burning leaves on an autumn wind.

Pendefyre.

I hold fast to the invisible thread between us. I do not let go as the maids finish their work. As I cross to the wardrobe to retrieve my fur-lined cloak. As I shove my feet into boots and walk out the door, ignoring the concerned cries of the two women left behind in the chamber.

The thread strengthens as I follow it down the many stairs,

through the empty banquet hall, and out the doors of the keep. No one stops me as I wander across the dark flagstones to the front gates, though the guards stationed there shoot me inquisitive looks as I pass between them onto the bridge. The lake is dazzling in the morning sunshine, its surface peppered with sleek craft. By the shore, several men are fishing—casting weighted round nets out into the shallows, hauling in writhing yellow-scaled perch.

The scent of spices hangs heavy in the air as I meander down a boardwalk lined with vendors. They call out to me and the other shoppers, showing off their wide array of wares. It reminds me a bit of my trips to Bellmere with Eli, when we'd visit the markets to stock up on medicinal supplies and healing herbs—only the produce here isn't half-rotten.

My head whips around, taking it all in. Fresh vegetables, wheels of cheese, cured meats, salted fish. Vats of mulled cider stirred by women in starched white aprons. In one stall, a man is roasting chestnuts over a rotating spit. He pauses to grin broadly at me. He is missing several teeth.

I grin back, wishing I had some money to exchange. I doubt the bag of Llŷrian coins Soren left me will work here. Even without being able to buy anything, I linger a while, fascinated by the bustle of activity. Many curious eyes follow me as I move through the crowd, but no one approaches or speaks to me. A few times, people make a strange hand gesture in the air as our paths cross—two fingers moving in the shape of a diamond. Whether they are cursing or blessing me, I do not know.

Eventually, I leave the outdoor marketplace behind, following my invisible tether along the shoreline to a crop of low-slung structures built into the base of a particularly sharp cliff. A massive stable sits alongside an armory and a blacksmith. The forges are ablaze, the masters within hard at work—hammers rhythmically striking anvils, filling the air with the music of meticulous labor.

A string of barracks ring a central courtyard of sparring pits, practice dummies, and archery targets. Soldiers mill about everywhere, hurling spears and shooting bows. Some are in full uniform, heading out on patrol with sword and shield, but most are dressed casually in simple breeches and shirts.

A large cluster of spectators is gathered by the centermost pit. I slip unnoticed through the rapt throng, moving until I am pressed up against a post-and-rope railing. The men inside are circling each other, trading blows with a ferocity that steals my breath. I recognize them even without seeing their faces.

Cadogan and Penn.

They are both shirtless, skin gleaming with sweat from their efforts. As I watch, Cadogan lands an uppercut to Penn's stomach that makes him reel back with a grunt of pain. His torso twists around and I get a glimpse of the dark whorls that feather across his pectoral.

His Remnant.

It is a mirror of Soren's mark—a triangular design that spirals across the right side of his chest like smoke turned flesh. I cannot see the details clearly from this distance, but there is something in the design that dances like living flame, the pointed whorls and furls reminiscent of fire in a hearth. I can't help thinking that the real thing is infinitely better than the version gouged into the leather cover of the tome stashed under my pillow in the spire.

Penn's fist flies out, clipping Cadogan across the mouth. A spurt of blood hits the sand floor of the pit.

"Yield?" Penn asks, grinning darkly.

Cadogan shakes his head, wipes his bleeding mouth, and lifts his fists. They continue to prowl around each other for a few moments. I flinch each time another blow lands. The other spectators cheer and heckle, making bets about which man will finally admit defeat. Very few bet against Penn—possibly because he is their prince, but more likely because his skill is apparent to anyone with eyes.

I'm so enraptured, I do not even notice Mabon, Gower, and Jac in their midst until they materialize around me.

"Hello, boys."

"Ace," Jac greets, elbowing me lightly in the side. His eyes do not leave the ring. "Fancy meeting you here."

"Was I supposed to sit in my tower like some tragic heroine in a folk tale for children?"

"No. But you could've at least told someone where you were going."

"I don't need a nursemaid." I touch my cloak pocket, where the sturdy hilt of my dagger presses against my thigh. "I can take care of myself."

"Be that as it may, your life is too valuable to put in jeopardy. Penn will have our heads if he finds out you've been wandering around unprotected. Especially outside the castle grounds."

Mabon grunts in agreement.

Gower, per usual, glares at me like I am a bug to be squished.

"Fine." I swallow some of my petulance. "Next time, I'll let you know before I leave the keep."

"Much appreciated, Ace."

We watch the sparring match for a few moments. The way the two men move around the ring is so fluid, they could be waltzing in a ballroom—if not for all the blood.

A faint ruckus sounds from behind us as someone forces their way through the crowd. I turn just as a man with a crop of copper-red hair emerges, carried forward by a set of wooden crutches.

"Farley!" I cry in delight.

"Well, well, well. If it isn't Miss Bullseye herself!"

"How's your leg?"

"On the mend, thanks to you." He grins at me. "I'll be back in action in no time."

I drop to my knees, gown pooling in the dirt as I examine his splinted bone. What I can see of his leg beneath the bindings looks healthy. I probe the flesh, pleased to find no swelling or crookedness.

"It's healing well," I say, rising back to full height. "But you shouldn't be up and about yet. If you overtax yourself, the bone won't set properly."

He rolls his eyes. "I get around well enough on these crutches. I refuse to spend one more day sitting on my ass. The cart ride from Vintare took an age."

"And he hasn't stopped complaining about it since," Jac mutters.

Mabon laughs.

Gower is still too busy glowering at me to express any amusement. His mood is black as the limp hair that falls around his face.

I frown at Farley. "Let's at least get you out of this throng. If you topple over, there'll be no getting you up again."

"I'm not going anywhere, Ace. I've got twenty crowns on Cadogan pulling this off."

"All my hard work in fixing you will go to waste if you're stomped to a pulp."

"She's not going to relent, is she?" Farley whines.

"Nope," Jac replies, watching Penn sweep Cadogan's feet out from under him. The crowd pulses with cheers. "There go your crowns. Might as well go with her, mate." He pauses, eyes shifting to mine. "Just . . . don't go far."

I sigh. "Yes, O devoted nursemaid."

The crowd of soldiers surges forward as more blood spills in the pit, pinning me against the fence and nearly knocking Farley over. I reach out to steady him.

"Fine, Ace." He grips his crutches tighter. "I'll go with you. But fair warning, you'll be forced to entertain me if I do."

"Oh? And how, exactly, am I going to do that?"

"Ever hurl an ax?"

I shake my head. "No."

"Toss a javelin?"

"No."

"Surely you've thrown spears, then."

"No, Farley, I can't say I have much experience with spears." My eyes shoot to Jac when he makes a strangled sound. "Don't say it."

His mouth snaps closed, cutting off a chuckle. "Say what?"

"Whatever impulsive, inappropriate comment was no doubt brewing in your mind."

"How do you know it was inappropriate?"

"When do you ever say anything appropriate?"

He merely grins.

"If you two are quite finished," Farley says, pivoting on his crutches. "I think we'll save the throwing instruments for when I'm back on both feet. Stick with something we already know you can do."

"Which is?"

"I saw some open archery targets by the back barracks," he calls over one shoulder as he disappears into the mob. "Let's see how good your aim is in the light of day, Ace."

A nother one!"

"How many is that?" Farley calls grumpily from behind me.

"A clean dozen." Smiling, I lower my bow and turn to face him. "Pay up."

"You'll rob me blind, woman."

I shrug, unconcerned, as I walk back to the low stone fence surrounding the archery arena where I've spent the past half hour hitting every target with a precision that impresses even myself. A crowd of spectators has gathered to watch as I shoot bullseye after bullseye. I suspect most of them are more interested in getting a closer look at the Air Remnant than actually seeing my skills with a bow, but they've placed bets nonetheless. This final round involved me hitting all twelve dummies directly through the heart. Farley had staked fifty crowns I'd miss at least one.

"He's already half-lame, Ace." Jack looks pleased as punch as he pockets the winnings from his copper-headed friend. "You want him out on the streets begging for coin as well?"

I bump shoulders with Farley as I take a seat beside him on the stone wall. "I need the spending money. And, seeing as you wagered against me, I can't muster much sympathy."

"Don't hold a grudge." Farley's shoulder bumps mine in return. "I wasn't the only one betting against you! At that distance, only someone daft would guess you'd hit all twelve."

"Why?" My eyes narrow. "Because I'm female?"

"*Oi!* Don't be putting words in my mouth." He eyes the stretch of earth between us and the targets. "Doubt even our top marksmen in the Ember Guild could manage to make those shots without a single bogey. You're a sorceress, I'm sure of it."

"I'm no such thing!"

Jac crosses his arms over his chest and stares at Farley. "She doesn't need sorcery, you fool. She's the bloody Remnant of Air."

"So?"

"*So*, it's no great shock she can outshoot our best marksmen. There's likely no target in the realm she won't be able to hit if she puts her mind—or her power—to it. She can control the damn wind currents. Her arrows will always find their marks."

"What?" Farley explodes. "Ace! You could've told me, you little cheat!"

"I'm not a cheat! Don't cry foul because you underestimated me."

"Jac just said—"

"Jac doesn't know what he's talking about. I'm a good shot. A natural. That has nothing to do with my Remnant."

"Mm-hmm." Jac snorts. "I hate to break it to you, Ace, but your talent with a bow has everything to do with your powers. Half the time you don't even set your stance or aim properly before you shoot—yet you somehow still hit the targets every time. How is that possible? I'll tell you: *it's not.* Unless you're influencing the wind, sending those arrows sailing through the air with zero resistance. Just because you don't realize you're doing it doesn't mean I'm wrong."

I blink slowly at him, baffled into silence. Can it be true?

Have I been unconsciously tapping into my power? It seems impossible. But perhaps being a wind weaver is so deeply ingrained in who I am, it bleeds into my most mundane actions without any actual intention.

"Don't look so dismayed, Ace. You're not the one with an empty coin purse." Farley grins at me. "Though, in the future, I'll know better than to bet against you."

"I didn't know . . ." I trail off, shaking my head. "How could I be using my power without even realizing it?"

"Be grateful it came out in your superb archery skills," Jac says. "There are much more unpleasant ways Remnant maegic can manifest. Trust me."

I think of the sparks jumping from Penn's fingertips. Two handprints scored into a wood fireplace mantel. Taper candles boiling into rivulets of wax on a banquet table.

"How out of control does it get?" I ask softly. "The prince's power?"

Both men glance at me sharply. All traces of humor are abruptly gone from their faces.

"You'll have to ask him about that." Jac's eyes are very solemn. "But you should know . . . the birthright he carries is not an easy one to bear. It's not hard to understand why. Of all the elements, fire is perhaps the most . . . volatile. The most unpredictable. Arguably the most destructive. He battles with that reality every day. Most days, he wins."

"But not all."

"Not all," he agrees. His voice drops lower, out of earshot of the other soldiers milling around the archery arena behind us. "That day on the range, with the Reavers, after he summoned the flame . . . I wasn't sure we'd get him back. The battle fury burned so hot inside him, it was like his very skin was aflame. We had to dunk him in ice-cold river water to cool him down. Three barrels of it. They burst at the seams around him, split open like melons, one after another. And the water didn't just boil over . . . it *evaporated*. I didn't think we'd ever manage to quell the fire."

"The Reavers—"

"It wasn't the Reavers," Jac cuts me off. "I've battled by his side a hundred times. A hundred enemies. Monsters, men, everything in between. I've never seen him lose control like that. Never seen him so close to the edge." His eyes hold mine captive. "It wasn't about the godsdamned Reavers. It was about *you*."

My mouth falls open. But any response I might have mustered is swept away by the sound of approaching footsteps. I do not turn to look. There is no need—the faint tug on the invisible thread looped around my heart tells me clearly enough who stands there. Several soldiers murmur greetings to their prince, but he says nothing. His words, when they come, are for me.

"What the hell are you doing here?"

My shoulders stiffen. Could he never spare a kind word? Could he never utter a simple greeting? It takes all my effort to keep the glare off my face as I glance at him. I mean to meet his eyes, but my gaze snags on his chest. He is still shirtless, his mark on full display. It is even more intricate up close, the design etched in stunning detail. I cannot seem to look away.

"Rhya."

My eyes sail upward. Color burns across my cheeks. "What?"

"I asked what the hell you're doing here."

"What does it look like?"

"It looks like you disobeyed my direct orders to stay in the tower."

"You never gave me any orders. You weren't even there when I woke up, in fact."

His teeth clench together. "Do not test me. I'm not in the mood."

"As far as I can tell, you're only ever in one mood. *Grumpy, gloomy, grouchy...*"

Farley and Jac swallow laughs.

"Get up." Penn glares at me, unamused. "Now."

I glare back at him, stubbornly keeping my seat on the stone wall. He tolerates this show of defiance for about three seconds before he reaches down, wraps his hand around my biceps, and jerks me to my feet.

"Hey!" I snap. "Let go! We're in the middle of target practice! And Jac is about to teach me some dagger play."

"Not anymore."

"But—"

"Say goodbye."

I cast a desperate glance at Farley and Jac as Penn tugs me away. Both of them are grinning broadly. Farley lifts one of his crutches and waves it at me as I am tugged around a corner, out of sight.

"Must you always act like such a brute?" I hiss.

Penn remains silent.

We do not take the main road, but divert onto a narrow back route that cuts behind the barracks and winds past the rear of the stables. It is far less busy than the market thoroughfare; we pass only a handful of young grooms mucking out stalls and polishing saddle leather. They keep their eyes respectfully averted as Penn forces me along, ignoring my visible struggles.

"Where are you taking me?"

"Back to the keep," he says, never pausing his long-legged strides.

"I thought I wasn't a prisoner."

"You aren't."

"Then why do I have to stay in the tower?"

"It's safer."

My heart quails. I battle to keep my tone even, but worry sluices through my words nonetheless. "I thought you said I was safe here. That no one could get to me."

"It's not *your* safety I'm worried about." He halts so abruptly, I trip over my own feet. Only his hold on my arm keeps me from careening into the dirt. "Until we know what you are capable of, I'm not letting you wander about causing trouble. Understood?"

"No, it is not *understood*. You can't keep me locked up there all alone for the rest of eternity. I'll go mad!"

"I can do whatever I see fit."

My temper flares hotly. "I will not spend my days locked behind walls, hidden from view, with only books and dust bunnies for company. I'm not your perfect, precious Enid, in need of constant protection."

His hand falls away from my arm like I've scalded him. "I'm acutely aware of that. You could not be more different from her if you tried."

"I . . ." My words die at the look on his face. Pain. Unmistakable pain. He hides it quickly, but not quickly enough. At the sight, my temper vanishes as suddenly as it appeared. On its heels comes a rush of regret at my hasty words. "I'm sorry. I should not have . . . It's not my place to . . ."

Penn's jaw tightens. "It's fine."

We lapse into terse silence, neither knowing how to proceed. I am rather ashamed of myself for resorting to verbal barbs. Why is it I have no problem passing easy hours with his men, joking and laughing, but the moment I get into his presence my tongue sharpens into a knifepoint?

In truth, I do not know enough about his relationship with the former wind weaver to rightly comment on it. Whether they were mere friends or something more . . . Penn has not told me and I have not yet summoned the courage to ask. Whatever they were to each other, she had clearly mattered a great deal. She still does, if the echoes of heartbreak haunting his expression are any indication.

"You have no idea how to properly control your power," he says finally, breaking through the heavy silence that presses in on us. "You could hurt someone."

"Then train me."

He jolts in surprise. "Excuse me?"

"You say I'm a danger—to myself, to everyone around me. Then help me. Show me how to control it."

He is quiet for a long time, staring at me. When he speaks, it is almost a whisper, though there is no one around to hear. "You would trust me with this? To teach you?"

"If there was someone else I could ask, I would. But we both know you are the only one I can turn to." I swallow hard, trying to get my racing pulse under control. "If not to train me, why bring me here at all?"

"To keep you safe. To keep you *alive*. If you die, gods only know how long it will take to find another like you. I will not spend any more years in the Midlands hunting halflings. I do not have the stomach for it."

"I am . . ." I search for the proper words. "*Grateful* . . . for your protection."

His mouth twitches. "Right."

"Gratitude aside," I hurry on, "I meant what I said before. I cannot spend my life locked in a stone tower. I'm not built for it."

"While you reside beneath my sister's roof, I'm afraid you must maintain at least some presence at court." He blows out a breath. "Do you think I would attend her bloody dinners if I had any other choice in the matter?"

"You are at least accustomed to this world. You grew up here. No one dares question your place." My voice drops to a murmur as my eyes drop to my feet. "I do not belong here. I am not meant for fine society. I feel no desire to overindulge in piles of gourmet food; I care nothing for stilted conversation with jewel-draped courtiers. I . . . I grew up in a cottage. In the wild, in the woods. The closest I have ever come to royalty before now is the queen bee of the hive in our gardens. I do not embroider or paint watercolors or play pianoforte or . . . whatever else the accomplished ladies of the court do to occupy their time. And I have no wish to. Why waste a whole day locked indoors when I could better use it hunting or healing?"

"Can you not simply rest for a time? Until you've some meat on your bones and some color in your cheeks? Until that haunted look has faded from your eyes and you stop flinching at every sudden noise?" Penn sounds more exasperated than I have ever heard him. "Or have you spent so long running, you've forgotten how to stop?"

My eyes stay locked on my shoes. The tips of my boots shine with fresh polish in the midday sun. "Do not speak to me of rest. *You* do not rest. One day home, and you're already at the sparring pits."

He grunts, a sound of begrudging agreement. "Court chafes after so long away. It will pass. You will settle. Give it time."

I shake my head. "I won't—"

His hand latches on to my chin without warning, cutting off my words. He jerks my face up to his, so I can no longer escape his eyes. They smolder with a conviction that catches me off guard

"You say you have no place here? You do. Your place is with me. So long as I am here, no one will dare lift a hand nor utter a word against you. Do you hear me?"

"I . . ." I swallow hard; his eyes track the movement. "I hear you."

"Good."

"Still, you must at least give me the freedom to be outside during the day. To feel the wind and the sunlight and the grass beneath my feet. You must let me have a purpose here, beyond that of a rare butterfly pinned behind glass."

He stares at me, still holding my chin. I can see the thoughts working in his eyes but I cannot decipher them. I sense nothing from the link that stretches between us, a band of tension from the exposed mark on his chest to the concealed one on mine; not the slightest hint at what he might be feeling. So I am utterly surprised by the words that come out of his mouth.

"You are nothing like her."

I flinch, thinking it an insult.

Until he keeps talking. "Enid . . . She was many things. Gentle. Kind. Intelligent. But . . . not strong. Not fearless."

My lips part. He watches my soft exhale of surprise slip out, his eyes lingering on my lips so heavily I dare not draw another breath. "I'm not fearless."

He does not answer. But his hold on my chin changes, morphing from a restraining grip to almost a caress. My breath snags in my throat as the strong pads of his fingers slide along the sharp line of my jaw, then trace down the slope of my neck. I tremble as I feel the rough scrape of calluses from his sword.

There is such strength in those hands. Such power. They could break me with minimal effort, snatch my life away in the lull between two heartbeats. Yet they are unbearably gentle as they move against my skin. His thumb strokes over the highly sensitive hollow of my throat, tracing the pulse that throbs in my jugular. It pounds in double time, as though I've just run a great distance. Ironic, as I have never stood quite so still. My feet are firmly planted against the dirt. In this moment, I would not move for anything.

"Penn," I whisper.

The word breaks whatever spell has fallen over us. His eyes tear up to mine, pausing briefly at my mouth along the way. With one final swipe of his thumb over my pulse, his hand falls back to his side.

"You want to learn about your powers?" His voice is full of gravel. "Then, come. I will teach you what I can."

I blink. *"Now?"*

"Unless you have something more pressing to do with your afternoon," he calls, turning on his heel and striding past the back side of the armory, toward the distant keep. I watch his bare back disappear around the side of the building, a play of rippling bronze muscle in the sun.

After a long, steadying breath, I follow.

WE STAND FACING each other across the hidden ledge of rock behind the falls. Tucked below a ceaseless cascade of water, the half cavern is totally concealed from view. It is a secret place—the sort you'd never stumble upon accidentally, accessible only by a slippery climb up roughhewn rock steps through the mist. Strange symbols are etched into the volcanic ash walls. A code of glyphs, indecipherable and ancient. I wonder what they mean, and who carved them. If they have been here as long as the city itself. Perhaps even longer.

The water is a constant roar all around us. We have to shout to hear each other amid the din, even standing a handful of paces apart.

"Focus, Rhya. Find your center."

"I'm trying."

"Not hard enough, apparently. I can feel your anxiety through the bond. Your fear. It's swamping you."

I narrow my eyes at him. "Stop reading my emotions!"

"Then conceal them from me. Push me out."

"You make it sound so simple."

"It is simple. Simple as closing your eyes or blocking your ears."

"You forget this is all new to me. You've been doing this a lot longer than I have." I pause, tilting my head in contemplation. "How old are you, anyway?"

"Old."

"That's not very specific."

His brows knit together. "Older than you, not quite as old as Soren. Old enough to know that putting a number on the age of someone immortal is about as useful as selling ice in the Frostlands. Now, can we get back to more important matters?"

"Fine," I grit, closing my eyes once more. "I'm *focusing*."

I hear him sigh. I try to ignore it, turning my senses inward to the storm that swirls ceaselessly within. It is less difficult to shut out the roar of the falls or the man standing across from me than it is the worries of my own mind. Penn is right—I am afraid. Afraid to tap into my Remnant again. The last time I did so, I'd spent the following two days unconscious.

Penn speaks again, much nearer this time. "So long as you're afraid of your own power, you're letting it control you. If it controls you, it can overwhelm you. Harm you . . . along with everyone else around when it inevitably leaks out."

"So how do I get over the fear?"

"Face whatever it is that makes you afraid." He pauses. "What scares you so much?"

I swallow hard, hearing Soren's words in my head.

It will crack your mind like the shell of an egg . . .

"Rhya. Look at me."

I open my eyes and stare straight into Penn's. His face is close—shockingly so.

"Think of your Remnant like a gate, containing all your power inside," he murmurs lowly. "When that gate opens, you let a short burst slip through. In the past, that's only happened when you've been scared or when your life was threatened. You've unconsciously cracked that gate open, let a bit of your power spill out. Enough to keep you alive, enough to protect you."

"On the bridge."

"Yes, the bridge. The Red Chasm. The mountain." His eyes narrow a shade. "A crack is fine—so long as it's controlled, so long as you can shut that gate again when the danger has passed. But any more than that . . ."

My brows lift, a silent question.

"You don't want to let so much power flood out that it takes the gate right off the hinges," he says carefully. "You may never get it closed again."

I shiver.

"Don't worry. I will teach you to keep it contained. I will teach you control. You just need to be vigilant."

"You make it sound like my Remnant is a foe to be fought."

"It is. I fight a war against my own power with every breath. I still struggle to keep it in check—and I have been doing this for far longer than you've been alive. I can only hope you have an easier time than I do."

"But you use your powers."

"I do. Reluctantly. In moderation. And only in the absence of any better options. It is not a party trick to be used for amusement."

I think of Soren and his water goblet, the dance of droplets. I'm not sure the Water Remnant would agree. "Why?"

"You saw the wildfire on the mountainside. How it raged. You said yourself it was unnatural. Untamable." He does not look away from me, even for an instant. "Why do you think I was so desperate to get you away from there?"

"The battle—"

"Not the battle. *Me*. I was protecting you from me. I knew what would happen when I unleashed my flame. I knew it would burn out of control. I knew there was a chance I'd kill everyone within my radius. Including Jac, Mabon, and Uther."

I suck in a startled breath. "But you didn't."

"No, I was lucky. This time, I managed to lock it down before I took any innocent lives." His eyes are haunted, full of fiery ghosts I cannot decipher.

This time.

There had been other times when he could not lock it down. Could not contain it. And others had paid the price.

I suddenly see his desperation to get me off that mountain with fresh perspective. I see *him* with fresh perspective. He exercises rigid control in every aspect of his life not because he is a dictator by nature, but because deep down he is terrified of the hell he could unleash, should his restraint slip at any given moment.

"It must be exhausting," I whisper.

His brows lift. "What?"

"Keeping it in all the time."

I do not just mean his power. I mean his agony. His despair. His deep loneliness. There is no one around him who can ever truly understand the weight that rests upon his shoulders. Upon his soul.

Penn watches me for a heavy beat. His voice, when it comes, is hardly more than a murmur. "It is better to exercise control than suffer the consequences of losing it. Now, shut your eyes and focus."

I press my lids closed, again seeking the swirling storm within. The wind rises instantly, a howl beneath my skin that vibrates along my limbs. Every hair in my body stands on end as

I let the power pulsate. The Remnant is a steady throb at my breast, cold as ice, beating along with my frantic heart.

"Quiet your mind."

I nod as I seek out the eye of the storm, where all is calm and centered. It takes a moment to find my way there through the roiling surf and screaming wind, but once I do, a serenity settles over me. A sort of clarity I only ever feel there, bobbing in tranquil waters as the hurricane circles at a safe distance.

"Good." Penn takes my hands without warning, pressing his large, callused palms firmly against mine. My heart lurches into my throat as a white-hot pulse of power jumps from him to me, like a static shock. In my mind's eye, the water I am floating in warms by several degrees, as though he's blasted fire down the bond between us.

"What—what are you doing?" I breathe, cracking open my eyes to look at him.

He sends another pulse shimmering down the bond. "Do you feel that?"

"Y-yes," I stammer.

"There is a natural symmetry between the maegic that whispers through your veins and that which burns in mine. A tactile connection helps at the beginning when the connection is still . . . new." He pauses. "When you used the bond to find me today, what did it feel like?"

"Like tugging a thread or following an unspooled skein of yarn."

"Faint?"

I nod.

"It will strengthen. Eventually, with a bit of practice, you will be able to locate me much more easily. And to feel my fire, along with my physical presence." Heat blasts down the link again; I start at the sensation of warmth spreading through me. "To channel me, in a sense. And vice versa."

"Channel you?" My heart is thudding madly. "You mean tap into your power?"

"Yes. It is sometimes possible to channel the power of another Remnant."

"Not always?"

"Just as air fuels a fire and water extinguishes it, the four Remnant powers can fuel and feed from one another. There are innate compatibilities. And, with them, innate limitations. Some elements work better in combination than others. For instance, fire and air are . . ."

I arch a brow. "Combustible?"

"They can be, yes. Your power and mine work well together, as air feeds a burgeoning flame to new heights. But when it comes to fire and water . . ." His sun-bronzed shoulders lift in a slight shrug. "Soren and I are not only opposites in personality. Our powers are at opposite poles of the tetrad."

I think of their Remnant marks—Soren's flowing across the left side of his chest, Penn's furling over the right. Their placements mirrored, yet aligned.

"So you can't channel his power? Can't link with him?"

"It would not be easy. Nor, I imagine, comfortable for either of us. Even when we were on better terms, we never found occasion to try."

"You're natural foes, then? Enemies by design?"

"Not foes, exactly. *Foils* would be more accurate. You will likely experience a similar sensation with the Remnant of Earth, if they are ever discovered."

"Why?"

"Earth and air are fundamental opposites, intrinsically at

odds. We are all connected, but some of those connections are more harmonious than others." His hands tighten on mine. "Even within the tetrad, there is a natural balance of power. None of the four can rise unchecked or wield their power uncontrollably, for we each have a foil."

My mind turns this over. It does make sense. "Water to quench fire, earth to tamp air . . ."

He nods. "And flame to boil the flood, wind to stir the soil."

"Does that mean air and water would also be compatible? That if I were to merge with Soren—" My words cut off sharply as a pulse of power—this one hotter, nearly scalding—shoots down the bond at the mention of Soren's name. My wide eyes scan Penn's rage-suffused expression.

Perhaps it is not wise to mention Soren at the present moment.

Penn swiftly recovers from the slip. His nostrils flare and his jaw clenches with effort as he scales back the unexpected heat.

"I'm sorry," I murmur, feeling sweat drip down the back of my neck. My body temperature has yet to regulate from his blast.

"Don't be." There is the ghost of a chuckle. "Here I am trying to teach you control, and I practically lose mine before we've even begun."

"It's okay."

"It's not." His teeth grind together. "It's just what you said—*merge*."

My brows lift. "Is that not the same as channeling?"

"No. It is not. In the time before the Cull . . . to merge with another fae . . ." His eyes lock with mine. "It was akin to a mating bond. An unbreakable, irremovable covenant. A soulmerge."

"Different than the Remnant bonds?"

"Yes." He pauses tightly. "Two separate powers unify into one intractable maegic. A joining of souls that cannot be forced—and cannot ever be undone."

"I've never heard of such a thing."

"Nor would you. Even in the days of the empire, soulmerges were exceedingly rare. Some claim they were no more than legend. Others believe the emperor himself was the product of such a union, that his parents had soulmerged and, in creating him, passed on a potent medley of elemental power."

"Is that even possible?"

"I'm not certain. But it is said he could wield more than one element in his heyday."

"Which ones?" I ask, heart beating rapidly.

There is a bated beat of hesitation. "Fire and air."

Our eyes hold for a long time, neither of us saying any more. Eventually, Penn's hands squeeze mine and he seems to snap out of the daze he's slipped into.

"We've veered off topic. Let us get back to more important things before we lose the daylight. Close your eyes."

I am all too happy to oblige, suddenly desperate to escape the intensity of his gaze. When I've refocused and am once again bobbing in the still waters of my mind, he sends a short blast of heat down the bond.

"You feel it? The pulse?"

I nod.

"Good. Now, I want you to send it back to me."

"What? I can't—"

"You can. Just like you did on the mountain, when you created your air shield to keep the fire at bay. But instead of blasting it physically outward, channel it internally down the bond. Into me."

"What if I send too much?" I ask, nervous at the prospect of losing control. "What if it overwhelms me and—"

"This is a safe place. The sigils carved into the walls of this cavern are wards. Any power you expel here will be absorbed into the volcanic ash. If your control slips, you'll provide the barriers that protect Caeldera with a surplus charge. So even if you fail, you'll be helping. Not hurting."

That soothes me some. My voice is small as I put words to my final worry. "But you're here with me. What if I hurt you? What if—"

"You won't hurt me."

"But—"

"*Trust*, Rhya." His hands tighten almost to the point of pain. "Trust me. Trust yourself."

The dark storm clouds of my power swirl faster, pressing in on me. In the distance, lightning cracks down over the water, a splinter of untempered power. Wind, raw and ravaging, howls in my bones.

"Now," he urges. "Release it. Give it to me."

I do.

It ripples outward, a shock wave blasting through me. Out of me. From my skin. From my soul. As it had on the mountain, but magnified tenfold. Penn jolts backward as it passes through me into him. The bond between us grows taut, pulled tight as a bowstring, screeching under the sheer force of power flowing between us. My hands flex against his, holding on with all my strength, afraid to let go. Afraid, if I lose hold of him, I will also lose hold of the maegic that threatens to overwhelm me.

I try to keep it contained. To keep the power from breaching the confines of my mind. But even as I struggle, the storm clouds that ring that quiet, safe place within turn to pitch, blacking out the sky as they close in from all sides. The waters in which I bob, once warm and still, turn to froth as unpredictable swells churn riotously around me.

I feel the moment I am swept away—feel the moment the cavern around us goes static, the wail of power in my bones, in our bond, turning to a real, visceral howl in the air as incorporeal power turns concrete.

"Rhya!"

My eyes fly open as air tears violently at our clothes, a swirling vortex of mist and dust. Penn is there, chestnut hair whipping around his head, eyes burning into mine. The maegic in them smolders close to the surface. He is holding my hands, absorbing the shock waves of my power. All around us, the wards in the walls are aglow in the gathering dark, scores of red burning against the black volcanic stone as the wind surges out of control.

"Rein it in!" Penn shouts over the screaming gusts. "Find your mind's center!"

But I am lost in it—lost in the storm, lost in the chaos of wind currents that have strengthened so quickly into an uncontrollable tempest. The floodgates are open, just as I feared, and I am ill-equipped to slam them shut again. My head aches as if it is being split in two, the bones of my skull creaking like they will burst apart at any given moment.

I hear Penn shouting my name, calling out commands, but his voice seems to come from a great distance. I can no longer feel the grip of his hands on mine. I can no longer feel anything at all.

Nothing but wind.

Nothing but cold.

At my chest, the Remnant burns. Breath stealing. Blinding. It pulses painfully—once, twice. A third time. And then, just when I think I might die from the agony, just when the thrashing wind threatens to lift us both off our feet and hurl us into the falls . . .

My mind gives way.

Consciousness flickers out.

And I tumble blessedly into darkness.

TWENTY–TWO

I dream again of the great, dark sea. It swirls around me with violent rhythm. Lulling with languorous caresses designed to swallow me whole. To drag me under, to the depths, where no light or sound can permeate.

Strangely, I feel no fear. Even as I sink, disappearing into the colorless fathoms, I am not afraid. Only curious about what, if anything, might await me at the bottom.

I am not destined to find out. Not this time, in any case. For just as the world far above fades out of view, a tether coils around me in the abyss—warm and insistent, tugging me back to the surface.

Back to the air.

Back to consciousness.

A hand skims over my forehead, smoothing back the hair at my temples. *Eli*, I think immediately, my sluggish mind conjuring impossibilities. But no. It cannot be Eli. He is long gone, and besides, the hand that now moves with such halting gentleness over my skin is large and riddled with calluses. And hot. So hot, it sets off a fever inside me, burning low in the pit of my stomach.

The hand moves to my neck. A thumb traces the frail thud of

my pulse as something else grazes my forehead. A pair of lips. They are whisper soft as they press against my skin in a fleeting kiss that lasts no longer than a heartbeat.

Surely, I must still be dreaming.

I am utterly immobile, taking not a single breath, even as the silence stretches into a small eternity. Even as my lungs begin to sear from lack of air. For if this is a dream, I am not yet ready to abandon it. And, if it is not . . .

"I know you're awake."

My eyes flutter open at his soft words.

Penn is there, *right there*, his eyes locked on mine as reality slams back into place. His hand is still at my throat, but he pulls it back when I struggle to sit up on the bed. It takes more effort than it should. Exhaustion sweeps through my body in great, un-yielding waves. He reaches behind me to adjust one of the pillows as I collapse back against the headboard.

Breathing hard from the effort, I take my first look around. I am in the tower. In Penn's bed. I have no recollection of getting here. Heat sears my cheeks at the realization he must've carried me.

"What happened?" My voice cracks.

"You lost control. Then you lost consciousness."

"I remember being in the cavern . . . Trying to call the wind. Trying to contain it . . ." I shake my head. "It was too much. Too much power, too fast to rein it back in."

His fingers flex against the dove-gray blankets that cover me from the waist down. I jerk them a little higher up my body when I realize I'm wearing nothing but a thin white nightgown.

"It's my fault," Penn says bluntly. "I knew you weren't ready. Yet I let you talk me into a lesson you couldn't handle. I let you push yourself past your limits."

"It's not your fault. Like you said, I'm the one who talked you into it."

His jaw tightens. "You asked me to help you. Instead, you wound up hurt—"

"I'm fine. Look at me."

Look he does, eyes scanning my face intently. He appears unconvinced.

"Really. I'm all right." I fight off a yawn. "Nothing about six years of sleep won't cure."

"I'll let you sleep for six decades if it means you stay safe. This is exactly why I did not want you attempting to use your powers."

"I have to learn my limits. If I never explore them, if I walk around blindly suppressing them, as I have for most of my life . . ." I stretch out my arms as I speak, wincing at the soreness of my muscles. "It could end up in a far worse disaster than a bout of unconsciousness. Which you already know. You're just too stubborn to admit it right now."

He scowls at me.

I smile at him. "How long was I asleep, anyway?

"A full day."

I press my lips together, absorbing the news. An improvement over the last time, but not by much. It is nearly dusk outside, twilight slanting through the misty tower windows all around us. My lips curl up at one side. "On the upside, I got to skip another loathsome dinner at court."

His eyes flare with humor, but his grave expression does not so much as flicker. "I take full responsibility for what happened. Next time—if there is a next time—we'll be more careful. Much more careful. I promise."

"I don't blame you, Penn."

Without thinking, I reach out and place my hand on top of

his. His whole frame jolts, a tiny earthquake rocking his bones. With aching slowness, he looks down at my fingers—slim and pale against his sun-bronzed skin. I doubt his expression would be more bewildered if he'd glanced down to find his hand intertwined with an ice giant's.

I tell myself to pull back, to pull away, but my body no longer seems to be cooperating with rational thought. For a long moment we simply sit there, in the twilight stillness, neither of us daring to move or speak.

"You should know, I . . ." Penn hesitates. "If I'd thought for a minute that . . ."

"That what?"

"You have a great deal more power than I was expecting," he admits, almost reluctantly. "For someone with such a limited grasp on her abilities, you are able to expel a great deal of raw strength."

"Really?"

"You nearly hurled me into the godsdamned waterfall."

I blink. "I did?"

"You did."

"I don't remember that."

"That's not surprising. When you let the power course through you unchecked, it overrides all your other senses." His stare turns severe. "That's why I have been stressing the importance of learning to contain it. You're lucky you lost consciousness before it killed you. Before it killed the both of us."

I remember the agony I felt before I passed out in the cavern— the splitting pain that threatened to cleave my head in two. Never in my life have I known such pain. I have little desire to experience it again. Still, I need to learn to use my power properly. Otherwise I risk it lashing out unbidden, and potentially harming anyone in my path when it does.

"So, what now?"

"Now you rest. You recover your strength." He sighs, a soft huff of air. "Then, when I decide the time is right, we try again."

"What if I can't learn to contain it?"

"You will."

"But what if I can't?"

His hand pulls away, leaving mine cold and empty against the blankets. His tone is hard as brimstone. "You will, Rhya. Because you must. I will not see you hurt yourself or anyone else. I will not allow your conscience to be blackened by the consequences of losing control."

"You . . ." I'm almost afraid to ask. "Have you ever lost control, then? Hurt someone with your power unintentionally?"

He nods curtly, lips pressed in a thin line, but does not offer any further explanation. Instead, he pushes to his feet and begins to pace along the footboard of the bed.

I force out the question. "When?"

"A long time ago."

"What happened?"

His head shakes—one sharp jerk of rejection. He appears to be battling inwardly, his hands clenched to tight fists. I wonder how near the surface his fire burns; how close that inferno is to breaking free at any given moment.

For a fraught stretch of time, I stare at him, summoning my courage to speak. "When I was at the Acrine Hold with Soren—"

A muscle leaps in Penn's cheek.

The fire flares in the grate.

I hurry on before I lose my nerve. "He implied that . . ."

"That *what*?"

"That you are somehow responsible for Enid's death."

Penn's stride falters—not quite a stumble, but nearly. Thick silence settles, only the sound of his booted feet against the floorboards to disturb it as he resumes pacing. When he finally speaks, it is with a coarse rasp of self-loathing that makes my heart contract.

"What happened with Enid was the greatest tragedy of my life. And the greatest shame."

I dare not speak.

"She was so fragile. So sheltered. For a girl like her—a girl who had spent her life under lock and key, hidden away from the atrocities of the world—to witness what she did, to live through the horror she suffered . . . Her family slaughtered, her home destroyed . . ." He swallows roughly, the apple bobbing in the broad column of his throat. "She was not equipped to deal with it. It broke something inside her. Cracked her foundation to irreparable pieces. And those cracks . . . They allowed her power to seep out in unpredictable ways. They made her unstable. Not only emotionally. *Elementally.*"

I suck in a breath.

"I thought bringing her here would help save her. I thought I could fix the damage that had been wrought. That, together, Soren and I might somehow repair the parts of her that were shattered, using our powers to keep hers in check. To soothe the raging wind within her before it swept her away completely." He pauses. "But I was wrong. Gravely wrong. And it was Enid who paid the price for my miscalculations. Paid with her life."

My fingers twist in the bedding, so tight my knuckles go white. "She . . . Then, she died because of . . ."

I break off, unable to ask the question. He nods an affirmation, equally unable to answer it.

She died because of him.

She died at his hands.

In the wake of my soul-deep exhaustion, the bond between us has flickered into numb silence. But I do not need a psychic connection to know what he is feeling in this moment. The pain on his face is so sharp, so piercing, it makes my throat catch and my eyes smart. I want to fly across the room to him. To take away his agony any way I can. Yet, I know him well enough to realize any comfort I offer will be spurned.

And so I remain perfectly still, doing nothing to console him as he stands there, balanced on the sword's edge of a particularly cutting part of his past, radiating shame and scorn in waves so thick they make it hard to draw breath. I force myself to hold his eyes, keeping my face free of the condemnation he seems to be waiting for.

He expects me to loathe him for this. To flinch back. To shy away. And there is a part of me that instinctively wants to do just that. But I push that part down, bury it deep. I match his gaze—unblinking, unflinching—until he is the one forced to glance away.

"Soren blamed me," he says finally, staring at the red-veined wall. "Still blames me. He thought himself in love with her, you see. As if someone like him is even capable of love."

"And you?" I ask, a tremble in my voice. "Were you in love with her?"

A biting, bitter scoff flies from his lips. "Who could not love a bird with a broken wing? Who could resist the urge to take her in, to set her bones, to keep her safe until she was strong enough to fly?"

My heart pangs in sympathy—and in something else, something I am both afraid and ashamed to feel. I chew my bottom lip, unable to say a word. I can see Penn's face only in profile. It is carefully empty of emotion as he speaks.

"For a long time, I thought there was nothing I would not do, no length I would not go to, if only to undo it. To rewind that day. To bring her back. To make it right." He sucks in a breath so deep, his whole frame expands. "It is only lately, for the first time in seventy years, that I have felt my first bit of respite from those pointless longings. For if she were still here . . . you would not be."

My heart pangs again, a painful jolt against my rib cage. That low, feverish ache in my abdomen—the one that began the moment I regained consciousness and found him there, mere inches from me on the bed, waiting for me to awaken—intensifies until I can scarcely sit still. "Penn—"

"You need to rest. And I need to get down to the Great Hall. I'm late for Vanora's dinner." He is still not looking at me. "The servants will be up soon with a tray of food for you. When you feel strong enough, they'll draw you a bath."

"Okay," I whisper, hardly knowing what else to say.

"Sleep here. Don't risk climbing the ladder to the spire. You're still too weak."

"Okay."

"Help yourself to the books."

"Okay."

"I will see you in a few days."

"Oka— Wait. Did you say a few da— *Wait!*" I cry, but he's already crossed to the far side of the chamber and stepped through the door. It clicks shut firmly at his back.

Glowering at his high-handed exit, I slide down into the fluffy mass of pillows stacked around me. As I burrow beneath the blankets, I'm annoyed to note that they smell like Penn. Spiced smoke, dark fire. I am even more annoyed to find that there is a part of me that quite likes being here, in his bed, breathing him in with each inhale, my senses engulfed by his lingering presence.

My head is awhirl with thoughts of Enid—for though he told me of her untimely death, it was in but the vaguest of terms. I still have questions. More than I can put words to. Yet they are already slipping from my tired mind as the waves of exhaustion I've been battling since the second my eyes peeled open lull me back beneath their thrall.

Tucked safe and warm beneath the blankets, I allow my eyes to slip shut and fall into a deep slumber. If I dream at all, I do not remember.

⁓

I AM KEPT abed for three endless, excruciating days.

My maids, Keda and Teagan, are lovely women who do their best to keep me happy and healthy as I slowly regain the strength my failed training session sapped away. But even the most kindhearted prison guard is still resented by their prisoners. Especially as the penal sentence stretches on without reprieve.

By the end of the first day, I am physically recovered—the ache gone from my bones, the cold prickle of power gathering once more within my chest, only the slightest hint of fatigue lingering when I overexert myself. By the second afternoon, I am chafing to be released from my increasingly dull confinement. By the third morning, I have abandoned all attempts at civility in favor of brooding in sullen silence—except when asked a direct question, at which point I become so curt and churlish, it is enough to make me flinch.

I tell myself that my general grouchiness has nothing at all to do with the absence of a certain cantankerous prince. For Pendefyre has not shown his face even once since I first awoke and found myself in his bed. I wonder where he is sleeping—and, in weaker moments, whom he might be sleeping with, as Vanora's serpentine voice snakes an ugly path through my head.

I do hope she's not another one of your whores. The last one made such a spectacle of herself when you grew tired of her charms.

It does not matter whose bed he sleeps in. It is no business of mine. Yet I am unquestionably irritable as the days creep on without a visit from him—a sensation that only intensifies when I realize I can no longer sense his presence through our bond. Not a flicker, no matter how long I sit on the settee by the fireplace and cast out my senses in search.

Just when I was beginning to grow accustomed to the invisible tether between us, it's vanished with an abruptness that makes my eyes sting unpleasantly. I narrow them into a scowl—rage is a safer emotion than anything else I might be feeling—which I then direct at the empty spot on the desk where a gleaming black battle helm once sat beside a bandolier of slim, lethal blades.

Keda, ever observant, notices my dark look and promptly informs me that the prince has left the city on official business.

"No doubt seeing to some of the Fyremas preparations," she breezes, running a boar-bristle brush through my hair in long strokes from the crown of my head all the way to the ends where they fall against the small of my back. "It's only a fortnight away. The whole castle is in an uproar getting everything ready. I'm sure the prince is as busy as the rest of us."

"When will he be back?"

"No rightly idea, miss. Don't fret, it's nothing unusual. He's often away from the keep settling trade disputes, or consulting with Commanding General Yale in the northern provinces, or attending diplomatic summits in other kingdoms . . ."

"Oh."

"Now that he's returned, His Highness will be resuming most of his responsibilities outside the capital. More than before, I'd guess, seeing as the queen has no heirs and Her Royal Majesty does not often stray far from the keep, being of advancing years and failing health. We won't be seeing much of Prince Pendefyre around here for a while, I reckon."

The news makes my heart clench in a completely unwarranted manner. I try—with questionable success—not to sound too crestfallen when I ask if he'll be back for the festival.

"Most certainly," she assures me. "He never misses Fyremas."

"What is Fyremas, exactly?"

"Did your old kingdom not celebrate the equinox, Lady Rhya?"

I shake my head.

"What a shame! It's the most wonderful of days." The brush hits a snag and she pauses her ministrations momentarily. "It marks the start of the spring thaw and the recharging of the wards around the city. There's a ceremony where the prince . . . Well, I won't ruin the surprise for you. Best to experience it for yourself." Her wink is quick. "Afterward, there are parades in the streets, processions of flowers and flame-dancers. Food and drink everywhere you look. Musical performances from Dyved's best bards and minstrels. Oh and *fires*, of course! Everyone lights the torches in front of their houses and leaves them burning all night, dusk till dawn, so the streets are lined with flames." She sighs dreamily. "There's even a fireworks display over the lake at midnight. Have you ever seen fireworks?"

"No."

"You'll just love them. They're dazzling to behold." Her smile flashes bright in the reflective surface of the age-fogged mirror as she resumes brushing. "Of all the festivals, Fyremas is my favorite. Though I expect it's most folks' favorite."

"People are happy to bid winter farewell."

"True. Especially in towns on the upper plateau, where the snows are deep and the air is chill. We're lucky to be spared the worst of the frost here in the capital."

"Handy to have a Fire Remnant for your prince, infusing the whole city with maegical warmth."

"Indeed, miss. Indeed." Her smile widens. "But that's a big part of why Fyremas is so popular. It's the prince's personal holiday."

My brows shoot up. "He has a *personal* holiday?"

"It's mostly to celebrate the start of the new planting season, like I said. But it's become something of a tribute to Prince Pendefyre over the years. You see, no matter how long he was away, he'd always make a point to come home to Caeldera at Fyremas to recharge the wards that protect us. Always. No exceptions. Some years, that was the only time we saw him for ten or eleven months." Her brush stills against my scalp and her expression turns solemn. "We're all very glad to have His Highness home for a longer spell, now that he's finally finished his work in the south. Now that . . . well, now that he's found you, miss."

My fingertips dig into the fabric of my gown.

"Listen to me prattling on." Keda shakes her head and resumes brushing. "I'm sorry. I'm chatty by nature. My ma always says I could out-jabber a blue jay."

"Don't apologize."

Her eyes widen suddenly. "Oh! You'll be needing a dress."

If I look confused by her sudden proclamation, it is because I already have a whole rack of new dresses, carefully delivered into Penn's wardrobe by my maids during the first day of my captivity. I gesture down at the simple ivory gown they've dressed me in today. "I'll just wear this one."

"Oh no, miss. That won't do. That won't do at all. You're the Remnant of Air! You'll be at the very front during the ceremony. Likely during the fyre priestesses' procession afterward, as well. A position of great honor—one that calls for more than a plain old day dress, that's for certain.

"Day dresses are all I have," I tell her, even as the image of the many-hued blue Llŷrian gown flashes in my mind. "It will have to do."

"I'll make some inquiries with the royal dressmakers. See if they've made any plans for you."

"That's not necessary. Really. I don't want to be a burden here."

"Oh, miss, I didn't mean to imply—"

"You didn't imply anything of the sort." I shoot her a reassuring smile. But it must not have the intended effect, as Keda lapses into troubled silence—and remains so as she finishes arranging my hair, then scurries out the door without a backward glance at me.

Several times throughout the day, I catch her in hushed conversation with Teagan, the two of them whispering to each other as they eye me across the chamber. It makes me uneasy and, despite my best efforts to remain upbeat, likely contributes to my increasingly vexed disposition as yet another night falls with no sign of their dearly beloved crown prince.

⌒‿

LOCKED AWAY IN my turret, I finally find the time to crack open the book Soren gave me when I left the Acrine Hold. The first chapter is a rather dry account of things I already know, about the Cull and the fall of the empire. With my recent conversation about the elemental courts fresh in my mind, I skip ahead until I find a section discussing them.

My eyes scan the page, drinking in the bold letters.

> Before the Cull, the four elemental strongholds of Anwyvn stood for thousands of years in their respective locations. Ruled by the emperor's appointed sovereigns, whose reigns sometimes lasted for centuries, each House eventually established its own unique cultural practices, criminal proceedings, and court hierarchies.

Interesting, if not entirely new information.

I keep reading.

> Prior to their sackings, the strongholds were considered by many to be impenetrable. Yet, two of the four would fall almost immediately when the empire was overthrown. A more complete account of the individual battles can be found in Chapter XXVI.

In the margins someone has scribbled an addendum to this paragraph in sloping masculine script. *Skip Chapter XXVI. Bloody dry read. Spends more time describing bulwark structure than actual battle strategy.*

I can almost hear Soren's deep, melodious voice whispering the words into my ear. From a full kingdom away, he feels annoyingly present in the room with me.

I roll my eyes and read on.

> Below, you will find a chronicle of the four elemental houses, detailing their unique characteristics, from climate to culture to court dynamics. For an in-depth list of lineages and leadership, please refer to Chapter XLIII.

Skip XLIII, too. Nothing but an endless list of old, dead fae who didn't have the sense to see the Cull coming.

I jerk my eyes away from Soren's snarky advice and steer them back to the pertinent subject matter. The chapter is divided into four main sections, each discussing one of the elemental courts. I skim the first avidly, my curiosity too strong to suppress for another moment.

HOUSE OF LLŶR: THE WATER COURT

Located in the easternmost stretch of the Northlands, the prominent kingdom of Llŷr has long been
the source of aqueous maegic. Ruled from the island city of Hylios, the vast territory includes the
semiautonomous regions of Daggerpoint and Prydain. Despite numerous conquest attempts by mortals, the Water Court remains intact to this day.

SIGIL: The Drowning Sun
SOVEREIGN: King Soren, Remnant of Water
HEIR: None (potential bastards remain unknown
to this author at the time of printing but cannot be
entirely discounted as a possibility)

My eyes slide of their own accord to the margins, where Soren
has scribbled, *Rather judgmental, this author, is he not?* I suppress
a smile—my first in days, since I found myself in seclusion.

There are a few more paragraphs detailing the ins and outs of
Hylios, but I move impatiently past them to the next prominent
section.

HOUSE OF DYVED: THE FIRE COURT

Sprawling across the westernmost corner of the
Northlands, the snowbound kingdom of Dyved sits
atop an elevated plateau that stretches from the
North Sea to the Cimmerian Mountains. As the
home of fire maegic, it is perhaps especially fitting
that the capital city of Caeldera should sit within
the crater of a long-dormant volcano. The unique
geographical formations of the kingdom keep it

shielded from invasion attempts by numerous Reaver clans in the west, who occupy the neighboring ice shelf, as well as the marauding Frostlanders, who regularly encroach from the east.

SIGIL: The Flaming Mountain
STEWARD: Queen Vanora
HEIR: Crown Prince Pendefyre, Remnant of Fire

Next to Penn's title, Soren has tacked on, *And pompous git*. I sink my teeth into my lip to smother a chuckle and move on to the next section. The smile fades as my eyes process the words I am reading.

HOUSE OF TARANIS: THE SKY COURT

The so-called Court of Clouds was once considered the most beautiful of the four maegical strongholds. After the kingdom of Taranis fell during the Cull, many of its unique structures were reduced to rubble. The ruins are located in the southwestern region of Anwyvn, bordered by Lake Lumen and the Westerly Sea, in a territory currently occupied by mortals.

SIGIL: The Falling Star
SOVEREIGN: Queen Arianrhod (killed in battle defending her throne)
HEIRS: None (all deceased)

Soren has not written any pithy notes in the margins here. Perhaps he knew I would be in no mood to jest after reading about my own court's destruction. I am so unsettled, I can do no more than glance at the fourth section, which is labeled **HOUSE OF AMAETHON: THE EARTH COURT**, before I close the cover with a dull thud.

My spirits were already low enough before the rather depressing reading session. They plummet farther as I set the book aside. It is my fourth morning of seclusion. I watch Teagan and Keda toweling up the tepid water that runs across the tiles over the top of my untouched breakfast tray. My offers to help them sop up the mess after my morning bath had been gently but firmly rebuffed, as had all my previous attempts to aid in tidying the tower, dressing myself, brushing my hair. I'm surprised they permit me to lift the spoon to my own mouth while eating my porridge.

Inside, I'm quietly seething that Penn has left me up here to rot. One day of rest was plenty restorative. This forced confinement only serves to make me crazed. My hands itch for my bow. For the comforting monotony of grinding herbs in my mortar and pestle. For the busywork of formerly avoided chores in Eli's tidy stockroom, if only to occupy the infinite hours that tick by with mind-melting slowness. My appetite—for food, for amusement, for life itself—has withered into nothing.

"You've not touched your breakfast, miss," Teagan chastises, calling me out of my reverie as she drops her wet towel in the bucket and bustles over to me. "You must eat."

"I'm not hungry."

"Still, you must eat. You need to regain your strength. Prince Pendefyre instructed—"

"Oh, I don't give a fig what he instructed. Another day locked up here, I'll hurl myself from the balcony just for a change of scenery."

Teagan wrings her hands. Her curls are escaping her kerchief again. "Miss, you mustn't say such—"

"I did have an idea," Keda interjects. "Something we could do . . ."

"Keda!" Teagan hisses warningly. "As we've discussed already, it's not an option."

I perk up. "What's the idea?"

"Our chat yesterday got me thinking. There's a dressmaker here in the city—an old friend of mine from our early years of schooling. She's married to a member of the Ember Guild, so we don't see much of each other anymore. Different social circles, you understand." The brown skin of her cheeks tinges pink, but she perseveres. "We still keep in touch every now and then. And I just know, if I bring you to her, she'll be honored to create a dress fit for the Remnant of Air."

"Keda," Teagan scolds. "You know Queen Vanora has a gown being prepared for her already by the royal dressmakers!"

"She does?" I ask.

Keda's slim face contorts in a grimace. "*That* awful thing? You cannot be serious! It's the color of pus! Not at all suited to Lady Rhya's coloring. Not that you'll even be able to see her face with so many ruffles at the collar . . ."

My lips twist. "How very . . . considerate . . . of Her Royal Majesty to think of me."

"You're a lovely woman. You'll look . . ." Even while wringing her hands in distress, Teagan cannot bring herself to lie. "You'll make the best of it, no matter what the gown looks like."

"She's to be presented to the whole city!" Keda practically screeches. "You'd have her look like a pustule?"

"Don't put words in my mouth, Keda! You know I don't want Lady Rhya looking like a pustule!"

"I also would prefer not to look like a pustule," I chime in. "For the record."

They both ignore me, busy glaring at each other.

"Are we certain I even have to attend?"

"You have to attend," they say in unison.

"Then I vote we pay this dressmaker friend a visit." I rise to my feet. "Gods know, right now, I'd walk to the guillotine just for a chance to stretch my legs."

"It's settled, then. We'll pay her a call this afternoon. You can speak to her while we run our errands at the market, and we'll collect you on our way home."

Teagan makes one final appeal. "The prince won't be pleased when he hears of this . . ."

Keda plants her hands on her hips in defiance. "What do you think will displease the prince more—returning to find she's slipped out of the tower for a few hours under our close supervision? Or splattered against the rocks beneath the falls because she's been driven mad by boredom in his absence?"

"I'm guessing the latter," I murmur.

Both women studiously ignore me for the second time in as many minutes.

"Come now, Teagan. Surely you can agree she's in need of some diversion," Keda wheedles. "I don't see the harm in it. We'll be with her the whole time!"

"But the prince—"

"Stay here, then!" Keda throws up her hands in frustration. "If you're so worried about breaking protocol, stay here. We'll be gone but a few hours."

"I'm not staying here! Gods only know what kind of trouble the two of you will find yourselves in without me there to talk you out of it!"

And so we go—the three of us, together. No one moves to stop us as we make our way down the many stairs and through the drafty stone passages of the keep below. No one pays us any

mind whatsoever. Keda was right; everyone is far too busy preparing for the upcoming festival to notice two brown-clad maids
and their blue-cloaked charge slipping out the front gates and
hurrying across the bridge.

The minute the sun hits my face, my spirits soar. To either
side of us, the lake sparkles like facets of a teal gemstone. We pass
a fleet of arriving tradesmen, their horse-drawn wagons piled
high with foodstuffs, flowers, fireworks, fresh vegetables, and
festive decorations. Some are strapped down with cages of chick-
ens, geese, and other live fowl; others have pigs leashed behind
them, waddling to their deaths with smiling snouts. The line of
merchants stretches nearly the length of the bridge, all waiting
for their chance to unload at the front gates.

The market is similarly crowded—even more so than the
first time I saw it, each stall packed with shoppers. Keda marches
through the bustle with a purposeful stride, clearing a path with
the sheer force of her gaze. People scurry out of our way like
cockroaches in torchlight. With her in the lead, it does not take
us long to clear the throng.

Only moments later, we are in a part of town I've never been
before. The streets are cobbled, the sidewalks lined with flickering
lampposts. The buildings are cramped close together, one running
right into the next—a mix of shops and storage depots, narrow alleyways and stone-faced warehouses. We bypass a stately bank
building, where a constant stream of patrons flows in and out the
tall front doors, exchanging crowns from fat purses at their belts.

Eventually, we turn off the main thoroughfare onto a pleasant
avenue lined with squat manicured trees and several glass-
fronted shops that exude elegance. I note an apothecary, a cobbler, and a delicious-smelling chocolatier before we come to a
stop outside a pale blue building at the end of the block.

Several fabulous ball gowns are on display in the window, a blend of intricate beading, bold cuts, and eye-catching needle-work. One looks like a golden bird in flight, with a feathered bodice and fluttering wing sleeves. Another seems fit for a mermaid beneath the sea, with a pearl-lined bodice and a long train of shiny disks that shine like scales. The front door is propped open to allow the breeze inside. The wooden shingle hanging above it declares PREMIER CLOTHIER in ornate carved letters.

"This is it," Keda announces, stopping abruptly. "Carys's shop."

"Carys? Your friend is called Carys?"

"Do you know her, miss?" Teagan asks.

"No," comes a lilting voice from the doorway, where a woman has just appeared. Her shiny black hair is braided in a perfect circlet, her light-green eyes are glittering with warmth, and her hands rest on her heavily pregnant stomach. "But she knows my husband quite well."

CHAPTER
TWENTY-THREE

"W elcome, Rhya." Carys extends a hand of welcome. "I've heard so much about you."

I clasp her palm against mine, smiling tentatively back at her. "I wish I could say the same, but truthfully I had no idea this was your shop."

"Small world, isn't it?" Keda steps forward to greet her childhood companion with a light embrace. "You're a bit rounder than the last time we met, old friend."

"And you're cheeky as ever!" Carys grins. "Seeing as it takes having a baby to get you to pay a visit."

"I had no idea you were expecting! You should've written."

"When I next find a spare minute that my fingers are not hemming a bodice or threading a needle, you'll get a lengthy letter."

"Forgive me if I don't hold my breath. I know how busy you are." Keda heaves a guilty sigh. "I hate to pile on your workload, but we're not here for a social call. This is official business with the best dressmaker in town. Lady Rhya is in dire need of a gown for Fyremas. It seems the royal dressmakers are hard at work on a ruffled yellow monstrosity—no doubt following Her Majesty's orders to make her look as ridiculous as possible during the procession."

"That does indeed sound like a scheme our magnanimous queen would concoct." Carys glances at me. "Don't worry. We'll find something better suited for you. There's no time to make something from scratch, but I have several gowns in my inventory that can be altered before the festival."

"Truly, I don't want to cause—"

"You're an angel, Carys!" Keda cuts me off, beaming. "I knew we were right to come to you."

"Do make sure to tell the incensed royal dressmakers of my angelic character when they discover I've subverted their efforts." Her hand sweeps the air, beckoning us forward. "By all means, come inside."

Keda's lips flatten in remorse. "I wish we could stay, but Teagan and I have errands to run at the market. It's chaos at the palace, pure chaos. We've a list of orders a league long. We'll head off now, then circle back in an hour or so to collect Lady Rhya."

"Only if you're up for company, Carys," I interject. "If you're too tired—"

The dressmaker waves away my words. "I'm delighted to have some company."

After we bid Keda and Teagan farewell, Carys ushers me into the shop, sage eyes twinkling with happiness, gait shuffling from the heavy burden she carries. It is a bright, clean space stocked with fabric—bolts and bolts of it lean against the wall, along with dozens of bundles of satin ribbons and lace trimmings. There are spools of thread in every conceivable color, racks of needles of every length and thickness. Several completed gowns are displayed on the hanging racks, their designs just as elegant and eccentric as the ones in the window. Others are pinned in various stages of development against fabric mannequin forms near the back.

"Your shop is lovely, Carys."

She shoots me a warm glance as she leads me to a cozy sitting area by an array of floor-to-ceiling mirrors, furnished with two upholstered chaises and a matching set of armchairs.

Carys promptly collapses into one of the chairs. "You'll have to pardon my lack of hospitality. I'm usually a much better hostess, but in this condition . . ." She grimaces down at her protruding stomach. "I feel ready to pop and there are still weeks to go."

"When are you due?" I ask as I settle across from her.

"A fortnight. Just in time for Fyremas."

"You must be very excited."

"To be able to see my feet again? Tie my laces? Go for more than an hour without using the toilet?" She snorts. "Surely."

I laugh. "Uther is bursting with pride. I've never seen him smile so much as when he spoke of you and your child."

"*Och!* If he had his way, I'd be confined to my bed under lock and key for the next two weeks, the scoundrel. I told him: I'm carrying a child, not a cargo of explosives. A bit of movement is healthy."

"He worries."

"He *hovers.*" She scowls, but I can see the love blazing in her eyes. "Though I suppose I can't complain about that at the moment. He's off on a mission with the Ember Guild. Don't tell him—I'll never admit it if you do—but I'm actually bored to tears without him here to monitor my every sneeze and hiccup."

"Will they be back soon?"

"A few days, I should think." Her eyes glitter knowingly. "Eager to see Prince Pendefyre again, are you? I've heard you two are quite inseparable."

"I—" My cheeks flame. "No, I—"

"Are you truly staying in his chambers?"

"Well, yes, but it's not—"

"Oh, look how red you are! I'm sorry! I'm only teasing. Terrible of me, when you're the first diversion I've had all day." She heaves a sigh. "Truth be told, I have no real notion of when the men will be back. All I know is that there was another earthquake a few days ago near the border, not far from the range."

"I didn't know the quakes had moved so far north," I murmur, brow furrowing at the news. Land tremors were far from uncommon in the Midlands. Eli had told me they were even worse in the far south—strong enough to flatten whole towns. But that was not the case in the Northlands.

At least, not until now.

"I've lived in Dyved all my life, and never have there been so many tremors as in the past few years." Carys shakes her head slowly back and forth. "Many are saying it is a bad omen of things to come. A warning that the blight is spreading more quickly, creeping past the mountains that have protected us for so long."

"This quake, was it a very strong one?"

"Apparently strong enough to trigger an avalanche. An entire trading post at the base of the mountains was buried in snow and ice."

"That's terrible." I expel a short breath. "Were there any survivors?"

"I expect the Ember Guild went to find out just that. That's what they do when they aren't off fighting some campaign or other against the Reavers and Frostlanders. They go where they're most needed, often at a moment's notice, whenever the prince asks."

"Asks?" My brows arch. "*Commands* would be more accurate, would it not?"

"Perhaps you're right. His men would follow him out of sovereign duty. But I suspect even without a royal title, they would follow Pendefyre to the ends of the earth. He has long since earned their fealty. He is a good man." She pauses. "Surely, you know that better than anyone."

I keep silent, at a loss for words.

Her green eyes are sharp as blades, belying the softness of her voice. "Did you know, before the avalanche took him south, he spent two full days going door to door through the city, visiting the widows and widowers of Uther's slain unit? Every man and woman who lost a husband against the Reavers; every child who lost a father. More than thirty households."

"No," I breathe. "No, I didn't know."

"The bodies were retrieved from the Cimmerians and delivered for exequies the same day you arrived here. Uther told me the prince personally arranged and attended each funeral."

My throat feels oddly thick. I swallow hard to clear it.

"Many of those widowed are my friends. So I feel confident sharing with you how much it meant to them to have their prince there as the pyres burned and the ashes scattered. To have their men put to rest properly. To give such senseless loss a purpose." She studies me carefully. "Prince Pendefyre is a good leader and an even better friend. He may not be a perfect gentleman, he may across as gruff and arrogant and short-tempered . . . but there is a heart that beats behind the thick defensive walls he shields himself with." Her lips twist wryly. "One must merely be clever at climbing."

"His heart does not beat," I mutter under my breath. "It bleeds like an open wound."

"What was that?"

My gaze moves back to hers and I raise my voice to an audible level. "He does not want me scaling his walls any more than I want him burrowing under mine."

"Are you sure about that?"

I hesitate for a long beat—long enough for Carys to clap her hands together and change the subject.

"In any case, they've gone to aid however they can. I expect they'll be gone at least a week. But so long as Uther returns before the little one makes his or her grand debut, I'll be glad enough."

"If he is not back in time, do you have anyone to be with you?"

"I have a girl—an apprentice of sorts—who comes each morning to tidy the shop and check in on me. Though she has precious little to do these days. I'm not taking on any new commissions until after I've delivered."

I nod. "And your family? Are they close by?"

"My parents passed on several years ago, as did Uther's."

"I'm sorry."

She looks down at her stomach. "It will be nice to be more than just the two of us around here. Gods willing, the delivery will be an easy one."

Gods willing.

The few births I attended in the past had been many things—*easy* least among them. I try to keep the worry from my voice as I inquire about the city's midwives.

"There are several who live within a half day's ride," she assures me. "All quite skilled. And then there's the Life Guild—the city's healers—if things go truly awry. I'll be in good hands when the time comes. I just . . . I don't want Uther to miss the birth. We tried for so many years to conceive, but the gods did not see fit to bless us until this year." Her eyes grow a bit misty as her hands stroke her stomach. "In many ways, this child is our miracle. And should he or she be our *only* miracle, my husband should be here to witness it."

"I'm sure he'll be back in time."

She forces a smile through her gathering emotions. "Och! Look at me, sappy as a maple tree. You'll have to trust me when I say I'm usually made of sterner stuff. These days, I cry at the drop of a hat."

"There's no need to apologize, Carys. It's quite common for expectant mothers to grow emotional as the delivery approaches."

"Of course, you'd know of such things. Uther said you are an accomplished healer."

"I have some skill."

"Just *some*? I saw Farley's splint when he hobbled over for a visit the other day. You did a fine job. Thanks to you, he'll walk without a limp. Even ride again someday. He didn't stop singing your praises until Pendefyre threatened to rebreak his legs." She giggles. "It made for much more interesting conversation than their usual talk of weaponry and war tactics."

My brows arch. "Do they often meet in your shop?"

"Not in the shop, but above it. Uther and I live in the apartments upstairs. The prince's closest advisers often wind up sitting round my table through the wee hours, discussing the ins and outs of soldiering. Though, in recent days, you've been a more frequent topic of conversation."

"Me?"

"Oh, yes. You have a burgeoning fan club among the Ember Guild. They're all exceedingly fond of you." She pauses. "Well, not Gower, but I wouldn't take that personally. He's not fond of anyone. And you're likely to get the worst of it, seeing as he's been ordered to stay behind and watch over you."

This is news. "He has?"

"On direct orders from the prince himself."

"I've seen no sign of him."

"Mmm. Keeps to the shadows, that one. Always skulking about like a vampyre." Pausing, Carys arches one slender black brow at me. "Surely you did not think the prince would leave you here completely unattended?"

I had, in fact. "A girl can hope."

"Don't look so sour. He cares about you." Her lips curl in a playful smile. "Though I can't say how much, since it's Gower he left behind to watch over your welfare. Miserable fellow. I've known him for years, never seen him crack so much as a smile."

"I'm glad it's not just me who makes his eyes shoot daggers."

"Not at all. He rarely fraternizes with the other guild members, so it shouldn't be difficult to avoid him. Next time they all crowd into my kitchen, you'll come along. You can keep me company while they prattle on."

"I doubt Penn will allow that. If he had his way, I'd spend the rest of my life locked in the palace." My eyes narrow. "Which is totally hypocritical, seeing as he himself spends as little time there as physically possible."

"He's never been one for court. He and his sister do not get on well. They are very different in temperament—and in their priorities for the kingdom. The prince, for instance, has always taken a special interest in his subjects, whether they are here in the capital or on the farthest reaches of the plateau. Whereas the queen, throughout the course of her exceedingly long reign, usually cannot be bothered to peel her eyes away from her vanity mirror long enough to help anyone. There are few who will miss her when she finally vacates the throne." She grins suddenly. "*King Pendefyre* has a lovely ring to it, don't you think?"

I start. I have not allowed myself to properly consider the fact that Penn will one day rule the entire kingdom. Another weight on his shoulders, another responsibility to bear. It is a wonder his knees do not buckle beneath the strain of it all.

"What is it?" Carys asks softly. "You look distressed."

"I'm fine. I just . . ." I shake my head to clear it. "Keda told me the Fyremas Festival is essentially his personal holiday. I'm beginning to understand why he is so beloved here."

"It's true, Fyremas has become something of a tribute to him. I'm sure it will pale in comparison to his wedding day."

My eyes drop to the elegant rug by my feet. My pulse is suddenly pounding quite fast. "Is he to be married soon, then?"

When Carys doesn't answer after a few excruciating seconds, I glance up to find her grinning at me again. "Why?" she probes, eyes twinkling. "Would you be bothered?"

"Of course not! It's no business of mine." My cheeks are aflame. "I'm not even sure why I asked."

"I know precisely why you asked." Peals of laughter spill from her lips. "Oh, you've gone bright red again. That was the last of my teasing, I promise. Besides, we should move on to more important business—finding you something exquisite to wear for Fyremas." She thrusts out a hand and waggles her fingers. "Help me up, would you?"

Rising from the chaise, I eye her speculatively. "You don't have to do this, you know."

"Of course I know. I don't do anything I don't want to do. Just ask my husband."

I snort. *Poor Uther.*

"I want to do this," Carys declares adamantly. "Firstly, because I'm bored out of my skull. Secondly, because I heard all about Queen Vanora's attempts to humble you at her banquet by dressing you like a servant. And thirdly because it would give me no greater pleasure than to undermine the royal dressmakers and their precious Stitch Guild, who traipse through this city as though their needles are made of solid gold and their patterns are drawn by the gods themselves."

I snort again.

"Now, are you going to help me up? Or must I struggle to my feet like a fish on dry land?"

Grinning, I grasp her hand and help her up.

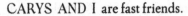

CARYS AND I are fast friends.

After that first afternoon, visiting her shop becomes a daily ritual. Everyone at the palace is far too busy with Fyremas preparations to keep close watch over me. Even Teagan and Keda have been pulled into the fray, appearing only in the early morning to deliver my breakfast tray and at the very end of the night to drop off my dinner. I may be fully recovered, but not so much that I will brave the Great Hall on my own. I plan to keep taking meals in the tower for as long as I can get away with it.

If anyone questions me about my activities beyond the palace walls, I have the perfect excuse to return to the shop on High Street: Carys is gradually altering the dress we've chosen. Originally designed for a much taller woman, it needs all manner of hemming and tucking to fit my petite frame.

In truth, I would happily visit even without the alibi of alterations. I have never before had a proper friend. Carys is a decade older than me, but we get along like we shared a womb. She has a quick wit and sharp eyes, laughs often, and teases me mercilessly when the occasion suits her.

It suits her often.

At Uther's insistence, she's stopped taking on new couture commissions as her due date approaches. Without work to busy her hands or a constant stream of customers to keep her entertained, Carys is nearly as bored as I've been locked alone in my tower.

We pass our time chatting and sipping cups of herbal tea, either in the shop's cozy sitting area or upstairs in the elegantly decorated living quarters. The apartments are small but homey, warm in all the ways the palace is cold. Carys's taste is flawless, from the tapestries on the walls to the meticulously arranged antique furnishings to the lovingly decorated nursery she's prepared for her child. I feel at ease there—more at ease than I have in many months.

In her calm, quick-to-smile presence, it is easy to share stories of my childhood in Seahaven. I tell her of Eli's cottage with its lopsided shutters and sprawling gardens. Of my favorite beach, where the sand was so white it looked at times like Cimmerian snow. Of the Starlight Wood, a hallowed place of ancient power, where the tree bark glowed even in darkness and the leaves were veined with silver. I even tell her of Tomas, my ill-fated summer romance, destined to end whether or not he survived the burning of my village.

In return, she tells me stories of her own formative years in Caeldera, growing up the daughter of a foot soldier and a seamstress, elevated to her current social standing through her marriage to Uther—who is, I learn, a distant relation to the royal family. Vanora's cousin—albeit several times removed. Sometimes, she tells me stories about the Ember Guild's many campaigns and conquests. She is careful not to harp overmuch on anything related to Penn. I think she can tell speaking of him only serves to upset, anger, or embarrass me.

I quickly become accustomed to our effortless camaraderie. Which is perhaps why on my fifth visit to High Street, when Carys leads me into the sitting area, I am stunned to see she has another guest already there sipping tea. Even before I see the crutches leaned against the chaise or the copper hair shining in the midday sun, I hear the warm boom of his voice shouting my nickname.

"Ace!"

Farley—left behind by all his friends in the Ember Guild

while he recovers, and openly seething about it—is as desperate for company as me and Carys. Perhaps more so. Thus, we fold him into our daily ritual, our party of two becoming three. Soon to be four, given the dressmaker's ever-expanding girth.

I eye her with a healer's concern when she is not looking and cast silent prayers to the gods above that Uther is already home-bound. She is carrying low. The babe will not come in weeks but mere days, if I have to wager.

"You look exhausted," I tell her bluntly when she pulls open the door a week after our first meeting. I duck inside without preamble—it is raining hard, and the parcel I clutch beneath my cloak is in danger of getting drenched.

"Probably because I am." Her face contorts in a mask of dis-comfort. There are deep circles beneath her eyes. "The babe has been kicking nonstop since yesterday afternoon. I didn't get a lick of sleep."

"You should rest. I'll come back tomorrow."

"Don't you dare! I've not seen another living soul all day. Be-sides, I'm quite used to being tired. I doubt I've had a decent night's sleep since Uther was promoted into the upper ranks."

"You worry about him."

"I do, though there's no need for it. He's so skilled, so capa-ble." She sighs as she leads me to the narrow staircase at the back of the shop. "Gods, but I love that man. I can't blame the prince for promoting him. He recognizes talent. Rewards it, too."

I help her climb the stairs to the apartments, keeping one hand on her back for support. Through the fabric of her gown, I can feel the rapid flutter of her breathing. This short climb will soon be too strenuous for her to manage. By the time we reach the upper landing, she has to lean against the wall to catch her breath.

"Sorry," she rasps, panting hard. "The stairs—"

"You shouldn't be going up and down, Carys. It's not good

for you to exert yourself like this. You'd be better off resting in bed."

She waves away my words, pushes off the wall, and waddles into the parlor room. Leaving her to recover on the sofa, I walk straight into the kitchen and put on the kettle, as has become our custom. I retrieve two mugs from the cupboard above the sink and spoon a lump of sugar into each one while the water boils. I do not use the tea leaves Carys typically favors, instead pulling out the tin of herbs from the parcel I brought along with me.

The stop I'd made at the apothecary down the block cost me all the coin I won wagering on my archery skills, plus the handful I found rattling around the bottom of Penn's desk drawer. I figure he will not notice it missing. Even if he does, I have no qualms about my thievery. It is for a good cause. And if eight crowns are enough to break the royal bank, he has bigger problems to contend with.

Carys is still breathing heavily when I return to her, color high on her cheeks. Her face screws up in disgust when she takes a sip of tea.

"*Och!* That's not chamomile!"

I sip my own steaming cup—plain peppermint—and smile. "No, it isn't."

"What is this dreadful concoction?"

"Goldenrod and gingerroot. It will help with the swelling in your feet."

"It tastes like dirt."

I shrug, unbothered. "No Farley today?"

"The rain must have kept him at the barracks. I'm surprised you made the trek down from the palace. It's pouring buckets out there."

I squish my toes inside my sodden boots. "I don't mind the rain. It matches my mood of late."

She takes another sip of her tea and grimaces. "Mmm. And

would this unhappy attitude have anything to do with the continued absence of a certain man with a penchant for fire?"

"*No.*" I grit my teeth. "It's not about Penn. It's my utter lack
of purpose here."

"Perhaps purposelessness can be your purpose."

"Clever."

"Have you been back to the cavern behind the falls?"

I press my lips closed, knowing my answer will displease her.
The past few mornings when I set off to walk to her shop, my feet
have turned me in a different direction—leading me not across
the bridge, away from the keep, but behind it, into the thick mist
of the thundering falls. Up a flight of slick stone steps. Into an
ancient cavern with glyph-gouged walls.

When I'd been there with Penn, the glyphs were aglow, red
as the tips of a blacksmith's tongs left too long in the forge. Now
they are quiet and still, the same gray-black shade of petrified ash
that characterizes the rest of Caeldera's foundations. And yet, as
I lift my hand to trace the indecipherable patterns, I feel a deep
thrum of maegic beneath the tip of my finger.

I spend hours meditating in the cavern, seeking out the inner
point of stillness inside my head as the water cascades all around
me. It is growing easier to locate the eye of the hurricane; to im-
merse myself in the calm waters at the center of the cyclone. But
even as I bob there undisturbed, I never lose awareness of the
danger surrounding me, not so far in the distance. Pressing in
with the dark promise of infinite power—and unimaginable pain.

Penn wants me to learn to tame that storm. To draw it close
and somehow hold it, like a breath pulled deep into one's lungs
but never released. It seems impossible to contemplate, let alone
achieve. Regardless, I have to try. After hearing his story of
Enid, the stakes are too high not to attempt.

I will learn to keep the gate shut, I tell myself over and over, jaw clenched with determination. *I will learn to contain this brewing storm inside.*

There is no other choice.

Carys frowns at me, gleaning the truth from the stretching silence. "I don't think going there on your own is a good idea, Rhya."

"You've made your thoughts on the matter quite clear, Carys."

"After what happened the last time, I can't believe you're even thinking about testing your powers again. What if you slip up? What if you get hurt?"

"I'm not going to lose control again."

"You seem quite confident for a girl who recently spent a full day unconscious." She narrows her green eyes at me. "I'm going to be exceedingly annoyed if all my hard work altering your Fyremas gown goes to waste because you wind up offing yourself accidentally."

I laugh.

She does not. Her tone is deadly serious. "You should wait for Pendefyre."

I purse my lips in lieu of a response.

"Why is it so important you do this alone?" Carys persists.

"I don't want to depend on anyone. All right? Especially not on . . . *him.*"

"He seems like the *only* person you truly can depend on. The only one who understands what you are going through. Are you not cut from the same cloth?"

My scoff is indignant. "We could not be more different! He is the most headstrong, high-handed, hot-tempered male I have ever crossed paths with!"

"I have not known you long, so I cannot claim to be an expert on your disposition. But if the stories my husband brought back from your time in the Cimmerians are anything to judge by, you do display your own fair share of temper, Rhya." Her lips twist in a wry smile. "Perhaps if you'd stop being so intent on hating Pendefyre, you might find you actually have much in common."

"Humph."

"Why do you continue to deny the attraction between you two?"

"Attraction? Your pregnancy hormones have gone straight to your head, Carys. We are not attracted to each other."

Except maybe for a few fraught moments on the road when I'd catch his eye across the fire... Or during our fight in the clearing, when I thought he might kiss me... Or when I'd first seen him shirtless in that sparring pit... Or when I'd awoken in his bed and felt his lips on my forehead...

I shake my head to banish the unwelcome memories.

"We can't stand to be in the same room most of the time," I insist, trying to convince her as much as myself. "We've never shared a single conversation that did not end in yelling or bloodshed."

"So?"

"So? You've twisted reality to suit your own delusional romantic narrative."

"Explain it to me, then. How it really is between you two."

I hesitate. "We are . . . uniquely connected. There is a bond between us that cannot be severed."

"The Remnant bond. Yes, Uther told me about it. Is it true you can read each other's thoughts?"

"No, it's not like that." I shudder, aghast at the thought of having Penn inside my head. "It's more like . . . knowing someone is standing directly behind you when they haven't announced themselves. You can sense their presence in your bones, can pinpoint where they are if they're close by." I gnaw my bottom lip. "I haven't been able to feel his presence since he left the city."

"Mmm."

My eyes narrow at the knowing smile that curves her mouth behind her teacup. "Mmm . . . *what?*"

"I just find it interesting that you claim not to care about him at all, yet just admitted you continually try to sense his presence. It's a bit of a contradiction."

"It's always wise to be aware of the location of one's enemies."

Her eyes roll heavenward at my haughty declaration. "Tell me more about the bond. I find it all rather fascinating."

"There's not much to tell. We are tethered. Linked. Our bodies, our maegic, our emotions."

"Your emotions?"

"Sometimes, strong feelings can . . . spill over." I take my final sip of tea and set my empty cup back on the table. "I'm working on controlling mine."

"Why? I should think it would be nice to have my man know exactly how he's making me feel at any given point of the day without having to so much as open my lips."

"Penn is *not* my—" I scowl at the grin that splits her face. "You're teasing me again."

"Couldn't resist. Carry on."

"That's it, for the most part. Penn did say it was possible for the Remnants to channel each other somehow. But seeing as I can't control my own power with any kind of success, I highly doubt I'll be able to handle something like that." My scoff is scornful. "Perhaps the gods chose the wrong girl to fulfill their damned prophecy. This mark at my chest seems wasted on me."

"You're being rather hard on yourself."

"I'm being realistic," I correct. "Now, can we please talk about something else? *Anything* else. I'm not above begging."

Carys studies me for a long time across the polished wood tea table between us. Her green eyes see far too much, all the inner facets I would rather hide away. With a familiar knowing smile still curving her mouth, she shifts the conversation into blessedly safer waters.

"If the baby comes a few days early, maybe I won't miss the whole festival. I love fireworks more than anything. I would hate to be bedridden for the entire show . . ."

CHAPTER
TWENTY–FOUR

The rain has slowed from a downpour to a drizzle by the time I bid Carys farewell and start my sodden march back to the palace. The streets are empty as I have ever witnessed, the normal midday hubbub of the marketplace forced indoors by the elements. The vendor stalls are vacant. Even the chestnut roaster, who seems a steady fixture, is gone from his usual post.

I tromp through puddles, my skirts a damp slap against my legs. My cloak is soaked through. The constant patter of rain against the earth is the only sound except for my squelching boots. For once, I am eager to get back to the warmth of the tower, with its crackling fireplace and volcanic wall.

Cobblestones gleam orange and red, a sheen of moisture catching the flickering glow of the lamplights. The air is chill, but I barely feel it. My thoughts are directed deep inward as I hurry down the abandoned roadway, head bent to avoid the worst of the raindrops.

I am worried about Carys; worried Uther will not make it home in time for the birth; worried she will trip down the stairs and go into labor prematurely. I have half a mind to turn around and head back to High Street, just so she won't be alone, but I know my absence at the palace will certainly be noted if I'm not there in a few hours when the maids pay their nightly call.

"Tomorrow, first thing, I will go back and check on her," I mutter to myself as I walk past a row of parked merchant wagons. Next morning's deliveries, piled high with goods. "I'll ensure she does not overexert herself. And make her drink more of the healing tea she so loath—"

The fist comes out of nowhere.

It clips me across the mouth, hard enough to split my lip. I taste blood on my tongue, a rush of hot copper, and cry out in pain. The sound is swallowed up by a large hand that claps over the bottom half of my face. In a blink, a second arm bands around my midsection, hard as granite, and hauls me backward. I kick and claw as I am dragged between two parked wagons, but whoever has me in his grasp is barrel-chested, with arms like anvils. The speed at which I find myself subdued is laughable.

My eyes widen when I see where he is taking me. One of the wagons is open at the back. I know instantly that I am the intended cargo. My teeth sink into the fleshy part of his palm, hard enough that he loosens his hold for a moment. He hisses an oath as I drop low and twist away, falling face-first into a puddle when my wet skirts tangle around my legs. The skin tears away from my hands as I scramble for purchase on the rough sidewalk, dragging myself forward.

The instant I find my feet, I start running flat out. He chases me, boots pounding through the puddles so close, I can feel the splashes against my back.

Where the hell is Gower when I need him?

With each stride, the cold power at my chest coils tighter, searing through my cloak. I reach inward for the wind that might save me, but it slips uselessly through my fingers, dulled by the

fear and panic overriding my senses. Resorting to more tradi-
tional methods, I shove one hand into my cloak pocket to retrieve
my dagger while the other fumbles for the whistle hanging on the
cord at my throat.

I'm not too far from the soldiers' barracks. If I can signal for
help, someone will surely hear me. Someone will come running.
Someone will—

The whistle never makes it to my lips.

He clobbers me from behind with something much harder
than a fist. It feels like a plank of wood or the hilt of a sword.
Stars burst in my visual field, fragmenting the world around me
into a kaleidoscope of colors. I go down in a heap of limbs, landing face down in a puddle. I feel the dirty water seep through the
fabric of my dress, into my skin.

Then I feel nothing at all.

THE WAGON ROLLS along an uneven road, jolting painfully
each time we hit a divot. I am slumped on the floor in the back,
hands bound with coarse rope. There is a gag in my mouth, so
tight I can barely breathe. My tongue is parched as sand. My
head throbs so fiercely, it is a miracle I am able to see straight.

Struggling into a sitting position, I gingerly probe the back of
my skull and discover an egg-sized lump beneath my braid. No
wonder my head hurts. I wipe the crust of dried blood from my
lower lip with my damp dress sleeve. To my surprise, the split is
already healed—as are my scraped palms. My enhanced healing
abilities are well intact, at least.

Through a slotted window at the front, I can make out the
back of my captor's neck. He has not yet realized I am awake,
focused as he is on steering the pair of mules who pull us through

the gathering dusk. It is not yet full dark. A good sign. I was unconscious only briefly, which means we have not been on the road for long. We might even still be in Caeldera.

Pulse pounding, I press my cheek against the side of the wagon, trying to make out slivers of passing scenery between the splintered wood planks. I see no buildings. Only fields of barren, half-frozen farmland and pine trees piled with dripping snowmelt. The road beneath our wheels is not cobblestone, but hard-packed reddish dirt.

We are beyond the city limits.

Beyond the wards.

My heart sinks into my stomach as hope withers within me. I have been taken. For what purpose, I do not know. By whom, I do not know. All I do know for sure is that it is no one's fault except my own.

I trusted Penn when he said no one could get to me in the capital. I thought myself safe within the protective cradle of the crater, shielded from outside evils by an invisible barrier. I fancied myself untouchable in my new existence at the palace. And so, I had let down my guard, had dropped my constant vigilance.

All for . . . what? A handful of steady meals? A place to rest my head? A chest of warm clothes? A bit of kinship?

For that, I traded my life.

I am no better than a starving alley cat, won over with a few tossed scraps.

How quickly I settled into new patterns at the palace. How fast I forgot that I never meant to stay—not in Caeldera, not with Penn. Not permanently.

Where was my sense of self-preservation?

Where was the foundation of logic on which Eli raised me?

I had lost sight of everything that kept me alive, everything that carried me through those long months on the run. And now I would face the consequences.

My pulse leaps when we lurch to a stop. Muffled male voices call out to my captor, asking for his credentials. We are at a security checkpoint. Hope surges anew. But just as I am about to begin banging on the side of the wagon with my bound hands, my captor responds to the men in the tower, his voice gruff as it carries back to them through the twilight.

My soul stills along with my body.

I know that voice.

Recognize it.

"My *credentials*? I am Second Lieutenant Gower of the Ember Guild," he snarls. "I don't appreciate being delayed. Let's move it along, shall we?"

Gower!

There is a tense beat of silence. "We haven't heard anything about a transport . . ."

"Nor would you. This is Prince Pendefyre's personal business."

"Of course," the guard hedges. "But you must understand, we have certain protocols . . ."

My dazed mind struggles to make sense of this unexpected turn of events. Perhaps Gower has taken me on Penn's orders?

I dismiss the possibility almost as quickly as it arises. Penn would never allow anyone to lay a hand on me, let alone throw me into the back of a wagon under the cover of darkness and sneak me out of the city.

In a swift resurgence of desperation, I thump my bound fists against the side of the wagon hard enough to bruise. I scream, but the sound barely permeates the gag around my face. I yank it roughly down and try again.

"Help!" I yell. "Help! Back here!"

"What in gods' name is—"

The guard's question cuts off abruptly as Gower vaults from the driver's seat, his body weight jolting the wagon. I scramble toward the slot-like window at the front. I can see nothing. Nothing except the short, stubby manes of the two mules. But what I hear paints a clear enough picture.

The slide of a sword pulling free from its scabbard. A brief scuffle, thudding limbs, and traded blows. A short scream of pain. And then . . .

Chilling silence.

When Gower's face, red with exertion, appears on the other side of the slotted window, I backpedal so quickly I go down on my ass in a tangle of skirts. I stare up into his cold, dead eyes as waves of despair wash over me.

The guards are dead.

And with them, my chance at escape.

"Stupid bitch," he seethes. "If I weren't getting paid to deliver you intact, you'd feel the length of my sword for that little stunt."

I'm shaking with anger and fear as I get to my feet. "You killed them. Those guards outside—"

"And whose fault is that?" he roars, so incensed spittle flies through the slot. Lank black hair falls over his sweat-dotted brow. "If you'd kept your mouth shut, they'd still be alive."

I stare at him—at the crazed glint of hatred in his eyes—and know there is little point in arguing. Steeling my shoulders, I ask, "Why are you doing this?"

"I don't need to explain myself to the likes of you."

"Coin, then? It must be." My head tilts in contemplation. "I wonder, Gower . . . what is the going rate for betrayal these days?"

"I owe you no loyalty, bitch. I didn't betray you."

"Maybe not. But you betrayed your leader. Your prince. And I'm certain he will be less than forgiving when he finds out."

He flinches ever so slightly at my words. "He's not going to find out."

I laugh. "You're delusional. You really think you can kidnap me and no one will notice?"

"I have a plan—"

"I'm guessing whatever plan you had went to hell the minute you killed those guards outside."

Gower's eyes flash with wrath. "You know nothing!"

"I know Penn will kill you for this," I whisper in a bald voice. "There is no place you can run, no place you can hide. He will hunt you down wherever you go. His face will be the last you see before your pathetic existence is snuffed out like a flickering candle."

"I have fought beside Pendefyre for years. You have been around for . . . what? A handful of weeks?" His voice is sheer malice. "He may enjoy bedding you, but I assure you, he will hardly mourn your loss. No one will. You may be of importance to our enemies, but all in Caeldera will forget you long before I've reaped the rewards of this exchange."

His words knife through me, but I keep my expression still and calm as the waters at the center of my mind's eye. "Is that how you justify your actions, Gower? The reward purse outweighs your conscience? Assuming you have a conscience, that is. Doubtful, seeing as you've kidnapped me for a bit of extra coin."

"Not a bit of extra coin, you stupid bitch! Efnysien is offering immortality for the one who delivers you to him!"

I struggle to keep my shock buried beneath a mask of indifference.

Gower's eyes go unfocused, as though he is not fully there. Not fully seeing me or speaking to me. "Deliver the girl, get to live forever. His scouts have spread the missive far and wide. It's only a matter of time before someone takes him up on the bargain. Why not me? Why should I not benefit from your existence? Your life for mine. A fair trade if I ever heard one. Who in his right mind would resist such a reward?"

My eyes scan his face more intently. I have never looked at him—*really* looked at him—before. He is always scowling at me or storming off before I can study him with any sort of acuity. But now, seeing him up close for the first time, I notice a faint yellowing of his skin. A jaundiced undertone I have observed in sickly babes and dying men. His eyes, too, show signs of illness. They are ringed with deep shadows, their whites turned the dull shade of curdled cream. And there is a gauntness to his cheekbones at odds with the complexion of a healthy warrior.

"How long have you been dying, Gower?"

His gaze jerks back to mine, wide with shock. "*What did you say to me?*"

"You're dying. I can see it clear as day. Judging by your pallor, you've been ill for quite a while now." I take a swing in the dark, hoping my guess strikes home. "Has the vomiting begun? The bloody stools? The burning bile in your throat?"

"Shut up!"

"Your reaction suggests that it has," I say softly. "You must be in a great deal of pain."

"You have no idea. No idea what—" He chokes into silence, his teeth gnashing together to contain his words. "It doesn't matter. Soon, I will be healed. I will be immortal. And you . . . You will be dead."

"No."

His scowl darkens. "*No?*"

"No." I shake my head at him, almost in pity. "I will not die.

Not today, in any case. And not because of you, you miserable excuse for a man."

"You little—"

"You will be the one to die, Gower," I cut him off. "Long before you make it to Efnysien to claim your supposed immortality."

I must appear calm to him in that moment, with my serene expression and even tone. But inside, I am far from calm. Inside, I am a gathering storm. A churning cyclone, growing in strength. Rising to meet the rage that thrums through my veins as I stare at this traitor who intends to steal away my future.

I am not about to let him.

Not when I have the power to stop him coiled at the center of my chest, poised to strike with a viciousness I have only felt once before.

"What—what are you doing?" Gower's face is no longer full of scorn. It is full of fear as he shouts over the growing wind that fills the wagon. Planks of wood rattle as the entire rig rocks back and forth with increasing velocity.

"Stop this!" he screams, pulling his face back from the slotted window. "Whatever it is you're doing, stop right now!"

"Goodbye, Gower."

I close my eyes, surrendering to the storm the same way I had on the mountainside when I held back the inferno. The power bursts from beneath my skin, exploding out of me like a shock wave of electrified air. There are no ancient wards to contain it this time. No bond of support from Penn's formidable presence.

I am untethered.

Unencumbered.

Unrepentant.

My bonds rip away, snatched from my wrists like they are

made of paper. My back bows under the force of it—spine arching, head falling back. I hear the sound of splintering wood. My eyes sliver open and I see not the wagon's ceiling, but open sky.

Somewhere in the back of my mind, Penn is shouting at me to contain it. To lock it down before it kills me. I pay him no heed as another shock wave blasts outward, this one even stronger than before. So strong, it lifts me clean off my feet. I brace myself for a fall, but my body does not hit the earth below; instead, it rises toward the sky. I ascend into the air like a bird in flight—arms outstretched, hair billowing all around me, skirts fluttering like wings.

I hover there as the wagon combusts beneath me. Nails shudder loose from their holes, wheels fly from their axles, boards shred into shards. The team of mules bolts with a clatter of hooves, their tack trailing behind them in the dirt. I do not see Gower in the melee, but I hear him cry out in pain—a brief bleat of agony—before the sound is snatched away by the wind. All around me, the vortex kicks up a cloud of dust and debris as it lengthens into a towering funnel cloud that stretches from the earth to the clouds far overhead.

Someone is wailing—an unearthly, inhuman sound. It's me, I realize after a moment, feeling the strain in the hinge of my jaw as the cry spills out. Blood drips from my eyes like tears, tracking down my face into my open mouth.

It tastes like copper.

It tastes like pain.

It tastes like madness.

Raw power. Too much to hold without shattering. Too much to endure without my skull cleaving in two. It is cracking me open. Flaying me into fragments. I float there at the center of the tornado, losing myself in slow degrees as the pulses of power strengthen. My consciousness flags beneath the crushing mass of agony and air, beneath the biting cold at my breast that pierces my lungs and steals my breath. I am no longer me—no longer Rhya Fleetwood, Remnant of Air.

I am simply . . . air itself.

The wind itself.

Think of every breeze that has ever stirred between every blade of grass in every corner of this world . . . Think of every ripping squall that has ever filled the sails of every ship in every far-off sea . . . Think of every soaring current that has carried every bird that dared spread its wings in every distant sky . . .

Strange—it is Soren's voice I hear in that final second before my mind blanks entirely.

From a whisper to a scream, from the lightest puff to the wildest tempest . . .

All that resides within you.

All that and still more.

Another shock wave crashes outward, carrying with it my last semblance of strength. My mind tapers into darkness so suddenly, there is no time even to brace as I plummet from midair to the hard-packed roadway below.

If the landing hurts, I have no inkling of it.

I am already unconscious.

~

DAWN IS PEEKING over the horizon when I shake off my dreams, pushing out of the deep, dark sea where I am drowning, gasping awake as my head breaks the surface. I blink up at the sky, thoroughly dazed.

I am lying on a bed of splintered wood. Parts of the obliterated wagon litter the ground all around me, most no longer than the length of my forearm. The wind is gone; only the faintest whisper of a breeze stirs the blades of grass that line the perimeter of the road. Grappling with the familiar exhaustion that comes whenever I expend my powers, I haul myself into a sitting position. It takes a long time to get my limbs to cooperate. They seem made of jelly, even after a full night of sleep.

I suppose I should feel lucky no one came across me while I was unconscious. But it is hard to feel anything except horror as my gaze sweeps the site, taking in the full scope of the wreckage for the first time. Several pine trees are toppled, ripped out by the roots, their trunks resting against the snow-dappled earth. One has fallen directly atop what must have at one point been a guard post. It is naught but a pile of kindling now.

I try not to look at the bodies scattered beneath the detritus. The slain guards. Three of them, young and strapping, with sightless eyes fixed skyward. Their blades sit uselessly in the dirt beside them.

A muffled moan makes my head whip around. The sudden movement triggers a dizzy spell that takes several hard blinks to clear. When I am once again capable of focusing, I spot the source of the agonized whimpers. Gower. He is flat on his back in the road twenty paces from me, twitching occasionally. His hands clutch at his midsection—at the shard of wood that speared through him when the wagon exploded.

Skies.

I drag my way to him through the wreckage, fighting my fatigued muscles with every inch of ground I gain. Exhaustion batters at my temples, a relentless ache, but I banish it from my mind. I was asleep for hours. Since twilight. For a man to linger so long with such an injury . . .

I cannot fathom how much pain he is in.

It would have been a mercy to die right away, in the blast. Six inches higher, the spear would have pierced his heart and killed him instantly. But by some cruel twist of fate, it skewered the fleshy planes of his stomach instead, leaving him to a drawn-out death I would not wish upon my worst enemy.

"Gower," I whisper through parched lips, peering down into his face. "Gower, can you hear me?"

His eyelids flicker but do not open. He does not answer except to moan—a low, anguished mewl. He is pale from the blood loss. The earth around his body is saturated with red.

"Gower?"

"M-mercy," he gasps, the word garbled. *"Mercy."*

His head falls listlessly to the side, as though the effort of just that one plea is more than he can endure. His hand is wan and clammy when I take it in my shaky ones and squeeze with as much strength as I can muster. He does not squeeze back. I doubt he would even if he had the ability.

I've killed him, after all.

The lance in his abdomen is thicker than my fist. The finest healers in Anwyvn could not stitch him up. And even if they could, he would never survive the fever that followed. Not when his body is already so weak, his immunity so damaged by the cancer that gnaws at his insides.

Anyone who spends time around the dead or dying learns quickly—there is a scent to death. A particular aroma that plagues battlefields and sickbays alike. Not only blood or bile but something else. A grim harbinger of what is to come.

I smell it now. Pull it into my lungs like deathly perfume as I hold the hand of the man who would have passed me over to Efnysien without so much as a backward glance, all too happy to trade his life for mine.

Mercy.

He asked me for it. Begged me for it. His final request—for salvation from his agony, for deliverance from this lingering punishment. But why should I grant him such a thing? He had shown me none. He had all but condemned me to death at the hands of a power-hungry madman.

As I watch his chest rise and fall in shuddering, excruciating gasps, I feel no sympathy. Or so I tell myself, as my eyes smart with unshed tears and my throat thickens with grief. This is no more than he deserves: a direct consequence of his own self-serving choices. Traitors do not warrant an honorable passing of soul into aether.

This is the fate he has earned.

Still, I cannot stop from setting his hand down by his side. Nor from reaching down into his boot, where the familiar hilt of a blade pokes out, shining in the weak morning sunlight—my dagger, stolen back on the streets of Caeldera. For a moment, I trace the glyphs carved into its handle, wondering not for the first time what they mean. And then, with a steadiness honed by years of healing, I palm the blade firmly and lift it to Gower's throat.

Beneath the thin skin, I watch his pulse pound in the vein. It is thready. Weak. Unlike mine, which is racing at twice its normal speed as I adjust the angle of my dagger to rest beneath the hollow of his ear, where his neck joins his jaw.

"Your life for mine," I whisper, recalling the words he'd spoken earlier. "A fair trade if I ever heard one."

In one clean jerk, I slit his throat.

I DO NOT know how long I sit there in the dirt beside Gower's dead body, staring at the blood on my hands. Long enough for the sun to drift high into the sky. Long enough for the pain in my temples to subside from a blinding ache to a distant throb. Long enough for some of the power I spent in last night's outburst to re-form at the center of my chest, a faint furl of wind wrapped directly around my heart.

As the exhaustion begins to ebb, I take stock of my situation. I have no idea where I am. Moreover, I have no idea where I might go from here. Back to Caeldera? At the moment, that seems like the worst idea possible. It would be one thing if Penn were there . . . but he is not, and it may be days before he returns. Gods only know if anyone else will believe my story.

Kidnapped by a member of the esteemed Ember Guild. Forced to kill him to escape. And as for the matter of the slain guards and wind-blasted tower . . .

My head shakes, a slow rejection. I do not trust anyone in the capital to shield me from the repercussions of my actions. I certainly cannot expect any support from Queen Vanora or the members of her court. They already hate me. They are eager for any excuse to see me brought low or banished altogether. I would not be shocked to find myself thrown into the palace dungeons to rot.

Carys will stand by you, a small voice pipes up. *So would Farley. And Teagan. And Keda . . .*

I shove that voice away. I cannot put my new friends in such a position. I will not ask them for a show of loyalty that will jeopardize their livelihoods or reputations.

No.

I will not return to Caeldera. I will find a way to survive on my own. I have done it before. I can do it again.

When I feel strong enough to move, I force myself to pick through the wreckage for anything useful. In the ruins of the guard post, I find a cache of weapons—battle-axes and broadswords, all too heavy for me to wield. In a stroke of luck, I spot a hunting bow and a full quiver of arrows half-hidden beneath the branches of a fallen tree. Near the flattened remains of an old table, I pilfer a few stale bannocks, a store of dried fruits and nuts, and a large hunk of cheese wrapped in wax paper.

I close the guards' sightless eyes as I check their pockets, coming away with a tiny whittling knife and a suede purse filled with Dyvedi crowns and farthings for my trouble. I pack as much as I can carry into a dusty rucksack I discover by the last soldier's body. Slinging it across my back along with the quiver, I walk into the forest.

I do not look back.

CHAPTER
TWENTY–FIVE

Dyved's forests teem with life.

I see more animals in two days living in the woodlands than I have in all my prior years combined. The deer I used to hunt in Seahaven were starved, slight creatures—half-dead already by the time my arrows brought them down. The elk and doe that cross my path here are in peak physical form, magnificent horned beasts with gleaming coats and glossy, intelligent eyes. Cotton-tailed hares dart through the undergrowth so fast, it is difficult to spot them in the low brush. Exotic birds of several different varieties warble from the highest reaches of the pines, filling the air with strange songs.

When I come upon a stretch of trees where the music tapers off into abrupt quiet, and see the bark of many trunks scored with deep claw marks, I quickly change course. I have no desire to see if Dyved's bears are as healthy as its deer population. Or as hungry.

I do not much care which direction I walk in, so long as it brings me vaguely south. I have no true destination. I make camp the first night by the crook of a river, sparking a fire with foliage and kindling I find scattered in the thicket. Once the flames catch, I feed them with dry logs until they are burning steadily, high enough to ward off the shadows but low enough to avoid drawing unwanted attention. The spring thaw is well underway, and while a hint of winter's sting lingers, it is not intolerable. Especially with a thick, fur-lined cloak and sturdy leather boots.

A far cry from my last sojourn in the wild.

Hours lengthen into days, and a sort of peace settles in my bones. Things are simpler in the forest. There are no social customs to follow, no sneering courtiers to impress, no tripwire conversations to tiptoe through. Here, I am not a child of the prophecy or a meaningless dinner guest or a maegical being of great import. I am just a girl in the woods. If I am hungry, I eat. If I am tired, I rest. If I am bored, I make a game of naming the herbs and flowers creeping through the ground with pale green shoots.

Rose hip. Sagethorn. Tansy. Comfrey. Chicory. Yarrow. Myrtle. Dogwood. Fireweed. Juniper. Star grass.

I collect some of the more useful ones as I walk, using the dead guard's pocketknife to take cuttings. It is rather optimistic to think I might ever find a place to plant a medicinal garden, let alone nurture it to fruition. Yet I do not stop until my pack is full of carefully wrapped roots and stems. A nascent harvest, swaddled in cheesecloth.

As the days slip by, I gradually make my way south across the plateau. I do not lend much thought to where I am going. My plan, if you can call it that, hinges entirely on finding the Range Road we took from Coldcross, and making my way back there. There, or somewhere like it. Any neutral trade-post town will do, where I can disappear into the fabric of daily life without so much as a ripple. One more anonymous halfling in the patchwork of society, overlooked and ordinary.

I see no one in the woods, keeping far off the roads. Occasionally, I pass a bit too close to the outskirts of a settlement or farm, but it is easy enough to divert my course at the first signs of life. I do not know exactly how far I am from Caeldera; close enough not to risk recognition at an inn, no matter how much my tired bones and aching soles might appreciate a night's rest on a feather mattress instead of the rock-riddled ground. Besides, I do not yet trust myself around people. Not after the carnage I unleashed. Not after Gower—

I shove the thought away before it can fully register.

There is a tiny whisper in my head that suggests, in the small hours of the night when the world is darkest and my worst fears rattle the chains in which I keep them fettered, that I am not dealing with reality. That I am hiding in the forest—from what I have done, from who I am becoming. From everything.

I do not give that voice much credence.

I am fine.

Totally fine.

So what if I break down at the sight of my dagger's blade, stained with dried blood? So what if I douse it in the first creek I come across, plunging my hands into the frigid water and scrubbing, scrubbing, scrubbing until every trace of gore is washed away? So what if I keep on scrubbing, even when the blade is clean again, only ceasing when my hand slips and I slice a deep gouge into my palm?

I sit there on the bank and watch my blood welling, spilling, dripping—vibrant, vital red against the bleak blanket of dried pine needles that cover the earth—with vague detachment. Only my long-ingrained training convinces me to eventually tear a strip off the hem of my shift and wrap the wound until the worst of the bleeding stops and the cut begins to close. Unable to stomach the sight of any more blood, I leave the saturated fabric there on the riverbank and hurry on my way.

That night, the end of my third day of wandering, the sun is dipping toward the horizon when I come to a strange, silent section of the forest. More bears, I think at first. But no—this is a different sort of quiet. Absolute stillness seizes the air. No birds, no breeze, no sound at all. No rabbits race through the scrub, no soft-footed deer nip berries from the bushes.

The trees show signs of damage far beyond ursine claws. Some are stripped of their branches, as though a very tall animal has moved through with haste and snapped them off. Others are knocked over entirely, fallen sentinels left to decompose with their roots exposed to the elements.

When I see the tracks scored deeply into the soil—some as long as I am tall—I'm overcome by the urge to run. Run, *quickly*, away from this place, before I find myself face-to-face with whatever left such mammoth footprints behind.

I backtrack through the woods to the creek where I'd washed my dagger clean that afternoon, holding my breath until I hear the comforting chirp of songbirds and see a pair of rabbits racing each other to their burrow at the base of an ash tree. The sun has nearly set; a waxing moon is rising to take its place. I make a fire, taking extra care to keep it burning low. I have put a fair amount of distance between myself and that eerie stretch of woods, but I am still too rattled to take any undue risks.

My stomach growls in protest as I stare into the flames. I have not eaten more than a handful of dried nuts all day. I force myself to munch on a stale bannock as I watch the embers devouring the thin twigs, a defiant glow in the swelling shadows. My thoughts drift to Penn as I chew the flavorless bread. They often do when I stare into the flames. I doubt I will ever again see a fire and not conjure him in my mind. Those severe planes of his face. That cutting jawline. That rare smile. I allow myself only a moment to wonder if he has learned of my absence; if he thinks I left him of my own accord.

It does not matter, I tell myself again and again and again, until the words lose all meaning. *He does not matter.*

Tossing the remainder of my stale dinner into the fire, I settle back against the mossy hollow trunk of a fallen tree, tuck my cloak more firmly around me, and allow the gentle babbling of the nearby brook to lull me into a fitful slumber.

SOMETHING WAKES ME in the dead of night.

I jolt into consciousness, eyes snapping open. It is black as pitch. The fire has nearly gone out. I push out of my slumped position against the hollow tree and find my feet, glancing around for signs of monsters in the dark. None materialize. My ears strain for sounds—anything that might indicate I am not alone in the clearing where I've made camp. There is nothing save the soft hoot of an owl soaring overhead.

Dismissing my paranoia, I stoop to toss a handful of fresh kindling onto the embers. I've barely risen back to full height when a large hand claps itself across my mouth from behind.

I scream.

"Quiet," Penn murmurs, his breath stirring the hair at my temple. "There are creatures in the Forsaken Forest you do not want to call down upon us."

The scream dies in my throat. I swallow hard, trying to slow my racing heart. As my breathing evens and sense returns, for the first time in more than a week, I feel the pull of an invisible tether in the center of my chest. My breath catches at the sensation. I had not realized how much I longed to feel the Remnant bond again—to feel Penn again—until it was snatched away from me.

"Are you calm? Can I remove my hand?"

I nod.

His arm falls away and he steps back. I inhale a deep gulp of night air and set my shoulders before I dare turn to face him. He wears the dark helm he had on when we first met, the serpentine nose bridge accentuating the fierceness of his severe expression. A thick growth of stubble dots his tight-clenched jaw.

"What are you doing here?" I whisper haltingly.

"I should ask you the same." His brows are furrowed, his dark eyes moving rapidly over me as though memorizing every detail. "Do you have any idea how long I've been searching for you? Two full days in this damned forest, going round in circles looking for tracks. You move like a bloody ghost."

My chin jerks haughtily. "Why?"

"Excuse me?"

"Why have you been searching for me?"

"Is this some sort of jest?"

"I'm perfectly serious." I stare at him. "Do you intend to drag me back to Caeldera to face trial? To throw me in the dungeons to rot? Because I'd rather you just kill me here and now. Be done with it."

As I speak, Penn's expression grows thunderous. "You think I've spent my time tracking you through the wilderness because *I want to punish you*?" He practically vibrates with rage. I am surprised smoke does not leak from his ears. "You think, after I felt the burst of power you expelled three days ago . . . after I felt your distress, your pain, your fear . . . after I came across the ruins of that wagon and saw the ground littered with bodies . . . and felt *nothing* from our bond, not a single fucking *flicker* of your presence . . ." A muscle leaps in his jaw as he struggles for control. "You think after all that . . . I want to hurt you?"

"I . . ." The ground beneath me seems suddenly shaky. "I didn't . . ."

"*Gods*, Rhya!" He half shouts, careful to keep his tone subdued even in his agitated state. "What do I have to do to earn your trust? What do I have to do to prove to you that I'm not going to hurt you? That I would do anything—*anything*—to keep you safe?"

"I . . . I don't know."

His hands curl into fists at his sides. "You are the most infuriating, obstinate, impossible woman I have ever met. And I have been alive for well over a century."

My spine goes ramrod. "If that's how you truly feel, why did you bother coming after me at all?"

"Like I said," he mutters. "*Impossible.*"

"Is it just because I'm the Remnant?" I wish my voice weren't shaking. "Just because of some stupid prophecy that makes you honor bound to protect me?"

"Fucking hell, Rhya!" His eyes bore into mine, aglow in the darkness. "I don't give a damn about the prophecy. Not anymore. I care about *you.*"

My heart is hammering. Too hard. Too fast. I cannot think straight, cannot even attempt to articulate everything I am feeling. Especially when he is looking at me like that. "You don't understand. I can't go back. Not after . . ."

"You killed him. Gower."

I reel back, like he's dealt a physical blow. *Of course.* He'd seen the gruesome scene. Of course he'd know what I've done. My stomach twists into an ugly knot. "But how did you— When did you—"

He takes pity on me when I choke into silence, answering the questions I cannot quite voice. "You had not been gone more than an hour before your maids realized something must've happened and sent up the alarm. I was already on my way back from the border with a unit of men. By the time we rode through the front gates, two merchants had come forward claiming they witnessed you being shoved unconscious into the back of a wagon by a man wearing an Ember Guild uniform. The guards posted at the tunnel confirmed its was Gower who passed through." His teeth grind together in frustration. "They didn't think to search the wagon when he claimed he was on official business for the prince."

I nod. "He tried that same tactic with the other guards. The ones at the outpost. But they were skeptical from the start. And when they heard me banging in the back of the wagon, they knew something was amiss. They tried to help, but . . ."

"Gower killed them."

I have to look away. His eyes are too intent, too knowing. I stare at the fire instead as I speak. The embers smolder, red as blood. "He was desperate, you see. Dying. A slow death, his insides eaten away bit by bit. I have seen such illness before, back in Seahaven. I doubt he had more than a year left to live."

There is a heavy silence.

"Apparently, Efnysien is offering immortality to the lucky individual who turns me over."

The silence grows electric with rage.

"I thought . . ." My voice falters. I swallow hard and try again. "I thought I was safe in Caeldera."

A pulse of guilt pierces the bond, sharp as a needle between my ribs. "So did I," Penn says with a heavy sigh. "I thought the wards would be enough to keep our enemies at bay. I did not anticipate being betrayed by one of our own. Certainly not one of my top men."

I press my lips together, unsure how to respond to that.

"The members of the Ember Guild are handpicked," he continues. "They train for years before they earn a rank akin to Gower's. I had no reason to think you were in danger where he was concerned."

Still, I remain silent. I do not trust myself to speak. My emotions are too raw, my reactions too untempered.

"Rhya," he prompts after a moment. "What are you thinking, right now? Give me some small indication."

I shrug and run my hands through my tangled hair. My thoughts feel just as raw as my emotions. It will do me no good to allow them to lash out at him.

Penn's voice goes rough with frustration. "What do you want me to say? That I'm sorry? Gods, Rhya, you know I am." He sucks in a breath to steady himself but cannot quite disguise the flash of temper. "That said, you were supposed to stay in the palace until I got back."

My whole frame stiffens. Finally, I find my powers of speech. "Well, you never should've left in the first place."

"In case you haven't noticed, I have other responsibilities besides catering to you. I have an entire kingdom to run. I can't spend every minute making sure you're not walking blithely into death traps—"

"*Blithely?* So it's my fault I was taken?"

"I didn't say that," he snaps. "But if you'd not been wandering around unattended—"

"I wasn't unattended! I had *Gower* looking out for me!" I snap right back at him. "I guess I should've somehow foreseen that he was going to knock me over the head, shove me into a wagon, and attempt to barter me to Efnysien like a prized lamb for slaughter!"

"Rhya—"

"You know, I almost don't blame him," I cut him off. My laugh is biting. Bitter. "Gower. He would've tried anything to live. It wasn't personal."

"Do not," he grits out between clenched teeth, "make excuses for what he did."

"I'm not excusing it, I'm just saying—"

"Enough." His eyes press closed. "Tell me the rest. Finish it."

"Don't order me around like one of your men. I don't snap to your commands, O great princeling."

"Rhya."

He sounds weary enough to garner cooperation. I heave a sigh and then, in a flat voice, describe the tornado I summoned in the sparsest details. The blast that destroyed the wagon, that sent the spear into Gower's gut. Penn listens without interruption for the most part, but I hear his sharp intake of air as I reach the final piece of the tale.

"I slit his throat," I whisper starkly. "He was gone in the space of an instant."

There is a long silence, during which he takes several deep breaths. When he finally speaks, his voice is a guttural rasp, brimming with vengeance. "You should've left him there to writhe. To rot. He did not deserve such a merciful end."

Startled, my eyes flash to Penn's face. "He was one of your most trusted men. A loyal lieutenant for years."

"A miscalculation I will not soon forget," he vows coldly. "I hold no quarter for traitors. He will receive no funeral pyre, no last rites. Let him lie there until the animals carry off his bones to bleach beneath the sun. Let his soul wander for an eternity of banishment."

"Penn—"

"He was meant to keep you safe! I entrusted him with the most important of duties in my absence. The most sacred. And at the first opportunity, he betrayed me. Betrayed you. Betrayed all of us, for if you are lost, so is our best hope."

"But, Penn—"

"No. *No.* I will not hear another word spoken in his defense. He would have taken you from me. He would have condemned me to a life without you." The words are uttered with such seething wrath, my heart skips a beat. "If he were not already dead, I'd kill him myself. And, Rhya . . ." His eyes hold mine; there is no mistaking the sincerity in them. "I would enjoy it."

Beneath my cloak, I wrap my arms around myself. In part to keep from trembling. Mostly, though, to keep from reaching for him. The urge is so strong, it takes all my focus to resist. I find myself wishing that, just once, Penn would allow his own unflagging self-control to crack wide open. That he would let go of his own resistance, pull me into his arms, and . . . and . . .

"Put out the fire and gather your things. It's time to go," he says, his fury buried—along with my foolish fantasies. "We have a long journey home."

I don't move. "Caeldera is not my home. I'm not going back."

"You are."

"No," I whisper tersely. "I am not."

"Where are you going, then?"

Scowling, I glance away. "Does it matter?"

"Damn it, Rhya—"

"Just let me go! You said it yourself, you have a million other responsibilities to deal with. You don't need me there to complicate your life."

"And what if I want you there?" he asks softly—so softly, my eyes jerk back to his face before I can stop them.

"Penn—"

"What if I want you complicating my life? What if I told you I can't sleep or see straight without knowing you're safe? What if I said just the thought of you being hurt, being killed, is enough to tear me to shreds?"

I can only stare at him. There is no way to speak—not with my heart lodged in my throat. But the bond between us speaks for me. It aches like a knife twist. My emotions spill out like lifeblood.

Regret and remorse. Fear and foolish hope. Most devastating of all, *longing*. Such longing, I lose my breath. Such longing, it nearly crushes all my convictions.

"You're running," Penn says, his eyes holding mine captive. "Running scared."

"I'm not."

"You are and you know it."

"And what do I have to be scared of?" I scoff to cover my fear. "*You?*"

"Yourself. Your own capabilities."

My teeth clench. "I'll learn to contain my power. To control it. I just need more practice. More time."

"I wasn't talking about your Remnant, Rhya. I was talking about Gower."

There is no concealing my flinch. "I don't know what he has to do with this."

"You killed a man."

I flinch again. My voice cracks out like a whip. "It was mercy. He was dying."

"Dying from a wound you caused when you unleashed that tornado," Penn says with a gentleness that makes me want to weep.

"Are you calling me a murderer?" Tears spring to my eyes unbidden. "He kidnapped me. He would have killed me."

"I'm sure that's true. Make no mistake, he deserved to die. But no amount of justification will change how you feel about what you did." Penn shakes his head slowly back and forth. "If it were me, I wouldn't think twice about driving my sword through his gut. I would relish the chance. You, though . . . *I know you.* I know how closely you guard your heart. I know, despite everything you have endured, you still believe in good and evil. In morality. So, whether or not he deserved to die, his death is a scar you will carry for the rest of your days."

I cannot stand to look at him anymore. Or perhaps I cannot stand for him to look at me. Not with the pressure gathering like storm clouds behind my eyes, threatening a torrent of impending tears.

Penn steps closer, directly into my space. His hands slip around my neck, a soft scrape of calluses against the thinnest skin. I close my eyes as his warmth sinks into me, pressing my lips tight together to keep my whimper of despair contained.

"Rhya." His voice is very nearly a caress. "Some grief is too heavy to carry alone. Let go of it. Give it to me. I will carry it for you."

The whimper slips out.

His hands tighten at the sound. Yet his words remain whisper soft. "Stop running from a past you can't change. Walk forward with me instead."

I thought, after all this time together, I had seen every side to Prince Pendefyre of Dyved. But here is one I have never before witnessed.

Gentle.

Considerate.

Caring.

It is such a far cry from his typical gruffness, from his finely honed scorn and blunt brutality, it undermines the last shred of my composure. The tears I have worked so hard to hold at bay rush out in a hot flood, pouring down my cheeks unchecked. They do not have a chance to fall, for Penn pulls me closer, flush against him, and before I know what is happening, my face is buried in the crook of his neck.

I allow myself to weep against his skin, to release all my grief into his strong, solid frame. As if he really can take the pain from me, absorb it like a sponge until I am wrung out and empty.

I cry for the life I have taken. I cry for the blood on my hands—on my heart. I cry for the girl I used to be, who saw the world with perfect clarity. Right and wrong. Good and evil. Sinner and saint. Mostly, though, I cry because I know down to my very core that I do not regret the choice I made. If I could go back to that moment in the wagon, when I chose to unleash the wind . . . I would do it again. I would save myself a thousand times over.

Even if I had to kill to do it.

I am not sure how long we stand there—my arms wrapped tight around Penn's back, his fingers laced through the thick fall of my hair. When my sobs finally subside into ragged gasps of air, when my shudders lessen into minor shakes, when my eyes are swollen and aching . . . I tilt my head back to meet his stare.

His eyes soften when he sees the tears still glimmering on the surface of mine. Our faces are so close—a hairsbreadth apart. Our breaths mingle in the scant space between our mouths. Mine are coming faster and faster as I try to remind myself of all the reasons closing that tiny shred of distance would be a bad idea, an irreversible one with repercussions that will echo far into the future, one that will change everything between us in fundamental ways . . .

But then, *he* moves.

All my reasons drift away, scattering to the wind like dandelion fuzz. My hesitations vanish in a blink; my excuses evaporate like they never existed. Because Penn's mouth is on mine, sinking down to claim my lips in a breath-stealing crush that makes my chest cave and my mind blank.

He kisses me with the same ragged desperation that buzzes through my own veins. With the same pulsing desire I feel mirrored in the bond that flows between us. Not just between us, now, but winding *around* us, twining us together like invisible rope. Tighter, tighter, tighter. Until I forget where I end and he begins.

I kiss him back, kiss him with everything I have—all my pain and rage and yearning, all my pent-up need from weeks of lying to myself that this, right here, is not exactly what I've wanted from him for longer than I care to remember. That this—his mouth on mine, his hands in my hair, his heartbeat thrumming in time with my pulse—is not what I have longed for each time we've bickered and butted heads and goaded each other with verbal barbs.

His head slants, deepening the kiss as my hands slide up his chest. A deep rattle moves in the back of his throat when my fingers brush the nape of his neck, where the thick hair curls below the rim of his helmet. The nose bridge is cold against my feverish face as I push up onto my toes, needing to be closer to him. Needing more of this. More of everything. More skin, more warmth, more fire in my blood.

More Penn.

His arms wind around me, steely bands that lock me firmly against him. I'm grateful he's holding me up, for there is no way my legs will support my weight, no way my weakened knees will keep from buckling under the immensity of my emotions.

The wind is a wail, stirring the leaves at our feet into a vortex, sending up sparks from the campfire into the sky. I try to get my power under control, to keep from setting off a squall, but Penn is all-consuming. I am swimming in his taste, his touch, his scent. Unable to concentrate on anything except the way his hands slide down my spine, a heated exploration. The delicious press of my breasts against his firm chest as I bow against him, lost to sensation.

Skies.

I gasp, and the second my lips part, Penn's tongue sweeps between them. I go fully pliant in his arms, allowing him to plunder my mouth without an ounce of protest. He is conquering me, bit by bit, but there is something beautiful about the surrender. He takes command of my mouth with the same unrelenting ferocity I have seen him exhibit in sparring pits and on fields of battle—no hesitations, no second-guessing.

I can only cling to him as his lips lay siege, driving my desire to a new height never previously experienced. At least, not until his hand slides up my side beneath the cloak and finds the soft swell of my breast. A moan moves in my throat—a ragged, hungry sound— as his thumb ghosts over my hardened nipple through the fabric of my gown.

The leaves and campfire sparks continue to swirl around us, faster and faster, until the world is naught but a blur of wind and flame. We'll set the whole wood ablaze if we keep this up much longer.

In this moment, I can't seem to make myself care.

"Gods," Penn mutters, his mouth ripping away from mine long enough to drag in a much-needed breath. I'm panting hard, too, my lungs screaming beneath the piercing cold of my Remnant. But that doesn't stop me from yanking on his nape, pulling him back down to me. I am not yet ready for this moment to end, not yet willing to let the building fervor between us sputter out.

I need his mouth.

I need his touch.

Never in my life have I needed anything so much.

His lips claim mine again in a bruising, brutal kiss I feel in every corner of my body. He's touching me, his warm hand palming my breast, the heat of it sinking into my flesh, igniting my bloodstream. Setting off a drumbeat of passion that increases with every pound of my frantic heart.

The smell of burning foliage tinges the crisp night air. Scorched leaves sail around us, their dry edges smoldering, caught up in wind currents I cannot control. I do not even try. My emotions are too raw, too immense to tamp down. They singe back and forth down the bond between us, growing hotter and hotter, until it is a potent channel of pure, fiery desperation. Mine, Penn's. They tangle into one. I can no longer separate our feelings, can no longer discern my own desires from his.

I hope, *gods*, I pray he is feeling the way I am right now. I hope his need for me is threatening to set his very skin aflame, for mine feels mere seconds from kindling.

I pour all my heat into the kiss, conveying with my body all the things I have spent weeks too afraid to put into words. My pulse spikes when his other hand slides down to cup the curve of my ass, pulling me flush against him, and I feel the hard evidence of his own passion pressing firmly against my midsection.

He is burning for me, too.

A wildfire in his blood, in his body—one I sparked. One I want, with sudden wild longing, to stoke until we are both utterly consumed by it. Until the past burns away, leaving space for something new to grow between us.

The realization is enough to send my mind reeling. My thoughts are fractured splinters I cannot cobble together into a cohesive thought, let alone put into words.

I want more.

I want him to—

A sudden, strange bellow in the distance splits the night, so loud I think it's thunder. It echoes violently enough to shake the heavens. Not the roar of a bear or the howl of a wolf. Throatier. Harsher. Infinitely scarier.

We jerk apart, both breathing hard. Penn stares at me with a half-dazed, half-desperate expression I'm sure is mirrored on my own face. But with several hard blinks, the fog of lust lifts and his frame goes rigid against mine. His hands leave my body and he pushes me out of his arms with the same urgency he used to pull me into them.

"We need to go," he tells me in a muted clip. "*Now.*"

The strange bellow comes again, rending the sky, and his jaw tightens.

"What is that?" I whisper, looking around in the darkness. Alarm suffuses my bloodstream, banishing any residual passion. It sounds like no animal I've ever heard. It sounds like—

"Ice giants." Penn's eyes are fully clear of the burning desire I saw in their depths only seconds ago. "There's a colony nearby."

I gasp. "*What?*"

"It is not called the Forsaken Forest without due cause. There is a reason these woods are given a wide berth. Each year when the Cimmerian snows begin to thaw, they make themselves at home here in bone-riddled caves, feeding on anything stupid enough to wander into their path before they go into hibernation for the summer months."

He glances over my shoulder, into the dark. His body is alert with tension. As if, at any second, we might find ourselves face-to-face with a mythological hoarfrost monster. My heart quails when I think of the strange copse of trees I'd found myself in only hours ago, with its snapped branches and deathly stillness. I press my lips tight together, wondering just how close I had come to death at a set of gargantuan hands.

"You are lucky you did not stumble straight into their midst," he mutters lowly. "Or we would not be having this conversation."

"Right," I say weakly. "*Lucky.* That's me."

He doesn't seem to notice the wry twist in my voice. He's busy stomping out the embers of my fire with his boots. He collects my belongings from their spot by the hollow tree, passing me my bow and quiver to sling over my shoulder as he jerks the rucksack strap up onto his own.

When our eyes meet again there is a moment—a moment of unspoken words, a moment of unfulfilled promises—that suffuses the air between us so thickly, neither of us draws breath. A moment that begs for *more* than a moment; for hours, for days, for a whole bloody month to finish what we started.

"Home?" he whispers finally, voice gruff.

Such a small word.

Such enormous implications.

It scares me, but I say it anyway. *"Home."*

Fire flares in his eyes, there and gone so fast I'm not entirely sure I haven't imagined it. His hand reaches out and twines with mine, his strong fingers squeezing like he'll never let me go.

I squeeze back.

Together, we leave the woods behind.

We make for Caeldera.

For . . . *home.*

CHAPTER TWENTY-SIX

I stare dubiously at the arch of intertwined vines. Thick and covered in razor-sharp thorns, they defy the laws of nature, twisting up from the ground in two gnarled columns that curve to meet in the shape of a large doorway.

"*This* is a portal?"

"What were you expecting?"

"I don't know." I shrug. "Something a bit more maegical. This just looks like part of nature."

"Maegic is part of nature."

I fight off an eye roll. "You know what I mean. It doesn't glow, doesn't pulsate . . . It doesn't do anything."

"I assure you, it does." He shoots me a bemused look. "Besides, portals are not designed to stand out to any common traveler on the road. Most folks are not even able to see them. They emit a glamour that keeps them hidden from all but those with strong fae blood. To a mortal, to most halflings, this place would appear as nothing more than an empty glade."

I glance around the clearing. It is set at the very heart of the Forsaken Forest, where the trees are so wide around, it would take a dozen grown men with arms outstretched to encircle their trunks. The ground is thick with moss and ferns, a green carpet that glows faintly beneath the press of each footstep. Thousands of fyrewisps drift in the air, twinkling like living stars until the first hint of dawn chases them away.

It had taken us hours of walking to reach the portal. The journey would have been much quicker with Onyx to carry us, but Penn said he would not risk bringing his stallion into the path of ice giants. Let alone any of his men.

"How does it work, exactly?" I examine the arched vines with sharper focus. A slight shimmer infuses the air of the entire glade but, other than that, I detect little in the way of power.

"The portals are like a network of doors, all connected. You step through one, exit through another."

"That simple, huh?"

His lips twitch at my incredulity. "The trick is to stay focused on where you want to end up. Only attempt to travel between portals when you know their precise locations. Otherwise . . . you can get lost."

"Lost where?"

"In between. Within the fabric."

"That sounds less than ideal." I narrow my eyes at him. "Why can't we just go back to Caeldera on foot?"

"Besides the fact that these woods are rife with monsters . . . that would take more than a week's time. Time we do not have. We've been away too long already. Fyremas is days away and one of my most trusted lieutenants is about to become a father—"

"Oh! *Carys!*" My heart seizes with sudden guilt. I have all but forgotten my friend during the drama of the past few days. "She must be worried sick!"

Penn's gaze sharpens at the familiarity in my tone, but he chooses not to comment on it. "All the more reason for us to get back as soon as possible. That means a portal. I assure you, it's perfectly safe."

"Unless you accidentally lose focus and wind up wandering the fabric of time and space for all eternity?"

"I'm certain you would find your way out eventually. There are plenty of exit points to choose from—even if you can't be entirely sure where they'll drop you."

"How many portals are there?"

"There's no way of knowing. Some have been lost to time, destroyed by the blight, or demolished by mortals when they sacked the sacred places of power. But there are a handful of them still scattered throughout the Northlands."

"Where did they come from?"

"They were built by our ancestors. Ancient fae. They wanted a way to connect the strongest leylines of the land. To travel quickly between the four courts."

"I've heard of leylines, but I'm not certain I truly understand what they are," I admit.

"If Anwyvn were a man, the leylines would be the veins beneath his skin. Instead of blood, they ferry maegic. Usually, they are invisible to the naked eye. Inaccessible. Except in spots where the maegic is particularly potent."

"Like the cavern behind the falls?"

He nods. "There are certain spots where the fabric of the world stitches together. Like a seam joining two sides of a garment. Power pools naturally in those places. You've likely come across them before, even if you did not recognize it at the time."

"The Starlight Wood," I whisper. "In Seahaven. There was a feel to it. A current in the earth. Like untapped power."

"Probably a portal."

"If it was, it is naught but ashes now. The wood was set aflame by soldiers the night I fled my home . . ."

I meet his eyes and find him watching me carefully. I have

never before voluntarily shared any information about where I came from, what my life looked like before our paths crossed.

Perhaps it is finally time to change that.

"One of the Midland kings sent soldiers." I swallow the lump in my throat. "So many soldiers. They overran the entire peninsula, laid siege to every settlement. They killed everyone. My entire village."

"Your family?"

"My mentor. His name was Eli Fleetwood. He was mortal. A healer by trade, and a skilled one at that. He could've set up his practice in Bellmere, in any big city, but he preferred to live in a cottage by the sea. People would travel all across the realm for his aid. He's the one who taught me to set bones and mix salves and brew tonics. He kept me safe—kept me shielded—for years."

"And . . ." Penn's voice is halting, as if he is afraid to push me too far. "Your parents?"

"I never met them. As far as I know, they abandoned me the day I was born. Eli found me squalling in a wicker basket on the shores beyond the Starlight Wood. Left there to wash away with the tides, like some sacrifice to the gods."

Penn absorbs my story in silence, then murmurs a soft, "I'm sorry."

"About my parents? Don't be. You cannot grieve something you have never known."

"Not about them. About your mentor." His eyes are very dark in the predawn morning. "You must miss him."

I do not say anything. I merely nod and look away. And Penn, being Penn, understands that there are some things I am not yet ready to discuss. Some wounds still too raw to poke or prod.

"This portal is currently dormant," he says, swiftly changing the subject. "If we stepped through now, we would merely find ourselves on the other side of this clearing instead of back in Caeldera."

"So how do you activate it?"

"Blood."

My brows lift. *"Blood?"*

"Specifically, maegical blood. Blood of a high fae. Blood like ours."

"That seems a bit barbaric."

"However you travel, be it by horse or ship or sled, you sacrifice something. Time, sleep, stamina, coin. This particular sacrifice is simply paid up front in exchange for safe passage." He stares at me, seeing the trepidation in my expression. "Don't worry. We'll go through together this time."

Before I can say anything else, Penn yanks one of the blades from the bandolier strapped over his chest and slashes a deep cut across his hand. He does not even wince. I am so busy staring at the blood welling into a pool in his palm, I don't realize he's taken hold of mine until I feel the sudden bite of the blade against my skin.

"Ouch!"

"Come. Quickly," he mutters, tugging me toward the portal. "Before they heal."

Clasping his bleeding palm with mine, he jerks me to a stop directly in front of the archway. At this distance, the thorns look sharp as daggers. The vines are more than simply twined; they are fused together. Inseparable, even with the sharpest instrument.

Our interlocked fingers drip red as Penn lifts them into the middle of the portal. It shimmers—once, twice—then begins to glow, a steady flood of light so bright, it is blinding. The whisper of maegic that tinges the atmosphere here at the heart of the forest crescendoes to a thrum that vibrates the air itself. My Remnant tingles, as if absorbing some of the residual power that flows all around us.

I glance to Penn for guidance.

"Whatever you do . . ." He grins at me, a rare flash of straight white teeth that steals my breath. "Don't let go."

Without another word, he leads me forward into the light.

TRAVELING BY PORTAL is like being slingshot directly into the sun. It is dizzying. Disorienting. A rushing spectrum of color, a ceaseless buzz of white noise. The world contracts down to nothing, then expands into infinity. It tips sideways, turns upside down. Spins like a wobbling top across a wood plank.

There is no substance—not to the world around me, not to the man beside me. Not to *me*. My bones dissolve into particles, scattered like dust as we hurl through a beam of pure light. I do not see, so much as sense. Do not touch, so much as feel.

I am sunlight.

I am time.

I am air.

No, not air, but . . .

Aether.

We hurtle across the network of leylines, gossamer and glowing like a spider's web in sunlight, intersecting and branching across the whole continent. It is too much to hold in my head at once, too vast to process without fracturing into pieces. I want to shut my eyes, but they are not there to shut. I wonder how it is I can still be holding Penn's hand when I have no hand left. I wonder how I can wonder anything at all with no mind, no skull, no self.

The journey lasts an eternity and also, somehow, less than a second. A lifetime wrapped within a single blink. With a jarring thud that makes my soul spasm, we slam to a halt. I feel my scattered particles reassemble, dust becoming blood and bone, all that was diaphanous returning to solid form.

And then we are back. Back on solid ground, back in the world. Feet in my boots, breath in my lungs. Penn's hand squeezes mine, warm and steady. Gulping in ragged gasps of air, I fight off waves of nausea churning at my middle and blink to clear the starbursts from my eyes.

We stand in a round cavern much like the one concealed behind the waterfall, only larger—and significantly drier without a constant blanket of mist to dampen the air. The stone walls around us bear glyphs in the same ancient, etched style, but these do not encircle the entire room. Instead, they form a doorway.

A portal.

It is roughly the same size and shape as the vine arch we passed through in the woods. As I watch, the glyphs fade from a bright-red glow to their natural shade of dark ash as the portal goes dormant. In mere seconds, it looks like nothing more than ancient artwork carved into the stone.

"Where are we?" I ask, voice hushed.

"See for yourself."

Penn does not drop my hand as he leads me to the mouth of the chamber. Stepping out onto a narrow ledge, I find myself staring down at Caeldera. We are at the very top of the crater, with a view of the entire capital sprawled out beneath us. Directly opposite our vantage point, the palace glitters amid the roaring falls. Its turrets refract the first beams of morning light, painting the typically gray facade in the pastel palette of sunrise.

I gasp at the sight, awed by the beauty unfurled like a carpet at my feet.

"This is my favorite place in all of Caeldera."

Tearing my eyes from the view, I glance at Penn. "It's not difficult to see why."

"I come here to clear my head." His lips tug up at one side. "Or to escape Vanora."

"Has she always been as she is now? So . . . calculating?"

"Vanora was born with no fire maegic. She burns with resentment instead. Her need for adoration is a flame that will never go out." Finally releasing my hand, he reaches up and removes his helm. It hits the stone parapet at our waists with a heavy thunk. I try not to watch too closely as he runs his hands through his hair, mussing the flattened strands. The sight is somehow more riveting than the view of the city.

"She resents me most of all," Penn continues, bracing himself against the stone. "We share no blood, no true familial bond. She is the daughter of King Vorath—the first Fire Remnant, who was born into the chaos of the Cull and claimed the throne when he came of age. And I was the son of a common blacksmith."

"*Was?* Are you not still?"

"The day I was born, mere minutes after I was delivered, they took me from my mother's arms and brought me here. To the palace. I was presented to Queen Amitha, Vanora's mother." He pauses. "You must understand, here in the Northlands, it was seen as a great honor to give birth to the next Remnant. I was not hidden away like Enid, not abandoned like you. My birth parents were elevated in social rank, lavished with gold, given great jewels and a parcel of land by the North Sea in exchange for producing me."

"For giving you up," I correct softly.

Penn shrugs. "Might makes right, as they say. Queen Amitha raised me well enough, for all that she could not give me a true mother's love. Even in her grief, she was not cruel. She was soft-spoken. Gentle. Too gentle, perhaps, since she joined her husband in the skies only a decade after his soul departed."

"A pity her daughter did not inherit those same traits."

"Vanora was born simmering with a bitterness no amount of love could sweeten. I don't think she ever accepted my sudden arrival in her life—especially as it coincided with her father's death. His pyre was not even cold when I was brought to Cael-dera, a newborn babe, a commoner at that, bearing a Remnant mark . . ." His expression is torn between amusement and apathy. "At the age of five, she could not understand why I possessed that which she was denied. Why his legacy had passed to me instead of her, a child of his own blood. Her bitterness, already steam-ing, boiled over."

"And your birth parents . . . you never saw them again?"

"No. They relinquished all claim to me. But that is not ab-normal. In the fae courts, it has always been so—the strongest of us taking up the reins of rule, steering the kingdoms. After the uprising, when the emperor was killed, when the maegic fled, it became even more essential. There was no one to unite the four elemental courts. No singular power to protect our borders from invasion, to shield our people from slaughter. We were on our own." His deep voice is reflective. "Two of the strongholds fell shortly after the wars began. To this day, they sit in ruins."

"Air and Earth," I murmur. "You told me once before."

And, since, I had read more about them in Soren's tome. It was a bevy of interesting information—even if the author's descrip-tions were dry and left something to be desired. Just last week, before I'd been kidnapped, I'd read a passage about the slow ero-sion of maegic, even in the strongholds that had survived the Cull.

Maegical gifts grow rarer with each generation.
Even among the oldest high fae bloodlines, where

power was once a guarantee, there is no longer an assurance that a child will be born with even the most basic abilities in wielding an element. Several families interviewed for this account confessed, under the condition of anonymity, that their newest offspring cannot spark a candle or fill a goblet, let alone heal after an injury.

Others say they have been in incapable of conceiving at all, leading to rising fears that the entire maegical race may die out within the next century. And while it is speculated that a child born to one of the Remnants—or, perhaps, a pair—might produce a stronger elemental talent, thus far there has been no evidence to confirm those hopeful theories."

In the margins, Soren had scribbled, *Surprised he didn't take the liberty to comment about my legions of potential bastards.*

Only he could make a joke out of the total eradication of our people.

"Yes," Penn says, calling me back to the present. "The Fire Court survived, but barely. Thousands were killed at the hands of Reavers and Frostlanders, who'd joined the mortal usurpers in their bloody regime. Dyved's armies fought them back, but at great cost." He stares at his home, brows furrowed, fingers flexing against the stone. "Afterward, King Vorath used what power he possessed to hold the kingdom together. He sealed our borders from all outside the plateau, closed the trade routes in and out. His reign was a time of rigid control and strict compliance. Of isolation and suspicion and fear. So much fear. That was the Dyved of Vanora's childhood. That was the clay from which she was molded."

"It does not excuse her actions."

"Excuse them? No. Explain them? Possibly. She was no more than a young girl when her father pushed his powers too far, trying to keep the wards up. He died in the process. And then . . ."

"You were born."

"Yes. The next Fire Remnant," he agrees with a hint of acerbity. "Vanora was Vorath's heir by birth. But I have his power. I have his flame." His hand lifts to his chest, pressing against his bandolier, against the mark I know lies etched on the skin beneath. "There are many who want me to step in and take the throne. It is mine by right—far more than it has ever been hers."

"Why not take it, then?"

He looks at me, brows high on his forehead. "Vanora may be vain and self-centered, but she has not been a bad steward of the throne. Dyved thrives. The people are happy. For more than a century now, she has been a decent enough ruler. I allow her lavish dinners and ridiculous balls and aggrandizing displays. In exchange, I keep my freedom. Freedom to travel beyond the plateau. To reopen our borders, reestablish our trade routes. To make alliances that once seemed an impossibility." He glances back at the city. "I was barely out of my leading strings when I set out to the Water Court for the first time with a contingent of trusted soldiers at my back. I wanted to see if it still existed. When I saw that it did, I demanded a meeting with the king."

"Soren?"

His nod is short. "Gods, he must've been amused by the sight of me, half-grown, rattling his gates with my list of demands. But he did let me in. More, he actually listened without dismissing my idea for a treaty outright." There is a pause. "He may be a miserable, misanthropic bastard, but he is true to his word. We have been allies ever since, sworn to aid each other in war. To hold the Northlands against invasion. To stave off the blight as long as possible."

"When we were leaving the Acrine Hold, he mentioned your royal obligations to attend his sister's wedding?"

"Princess Arwen." Penn sighs. "She is to be married at midsummer. I suppose I will have to make an appearance. Even if she were amenable to the idea, Vanora is now too frail to travel as far as Llŷr."

I chew my lip. "And me? Am I to attend?"

The air turns static with unspoken tension. "Do you want to?"

"I would like to see Hylios," I admit. "I am curious about the Water Court."

The silence lingers for a breathless moment. "As I have told you many times before, Rhya . . . you are no prisoner here. You may go where you wish. I have no right to keep you."

My gaze traces the lines of his profile. Two dark eyes, turned away from me. The sharp, straight slope of his nose. That stubborn mouth, so often set in a frown. I have seen but a handful of smiles from that mouth, and far fewer laughs.

I catch myself wondering what the formidable Pendefyre of Dyved might be like, had he been born without that mark on his chest, without that inferno raging beneath his skin. Had he grown up the son of a common blacksmith instead of a child of the prophecy. A sudden image of him—strong shoulders unburdened by the weight of destiny, bright smile in a soot-streaked face, handsome enough to capture the attention of every girl in his village—flashes through my mind, there and gone in the space of a heartbeat.

"It is still months away," I say in a thick voice. "Let us first see if I survive Fyremas."

My words are only meant to lighten the mood, which has

turned decidedly somber, but they jolt Penn into action. He pushes away from the stone parapet and grabs his helm. "We should be getting back. The sun is rising and it's going to be a long day."

I open my mouth to say something—*anything*—to keep him standing here with me a little while longer, to prolong this fleeting moment of transparency between us. But I have no earthly idea what to say, and besides, he is already in motion. I fall into step just behind him, a silent shadow following him back into the rock chamber. We bypass the dormant portal, now almost undetectable against the far wall, and move into a narrow passageway that leads deeper into the earth. It is so dark, I can barely make out the silhouette of Penn's broad shoulders three paces ahead. But I can feel him there, even without sight, the bond between us tugging me along like a new colt on a training bridle.

When he stops at the end of the passage, I follow suit automatically. He lifts his hand and presses it against the wall. There is a brief red glow of a ward activating in the darkness. An instant later, I hear a deep rumble in the earth and the floor beneath our feet drops out. I shriek as my hands fly out and twist in the fabric of Penn's cloak.

"Penn!"

"Relax." Mirth threads through his voice. "It's a lift, built into one of the old mine shafts. There's a whole network of tunnels surrounding the crater. A few are still in use for storage and the like, but the rest are sealed off from the public."

My hammering pulse slows somewhat as the lift lowers, a surprisingly smooth descent. I force my fingers to release their death grip on his cloak.

"My ancestors mined the earth around the old volcano for generations, but as Caeldera flourished into a more cosmopolitan city, the practice fell away," Penn informs me. I get the sense he is talking mainly to keep me distracted. "Most of our gemstones and minerals now come from the foothills near the Cimmerian Mountains and the salt flats in the upper provinces."

I nod, only half listening as I wait for the journey to end. Taking shallow breaths of stale air into my lungs, I envision open sky, clear dawn breaking through the clouds. Claustrophobia claws at me viciously as the moments tick on. At last, we thud to a stop at the bottom of the shaft. The earth beneath my boots is blessedly solid as Penn guides me down another short passage and, finally, into the light. I suck in a deep breath, filling my lungs to capacity.

"I see a future career in mining is out of the question for you."

I glance over at Penn's sardonic remark. He is leaning back against the rock face at the base of the cliff, eyeing me with a mix of concern and amusement.

"I'm fine now." I exhale a shaky breath, feeling steadier already. "I have never been overly fond of confinement."

"Mmm. The deep earth is the antithesis to all that you are. You will never feel at home in places where there is no open sky. Just as I am not destined to turn my hand to sea captaincy. There are some things, for all our power, we cannot overcome."

I ponder this as we make our way back to the palace, moving through the quiet streets of Caeldera as they slowly come alive. Dawn breaks in full, bathing the clean-swept cobblestones with light. Roosters stir awake and announce the start of a new day with creaky crows. Soon, their owners will emerge, bound for the mills and the forges and the storehouses that dot the lanes around us. But for now, all is quiet. All is still.

I had once thought I might never return here, to this place. Yet in this moment, it feels like an indisputable homecoming. If I'm honest with myself, that may have more to do with the man walking beside me than it does with the city itself.

I do not share this sentiment with Penn. But between us, the invisible tether sings with such strength, such surety, I think if I dare lift my fist from its tightly clenched position at my side, I might run a hand across it, pulling music from our taut silence like a finger down the string of a harpsichord.

By the time we reach the palace, my fists are clenched so tight with the effort to keep them at my sides, my fingers have lost circulation.

CHAPTER
TWENTY–SEVEN

The alacrity with which I fold back into life in Caeldera
surprises me. In my time away, I gave little thought to how
those I left behind might feel to learn of my kidnapping. I was so
consumed by the blood on my hands, so convinced of my own
unforgivable actions, I never once contemplated that my return
would be one of open arms and raw relief.

But it is there in the wet eyes of my maids, blinking back tears
as they draw me a hot bath and brush the snarls from my hair. It
is there in the soft chuck of Jac's fingers beneath my chin when he
accompanies me down to dinner in the Great Hall. In Mabon's
muted smile, in Cadogan's quick wink. In the way Uther gently
pulls back my chair and takes a seat close beside me for the evening meal. In Farley's snarky request that the next time I go and
get myself kidnapped, I at least wait until his leg is healed enough
to help with the rescue mission. Don't I know he's the best tracker
in the Ember Guild?

They surround me in an impenetrable circle of protection and
warmth, telling me, without ever telling me, that there is no blame
for my killing of their comrade, no resentment for the taking of
Gower's life. This—their kindness, their understanding—is too
much to bear with any stoicism. I almost wish Vanora would

insult me again, if only to quell the emotional tide threatening to wash away any sense of composure. I choke down mouthfuls of turnips and keep my watery eyes on my dinner plate.

For all I see of his men, of Penn himself I see little. I had assumed, after what happened in the Forsaken Forest, that things would be different between us. That the newfound transparency we shared on the parapet would continue, now that we are back in the palace. That the fiery passion we had lit with our hands and lips and teeth in that dark stretch of woods would reignite, stoked by close proximity to each other, day after day, night after night.

And yet . . . that moment that had changed everything for me has evidently changed nothing for him. He is busy as ever, kept occupied by the not insignificant matter of running a kingdom. The fleeting moments our paths do cross are few and far between.

There is the nightly glimpse of him at the far end of the banquet table, of course. The more rare sighting of him swinging a sword or hurling a lance in the practice yards when I pass by on my way to High Street each morning, Farley hobbling after me on his crutches. And then, later in the evenings, long after dark, there are the long hours I lie on my pallet in the spire, still as stone, listening hard for the moment of his return.

The power in my chest coils tighter and tighter, a loaded spring, as I feel him approach through the bond and, eventually, hear the tower door creak open through the rafters. The muffled thumps of his boots hitting the floor. The click of a wooden chest opening and closing. The clatter of a scabbard returning to its rack.

These are all I have to live on—these ephemeral glimpses, these indistinct traces of existence. For he does not seek me out, not for training or for conversation. Certainly not for anything *beyond* conversation. It is as though he has erected an invisible perimeter around himself, designed specifically to keep me at bay. I am not sure why, or exactly when, it appeared . . . I only know that it has. And I am even less sure how to knock it back down.

I absorb this blow like it is no more than a minor perturbance, though in truth it is anything but. If Pendefyre regrets what happened between us, that is his prerogative. Not mine. If he wants to pretend it never happened . . .

Fine.

I can pretend as well as the next person.

But even as I tell myself I do not care to share his company, all too often I catch myself longing for it with a desperation that terrifies me. My mind is trapped in a perpetual spiral of anticipation, my senses heightened to a new sort of awareness each time I find myself in his presence.

Now that I know how he tastes, now that I know the devouring heat of his lips, now that I know how it feels to fit every curve of my body against the hard planes of his chest . . .

I cannot *un*know it.

I cannot forget it.

Even if he wishes to.

ON THE THIRD day after my return, I sit on a long neglected garden bed in the enclosed courtyard at the rear of Carys's shop, pulling weeds and planting the cuttings I took from the Forsaken Forest. The blade of the borrowed spade is streaked with earth.

Reposed on a low chaise beneath a slender white birch tree, Carys chatters absently as I work. Farley, sprawled on the twin chaise beside her, interjects occasionally with a witty remark or pithy comment. We have spent many such mornings like this, the three of us, bound together by our unique confinements.

"If this baby does not put in an appearance soon, I'm placing it in the care of the fyre priestesses at the Temple of the Gods," Carys decrees. "At this rate, I'm going to miss all the Fyremas festivities."

I pluck a particularly large weed, unperturbed by her threats. There is no heat in them. Besides, I have heard them all before, made with increasing frequency as her stomach grows rounder and rounder, her burden heavier and heavier, and still there are no signs of labor.

"And my husband. Where is he? After putting me in this condition, he simply vanishes?" She is scowling now, but the hands that stroke rhythmically over her distended belly are utterly gentle. *"Men."*

"Come now, Carys," Farley puts in bravely. "Uther is doing his best to help Pendefyre secure the Ember Guild. You know how tense things are within our ranks since—"

He breaks off suddenly. In the following silence, I can hear the words he does not say. *Since Gower.* Likewise, I can feel two worried gazes burning into the back of my neck as I bend lower over the flower bed, my skirts pooling around me in a cloud of fabric. They never voice their worries. Not to me, not aloud. We have hardly discussed my ordeal at all. That first morning, Carys had merely clasped my cheek with one of her fine-boned hands, looked deeply into my eyes, and murmured something about putting on the tea. As if she had been waiting only the span of a single night since our last visit. As if nothing had changed.

"Rhya, dear," she breezes now, forcing a light tone. "You're a healer. Tell me how I can hasten this birth along."

I sit back on my heels and wipe my hands on my apron. "Your babe will come when it's time. This is no race. There is no need to hurry if you are healthy enough to carry a few more days."

"Rhya." The faint whine in her voice is familiar. *"Please."*

"There are certain herbs to induce labor, but I would not give them to you for any reason besides as a last resort." I heave a martyred sigh. "Some claim spicy foods can trigger birthing pains. Others swear raspberry leaf tea does the trick. Then, there's the therapeutic massage of the pressure points, using sagethorn oil or rose-hip extract . . ."

"So? Which method shall we try first?"

"None of them, Carys."

"Whyever not?"

"Because the best way to hurry the babe along requires no tinctures or teas. You only need some physical activity. *Light* physical activity," I stress, seeing the excited spark in her eyes. "A very short walk. Or . . . well . . . activity of a different sort . . ."

"And what sort is that?" Carys prompts when I falter.

Farley snorts. "Can't you guess? Look how she's blushing! The sort of activity you need your husband for, I'd reckon."

I shoot him a look. "I am not blushing!"

"Red as a beet, Ace."

Ignoring him, I look at Carys with as much dignity as I can muster. "Annoying as he may be, he's not wrong. Some say that . . . intimate activities in the marriage bed are enough to . . . stimulate . . ."

"Farley!" Carys clips sharply. "Stop giggling like a schoolboy and go get my husband. Now."

"But—"

"No buts!" she snaps at the sulking redhead. "He's likely at the sparring pits. If you get a move on, even with those crutches, you can be back with him in no more than an hour."

"I'm not supposed to leave the two of you unattended," he says with great dignity. "Pendefyre said—"

"Och! Fine! Forget it!" With considerable effort, Carys pushes herself upright on the chaise. Planting her slippers on the flagstones, she struggles to her feet with a surge of determination. "I'll go get him myself if it's such a great imposition—"

Her words gasp into silence as a rush of water splashes down between her skirts, onto the slate. For a long moment, all three of us freeze, as though time itself has stopped. Carys looks down at her feet with a dazed expression. Her pink lips are rounded in a perfect circle of surprise.

"Oh," is all she manages to say. "*Oh.*"

I look directly into Farley's eyes. They are stripped of their usual mirth, wide with shock.

"Forget the sparring pits," I tell him. "Fetch the midwife instead. Tell her it's time."

IN ALL MY years of assisting Eli, I never once aided in a birth like the one of Carys and Uther's son. Given his hesitancy in making an appearance, when at last he arrives it is with a stunning, breath-stealing speed.

I have scarcely settled Carys back on the garden chaise when the first contractions seize her in their clutches. After that, there is no moving her up the stairs to the apartments. For beneath her skirts, I can see she is already well on her way to delivery.

Healer though I may be, I have not witnessed many births. Pregnancies grow rarer and rarer with each passing year as the blight grips the land in an ever-tightening hold. Most expectant mothers do not carry to term, and if they manage to, their babies are often born . . . *wrong.* Limbs twisted, eyes unseeing. Organs on the outside of their frail abdomens. Many come out blue and still, never taking a single breath of air beyond the womb. The few that do survive seldom live long, unable to breathe on their own.

And with the babies go the mothers. Whether their bodies fail during the bloody battle of childbirth or their souls flee in the heartbreaking aftermath of losing a child, fair few survive the ordeal. Sadly, what had once been common practice, natural as breathing, is now a rarity. Healthy deliveries in which both mother and child survive are a precious gift among mortals. Successful fae births are even more rare, a maegical anomaly in a maegicless era.

I do not allow myself to dwell on these realities as I examine my friend. My voice is level as I speak soothing words meant to keep her calm, meant to convince her there are no problems. Inside, though, I am counting the minutes until Farley's return with the midwife in tow. Inside, I am screaming that I somehow must move her inside, upstairs, to her bedchamber, where there are clean linens and fresh water and comfortable feather pillows to prop her against.

But how can I, with the babe bearing down so fast? How can I, when already her birthing pains are coming with alarming acceleration, one arriving directly after another, gripping her muscles with spine-bowing constriction and wrenching away all sense of autonomy? If she convulses thus on the stairs, there is no telling what will happen. She could fall. She could be harmed, the babe along with her.

I will not risk their lives. Not when I cannot be confident in how much time remains before the head crowns. Carys already seems far weaker than I'd like, her face white as a sheet, her breaths shallow and strained. Pain hazes her bright green eyes. And where, *gods*, where is all that blood coming from?

"Something's wrong." Carys moans, gripping my hand like a vise. "It hurts . . ."

"Nothing is wrong. I know it hurts, but you're doing well."

I swallow hard, trying to calm my own panic. It thrums fast and hot inside my veins, pricking at my Remnant mark with electrically charged fingers. I use all my self-control to keep my emotions in check, to keep my power locked deep inside. I cannot allow my rising panic to spill out in a wave that will turn a dire situation even more deadly.

I don't dwell on what it will mean for my friend if her babe becomes lodged. Or worse, descends breech first. For the thought of taking a blade to her is enough to evaporate any facade of self-possession.

"Rhya!" She gasps as another contraction seizes her. My finger bones grind together under her grip.

"This is what you wanted, Carys. What you prayed for. Remember? Your child comes, eager to meet you." I force a smile as my hands move over her stomach. The babe has already dropped quite low. "For one who resisted so stubbornly, they are now exhibiting remarkable haste."

"Just like their father. That streak of quiet obstinance . . . Gods help me, with two of them under my roof . . ."

"If anyone can handle them, it's you," I assure her. "Just keep breathing. That's it. Slow and steady. The midwife will be here soon."

But she is not.

An hour ticks by, and still, Farley does not return. Not with the midwife, not with Uther. Not with anyone. I fetch some basic supplies from the apartments upstairs, then do my best to comfort Carys as she writhes in increasing discomfort, distracting her with a low, constant stream of conversation. I speak until my voice goes hoarse, talking of everything and nothing—my childhood, my favorite foods, my dress for the upcoming festival. Keda and Teagan's latest squabble over the proper steps to the Dyvedi waltz. Farley's new infatuation with a particularly handsome member of the palace guard.

I sop sweat from her brow with a wet washcloth and hold her

hand when the pains have her in their grips. All the while, blood flows from between her legs, a deathly trickle.

Is this amount of bleeding normal? I wonder, heart racing. *Oh, Eli, how I wish you were here* . . .

The time to push grows nearer and nearer. Soon, there will be no more waiting. I feel the crown of her baby's head beginning to protrude and grip my friend's hand tight in my own.

"Where is he?" she wheezes. "Where is Uther?"

"He's coming. He'll be here soon."

"The midwife—"

"We cannot wait for the midwife," I tell her in as steady a voice as I can manage, dousing my hands with the strong spirits I found in her kitchen cupboard. "You're going to have to push."

"No, I can't. Not until—"

"You must. Carys, do you hear me? You cannot afford to delay, and neither can your child." I adjust the towel I've placed between her legs. The fissure of worry that's opened up inside me deepens further when I see more blood seeping into the white fabric. "I know this isn't how you wanted to do this; I know this wasn't your plan. But I'm here with you. I'm right here."

She swallows down her protests. Pulling in a deep breath, she looks at me—looks at me with such trust, such unwavering faith, it makes my eyes smart with tears. "Okay, Rhya."

"Can you push?"

She nods.

"I am here. I am with you," I tell her, positioning myself between her knees at the foot of the chaise. "You can do this. *We* can do this."

My voice sounds steady enough, I think. But deep within me, a voice is crying out—keening from my soul, screaming down the bond that links me to Penn.

Where are you?
I need you.
Please, come.
Come quickly.

THEY BURST INTO the back courtyard armed to the teeth and out of breath, ready to fight a battle long since ended. Uther, Penn, Mabon, Cadogan, and Jac. They all slam to a halt when they see me there, sitting in the dirt of the flower beds with the newborn babe in my arms. I am wrapping him in a soft blanket I retrieved from the nursery upstairs when Carys finally let him go long enough for me to clean him. She now dozes lightly on the chaise, exhausted from the aftermath of the birth and the sedating tea I'd forced her to swallow.

I myself could use a dose. My hands still shake. The past few hours have been some of the most harrowing of my life. Even now, with both mother and child breathing steadily, I cannot settle my own frazzled nerves.

For a long moment, the men merely stare, frozen, at the scene before them. Their stunned expressions are almost comical. Their eyes snag on the blood. I've wiped up the worst of it already, but there are still traces littered around me. On the flagstones. On my discarded gardening apron. On the towels and blankets piled beside the chaise. It is a jarring contrast to the peaceful domesticity of Carys's pretty courtyard.

Behind them, the door swings open once again as Farley jostles through it on his crutches. An ancient crone of a woman follows on his heels. The midwife. They, too, stop short when they see me.

"Took you long enough," I say to Farley in a glib voice. Beneath my flippancy, there is a deep undercurrent of untapped distress. "Did you cross the Cimmerians to find help?"

Uther is the first to recover his senses, rushing to his wife's side. He drops to his knees in the dirt, sparing hardly a glance at his newborn son. His gaze is for Carys and Carys alone.

"Is she—"

"She's perfectly fine," I assure him, noting the uncharacteristic fear in his voice. "There was a bit of bleeding, but it's stopped already with the help of a few stitches. We'll keep her under close watch for a few days, but I have no doubt she will live a long, healthy life." My eyes move to the swaddled babe in my arms. He has a dark crop of hair and a tiny rosebud mouth. The pointed tips of his ears are so delicate, I can nearly see through them. "So will your son."

"We owe you a great debt, Rhya," Uther says solemnly. He looks at his son, cradled in my arms, and his steady gray gaze glosses with emotion. "One I vow to repay, however I am able."

My airway feels thick. My emotions thrash and throttle, a raging storm within. I manage only a nod in response.

Carys's eyes crack open. She smiles weakly at her husband. "He looks like you, handsome. But he's got my lungs. You should've heard him hollering when he took his first breath . . ."

"I wish I had, my love. I'm sorry it took me so long to get here. We weren't at the barracks. We were on the upper plateau, securing the perimeter guard posts before the festival—"

"Shh." She lifts her hand to cover his as he strokes her cheek. "Rhya and I managed well enough on our own."

Uther looks to me. "Pendefyre felt your distress through the bond. He knew something was wrong. If not for that, we might never have known. It would've been hours before we returned."

I pass the child into Uther's capable arms and retreat to give the new family a moment of privacy. Before I make it two paces, Carys's hand shoots out and catches me around the wrist in a surprisingly strong grip.

"Rhya."

I turn back to her, brows raised.

"Thank you," she says. "From the farthest reaches of my heart. Thank you for being here."

"There's no need to thank me. You did all the work."

My words come out in a stiff voice that sounds nothing like my own. The emotions whirling inside me are edging into a place I can no longer control. Sweat beads my forehead. My heart is pounding. My stomach is a ball of lead. I have to get out of here, *now*, before I break down completely. Before the intensity of my feelings overwhelms me.

I smile at her with as much warmth as I can muster, then quietly extract myself. I might feel more guilty in fleeing if the midwife were not there, swooping in to examine Carys and her son with the shrewd eyes of an expert. She nods at me, a gesture of mutual respect, as our paths cross halfway across the courtyard.

Jac, Cadogan, Mabon, and Farley all speak to me when I reach their huddle by the door. Words of thanks, words of congratulations. For the life of me, I cannot focus on anything they're saying, even as they slap my back and smile down into my face. I am waging an inward battle against myself, fighting against the rising surge of power—suppressed while Carys needed my aid, now rearing its ugly head. My pulse is thunder in my veins; my nerve endings crackle like lightning. I place a hand against my Remnant, pressing hard through the fabric of my gown, as if to force it into compliance with sheer willpower.

It prickles defiantly.

Leaning against the far wall like he is carved from stone,

Penn takes one look at my face, grabs me by the hand, and leads me away without so much as a word of explanation to his men.

"Penn," I breathe, a note of desperation in my voice.

"Not here," he mutters, tugging me into the empty dress shop. "Not yet."

I say nothing more. In silence, we cross to the front door, passing bolts of fabric and half-pinned mannequins. We step out into the bright light of midday and cross from one side of High Street to the other, ducking between a parked cart of apothecary supplies and a towering stack of flour bags outside the chocolatier.

There is no need to describe to him how precarious the thread on which my control hangs; no need to share how the coil of power at my chest is threatening to come unspooled with each passing instant. My emotions are a raw current; my every feeling blasts through the bond without restraint. There is no way to hold it back, no way to tamp it down. He shares my searing agitation, my brimming disquiet, with each step we take down the cobbled streets of Caeldera, with each breath I pull into my shaky lungs.

The crowds are thick around us, throngs of shoppers and tradesmen lining the streets. Their faces are a blur in my peripherals, an undulating sea I cannot bring into focus. They give us a wide berth as Penn leads me back toward the palace. His hand is strong and warm around mine, grounding me when the emotions grow to a fever pitch.

All sense of light and joy is slowly being crowded out by darkness and despair. Visions flash through my head with each step.

My body, floating at the center of a ripping tornado. A shattered wagon in pieces on the ground. Gower's corpse, speared clean through. My little dagger slashing against the hollow of his throat.

A scene of devastation.

A scene of death.

At my own hand.

You killed a man.

I need a release. I am barely holding on. Try as I might to push it down, to keep it in, I have not yet learned whatever control will allow me to gather my power in like a breath but not release it in a gust that obliterates everything around me.

Penn was right, when he found me back in those woods. I am afraid. Afraid of my own capabilities. Afraid of whom I might hurt. I think of Soren—his nonchalant skill with the goblet, making the beads of water dance an intricate ballet for my amusement. How is it he learned to command his power with such nuance, when I cannot access my own without unleashing a wave of raw strength that sweeps me away? How is it he mastered his abilities when Penn, in nearly the same amount of time on this earth, seems scarcely able to tap into his without incinerating everything in his path?

There must surely be some middle ground between locking in my power and wielding it like an extension of self. But if there is such a balance, I have no idea how to strike it. When the wind rises inside me, it is like a cyclone. Unstoppable. Unfathomable. I cannot hope to prevent it. All I can do is seek high ground, or try like hell to outrun the worst of the fallout.

By the time we reach the cavern behind the falls, I feel as pale and shaky as Carys looked in the throes of delivery. Penn's strides never falter as he leads me up the roughhewn steps. Mist hangs heavily in the air, filling my lungs and slicking my skin. I press my lips together as though I might contain everything inside, no longer even daring to draw breath.

"Rhya."

I glance at Penn, barely seeing him. My eyes are turned inward, to the raging storm that rattles my bones. My lungs scream for air, but I do not comply.

"Breathe," he orders, gripping me by the shoulders. His fingers bite into my flesh hard enough to bruise. "You have to breathe."

I shake my head. I am afraid to part my lips, afraid the smallest breach in my external control will trigger the same inwardly.

"Gods, you *feel* too bloody much! That bleeding heart of yours is going to get you killed." He looses a low oath. "You need to separate yourself from it. Create distance between your mind and your heart. Between your heart and your power."

He makes it sound simple.

"Strong emotions are a liability. They are a powerful trigger for someone like you. For someone like me. Feeling anything too deeply—pain, panic, fear, joy, desire, or"—his voice catches—"*love*—" He clears his throat, hard, and continues. "Is far more dangerous than feeling nothing at all. It can make your control slip like this. It can make you spiral into chaos."

I struggle to focus on what he's telling me. His words are distant, muffled by a roar of wind inside my head.

"The things we want most in this world . . . The things that make us feel the most intensely . . ." His eyes are locked on mine, never shifting, trying to convey something he isn't willing to put plainly into words. "Those are the things we cannot have. Not without great risk."

I try to nod but can't manage it. Despite his urgings to distance myself from them, my emotions are still running rampant. My heart hurts almost as much as my screaming lungs. Though neither aches as much as the mark on my chest.

"You are stronger than your fear, Rhya. You are strong enough to push down the power. You just have to believe it." He shakes me so hard, my head snaps back. "You are the gate that holds the wind at bay. You are the sentinel at the threshold of chaos. You will not yield. You will not fall. Do you hear me?"

He's scaring me—almost as much as I'm scaring myself. And yet, there is some small part of me that responds to the violence of his grip, the uncompromising edge to his words. So I close my eyes and do as he says. I seek my center, find myself floating at the eye of a hurricane. The storm clouds are black as night, billowing with malice. The waters are not calm; they churn around me, a frothing portent of the tempest to come. I know I do not have long until the wind bursts from beneath my skin. I tremble as I tread water, fighting to keep my head above the icy swells.

"You can do this, Rhya," a voice is saying from somewhere very far away. "Contain it. Force it down. Force it deep inside."

The cyclone encroaches from all sides, an ever-tightening noose. There is no way to hold it back, no way to keep it from washing over me.

Every time I have tried to ride it out in the past, I have faltered. Every time I have attempted to outlast it, I have been swept away.

Not this time.

I push aside my self-doubt, my simmering anxieties that the gods have chosen wrong, that I am no child of the prophecy, that this destiny is a burden too great for my frail shoulders to bear. For, like it or not, there is no one else to bear it.

I am here.

This task, however insurmountable, is mine.

I am the Remnant of Air. I am the weaver of wind. I was born for this. I am stronger than my fear. And I will hold the line of chaos. I will keep the wind at bay. I will bolt the gate within.

Even if it kills me.

Inside my mind, I conjure an air shield like the one I made on the mountain, but taller, thicker, reaching all the way from the depths of the sea to the farthest reaches of the sky. Using all my focus, I blast it outward in all directions. Meeting the storm clouds head-on. Forcing them back, bit by bit, each handspan a hard-won battle, each sliver of space draining my resolve.

Still, I keep pushing.

Pushing and pushing and pushing, until the black squall fades into a gray memory. Until the waters lap like a summer lake. Until the hurricane retreats to the edges of my mental sea and the searing mark at my chest turns cold and silent.

The power is still there—it is always there; it will always be there—but I have done it. I have finally calmed the storm, contained the threat before it can burst forth. I have done the impossible, tethered the untetherable.

I have bested the wind.

Though the war has only waged inside my mind, I feel as though I have fought a battle. My muscles are sore, my mouth parched. My air-starved lungs are sharp blades of agony. I take a shaky breath, my first in far too long.

Cracking open my eyes, I find Penn standing before me. His face is so close, I can see every fleck of crimson in his dark ember eyes. And I wish, in that moment of quiet victory, that he'll kiss me again. I wish that more than anything.

He doesn't.

His hands slip up from their death grip on my shoulders and find my neck. His thumb strokes over my jugular vein, where the pulse patters in triple time. His words are turbulent with pride and relief.

"Well done, wind weaver," he whispers. "Well done."

CHAPTER TWENTY-EIGHT

The days preceding Fyremas slip through my fingers faster than I can find my grasp. I spend mornings at practice in the cavern, calling forth my power, then driving it back with my mental air shields over and over again, until it is, if not second nature, at least slightly easier to keep the wind from spilling out unbidden.

This I do entirely alone. Penn doesn't accompany me again—not to the cave, nor anywhere else. I see even less of him than I did before Carys gave birth. He goes out of his way to avoid me, holding me at arm's length with a front of chill civility whenever our paths inevitably cross. He leaves quickly if we find ourselves in the same room, excuses himself from conversations with his men that include me, and never returns to the tower until he's certain I'm already asleep.

It is probably for the best—or so I tell myself to cover the deep hurt his renewed indifference causes. I cannot afford to lean on him. This power is a burden I must learn to shoulder on my own.

I have never been so glad to have Soren's book as a guide. There are chapters discussing the many nuances of maegic each Remnant can wield—from water currents to fireballs—but I stick to the simpler sections, which detail the fundamentals of self-mastery.

Wind weavers especially should focus on breath work. The air in one's lungs is, after all, the very source of your power, the book tells me in one chapter.

Avoid enclosed spaces at all costs, it suggests in another. *Confinement will severely limit even the most proficient sky sylph.*

Be wary of mood swings, it warns finally. *Much like a sudden tempest, a wind weaver is prone to abrupt changes in temperament. They can appear from nowhere and overwhelm if one does not guard against them.*

Below this, Soren had written, *Remind me not to get on your bad side, skylark.*

After my first few solo power-summoning sessions, I leave the cavern on legs so shaky they scarcely last the climb back to the tower before giving out. But beneath my exhaustion is a newfound solace. For each time I successfully quiet my inner storms, I grow more confident in my abilities. I dare to hope that, someday, I might actually get a chance at a normal life. Not as the Remnant of Air, but as me. Rhya. For with my power locked deep within, I will no longer be a danger to those around me. I will no longer have to live in fear of what I might be capable of or whom I might hurt. I can simply . . .

Live.

Afternoons pass by in a blur of visits to Carys, Uther, and their new son. They've named him Nevin—their little saint—and the joy that suffuses the air of their apartments is strong enough to make my eyes sting with tears. I am not the only one who gravitates toward it. More often than not, a handful of Ember Guild members are there when I arrive, seated around the sturdy kitchen table discussing strategy in low tones so as not to wake the babe, or demonstrating swordplay techniques with fallen branches from the slender birch tree in the courtyard below, their blows no more than soft clicks of bark. I watch these displays of unexpected consideration with ill-concealed amusement as I tend the fledgling garden I've planted, trying not to laugh as Cadogan and Mabon's sparring match dissolves into an argument conducted entirely with vulgar hand gestures.

When she will let me—which is seldom, for she is quite reluctant to relinquish her son for more than a few moments at a time—I help Carys with Nevin. She has bounced back to full energy with remarkable speed and seems a tireless blur of activity despite my gentle rebukes to rest, my urging to recover her full strength. She is impatient to reclaim her dressmaking work, picking up the threads she was forced to set aside during the final stretch of her pregnancy.

As she checks the intricate stitching of my Fyremas dress for the hundredth time during Nevin's afternoon nap, I remind her that she has more important stitches to worry about—my own handiwork needs time to heal. But she merely waves away my words with a flippant remark.

"I'm a seamstress, dear friend. I know stitches. I should think I can manage to remove a few when the time comes . . ."

The shadows beneath her and Uther's eyes tell me their son's strong lungs are keeping them awake at night, but neither of them ever complains. Nevin is a long-awaited miracle. Their love for him burns bright, evident in the soft brush of their lips on his wrinkled forehead, in the gentleness of their fingers adjusting his blankets or rocking his cradle. I have never seen such undisguised affection before. Such unconditional devotion.

I catch myself watching them with a mix of fascination and deep longing that evening, the night before the festival. Wondering how any parent could feel such things for their child and still choose to abandon her; how any parent could wrap their new-born in a basket and leave her at the edge of the world, an offering for unknown gods.

I think I do a good job of keeping these thoughts clear of my expression as I examine the trio from beneath my lashes. But there is no hiding from Penn. I do not have to turn to see him seated by the wall, his tall form half in shadow, engaged in a hushed discussion with Farley and Cadogan. I can feel him there with such sharp clarity, like he is touching me; as though he has reached across the length of the room and run a finger down my spine, setting every nerve ending aflame.

I can hardly focus on the twyllo cards in my hand, let alone recall the wagering rules Jac and Mabon are attempting to teach me. Eventually, the sensation grows so heightened, I can no longer withstand it. Throwing down my hand, I jolt to my feet, an abrupt move that draws more attention than I want. Every set of eyes snaps to me at once.

"Rhya, love, are you all right?"

"I'm fine," I assure Carys. "Just a bit tired. I'm going to head back to the palace early and get a good night of rest before tomorrow's festivities." I look at Jac, who is frozen with his mug halfway to his mouth. His blue eyes are wide. "Will you walk me back?"

He glances fleetingly into the shadows where Penn sits before pushing to his feet. His mug hits the table with a low thunk. "Sure, Ace. Happy to escort you."

I grab my cloak from its hook by the door and whip it around my shoulders. My fingers fumble on the neck clasp, trembling under the weight of several intent sets of eyes, but eventually I manage to get it fastened.

"Are you sure you don't want to stay for dinner?" Concern feathers across Carys's features as she crosses toward me. "We've got plenty to spare."

"Thank you, but I'm not hungry." Before she can say another word, I cast a sweeping glance around the room, too quickly to lock eyes with anyone in particular. "Good night, everyone."

I bolt out of the apartments and practically run down the narrow staircase into the darkened dress shop, not pausing to wait for Jac until I hit the street. I lean against a lamppost, breathing hard. After a few moments, the front door swings open with a chime of bells at my back.

"I thought you'd be halfway to the palace by now, you ran out so fast."

Gods damn it.

My eyes press closed at the voice—a deep rasp that belongs not to the man I expected, but to the one I am trying so desperately to escape. I take a steadying breath before I turn to face Penn. Our gazes snag instantly. I have no earthly idea what to say to him. Where he is concerned, my thoughts have never felt so murky.

"Carys said you'd be needing this." He gestures to the flat white box tucked under his arm. A shiny gold ribbon ties its lid.

"My Fyremas gown," I murmur. I'd been in such a rush out the door, I forgot to grab the parcel Carys so lovingly prepared. "Thanks," I tack on belatedly, reaching out for it. My hands shake visibly.

"I'll carry it back for you."

"You?" My brows knit. "I thought Jac was to escort me?"

"Jac is well into his third ale. He's not escorting anyone anywhere. I'll walk with you."

"That's not necessary. I'm sure Mabon or Cadogan—"

"I'm heading back now, anyway." His dark brows lift nearly to his hairline. "Unless there's some reason you find my company objectionable."

"None at all," I say through clenched teeth.

"Lead the way, then."

I promptly begin marching down High Street. Penn falls into step beside me, matching my determined pace in easy strides. He is annoyingly long-legged. I scowl as I turn onto King's Avenue. Though it becomes difficult to hold on to any real sense of anger as the lively atmosphere of the city pulls me firmly into its embrace.

All around, the streets throb with life. It is the dinner hour, typically a quiet time, but tonight, instead of gathering around their tables, Caelderans fill their front walks, chatting animatedly as they ready their homes for the following day's festivities. Stoops are swept clean, doorsteps decorated. Wreaths are hung on windows. Garlands of holly and juniper wind their way up railings. The banner of Dyved flies from lampposts and awnings, the flaming mountain waving proudly in the breeze. Overnight, large metal barrels have appeared on every corner, each stacked high with kindling in preparation for the fires that will burn from dusk until dawn.

As we pass by, many set aside their tasks to wave in greeting, warm voices calling out to their prince. When they spot me at his side, several of them make a familiar one-handed gesture in the air—two fingers traveling in the shape of a diamond.

"What does it mean?" I ask Penn, forgetting my plans to ignore his existence all the way back to the keep. "The hand sign they make when we pass?"

"That is the sigil of the sacred tetrad. An honorary greeting of respect shown to the Remnants."

"They aren't cursing me, then?"

He scoffs as we pass the guard detail stationed at the foot of the bridge. "Quite the opposite. They see you as a blessing."

My stride falters, a tiny stumble of surprise.

Penn does not fail to notice my misstep. "Why is it so difficult for you to believe these people might welcome your presence here? That they would embrace you with open arms?"

"Past experience," I retort defensively. "When you've spent your life being hunted, the urge to bolt first, ask questions later, is not so much a choice but a deeply ingrained instinct."

He is quiet for a moment, absorbing this. We are about a quarter of the way across the bridge now. The palace looms before us, spearing upward into the mist. A row of fishermen trail lures across the lake's placid surface, their buckets of bait wafting like odoriferous cologne. Penn waits until we've left them well behind before he speaks again.

"You can try to hold the world at arm's length, but it's no use, Rhya. Like it or not, in the short time you've been here, you have already drawn a tight circle around yourself."

My shoulders tense. "I don't know what you're talking about."

"Yes, you do. Carys considers you a godsend after your help with the birth. Uther has vowed everlasting allegiance on behalf of his son. Farley owes you his ability to walk. All my men—Jac, Mabon, Cadogan, any of them—would lay down their lives for you without question. And I—" He breaks off abruptly, teeth clicking together.

"You *what*?" I ask, drawing to a sharp halt.

He stops as well but does not look at me. His gaze remains trained out toward the lake, where a young couple in a rowboat is floating between the lily pads, laughing as they fight for control of the oars. He seems the picture of composure—except for the muscle in his jaw, which ticks with telltale rhythmic tension.

"What is it you feel for me, Penn?" I ask on a tremulous whisper. "I thought I knew. Or that I was beginning to, at the very least. I thought, after what happened in the Forsaken Forest—"

He tenses at the reminder.

"—that I had some inkling of what we mean to each other," I continue doggedly. "But since we returned here, everything is different. You are different."

"Oh? And how am I *different*?" His tone is sharp. "I am the same man you've known since Eastwood."

"That's not true, and you know it!" Color fills my cheeks. Is he really going to make me say it aloud? "These days, you treat me like . . . like I am some sort of plague-infected scourge, best avoided!"

"Ah yes," he snarls softly. "That's precisely why I volunteered to walk you home."

"Don't be snide." I narrow my gaze. "You say I hold everyone here at arm's length? What is it that *you* do? Because, to my eyes, you are no better at letting anyone in than I am. In fact, you're worse. You keep an impenetrable shield around you, effective as the wards that surround your city. The minute anyone dares get close, you back away."

"I did not realize I was the subject of such intense study. Please, by all means, continue your assessment of my many flaws. I'm truly fascinated."

I stiffen at his biting sarcasm. I can feel his anger, his exasperation, palpable in the air between us. Thrumming through the bond, spilling over from him to me. It is a testament to how riled he is—usually, he's better at blocking me. My own frustration is a wild beast within, frothing and clawing for release after days of biting my tongue.

"I thought things had changed," I say bluntly. "I thought—but it does not matter what I thought. Clearly, I was wrong. We do not mean anything to each other. We are not"—I search for the right word to describe us, but there is none in the common tongue that can encompass our complexities—"*friends*," I finish, faltering on the word. "We never were. We are no different from the two strangers whose worlds collided beneath a hanging tree in a Midlands mire. What a fool I was to expect anything else."

He stares away from me, expression empty. If I expect him to contradict my words, I am in for disappointment. My stomach is a ball of lead as I reach out and snatch the ribboned box from his arms. He does not resist. His hands fall down to hang at his sides, curling instantly into fists.

"You told me so yourself, the other day in the cavern. I didn't understand then, but I do now. *Emotions are a liability. Separate yourself from them.*" I grip the box so hard, it threatens to cave in. "Thank you for the demonstration. It is a lesson I won't forget."

I turn to go but only make it a few steps before his pain-laced whisper halts me in my tracks.

"Rhya."

There is a war going on in his voice—and on his face as well, I see when I glance back at him. Emotions move through his eyes too quickly to properly decipher them. Rage and regret and resignation and something else, something so tormented it scares me.

"What, Penn?" I ask, voice thick. Tears are impending. I have no desire to be here with him when they break free. "What is it you want to say to me?"

His pause is tense as his posture. "You know my past. You know . . . The last time I cared for someone . . . The way things ended . . ."

Enid.

He's talking about Enid.

I suck in a sharp breath.

"Don't you understand?" A ragged note enters his voice. His eyes burn with flames as they hold mine. "I cannot do that again. *I will not do that again.* Not now. Not ever."

And there it is.

Finally.

The truth.

Whatever fleeting attraction he feels for me, he will not allow himself to explore. His avoidance since our return to the capital is suddenly so painfully clear, so devastatingly transparent.

The distance he's been keeping from me since the kiss?

His way of reestablishing control.

The new wall between us, impossible to scale?

His method of reclaiming any forfeit autonomy.

He deals with his attraction to me by blocking it out entirely. By pretending it does not exist at all. That *I* do not exist at all.

I might laugh if I weren't on the brink of tears. Because the true ache of it is, I *do* understand. I understand all too well. He would rather push aside any possibility of love than pursue something that could put his power into a dangerous tailspin. He would rather act like we are nothing to each other than expose himself to more hurt, more pain. To another lapse of his rigid self-restraint— a lapse like the one he endured seventy years ago. A lapse that claimed the life of the woman he loved.

His need for control is stronger than anything he feels for me. We are—and always will be—a risk he is unwilling to take.

Gods, but that hurts.

It cuts me open, flays me to the bone.

"If you want to pretend that nothing happened between us, that's what we'll do," I lie, heart hammering. "I'm happy to bury it. More than happy. Consider it dead."

His jaw is so tight, I'm surprised his teeth don't shatter. "Fine by me."

Another lance of pain skewers my heart. Surely, I am bleeding inwardly by now?

"Thank you so very much for the escort, Prince Pendefyre," I say with the icy politeness I usually reserve for Vanora and her courtiers. "I'll manage on my own the rest of the way. Have a pleasant evening."

With that, I pivot on a heel as I stalk away, feeling a bit more miserable with every step he fails to stop me. I'm lucky it is a straight path across the bridge, for the tears that stream from my eyes come with such speed, it's impossible to see where I'm going.

⁓

"OH, LADY RHYA!" Teagan exclaims. "You look just lovely."

In the mirror, a fair-haired stranger stares back at me. Weeks ago, I had gazed upon my own reflection and found a half-starved halfling with shadowed eyes, scarred wrists, and a broken spirit gazing back. The woman I see now is just as unfamiliar, yet no less shocking to the senses.

The benefit of steady meals and regular sleep cannot be denied. There is color in my cheeks and flesh on my bones. Some of my curves, stripped away during those long months on the run, have been restored to their former abundance. The gown hugs my frame and makes the best of my figure, plunging low at the bodice and cinching tight at the waist. Made of a pale gold silk, it shimmers in the sunbeams streaming through the tower windows.

Carys originally crafted it for a winter ball last Yulemas, but her customer had fallen ill on the eve of the event and so it sat, untouched, in her stockroom for more than a year. Despite its gilded luster, the design is rather simple at first glance—no frills or feathers to distract from its elegant lines or from my Remnant. But the back is spectacular. My spine is bare from nape to small. In lieu of simple sleeves, Carys has webbed panels of fabric together in a sinuous pattern that sculpts from the blades of my shoulders outward along the span of my arms.

Wings.

When I move, I look ready to leap into the skies. Each step

lends the feeling of flight. I feel like a magnificent bird, a rare creature of the aether—an illusion only enhanced by the gold diadem that circles my forehead and dips down toward the bridge of my nose in a beaklike point. At the very center of the circlet, a stunning amber-hued gemstone gleams each time it catches the light. It is my only adornment—a gift I'd discovered this morning, tucked in the depths of the dress box along with a note.

> Rhya,
>
> There are not jewels enough in all the mines of Dyved to adequately convey our gratitude. Please, wear this with our love. Happy Fyremas—your first of many to come.
>
> Uther, Carys, and Nevin

The weight of the diadem sits heavy on my forehead, setting off a warm glow in my bones each time I catch sight of it in the mirror. My hair, braided and pinned into a hundred intricate coils, shines like platinum. My eyes are rimmed with kohl, my lips stained pink, my skin dusted with pearlescent powder. I scarcely recognize myself. It takes effort not to reach out and touch the mirrored glass, to ensure the reflection is real.

"Carys outdid herself," Keda says with only the smallest note of smugness. "Can you imagine if we'd let the royal dressmakers have their way?"

All three of us look in unison to the corner of the room, where the ruffled monstrosity Vanora's henchman delivered this morning peeks out from the top of its parcel. My maids had not exaggerated—it is every bit as awful as they'd described. A swallowing sea of ruffles in a repugnant shade of sulfur.

"Her Royal Majesty is in for quite a shock when she sees you," Keda says, adjusting one of the hairpins at the back of my head.

"She won't be the only one," Teagan adds, smiling. "I'll bet His Royal Highness will scarcely be able to keep his eyes off you."

I nearly snort, catching myself at the last moment. If only she knew just how misguided her predictions are. After last night's argument on the bridge, I think it more likely Penn will never look my way again for the rest of our immortal lives.

"Is your primping finally finished?" I ask. "I'd love to go wander the streets a bit before the ceremony, or maybe even pay Carys a visit to show off her handiwork."

"There's no time for that, I'm afraid. It's nearly dusk. The ceremony is set to begin soon. Besides, there'll be plenty of time for you to join in the revelry after it's over."

I sigh and cross to the balcony, where I can watch the celebrations from afar. Technically, Fyremas does not begin until nightfall—kicking off with Penn's recharging of the wards, followed by a formal banquet in the Great Hall and, much later, a ball that lasts until daybreak. People will dance the night away, ushering in the spring with a celebration of life and rebirth, pausing only long enough to watch the midnight fireworks over the lake. Tonight, the palace gates are open to all Caelderans, a rare invitation for common folk to mingle with the most elite of Vanora's courtiers—though why they would voluntarily seek out such snobbish company remains a mystery to me.

Down in the city, the merriment began long ago. From my lofty vantage, I can see the throngs of people already congesting the cobbled avenues. I cannot hear their joy over the roar of the falls, but I imagine the air is thick with laughter, music, and chatter as food and drink flow freely. I would give much to be down there with them, rather than put on display as part of the royal spectacle.

"Almost time now." Keda looks toward the door, as though expecting a fist to knock upon it. "I'm sure Prince Pendefyre plans to personally escort you there . . ."

"Mmm," I hum doubtfully.

I haven't seen him since the bridge. He did not return until long after I retired to the spire last night, and it was barely daybreak when I heard him storm out again this morning, rattling the tower door on its hinges when he went. Our lingering animosity is the one sour note in my gathering excitement. It casts an undeniable pall over the coming evening.

Skies, everything was so much simpler when we were at each other's throats instead of under each other's skin . . .

As the time to depart grows ever nearer, my maids grow more and more dismayed. Keda is folding bedsheets to keep from wringing her hands. Teagan is chewing her bottom lip as she brushes nonexistent dust from the surface of Penn's desk. Both jump several inches off the ground when, at last, a fist raps against the wood.

"That'll be His Highness now!" Keda calls, racing for the doorway.

I do not have the heart to dash her hopes. The bond tells me plainly: whoever has come to accompany me to Fyremas, it is not Prince Pendefyre. He is far away, in a distant part of the keep, layers of stone and slate separating us. Even knowing this, I am still somewhat crestfallen to see Jac and Cadogan standing at the threshold, clad in a fancier version of their Ember Guild uniforms—maroon doublets edged in gold thread, dark suede breeches, and shiny leather boots to the knee. Embroidered black sashes slant across their muscular chests, the sigil of Dyved stitched directly over their hearts.

Sauntering into the tower without waiting for an invitation, they both stop in their tracks when they catch sight of me standing on the balcony. Cadogan seems stunned silent. The apple of his throat works rapidly, bobbing as he swallows. Jac only manages one word, muttered through clenched teeth.

"*Gods.*"

I look down at myself. "What? Do I look ridiculous? Wait, don't answer that. It's too late to change now. Besides, Carys made this dress for me. She'll be insulted if I don't wear it."

The men glance at each other.

"He's going to regret giving us guard duty," Jac says lowly.

"Immensely," Cadogan agrees.

"I'll wager twenty crowns he actually shows his face at the ball this year."

"Easy money."

"You're on."

"Um. Excuse me?" I clear my throat to interrupt their strange aside. "Would either of you care to explain what you're talking about?"

"No," they say in harmony, finally looking back at me.

Cadogan avoids my eyes. I swear, he is almost blushing. Jac, on the other hand, shows no such modesty. A slow smile spreads across his face as his gaze sweeps me head to toe, lingering in places that make my stomach flutter.

"You look good enough to eat, Ace."

I roll my eyes. "That's not saying much. I've sat beside you at dinner. Is there anything you won't eat?"

"We should get going," Cadogan interrupts. "It's a long walk to the throne room. Are you ready?"

"She's ready," Teagan says, giving me a tiny shove toward my escorts.

"She's *perfect*," Keda proclaims.

I allow the women to usher me toward the door. But when we

reach the threshold, I pause and tug them both into brief hugs, whispering words of thanks into their ears.

"Och! Off with you now!" Teagan scolds, pushing me away. "I'll not be blamed for your tardiness." Despite her harsh words, I notice she's blinking a bit too rapidly, as though holding tears at bay.

Keda merely winks merrily at me and whispers, "Have some fun, Lady Rhya."

"You, too," I order, squeezing her hands tightly. I glance at Teagan. "Both of you. You deserve to enjoy the festivities, after all you did to prepare the palace for them. Go dance in the streets. Eat something delicious. Drink a bit too much spiced wine. Seduce a handsome stranger. I expect to hear all about it tomorrow!"

They wave me off, into the care of Jac and Cadogan—one set of nursemaids swapped for another. Cadogan is mostly silent as we descend from the tower, an endless downward spiral, but Jac keeps up a steady stream of mindless chatter about the jousting tourney he'd competed in at the festival grounds erected just outside the city limits. Today, he'd been unseated by a burly fellow named Smithy; tomorrow, he would have his revenge in the hand-to-hand combat arena, gods willing.

I only half listen to him, using most of my focus to keep from tripping on my long train. The gold gown has far more fabric than the simple day dresses I've grown accustomed to wearing.

We reach ground level, then pass through the grand ballroom and banquet hall. The palace is bursting with folks from near and far, all clad in their finest attire. I knew, of course, that Dyved was rich in gemstones— Vanora's inner circle flashes them at every opportunity—but tonight, the display of wealth is staggering. Rubies, diamonds, sapphires, emeralds. Men and women alike drip with them as they make their way toward the throne room at the back of the keep. My gown, glorious as it is, looks understated in comparison to the sea of silk-draped courtiers swanning around us.

We join the crush, three minnows carried on the current of opulence. It would be easy to be swallowed up in such a crowd. But Jac and Cadogan keep a firm buffer of space around me as we walk, prohibiting anyone from getting within three paces. There is no blocking the curious stares or pointed comments as people spot me in their midst, however.

"That's her."

"The new wind weaver."

"Did you get a look at her eyes? Silver storm clouds!"

"I hear she and the prince are—"

I do my best to shut them out, to keep my gait steady and my chin high as we make for the impressive arched doors that grant entrance to the throne room. In all my wanderings of the palace grounds, I have never been here before. It is not often in use, except for formal matters of state or great celebrations. Located at the oldest part of the keep, it is more a cavern than an actual room, embedded deep in the bedrock behind the falls. Not so unlike the glyphed chamber where I have spent so many mornings at practice—except completely enclosed from the mist and utterly massive in scale.

The throne room is so large, in fact, I have difficulty making out the ceiling overhead. The jagged walls are the gloomy shade of petrified ash, full of crevices where the lava flows dried and hardened a millennium ago. With no windows to speak of, it would be pitch dark inside if not for the trenches of fire that run along the perimeter, burning steadily. Stone columns, wide as the tree trunks at the heart of the Forsaken Forest, shoot upward toward the ceiling. At their bases, more fires burn in sharp-toothed metallic cages, the flames licking hungrily at the stone.

I would have liked to pause at the threshold to properly take in the grandeur of it all, but we are caught up in the crush, already moving down a set of stone steps. At the bottom, the crowd parts in two—diverting to either side of a central aisle that cuts directly between the stately columns. The room is already nearly at capacity; folks stand shoulder to shoulder all the way to the raised dais at the far side. Despite the vast numbers, it is mostly silent, only a low murmur of voices as spectators find places to stand, jostling for better viewing positions. I make to follow them, but instead, Jac and Cadogan steer me toward the aisle.

"Where—"

Jac cuts me off before I can get more than a single word out. "You get a prime seat at the front, Ace."

I say no more as they lead me onward, aware that there are as many listening ears as watchful eyes trained in my direction. Cadogan and Jac flank me on either side, matching their strides to mine, their faces set in uncompromising masks, the broadswords strapped across their backs shining almost as brightly as the jewels adorning the crowd that surrounds us.

The atmosphere is rife with anticipation. The very air feels still, sacred, as though everyone is holding their breath. A full hush sweeps over the room in a wave as I make my way, one step at a time, down the aisle, deeper into the earth. I keep my expression clear, a mask of serenity concealing the chords of anxiety chiming in my bloodstream. It is more than being the center of so much attention; claustrophobia is rearing its ugly head, my natural aversion to being so far underground gripping me with sharp talons.

The stone walls are closing in, the heavy stone ceiling pressing down on my shoulders, flattening me toward the floor. Each step is an endeavor, each breath an enterprise. I taste soil in the air, inhaling the distinct flavor of confinement with every pump of my lungs. Visions of being buried alive, of opportunistic cyntroedi creeping and clacking and chewing at my bones, plague me.

I walk on.

The journey to the throne platform seems endless. The chill of the floor seeps into the thin soles of my gold slippers. I focus on the cold, envision it not as crushing stone, as confining earth, but as the crisp breeze of a winter evening, the icy kiss of the season's first snow. I am not here, not entombed. I am in the air. In the sky. A bird in flight, the golden wings on my back stretching wide as I soar.

These imaginings help a bit. But self-delusion only goes so far. By the time I reach the aisle's midpoint, my breaths are shallow, my skin clammy. I am teetering on the edge of a bottomless pit of panic, half-ready to turn and bolt from the room.

But then I feel it.

A jolt of warmth down the bond. A pulse of raw power, tugging me away from that dark edge.

Penn.

His presence cuts through the fog of panic in the interlude between two instants. I sense him with sudden clarity—as though he's been shielding himself but, in that moment, allows the shields to fall away. He is here, just ahead, not far at all. The tether tightens around my heart, reeling me in, urging me forward. I latch on to it, allowing Penn's reassuring strength to shore up my own flagging resolve.

My head lifts, eyes seeking him out, but he is nowhere to be found. At the end of the aisle, the crowd of courtiers to either side is replaced by two orderly rows of foot soldiers in starched brown uniforms. Standing at attention at the front of the brigade, a mountain of a man watches me approach through shrewd hazel eyes. The golden epaulettes at his shoulders give away his identity.

General Yale, who leads Dyved's armies in the northern provinces.

He is younger than I'd envisioned when the men spoke of him—no more than a decade or so older than myself. But those years have not been entirely kind. His dark hair is streaked gray at the temples and a ridged red scar runs the length of his left cheek from temple to jaw.

He surveys me with detached interest as the distance dwindles between us, his emotions unreadable. I get the sense there is not much his golden eyes miss. I breathe easier when we pass out of his sight line.

Beyond the brigade of foot soldiers, twenty elite Ember Guild line the throne platform, their maroon and gold uniforms identical to those worn by the men beside me. The dais itself is lofted several steps above the main floor. At its center is a heavy throne, crafted of the same dark metal that cages the fire at the base of each ceiling column. It is currently unoccupied. To its left side, one step down, on a smaller seat of similar craftsmanship, sits Queen Vanora. A position of honor—one befitting a kingdom's steward.

But not a true queen.

No wonder she does not often use this room, I think as her cold eyes lock on mine. *It is a perpetual reminder of her shortcomings, her lack of full sovereignty on display for all to see.*

"Wind weaver," she acknowledges when we come to a stop before the platform. Each syllable is scathing as it leaves her purse-string mouth. Her eyes sweep me head to toe and I see a glimmer of undeniable fury as she takes in the lack of sulfuric ruffles. She herself wears a resplendent gown of deep red, with a bevy of rubies to match. Her crown sits heavily atop her sleeked-back silver mane. "You are unforgivably late."

The hall goes utterly silent at her condemnation. Beside me, Cadogan and Jac both bend into swift bows. I sweep into a rather flimsy curtsy, more than happy to steer my gaze toward the floor.

"Apologies, Queen Vanora," I tell the stones.

"Do you think yourself more important than a warding ceremony that keeps all of us alive?"

"No, Queen Vanora."

"Do you think yourself above the protection of this city and its people?"

"No, Queen Vanora."

"Then be seated," she hisses, "before you delay us further."

I feel a different sort of pulse through the bond as I rise again—not reassurance, but rage. Wherever he is, Penn is close enough to hear his sister's vitriol. Yet, when I risk a glance into the shadows beyond the throne, I still cannot see a single trace of him.

My guard detail leads me away from Vanora's narrow-eyed scrutiny to a section of pew-like benches built along the bottom level of the dais. Carys and Uther are there, baby Nevin swaddled in his father's strong arms. I recognize several other highly ranked members of the Ember Guild in attendance, their wives tucked close by their sides. I smile at Carys; she grins back, green eyes dancing in delight as she surveys her handiwork.

Jac and Cadogan find an empty stretch of seating near the end of the pew, next to Farley. I frown at the redhead, noticing his crutches have been swapped for a simple cane. I've told him time and again, he ought to wait at least another week. The man is going to set back his recovery in an irksome display of masculine prowess. He merely shrugs, unrepentant under the force of my glare as I take my seat beside him.

My skirts have barely settled when Queen Vanora begins to drone, briefly welcoming her subjects before launching into a recitation of all she has done for the kingdom since the previous Fyremas—her allocation of funds to clear a tract of land by the North Sea where a new generation of farmers might homestead, her assignment of fresh troops to the southern borderlands where the Reavers threaten, her recent clearing of the Forsaken Forest where the ice giants had nested in previous weeks.

Her, her, her.

Nothing about Pendefyre. Nothing about General Yale. Nothing about the Ember Guild. She speaks as though she single-handedly carries the kingdom upon her back. As if every victory is hers alone, rather than the combined efforts of dozens, hundreds, thousands of Dyvedi citizens. After ten straight minutes of her self-accolades, Jac feigns a soft snore from my left.

I bite my lip, stifling a giggle.

Finally, the old crone runs out of steam. The hall seems to breathe a collective sigh of relief as her voice tapers into silence. Her hands curl around the arms of her chair, tension apparent in every arthritic joint as attention shifts away from her in one great whoosh of light and heat and sound.

All eyes soar upward, to the wall of shadow behind the throne platform, following the twin trails of fire as they streak from the floor trenches upward to the ceiling in two crackling lines, illuminating the back wall of the cavern . . .

And, with it, the Crown Prince of Dyved.

TWENTY-NINE

A collective gasp sounds as Pendefyre comes into view. My own lips part as I take in the sight of him standing on a ledge halfway up the cliff face in a hollowed-out natural chamber, his features awash in firelight. There are countless glyphs carved into the stone surrounding him, deep maegical scars that hum with untapped power.

He is dressed simply in plain black breeches—shirtless and barefoot, his Remnant on full display—yet he appears almost godlike as he stares down at us. And we stare back, necks craned, mouths agape. A congregation at worship of their deity.

"Fyremas is upon us," Penn calls, casting his eyes around the cavern from above, his voice reverberating with strength. "Once again, we celebrate the turn of the seasons. Winter to spring, snow to thaw. As our fields shake off the weight of slumber, as new life awakens deep beneath the earth, as we again take up the task of plowing soil and planting seed, we ask the gods to bless us with a fruitful harvest. We ask our ancestors to grace us with their favor, holding off the blight that erodes into our lands. We ask the wards to shield us, as they have for generations, from any who would do us harm."

He hauls in a deep breath, chest muscles flexing. "I have

walked the world beyond our borders. I have lived a life outside the lands we call home. I have tasted the ashes of ruined kingdoms in the air and seen the darkness that steals across all of Anwyvn firsthand."

His eyes press closed. When they open, he is looking directly at me. Even across such a distance, I can see—can *feel*—the heat in his stare. The intensity of it.

"In a time of widespread death and loss, we are fortunate to still have so much to safeguard. To possess so much worthy of protection. So on this night, above all else, we give thanks for the salvation already delivered. For the gifts already given. For the homecomings we thought might never come. And for the ones we love—the ones worth fighting for."

My breath catches.

"May the light of Fyremas burn bright until the dawn, a reminder that there is no night so consuming it cannot be endured; no gloom so heavy it cannot be cast out. We are Dyved. We are the flame in the darkness. And we will hold back the shadows, in whatever form they come."

Penn's arms rise from his sides. The crowd gasps again when they see, in the air above each hand, he holds a ball of white-hot fire. Everyone seems to hold their breath, awaiting Penn's next move. The effort to remain in control wears at him—his face is drawn; his brow furrows in concentration.

For the first time ever, all his shields are down, allowing me a rare glimpse into his psyche. Through our bond, I experience his emotions as if they are my own. That unflinching self-control, that undercurrent of intensity. There is no fear in him, no anxiety. He will not let those feelings take root, even if he feels them stirring to life within.

You are the sentinel at the threshold of chaos.
You will not yield.

You will not fall.

Tension thrums, charging the air like the sky before a lightning strike. Even at this distance, the raw strength he exudes threatens to make my knees give out. He drops into a crouch and presses his flaming hands to the stone. The earth gives a great shudder, a ripple moving through the cavern as Penn's power pulses, unbridled, into the thick layers of petrified ash. Into the wards beneath, embedded deep in the fabric of the earth. Into the leylines, those sacred seams of ancient maegic that hold our world together.

The trenches of fire flare along the floor perimeter, brightening the throne room nearly to daylight. The caged flame at the base of each column sparks higher, causing those standing closest to shy away in fear. The temperature rises by several degrees as Penn's maegic continues to pour out, wave after wave, pulse after pulse. A flood of raw energy. The glyphs in the chamber around him glow red—a glow that spreads outward through the walls like blood through veins, until the whole cavern is charged.

Maegic fills the air, thick and palpable. At my chest, my own Remnant stirs awake in response. I clench my fists, trying to hold on to my own control. I can no longer tell which emotions are mine and which are Penn's.

Is it my fear or his that lumps at the back of my throat?

Is it his worry or mine that prickles at my eyes?

I let his power wash over me, through me, and seek the tranquil center inside my mind—calming my own inner storms before they are magnified by the one Penn has unleashed.

It ends with bone-shaking swiftness. His power shuts off all at once, like the turn of a valve, a stopper shoved into a bottleneck. One moment the world is abuzz with maegic, the walls aglow, the air shimmering . . . and then, in a blink, the flames return to normal height in their trenches. The heat recedes; the air clears. The only trace of what just occurred is the red-veined lava flows, still glowing all around us, pulsing faintly like the earth beneath our feet has a living, beating heart.

His control is absolute, his skill astounding. I am not sure whether to be more awed by his discipline or more anxious I cannot manage anything akin to it.

The crowd bursts into applause—boots stomping, palms clapping, mouths calling out cheers of celebration. Farley lets out a whoop of glee. Jac grins as he jostles me with an elbow. Even Cadogan is smiling.

Fyremas has officially begun. It is time to celebrate. The wards are charged, the ceremony ended. But as the tide of jubilation sweeps through the room, I find myself the sole point of stillness, staring upward to the back wall of the cavern.

On the cliff face, the ceremonial chamber is empty.

At my chest, the Remnant bond is eerily numb.

Pendefyre is gone.

~

"JAC!" I YELL, breathless. "Enough! I'm dizzy."

He grins as he twirls me yet again, spinning me with the skill of a man who has significant experience holding women in his arms—both on the dance floor and off it. It is our third jig in a row. My breaths are short; my head is awhirl. The cups of strong mulled wine I consumed over dinner may be contributing to my dizziness, but my partner's increasingly wild moves are not helping matters much.

"Not my fault you can't keep up, Ace!"

"I should've asked Cadogan," I retort, catching sight of the second member of my guard detail as we whirl across the expanse of flagstones. His blond hair is a bright beacon even in the shadowy corner where he stands keeping watch.

For all the celebrations unfolding around him, Cadogan remains both sober and self-contained. He does not dance or drink. His eyes never stray far from me, even as the hours tick by and the party spills from the Great Hall to the grand ballroom to the courtyard. If he is not watching me, his eyes are scanning the crowd. Whenever I pause long enough to take a fortifying sip of wine, he instantly closes ranks, fending off anyone who gets too close for his liking. Several brave young men—a rather flattering amount, truth be told—risk making an approach and attempt to engage me in conversation, only to be turned around and sent on their way.

Cadogan takes his guard duties quite seriously.

Jac is a different story. He'd matched me drink for drink at dinner but soon outpaced me. By this point in the evening, he is glossy-eyed and loose-limbed. I'm surprised he manages to turn me with such success. Perhaps he relies on muscle memory, for he is long past thinking about steps or rhythms.

"*Brava!*" he cheers as the quartet of stringed instruments play their final refrains, his voice joining a chorus of whistles and applause. His blue eyes twinkle like stars when they meet mine. "Another?"

"No," I wheeze, pressing a hand to the muscle spasm stitching through my side. "A break."

"Weakling," he mutters, following me from the makeshift dance floor that has sprung up just outside the keep. There are hundreds of folks milling about, moving from the grand ballroom where Vanora and her glittering posse are gathered to the courtyard and back again. Some go farther, venturing beyond the palace gates, out onto the bridge that spans the lake and into the city itself, where the party rages on in the streets as all of Caeldera dances into spring. I imagine Keda and Teagan somewhere in their midst.

"Looks like Farley has found himself some company," Jac says, amused. "And here we were feeling sorry for him, not able to dance . . ."

My eyes follow the jerk of his chin and I stifle a laugh. Farley is reclined on a chaise near the refreshment tables with a swarm of admirers fluttering all around him. From his hand gestures alone, I can tell he is relaying the story of the cyntroedi attack. As he mimes two pincers snapping his leg, a raven-haired beauty strokes his cheek in comfort. A stunning man in amber silk reaches out to twine their fingers together, squeezing in sympathy.

"I suppose that explains why he was so adamant about ditching his crutches." My lips twist—I am half-amused, half-anxious. "He'd better not overdo it. Perhaps I should—"

"Oh, come on. Let the man have some fun, Ace. It's Fyremas, for gods' sake! He's not likely to rebreak his leg with a quick roll in the hay." Jac pauses. "Actually, more than one roll, by the looks of it."

"Is that a note of jealousy I detect in your voice?"

"Definitely."

"Go on, then. Find your own hay-roll partner. I don't need you watching over me."

"Penn will skin me alive if I leave your side tonight."

"Penn isn't here to know," I say stiffly.

In a rare moment of wisdom, Jac holds his tongue.

"It's not like you'll be leaving me alone," I point out. "I'll still have Cadogan watching me like a hawk."

"You don't truly expect me to abandon you on your very first Fyremas, do you? I may be an occasional scoundrel, but I'm not a *complete* scoundrel. Besides, left alone with Cadogan, you'd be bored to death. The man could find fascination in the drying of paint."

I choke back a laugh as we reach the subject of our conversation on the fringes of the crowd. More than a few hopeful admirers are lingering nearby, admiring Cadogan's burly form in the well-fashioned uniform, but he pays their preening no notice. His large hand is curled around a goblet—water, not wine.

"Where are Uther and Carys?" I ask him, brows lifting.

"Headed home to High Street."

"But they'll miss the fireworks! Carys said the fireworks are her favorite part."

"I'm sure they'll watch them from their own courtyard." Cadogan looks at me like I've grown two heads. "You cannot expect them to dance the night away with a newborn in tow."

"Of course not," I murmur, chastised. "I only wish I'd been able to say good night."

Jac snorts. "You're at Carys's shop damn near every day. A handful of hours separate you from a reunion."

"You're right." My lips flatten. "It's only . . ."

"What is it, Ace? Fyremas not living up to your expectations?"

"No, it's not that. It's wonderful, really. I just . . . I suppose I envisioned we'd all be together. If not for the celebrations, at least for the fireworks."

The men trade a glance.

"*We?*" Jac asks gently.

"We. Us. All of us." My cheeks flood with color. I wish suddenly I had something to sip—spiced wine, mead, ale, anything would do. "Farley, Mabon, Carys, Uther . . ." I trail off helplessly, swallowing down the final name that sits on the tip of my tongue.

"Well, Mabon pulled patrol duty at the tunnel tonight, the poor bastard, so he won't be back until dawn," Jac says, scratching at his collar.

"Farley looks a bit preoccupied at the moment . . ." Cadogan smirks as his eyes travel over my shoulder briefly, to the chaise lounge. The pair of admirers are now perched on either side of the cushioned seat, their bodies blocking most of our view of the reclining redhead. "But I'm sure we could peel him away—"

"No." I sigh. "No, that's not necessary. Forget I said anything."

"Ace . . ."

I wave off their concern. I feel rather foolish for harboring anything resembling disappointment. Never in my life have I attended a festival such as this. Back in Seahaven, Eli and I paid homage to the start of spring by taking a late-night stroll through the Starlight Wood, examining the new silver buds that gathered along the low-hanging branches, leaving blessings for the gods beneath the ancient Aurea Tree at the center of the grove. An honorable if unexciting tradition.

By comparison, Fyremas is a feast for the senses. Music everywhere. More food and drink than one could ever consume. Garlands of pine and juniper interwoven with the early blooms of spring, perfuming the smoke-hazed air. And firelight—firelight everywhere. Burning on torches and crackling in metal basins, reflecting in the eyes of everyone as they dance and drink and laugh. It all feels like a dream, some rapturous conjuring of imagination. And yet, beneath the joy that sizzles in my bloodstream, I cannot quite dispel the faint chord of discontent at the very core of me.

Penn's absence bothers me far more than I'd anticipated—far more than it has any right to, given the way we left things during our last encounter. After his vanishing act during the warding ceremony, I assumed he would eventually rejoin the festivities. Yet, he was not present during the feast, nor during the fire-lighting procession through the streets that followed, led by a

fleet of red-robed fyre priestesses bearing torches, casting blessings to the God of Flame. Even as the musicians took up their
strings and the dancing began, there was no trace of him—neither
before my eyes nor through our bond.

I cannot feel him at all, even when I cast out my senses as far
as they will reach.

Now the clock marches toward midnight, and his continued
absence itches at me like a scab on a freshly healed wound. I don't
want to ask his men where he is. To do so would be to admit that
I actually care for him . . . and that is something I am scarcely
able to confess to myself, let alone Jac and Cadogan.

So I keep silent, keep patient. Any minute now, he'll no doubt
walk out of some shadowy corner and say something equally infuriating and impenetrable . . .

"He's not coming."

My eyes jerk to Cadogan's. His handsome face is grave as he
watches me. "*What?*"

"Pendefyre. He's not coming." He glances at Jac, who hovers
by my side. "I'm sorry, we . . . We thought you knew . . ."

My face must betray my stunned disbelief, for Jac moves
closer and chucks me lightly under the chin. "Don't take it personally, Ace. It's not you he's avoiding. He never takes part in the
festivities."

"But . . ." I shake my head to clear it. "Where is he, then?"

They trade another glance.

"No one really knows where he goes—only that he does,"
Cadogan says, a hint of apology in his words. "We won't see him
until dawn at the earliest."

It's a surprisingly crushing blow to know that the moment I've
been holding my breath in anticipation of all evening is never to
arrive. I try to hide it, but I'm sure they both can see the disappointment that suffuses my features.

"Come on, Ace. Let's track down another cup of ale." Jac's shoulder bumps mine playfully. "Then we're heading back out on that dance floor whether you like it or not."

Summoning a smile, I cast my eyes heavenward. "Gods help me."

MINUTES BEFORE MIDNIGHT, a towering form materializes from the shadows beside me. My heart leaps in my chest . . . until I register eyes of lightest hazel, not dark ember; hair of peppered black in place of sun-streaked chestnut. His epaulettes shine bright as midday sun.

"General Yale, sir," Cadogan and Jac chorus in unison, both nodding in respect.

Yale's scar lends him an unearthly look in the wavering light of the torches as he nods back. His eyes are fixed on me. "I was hoping I might steal the wind weaver away for a waltz before the fireworks begin."

He phrases it like a request, but I know better. So do my guards, for they say not a word as I place my hand in Yale's proffered one and allow him to lead me onto the floor. He clears a path toward the center with ease, never releasing his grip on me as we maneuver through the crush of inebriated revelers.

The fiddlers strike their first note of a fresh waltz, a screech of bows on strings. On cue, Yale's other hand finds my waist. I suck in a sharp breath and try to focus on the steps. Keda and Teagan taught me the basics of some of the Northlanders' dances, but I am no expert. It did not matter so much when I was dancing with Jac. He is a friend. Yale is . . .

I am not yet certain what Yale is.

"You seem to be enjoying your first Fyremas," he says as we move in time with the music. It is a slower tune, a welcome relief from the constant lineup of lively jigs. I follow his lead, a marionette on strings. He moves with surprising grace for a battle-hardened warrior.

"I am," I agree, though he has not really asked. He has a habit of phrasing his inquiries as declaratives, as though he knows the answers to his own questions long before he puts words to them. "And you?"

"Fyremas is seldom a dull evening. This year is no exception. Though perhaps for different reasons."

My brows arch. "What reasons might those be?"

"Surely Pendefyre has already informed you of the Reaver rabble gathering along our borders, wreaking havoc with increasing persistence. They have taken several outposts in recent weeks. No matter how we drive them back, they seem intent on invasion."

"The Reavers have been a thorn in Dyved's side for years, have they not?"

"This is different. The clans have long been scavengers—striking opportunistically, sporadically, rarely twice in the same place. Not lately. For more than a month, they have been moving methodically and systematically, with a level of organization previously unwitnessed. Strange, is it not? Their newfound zeal. It makes one wonder what might be driving it. What—or *who*—they are so desperate to get their hands on."

A spiral of unease swirls in my stomach.

"But I don't need to waste my breath on these matters," Yale continues. "You must know more about it than anyone. After all, I'm told you are in the prince's closest confidence."

I swallow hard, saying nothing.

Yale's eyes are golden blades, whittling away any pretense. "Seeing your face in this moment, I think perhaps I need better informants. He clearly has not spoken of this to you."

"No, but it seems you are more than eager to. Or do you

merely mean to dangle information like a carrot for me to chase? I assure you, I have no intention of doing so. I am not a rabbit."

He smiles, a predatory flash of strong white teeth. "There's no need for snark, Rhya—may I call you Rhya?"

"That's my name. And, as I have no plans to refer to you as *General* or *Commander*, I'm fine with a bit of informality."

"Excellent. I'll call you Rhya. You can call me whatever you please. The men call me Yale. Friends call me Jareth."

"Yale will do, at present."

His smile vanishes. "You would be wise to court my friendship. The alternative may be less agreeable."

I do not care for his thinly veiled threats any more than I do the shrewd intelligence in his stare. But I keep my face clear and my tone light as we execute a spin, allowing him to twirl me within the circle of his arms. The tempo of the fiddler's tune is increasing, as is my heartbeat—though that has more to do with our conversation than the dance.

"I have friends aplenty already," I say stiffly.

"Yes, I have noticed that. Friends of great import, no less. The prince's inner circle has closed so tightly around you, I'm surprised I was allowed to steal you away for a dance." His hand flexes on my waist. "One might almost think your life was in danger."

"If you mean to scare me with vague implications—"

"Ambiguity is not my objective, I assure you. I'm delighted to enlighten you about precisely how much disruption your presence here has caused."

"*My* presence?"

"Do you have any concept of the time it took to comb through an entire army, weeding out anyone who might be tempted to collect the bounty Efnysien put on your head?" His eyes flash with rage—a lapse quickly concealed with frigid civility. "Do you have any idea how many soldiers I was coerced into diverting here on specific orders from Crown Prince Pendefyre, simply to protect *you*?"

My eyes widen. I knew that Penn increased security within the Ember Guild after the Gower incident. Ranks tightened, allegiances verified. I was not aware he'd ordered a similar culling within the rest of Dyved's armed forces, or that he'd commandeered some of the army on my behalf—an army typically controlled, with unequivocal authority, by the man in whose arms I currently waltz.

"What bothers you more, Yale?" I ask. "That Penn superseded your jurisdiction? Or that he did so to keep me safe?"

His grip tightens at my waist. The hand trapping mine feels like a set of shackles. "I should think even you would agree: it is neither sane nor prudent to protect one woman at the expense of the entire kingdom."

"An attempt was made on my life. Penn is merely—"

"I know what Pendefyre is doing. Just as I know about the traitor in his own precious Ember Guild. Second Lieutenant Gower, wasn't it?"

Yale's eyes are so cold they rival the Remnant at my chest, which has begun to sear at my skin as he speaks—an internal alert system warning danger is near. He's led me so far into the crush of circling couples, I've lost sight of Cadogan and Jac at the edge of the courtyard. Quite abruptly, I find myself surrounded by a sea of unfamiliar faces, a crowd so dense I cannot see beyond it.

"What do you know of Gower?" I ask, somewhat afraid to know the answer.

"Only that he did not succeed." Yale's tone suggests he may have wished for a different outcome. "Only that there are others like him out there—so many others, we cannot keep track of the threats. Some of them may be here tonight. Some of them may be on this very dance floor."

"And are—" I swallow against the lump in my throat. "Are you one of them?"

His lips twitch; I've amused him. "Me? No, Rhya. I do not need to eliminate you. I need only be patient. It is only a matter of time before one of Efnysien's lackeys succeeds where Lieutenant Gower failed."

My heartbeat is a roar between my ears, the rush of blood deafening. "What is it you want from me?"

"From you? Nothing."

"Do you mean to scare me off, then?"

The music is reaching a crescendo. He pirouettes me expertly, spinning me in a full circle. His chest presses close to my back for a brief moment as I turn in his arms. His mouth finds my ear to whisper, "Would that I could. You do not seem so easily intimidated."

Before I can retort, he spins me around to face him once more and we resume our waltz, gazes locked in a contest of stares I cannot escape. His puckered red scar catches the firelight, lending him a daemonic look. My skin crawls under his grip. I wish, with startling vehemence, that I could shove out of his arms, kick him in the shin, and find my friends. But my curiosity is too strong for me to walk away.

"Why this charade, Yale? Why ask me to dance if not to badger me into submission? I assume you are curious about more than my waltzing skills."

"Mmm. You could use some lessons on technique, though your natural grace makes you an easy enough partner to lead."

"False flattery seems rather gratuitous at this point, does it not?" I narrow my eyes. "Tell me what this is about or I shall take my natural grace and use it to remove myself from your presence."

"Quite a flair for dramatics beneath that calm exterior of

yours, isn't there?" He pauses artfully. "To be truthful, I wanted a closer look at you after watching so long from afar."

An unpleasant shiver moves up my spine at the thought of him—or his network of spies—watching me.

He feels my tremble; his lips curl up at the corners as he adds, "And to ascertain if the rumors are true."

"Rumors rarely are. That's why they're called rumors, not facts."

"Fair enough. But from what I have observed since I returned to Caeldera, it seems the whispers in the streets are not so far from reality. Prince Pendefyre has fallen in love again—with another wind weaver, no less. History seems doomed to repeat itself."

My teeth grit together. I have heard a similar refrain before, from Soren. I like it even less coming from Yale's smug mouth. "I would think the esteemed commanding general of Dyved's armies would know better than to listen to idle gossip."

"But it is not idle. He is in love with you. I have seen it with my own two eyes."

"Ridiculous." I bite out the word. "You have seen nothing, for there is nothing to see. There is nothing between Pendefyre and me."

Except in my memory.

Except in the farthest reaches of my foolish heart.

"Sometimes, affection is most apparent in the things left unsaid, the actions left untaken." Yale's tone is flat. "Sometimes, the deepest love disguises itself as indifference—for to reveal it would be to lay oneself bare. No man would willingly admit such a weakness. Perhaps not even to himself."

My pulse pounds. "Even if your laughable notions are true, I would think a man of your position has better things to worry about than the prince's love life."

"That's where you are wrong, Rhya." His strong lead never wavers, even as his voice grows intent. "Pendefyre is our rightful king. He will claim the throne. He will do it soon. I know this to be true. I also know that he is volatile. It is his nature, his very essence. The fire burns too strong within him, just as it did King Vorath." He shakes his head. "I cannot hold his temperament against him. But when a man like that—a man on whom the fate of my country, perhaps even my world, rests—falls in love, volatility can turn violent. When that man is also a king, violence has consequences for everyone. Only a very foolish general would disregard such a threat to all he is sworn to protect."

"You see me as a hazard, then. Something to be eliminated."

"I see you as an unpredictable variable. I don't like unpredictable variables. They tend to cause chaos."

"I have no intentions of causing chaos."

"Your intentions do not matter; only their outcomes."

"I think you overestimate my sway over Prince Pendefyre. Even if he is"—I nearly choke on the words—"*in love* with me, it will not affect his leadership."

"I have seen great men led astray by lust. I have watched the strongest of leaders cowed beneath the weight of despair over a lost lover, or driven into a blind rage in a fit of jealous temper. With a normal king, such provocations could be cause for disaster. With Pendefyre on the throne . . . I fear it will unleash utter devastation."

"What would you have me do, Yale?" I ask tightly. "Leave him? Leave Dyved?"

"I cannot answer that. I can only offer counsel when I feel it is necessary for the good of the entire realm."

"He will not let me go. He believes I have a role to play in all this. In restoring the balance. Fulfilling the prophecy."

"You may well doom us all long before you deliver that

heralded salvation," Yale says, his words stark. "In the strongest terms, I would advise against such a union. I would urge you to put a stop to this—before it is too late."

My heart pounds so hard it strains my rib cage. "And if I don't comply?"

"Then you should be prepared to face the consequences. I have been charged with the protection of this land. I cannot—I will not—let a threat go unchecked. Not even from a child of the prophecy."

The song is not yet over, but I draw to a halt, pulling back from his hold. My golden winged sleeves flutter as I lower my arms to my sides. I am quite finished with his false show of civility, with his camouflaged threats and ill-concealed judgments.

"Thank you for the delightful dance," I say in a tone that undermines my words. I do not wait for a response as I turn and bolt from him, cutting a blind path through the crush of gliding couples. But his voice follows me as I go, a sharp rebuke that cuts me to the bone.

"You would be wise to heed my warning, Rhya. I will not give another."

CHAPTER
THIRTY

The first firework explodes above me as I race across the bridge, ducking around clusters of people who line the railings to watch the vibrant display of sound and color. I jolt at the sudden boom but do not slow, do not stop. The crowd is dense but distracted—necks craned back to the sky, mouths agape in awe, eyes wide in wonder. No one pays me much attention as I race through their midst.

Flashes of color chase me all the way to the end of the bridge, then along the lakeshore. The water's surface reflects every detonation, a fluid rainbow in the night. Even more Caelderans are gathered at the banks, a thick throng of drunken revelers that's spilled out from the main square of the marketplace at the stroke of midnight.

The marketplace seems to be the epicenter of the evening's festivities, packed with spectators and entertainers alike. I do not pause longer than a heartbeat to watch the fire-eaters breathing mouthfuls of flame on the makeshift stage, do not hesitate more than a second to gawp at the painted contortionists writhing in suspended hoops above the crowd, pouring sparkling liquor from crystalline bottles between the parted lips of those passing below.

There is no time to linger. All too soon, Cadogan and Jac will realize I've slipped away from the dance floor, using the commotion around the fireworks display to camouflage my escape. They will pursue me, I have little doubt. But I do not think of that as I run, a streak of gold, through the firelit city streets, my flimsy satin slippers clapping against the cobblestones hard enough to bruise my soles. Nor do I consider that it is perhaps not the wisest course to abandon my net of protection as I round corners and dart past illuminated stoops, where couples sway in each other's arms and families of all sizes gather—especially in light of what I've learned from Yale.

We cannot keep track of the threats. Some of them may be here tonight. Some of them may be on this very dance floor.

I turn down a narrow street as a series of ear-splitting booms sound. Red, violet, blue, orange, a kaleidoscope of fiery powder flaring across the sky. I plow straight into a group of gawky youngsters with their wide eyes fixed upward, too transfixed to take notice of me. Their innocent enjoyment is a sharp contrast to the brimming conflict inside.

I cannot go back to the party. My thoughts are as jumbled as the feelings in my chest, where my heart races at twice its normal speed. My emotions are a gathering storm, mirroring the maegical one that rages deep beneath my skin.

Yale's words haunt my every step.

It is only a matter of time before one of Efnysien's lackeys succeeds where Lieutenant Gower failed.

I run on, faster, harder, trying to outrun his voice in my head. Even as I do, I know it is useless. I cannot outrun the truth. Not for much longer.

He is in love with you. I have seen it.

I am spinning out of control. Losing my grip on my emotions— and, with them, the gate within. My power rattles at it, desperate for release. Normally, I would go to the cavern behind the falls to recalibrate. Not tonight. There are too many people near the palace, too many watchful eyes tracking my every movement.

You may well doom us all.

I do not even consciously realize where I'm headed until I am there, standing at the base of the cliffside, staring at the shadowy mouth of the old mine shaft. Hauling a shaky breath into my lungs, I brace myself against the unpleasant sensation of confinement and enter the passage. Darkness engulfs me. Darkness and absolute quiet—such a glaring difference from the rest of the city. Even the booms of the fireworks show are muted by the heavy earth.

By the time I reach the lift, claustrophobia grips my lungs like a vise. My hand trembles as I raise it to the wall, fingertips guiding me where my eyes cannot, moving over the rough surface until I feel a series of gouges in the stone.

A glyph.

I have never activated one before—not intentionally, anyway—but I do not second-guess my own abilities as I pull a diaphanous tendril of maegic from the swirling storm clouds within me. It comes all too easily; my maegic brims very close to the surface tonight. On a sharp exhale, I send it pulsing out through my palm. Satisfaction fills me when I am instantly rewarded with a red glow.

The floor lurches as the lift activates, rising steadily through the shaft. I do not draw breath for the entirety of the journey. If there is any relief when I finally jolt to a stop at the top, it is quickly overridden by stronger emotions—the same ones that led me here in the first place. I make my way out of the tunnel, fighting my own feet to keep from running the final stretch of darkness.

I pass through the portal chamber, its glyphs dark and dormant against the far wall. Taking a ragged breath, I step out onto the precipice. The breath catches in my throat when my eyes land on the silhouetted figure by the edge.

He is here.

Of course he is here. That is, after all, why I have come—following the faint thread of our bond through the night without thought, without question, as soon as I was close enough to sense it.

He stands with his back to me, his forearms resting on the stone parapet as he watches the fireworks explode over his city. The view from this height is indescribable, its beauty almost impossible to behold, but I spare it no more than a passing glance. My eyes are stuck on Penn.

He is still shirtless, clad only in the loose black breeches he wore during the warding ceremony. He must've come straight here afterward. I watch his spine stiffen, his shoulders tense, and know he's heard my uneven gulp of air. Still, he does not turn to face me. He does not acknowledge my presence at all.

I had been sure—so sure, I did not pause to question it—that I would know what to say to him when at last I reached his side. Now that I have, my throat convulses around a lump of useless sentences that seem permanently lodged in my airway. I cannot force them out, no matter how I try.

In the end, it is Penn who speaks.

"You should not be here."

The utter weariness in his voice catches me off guard. I take a cautious step closer and whisper, "Neither should you."

His only response is silence.

"Are you all right?"

Again, silence. But the muscles in his shoulders ripple as tension courses through him.

"I was worried," I admit softly, taking another few steps. My slippers are soundless on the stone. "When you didn't come to the festival . . . I reached out, but I could barely feel your presence through the bond."

"Recharging the wards drains my maegic nearly to depletion. I'm surprised you can feel me at all."

"I couldn't. Not at first. Not until I got closer."

There is a terse pause. "I assume your highly adept guard detail has no idea where you are at the moment?"

My cheeks flush. "Don't blame Cadogan or Jac—"

"I shall blame whoever I bloody please," he snaps. Inhaling slowly, he takes great pains to steady his tone. "You should go back to the party. I'm not fit company for anyone tonight."

"I'm not *anyone*. I'm Rhya."

"All the more reason for you to go."

"Are you so determined to spend this night in solitude?" I close the rest of the distance between us, coming to stand alongside him at the parapet. In profile, his jaw is set like stone. There are deep shadows of exhaustion beneath his eyes. "I thought Fyremas was a night of unity and togetherness."

He scoffs. "Unity? This, coming from the girl who, at our last exchange, bolted from my presence like it was poison?"

I have no rebuttal. Pressing my lips together, I turn to look out over the city. I'd thought the fireworks were impressive from below, but at this vantage they are incomparable. Breathtaking. They swarm like distant fyrewisps, yellow then blue then red then violet, some giant and lingering, others flaring only for an instant.

Spread out below us, the entire crater is dotted with illumination. Torches and firepits burn from the bustling shores of the lake to the most precipitously perched homes halfway up the cliffs—a galaxy of earthbound stars.

"What upset you?"

Penn's sudden question makes my head whip his way. "Who says I'm upset?"

"Rhya, your emotions are damn near boiling over. Even with my maegic muted, I can feel you're close to losing control." He finally meets my eyes. "So just tell me. What—*who*—upset you?"

I want to look away, but I am trapped in the dark fire of his stare, trembling beneath the force of it no matter how I lock my knees.

"Yale."

"I should've known." Penn runs a hand through his hair in frustration. "What did he say?"

"Does it matter?"

"Of course it matters."

Now I do look away. "He doesn't like me, let's put it that way."

"Rhya."

"All right," I grumble, knowing he is not about to let the topic drop. "He said there are threats against me. So many of them, you redirected some of his troops to the city as extra protection."

"And?"

"*And*"—I force out the word—"he may have implied he won't be too shaken up when, eventually, one of Efnysien's flunkies manages to bypass all that extra protection and removes me from your life. Permanently."

"Fucking bastard!"

"Penn—"

"He's furious because I went over his head with the army. He's taking it out on you. That's all this is. Don't pay him any mind."

"Then I'm not in danger?"

His hesitation is telling. "Rhya—"

"I am!" I shake my head in disbelief. "Gods, Penn, were you going to tell me?"

"No."

"*No?*" I explode. "After Gower, I knew there were threats, I knew there was danger—more, even, than you wanted to admit. But this . . . How could you keep something like this from me?"

"Because I have it under control. We've doubled the perimeter guards at the towers around the capital—all across the plateau, in fact. The trade roads have checkpoints. Everyone who's come in or out of the city in the past week has been stopped for questioning and searched for weapons. The main tunnel into Caeldera is sealed shut with stone doors so thick, it would take a troll to breach them. Not to mention, I've just topped off the wards with so much power, I'm surprised I'm still conscious." The words come out in a harsh clip. "You are safe. I made certain of it."

"You still should have told me—"

"I wanted you to enjoy your first Fyremas!" he barks, stopping my protests. His voice softens a shade as he stares at me. "I wanted you to have one night—just one godsdamned night—where you could enjoy yourself. If I'd told you about the threats, it would've sucked all the light right out of your eyes. I've seen enough of that. I . . . You . . . You deserved more. I wanted to give you more. Is that so difficult for you to comprehend?"

"I . . . I don't . . ." I swallow hard, trying to find the right words as our gazes hold for a prolonged moment. My hand flutters uselessly up to my chest, pressing not against my Remnant but against my heart. It seems to be skipping beats. "Thank you," I finish lamely.

"You're welcome," he mutters.

We both tear our eyes away from each other at the same moment, looking back out over the city. The fireworks are exploding in rapid succession now, arcing like colorful ribbons across the atmosphere in a grand finale designed to stun the senses. I fix my sights on them, struggling to steady my breathing. I do not even bother trying to calm my racing pulse.

"Was that all?"

My brows shoot up my forehead, brushing the heavy diadem. "What?"

"Yale. Was that all he said?"

Heat flushes into my cheeks as Yale's voice echoes inside my head.

He is in love with you.

I am a bad liar.

I know this.

I lie anyway.

"Yes, that's all he said."

The air goes static. The longer the falsehood floats there between us unaddressed, the more the tension mounts. I feel I might combust out of my skin. Eventually, I can no longer stand it. Pushing away from the parapet, I turn to leave. "I'm sorry I interrupted your solitude. I'll go now—"

His hand on my arm is a vise, stopping me in my tracks. I do not dare draw breath as he tugs me around to face him. His gaze is the molten shade of fossilized amber—and I the helpless creature trapped within, impossibly frozen in place.

"Tell me what else Yale said."

"I told you—"

"You lied."

"I did not!"

"You can try to deceive me with words, Rhya," Penn growls, leaning in. His eyes flicker down to the low-cut bodice of my dress, where my Remnant is on full display between my breasts. My chest is heaving with each breath, a rapid rise and fall I cannot control. "But the bond between us does not lie."

"For the last time," I grit out. "*Stop. Reading. My. Emotions.*"

"I will, when you learn to shut me out."

"You are the most arrogant, hateful, obstinate— *Gods!* Sometimes I cannot stand you!" I jolt against his hold, but he does not yield so much as a finger. "Let me go!"

"Do you think I don't know how you feel about me? Bond or no, I am fully aware you despise me. How could I not be? You have told me time and again." His eyes narrow to slits. "I know you wish our paths had never crossed, that I had never found you, that I had never brought you here."

"That's not true!"

"Isn't it?"

"No!"

"Then what is the truth?" He shakes me lightly when I give no reply. "Honestly, do you think I *want* to read your emotions, Rhya? Do you think it is pleasant for me, day after day, to remain near you, mere paces away, and not be affected by all you feel? Do you think I enjoy trying to hold myself in check when your emotions blast at me in a constant torrent?" He yanks me closer— so close, our noses bump. "Everything you feel pours straight into me, from your heart to mine, no matter how I try to keep you out. No matter how I try to hold you at arm's length. Trust me, I wish more than anything that you would learn to shut me out. *Fucking hell!* Do you think I am made of stone?"

I reel back, as though he's struck me a physical blow. I do not get far with him still gripping my arm in a granite hold.

"I'm sorry it's so unpleasant to be around me!" I seethe at him, seeing red. "I suggest we return to your plan of mutual avoidance in the future. I promise not to seek you out again, since being near me is such an *intolerable* burden for you!"

With that, I manage to wrench my arm out of his grip and whirl around. I am suddenly desperate for distance. I am very close to tears; the last thing I want is for him to witness them. But

I only make it a handful of steps before two hands close around my biceps from behind, halting me in my tracks yet again.

I let out an angry half scream. But the sound evaporates in my throat as the warm plane of Penn's chest presses against my back. His head lowers to the crook of my neck, his lips brushing the sensitive lobe of my ear, and I go still.

Still down to my soul.

"Rhya," Penn whispers, his voice cracking. "Don't you understand? You . . . You have undone me completely. I look at you, I touch you, I sense you near me, and I . . ." His voice pitches lower, barely audible. "I pride myself on staying in control of all things. I am a master at it. But these days, I hardly recognize myself. I am a raw nerve, run ragged from trying to keep myself in check each time I'm near you."

"And how do you think I feel?"

His whole frame tightens.

"*I* was not the one who created distance. *I* was not the one who put up this new wall," I remind him, voice thick. "You are the one who wanted to forget what happened between us."

"Rhya—"

"You made me feel like you regretted it," I cut him off. "Regretted *me*."

His forehead presses against my nape. "I know. I know, and I'm sorry. Gods, I know this isn't fair to you. I know that I've hurt you, pushing you away. But I do not know how else to be around you without . . . without . . ."

"Without what, Penn?" I ask the shadows, wishing I could see his face. "Without admitting you cannot contain every emotion every minute of every day? That you are just as fallible as the rest of us—and just as capable of feelings, even if you see them as a liability?"

"They *are* a liability."

"Perhaps to you, but not to me!" My anger lashes out like a whip. "You see us as a risk not worth taking, but I never saw us that way! At least, not until you started holding me at arm's length. Not until you started acting as though we mean nothing to each other."

"I have responsibilities. I have a kingdom I am accountable to. I do not have the luxury of chasing after the things I want without a thought to the consequences." He pauses, voice dropping to an almost inaudible volume. "I would rather you hate me and be safe than put you at risk by . . ."

"By what?" Tears gloss my eyes. "By *loving* you?"

He presses closer, his body straining to erase our distance even as his dark words push me away. "It would be better if you hated me."

"For who? Certainly not for me." I shake my head slowly back and forth, devastation ripping through me. I know he can feel every excruciating pulse of it in the bond. And in this moment, I don't care.

I want him to feel it.

I want him to know.

He makes a pained sound, sharing my anguish.

"Do you want to know the saddest truth?" I ask, voice breaking. "I never hated you. Not even at the very start. Not even when we were enemies. Not even when I thought you wanted to *kill me*. Because even then, there was still a part of me that was drawn to you. Air to open flame."

His entire frame shudders. His emotions have never been so raw, so accessible to me. Tonight, he does not have the strength to hide them away.

"How can you possibly think, after all we have been through together"—I am crying freely now—"that I would ever be able to hate you?"

"*Stop.*" A shattered plea. "Don't say any more, Rhya. Don't say things you can't take back."

"I don't want to take them back!" I thunder, determined. "You may want to live a lie, Pendefyre, but I don't. Not anymore. If you don't want me, tell me. I'm tired of trying to sort out the truth from the pretending."

There is an endless pause. I think he's going to let me go, let me walk away. But instead, he groans low in his throat.

"You think I don't want you? *Gods.*" His lips skim my neck, a trail of flame. "All I can think about is your mouth on mine, your hair in my hands, your fingers on my skin. I lie in my bed at night, listening to you toss and turn, and it takes everything in me to keep from ascending that ladder. To keep from carrying you straight back down it, putting you in my bed, and letting the fire we sparked in that forest finally burn itself out."

Heat furls through me at his words, coiling in my very core. *Skies.* If I'd known, all those sleepless nights, he was lying just below me, sharing my torturous thoughts . . . sharing my secret desires . . .

"Why didn't you?" I whisper.

"Because I know better!" His grip becomes bruising, his fingertips biting into my upper arms. "I know these things I feel for you are dangerous—for you, for me, for both of us. For bloody everyone."

Yale had said much the same back on the dance floor. Hearing it confirmed from Penn himself is like a sword through the heart.

"Then why are you still holding me?"

"Because, gods help me, *I don't care anymore!*" His voice breaks. "I don't care about the risks. I don't care about the repercussions. I have tried. Tried not to feel this way, tried to lock in my feelings. It's no use. I'm not strong enough. Not when it comes to you."

He pulls in a ragged breath, his bare chest pressing more firmly to my exposed spine. Skin to skin. The evidence of his desire is hard against my backside. Undeniable. Feeling it there only intensifies the hollow ache building at the very core of me.

"Wanting you is all I do, Rhya. Waking or dreaming, avoiding you completely or seeking out your presence. I want and I want and I want . . . And . . . *It. Fucking. Terrifies. Me.*"

"You think I'm not just as terrified? You think the things I feel for you don't scare the breath out of me?" I pause, heart pounding. And then, unable to stop myself, I turn in his embrace. He sucks in a breath as I reach up to take his face into my hands. Beneath my fingertips, his skin is like a furnace. My eyes drift to his lips. "Please, Pendefyre . . . Don't let me walk away again."

"I could hurt you." His admission is agonized. "The way the fire rages in me, the way my emotions fuel it . . . If I lose control, if I slip—"

"You won't slip. You won't hurt me."

"You cannot know that."

I meet his eyes. They burn into mine, volcanic with so much yearning, I can't see anything else. Can't feel anything else. "I'm not afraid of you, Penn. I'm not afraid of your fire. I'm far more afraid of what we will forfeit if we never try. If we let fear win."

The words have barely left my lips when his mouth comes down on mine, a crushing impact. His kiss is a firestorm—unpredictable heat, uncontrollable desire. It blazes through my body, an inferno that singes me from the inside out, frying my nerve endings.

This—*this*—is what I came here for. Not to tell him about Yale, not to see if he was all right, not to bicker with him. This,

right here, his lips on mine, his heated body flush, so close I think
we might slip inside each other's skin and never come out. He
invades my senses, floods every part of my mind. The bond between us catches fire, a channel of invisible flame, burning hot
enough to scorch my soul as emotions spark back and forth from
his mark to mine.

Penn deepens the kiss. It turns raw. Relentless. Wild. My
head falls back on instinct as his lips lay siege. My body arches
like a bowstring as his hands slide up my bare spine to find my
neck. He presses his thumbs into the hollow of my throat, where
my pulse races at double time, and I moan into his mouth, an
unstoppable sound of pure want.

The noise unlocks something in him. Shatters the last bit of
his self-control. One minute I am standing in his arms and the
next I am lifted clear off my feet, carried three steps, and set on
the edge of the parapet. He barely lets me settle before his hands
reach for the slit of my skirts. With a rough jerk, he parts my legs
and moves between them. Any hesitation is a distant memory
now, any repercussions a far-off consequence. We think of neither past nor future, consumed in the immediacy of our hunger
for each other.

When Penn spots the dagger strapped in the leather sheath
around my thigh, he grins, a flash of white in the dimness. His
lips are still curved when they reclaim mine. But all amusement
ignites like paper as I wrap my legs around his waist, locking in
his tall frame as my arms twine up around his neck. His passion
is a throbbing press between my legs, matching the need that
pulses through my veins. I suck his lip into my mouth at the same
moment I delve my fingers into his hair, as I have wanted to for
so long, reveling in the feel of its thickness.

"Gods, Rhya." He gasps into my mouth as his hips grind

against mine, a delicious move that dizzies all my senses. "If you keep touching me like that, I'm not going to be able to stop."

"I don't want you to stop."

With another rumbling groan, he kisses me again. His hands imprison my hips, holding me firmly. Creating delicious friction that makes me gasp. Taking advantage of my parted lips, his tongue slides between them. My desire spikes higher as our mouths move together, a ravenous dance it is hard to breathe around.

But who needs to breathe?

Pendefyre is finally kissing me.

Breathing can wait.

My pulse is a drumbeat, the tempo increasing faster and faster as we let the flames consume us. Air and fire, an inextinguishable passion. Igniting together into pure, unadulterated . . .

Combustion.

One of his hands traces up the sensitive skin of my thigh, lingering briefly at the dagger sheath. He toys with the leather strap for a torturous second before his hand moves even higher—this time not stopping until he's found the heat burning at my core. A heat that magnifies a hundredfold as he palms the most intimate part of me.

Gods.

Yes.

Clinging to his shoulders, I rock my body against his hold, feeling my mind start to fray into delirium. Feeling like this passion we have unleashed will never burn itself out, no matter how long we touch, no matter how far we let ourselves go tonight.

As his fingers move, working my passion to new heights in slow, rhythmic circles, my own hand slides down his bare chest— hesitating only for a moment at the raised skin of his Remnant—

to find his length. I stroke him through the fabric of his breeches, satisfaction furling through me as he looses a low growl into my mouth. The sound makes my thighs clench arounds his fingers.

"Rhya," he says warningly. His hand stills between my legs. "Maybe we should—"

"No more maybes," I cut him off, voice breathy. "And no more excuses. We've done enough talking, Pendefyre. Just . . . *Touch me.* Please."

His hesitation goes up in smoke. His mouth slams back down on mine, kissing me harder, wetter, deeper. It is a clash of tongues and teeth, a heated battle—one where both of us walk away winners. Our lips never part, even as our desperate hands move over hidden places. Places we have scarcely allowed ourselves to dream of touching, until this moment.

Buttons slip, hems shift. Penn hisses out a sharp breath when I take him into my grip. I love the feel of him, naked in my hands. Strong and sleek as every other part of his body. And he does not hide his own gratification when his fingers find their way beneath my undergarments. A rumble moves deep in his chest at the silken confirmation of my desire for him.

Our kisses ravage as we find new rhythms, carve out a new tempo that crescendoes until I think I will not be able to stand it without shattering to pieces. I shift in his arms—restless, needy. Aching for something I cannot articulate. Not with words, in any case.

The throbbing pulse inside me spikes to a fever pitch.

I can barely keep my thoughts from fraying, lost in the all-consuming nature of Penn's touch. Even with his maegic muted, the bond heightens our connection—feeding it, fanning the flames to something more than purely physical. Something more than I ever felt with Tomas, something more than I knew was possible.

This is a spiritual, soul-deep connection. One that only makes the urgent dance of our hands and mouths all the more intense. The bond tightens around us, an invisible tether, urging us closer, closer, *closer*.

When my breaths have been reduced to choppy pants, I can no longer kiss him properly. I pull back, only enough to draw air into my lungs, and stare into his eyes. Penn's gaze is locked on mine, a fiery hold I cannot escape. One I do not *want* to escape. The fire I see in him is a match for my own. I want it to consume me, spark by spark. I want it to catch into an unstoppable inferno. I want—-

Him.

I want him.

He is as close as he's ever been, and it's still not close enough.

"Penn," I whisper, the word cracking in my throat. "Please, I—I need you."

His eyes flare, molten with lust. His hands slide up to my thighs so he can shift closer, trailing heat across my skin in their wake. My breath catches, anticipation spiraling through me in a vortex, as I feel how close he is—how close *we* are. His lips hit my ear.

"I need you, too," he admits in a rough rasp.

Thank the skies.

My hands lock on his shoulders as my body arches eagerly against his. There is a fire inside me only he can extinguish. One that has been smoldering for months now, an exquisitely slow burn. Tonight, we will spark those embers into everlasting flame.

His grip tightens on my hips as he—

"Loath as I am to interrupt this touching display," a familiar voice, smooth like water tumbling over a bed of river rock, says from somewhere that seems at once very near and very far. "The three of us need to talk."

PENN AND I jerk apart like a bucket of ice water has been dumped on our heads. Which, in a way, it has. For standing not five paces away is the Remnant of Water himself.

King Soren of Llŷr, in the flesh.

He towers like a daemon, a harbinger of doom in a warrior's body. His bright-blue eyes are luminous in the dark. They move back and forth from me to Penn with catlike cunning, taking stock of every infinitesimal detail. Me, rearranging my skirts as I hop down from the parapet; Penn, adjusting his trousers slightly with shaking hands. Both of us breathing unsteadily, cheeks flushed and mouths kiss swollen.

"Soren." Penn's tone is pure ice. "What the fuck are you doing here?"

"Now, now." Soren crosses his arms over his broad chest. "Is that any way to greet someone who's just come to save your hide?"

"Send a raven next time," Penn growls.

"This is urgent."

"I don't care how urgent the news. You cannot come marching through my portals whenever you please."

"So possessive of your toys." Soren's eyes slide to me. His perfectly chiseled features are as difficult to read as I remember from our first meeting. "Speaking of toys, you're looking well, little wind weaver. Quite well. I must say, I might not have been so quick to let you go had I known a few months of regular meals would turn you from the waterlogged runt I found on that mountainside into—"

"I thought you had urgent news," I interject pointedly.

"I do." Sobering, he glances back at Penn, who looks fit to be tied. "You need to ready your forces."

Penn stills. "Why?"

"Not long ago, I received word from one of my generals. During a routine patrol of the range, some of her scouts went missing. She sent a unit after them to find out what happened." Two thick black brows furrow inward. "They followed the trail all the way to your southern border. Straight into Reaver territory."

"I'm sorry you lost your scouts," Penn says curtly. "But given the tribes' recent aggression toward my own people, I can't say I'm shocked—"

"Just *listen*, would you?" Soren sucks in a breath, steadying himself. His tall frame is ramrod with tension, lacking any trace of his typical airy nonchalance. "The report I received after the recovery mission was . . . bizarre. The bodies weren't mutilated or mangled, like most Reaver attacks. These were killed very precisely—arrows through eyes, throats garroted, heads bludgeoned. Very little blood, very few marks anywhere below the neckline. And they were stripped bare. Their attackers stole their uniforms after they killed them."

Penn digests this, clearly troubled. "Usually the clans take pleasure in ripping apart all traces of us—clothes and all."

"I thought the same. As did my generals. So we looked into it further. Sent a few additional scouts out onto the ice shelf two days ago." Soren's expression is intense. "They found more stripped bodies. Not Llŷrians, this time. They were Dyvedi men, Pendefyre. Your men. A whole legion of them, at least."

"I would have been informed if an entire legion went missing, Soren."

"Not missing. *Replaced*." Soren steps closer, gaze unwavering. "Think about it. The stripped uniforms. The strange deaths. The increased organization of their attacks. This is bigger than a decades-long dispute over some borderland."

"Let me get this straight—you think the Reavers are killing Dyvedi soldiers in secret and stealing their uniforms?"

Soren nods.

"For what possible purpose? To play dress-up as the fae they aim to eliminate?"

"To infiltrate your territory undetected," Soren snaps, his frustration breaking loose from its fetters. "You may not want to believe it, but it is happening all the same. The Reavers are moving against you. And they do not act alone. They have found a new ally. A powerful one."

"The clans can barely keep from slaughtering one another en masse every few years. They are not capable of conspiring with outsiders."

"So you thought. So we all did. It seems we were wrong. Unthinkable as it may be, the Reavers have allied themselves . . ." Soren's eyes glitter, dark sapphires. "With Efnysien."

My stomach lurches.

Penn shakes his head. "That's not possible."

"It is," Soren counters, gritting his teeth. "I would not lie about something like this."

"The Reavers hate the fae above all. They would never accept the help of someone who wields maegic—even the dark, distorted maegic Efnysien commands."

"They would if they thought it would finally win them what they have long coveted: control of Dyved. Eradication of your people." Soren's stare is as hard as his words. "Efnysien's red army has been gathering for months on the ice shelf, completely undetected. Gaining slowly in numbers. Stealing uniforms to slip into your lands unseen. Replacing fortified borders without raising the alarm. Biding their time for an opportunity to strike."

"Gods above," I whisper.

"From what my scouts witnessed, they are no longer waiting," Soren continues. "Even now, they are marching north across the plateau with their sights fixed on Caeldera. And they are not alone. Half the Reaver clans march with them."

I glance at Penn. His face is stark white in the starlight as his former friend's words begin to permeate. Still, he clings to hope. "Even if what you say is true, even if they succeed in cutting a path across the plateau, they cannot enter the capital. They will never get through the wards."

"They can." Soren takes two steps forward, so they stand face-to-face. His voice is grave as death. "With Efnysien's help, they can breach any maegical protections that would normally keep them out. You know I am right. His power was strong when I banished him almost a century ago; it is unparalleled now. Your wards will fall, Pendefyre. And your armies, however well trained, are both outnumbered and unprepared. They cannot win this fight."

Sudden horror grips my heart. "We need to warn everyone. We need to evacuate! Surely, there is somewhere safe we can go . . ."

When neither of them responds, my eyes fly from Soren to Penn and back again. They are engaged in a grim stare-down, communicating something without speaking aloud. Realization falls like a guillotine.

Caeldera is the safe place. It is Dyved's best stronghold. There is nowhere else to go, nowhere better to ride out an invasion on the whole plateau. If the city falls . . .

We will all fall along with it.

"How long do we have?" Penn asks—the only question that truly matters anymore.

"I don't know," Soren admits. "I didn't wait around for another status report. I came straight here to warn you. It could be tonight; it could be tomorrow."

He looks out over Caeldera, dazzling in its midnight beauty. Far below us, thousands of civilians still celebrate in the streets, blissfully unaware of the impending danger.

"If it were me . . . if you were my enemy . . ." Soren tears his eyes from the city below. "I would strike when you were at your most vulnerable. When your people were most exposed—gathered in the streets in great numbers, in the midst of a celebration, senses dulled by drink . . ."

"Efnysien will know my powers are drained tonight," Penn says bitterly. "He will know I cannot protect my people."

"A full battalion of Llŷrian troops will be here by daybreak." Soren nods firmly to underscore his words. "We merely need to hold out until then."

"If the wards fall—"

"Then we will fight," Soren vows. His eyes flicker to me. "You are not the only one with power here, Pendefyre."

I swallow a bleat of fear and, with a nod, echo him. "We will fight."

"You will not," Penn growls, turning to glower at me. His hand snatches mine in a bone-grinding grip. "Come. We need to get back to the keep, where you'll be safe. If Soren is right, we may not have long before—"

His words are swallowed up by the sound of a massive detonation. At first, I think it is another firework—a belated explosion going off at the lakeshore. But there is no shower of sparks, no cascade of color. The sky itself shudders, as though the heavens might plummet, and I know with a surge of paralyzing certainty that this is no party trick.

The atmosphere strobes bright as a bloodred dawn. A haze shimmers in the air—the same shimmer I'd seen mere hours earlier, when Penn's power poured into the earth back in the throne room. The wards are reacting to a great influx of power. Only this time, it is not shoring them up.

It is ripping them apart.

The rumble of the first explosion has hardly faded when a second boom blasts through the sky. As I watch the wards flare again, the red haze flashing like heat lighting . . . I know, without a word from Pendefyre or Soren, that whoever means to attack us is no longer on their way.

They are already here.

CHAPTER
THIRTY–ONE

We run.

Penn first, me in the middle, Soren on my heels. Down the passage, past the portal—still glowing faintly from Soren's journey—to the lift. None of us speaks as Penn activates the glyph and we shoot downward into the earth. The only sound in the jarring quiet is that of my breaths, thready and terror laced, pumping in and out of my lungs.

The lift ride lasts a lifetime. Each second drags into a day, a month, a year wasted. Time ticks away uselessly while those in the streets party on, completely unaware of the looming danger. I think of all the families I passed on my way here, necks craned backward to catch a glimpse of the fireworks show, grins splitting their faces in glee. Defenseless. Innocent. Unprepared. I nearly chew through my bottom lip trying to hold in my hyperventilation.

We hit ground level and charge, full tilt, for the mouth of the mine shaft. Another blast hits the wards just as we exit into open air. The sky flashes faintly red, a weak pulse. A cry goes up from the crowd, a medley of amusement and concern. Most, still caught up in the intoxicating festivity of Fyremas, assume it is just another facet of the celebrations.

"Sound the alarms!" Penn roars at two bewildered-looking soldiers stationed on a street corner as we hurtle past them. "We are under attack!"

We do not pause to see if they comply. We run faster. Impossibly fast. An unyielding sprint. At my sides, Soren and Penn seem tireless, their long legs eating up the ground without ever breaking stride. Somehow, I keep pace with them, my feet flying over the cobblestones as though I've grown true wings, the golden train of my gown whipping out behind me like a battle flag. I feel the cold burn of power coiled in my chest and realize I am unconsciously using the wind to propel myself forward, the air currents extending each bound farther, higher, longer than my petite legs could accomplish of their own accord.

Under normal circumstances, this might shock or even delight me. Tonight, there is no room in my mind for anything but dread. It poisons my veins, a toxic elixir, as we carve a jagged path toward the heart of Caeldera. When we reach King's Avenue, the main thoroughfare from the tunnel to the lakeside, we find it packed with people still dancing and drinking.

"Get inside!" Penn roars, over and over. "Take cover!"

Faces stream by in a flood—at first merely concerned, then increasingly terrified as yet another blast of maegic shakes the sky.

"Prepare for attack!"

A cacophony of confusion and terror rises in place of music and laughter. Just as we reach the main square, that terror reaches a fever pitch when alarms begin to sound—a shrill ringing that splits the night, warning of an imminent attack. Even the drunkest revelers know what it means.

People bolt for cover. Stalls overturn in the crush. Vendors desert their wares. The stage is abandoned, fire-eaters long gone. The contortionist hoops hang empty. We push against the tide, fighting our way upstream as folks flood from the lakeshore through the marketplace, onto King's Avenue. Their fear is palpable, infusing the air, mingling with the persistent scent of gunpowder from the fireworks.

The moment we reach the bridge, I know there will be no getting across. It is packed with people pouring from the palace, desperate to reach their homes and reunite with their loved ones.

"*Oi!*" Someone whistles sharply over the din. "Pendefyre!"

The three of us slam to a halt. In unison, we turn to see Jac, Cadogan, and Farley shoving their way toward us through the melee by the foot of the bridge. On their heels, about two dozen other members of the Ember Guild are forming orderly rows around us, buffering the panicked crowd. The sheer amount of weaponry strapped to their persons is mildly reassuring.

"Oh thank the gods. She's with you." Jac is staring at me like he wants to sweep me into a hug and throttle me simultaneously. "Damn it, Ace, we've been looking for you for almost an hour! If the sky wasn't falling, woman, I swear . . ."

"Sorry." I grimace. "If we live through the night, I'll make it up to you."

"Not sure what's going on," Cadogan cuts in, stepping forward to face Penn, "but we figured you might need these."

Penn nods in gratitude as he accepts his boots, broadsword, and bandolier of throwing knives. On all sides, people continue to jostle by, an unending stream. How quickly this night of warmth and light has darkened into shadows of despair. How fast these flames of joy have turned to ash. The sky flashes red again as another barrage of maegic hits the wards.

"Anyone care to explain what the hell is happening?" Farley shouts over the resounding rumbles.

"We're under attack," Jac says. "Obviously."

Farley rolls his eyes. "Bloody half-wit, you think I don't know we're—"

"*Enough!*" Penn barks as he straps on his bandolier with one hand. In the other, the naked blade of his broadsword gleams. "The Reaver clans have found a new ally in our old enemy. Efnysien. He's trying to bring down the wards. If he succeeds, they'll breach the tunnel and sack the city."

"Gods." Jac pales. "Can he do it?"

"Let us hope not." Penn glances past the flood of panicked civilians to the palace looming behind. "Where the hell is Yale?"

"Took it upon himself to protect the queen." Cadogan's face is a mask of contempt. "Our brave commanding general, barricaded in the throne room while his soldiers do battle."

Beside me, Soren snorts. The other men look at him, seeming to finally take note of his presence. Their thunderstruck expressions are very nearly comical.

"What the skies is *he* doing here?" Farley splutters.

"Helping," Soren fires back. "Which is more than I can say for you, tripod. Do you plan to swing that walking stick at every Reaver who comes your way?"

Farley's oath is overshadowed by another onslaught from outside the crater. The wards shudder weakly, strobing the diluted shade of inexpensive wine—as though their strength wanes with each strike. I am not the only one to realize this, for any verbal sparring is quickly brushed aside in lieu of rapid-fire battle orders.

"Cadogan, take your unit to the tunnel," Penn commands, jerking his chin toward King's Avenue. "Mabon should already be there with the rest of the guild and a contingent of foot soldiers. Grab as many able-bodied men as you can find on the way. If they're sober enough to stand, they're sober enough to fight." He pauses. "We have to assume anyone stationed outside the ward perimeter is already dead."

Cadogan nods, expression grim.

"Jac, go to the aviary," Penn continues. "Tell the master of scrolls to send ravens to every guard post and battle station across the plateau. We need reinforcements here as soon as possible."

"And afterward?" Jac asks.

"Meet us at the tunnel. We may yet have need of your axe."

Jac takes off like a shot, headed west along the lakeshore to the rickety stone tower that houses a flock of well-trained avian messengers. Cadogan, more somber than I've ever seen him, has already turned to the dual lines of battle-ready Ember Guild and rattled off their marching orders. Lump in my throat, I watch them go until I lose sight of their maroon uniforms halfway down King's Avenue.

"Where is Uther?" Penn asks, calling my attention back.

Farley shrugs. "Home with Carys and the baby, last I heard."

"No. I'm here," comes a breathless voice from just behind us as Uther jogs to a stop and joins our circle. His steady gray eyes sweep over me and Soren before coming to rest on Penn's face. "Where do you need me?"

"Uther, your family . . ." Penn hesitates. "Are you certain—"

"I said, *where do you need me?*"

Penn clasps his hand on Uther's shoulder. "Go to the barracks. Make sure any stragglers are out of bed, armed, and ready to fight. Bring whoever you can find to the front gates."

Uther nods. His eyes meet mine for a brief instant, shining with undisguised warmth, before he, too, races away into the night.

"Farley." Penn's attention shifts to the redhead. He looks grave, leaning heavily on his cane, bow and arrow strapped across his back, short sword hanging from his hip. "You'll be at the keep. The guards there already know the lockdown protocols, but I want to ensure people have a place to fall back, if necessary."

"The keep? You're joking."

"Farley. It's the safest place—"

"Fuck *safe*!" Farley's expression mottles with anger. "I want to fight!"

"Your leg is not recovered."

"I don't need my leg to swing a bloody sword!"

"I need you with Rhya."

Farley quiets.

I tense.

At my side, so does Soren.

"I'm with Farley on this," I interrupt, nearly shaking in my attempt to keep from screaming. "You aren't sidelining me. I'm not running or hiding. Not this time. Not while you all risk your lives to keep the city safe—"

Penn glowers. "Rhya—"

"She's right, Pendefyre," Soren says, surprising me. "We need her. Your powers are not at full strength—"

"I don't need you to tell me about my own bloody limitations, Soren. And I definitely don't need you putting ideas in her head. She has no training for battle."

"What have you spent these past weeks teaching her, then?" Soren asks, incredulous. "From what I witnessed up on that parapet, perhaps your lessons have been more focused on the bedroom than the battlefield."

Penn's expression darkens with wrath. "Be very careful what you say next, nymph."

"Why?" Soren's brows arch sardonically. "Is the truth too hard to swallow?"

"Stop it! Both of you." I step between the two men, cutting off

Penn's sight line to Soren before things escalate to bloodshed.
"Penn, please. Now is not the time to be overprotective—"

"We're under attack," he counters. "It's precisely the time to
be overprotective."

"You can't protect me from *this*!"

"I can bloody well try!" His words are a roar, right in my
face. But beneath his rage, I see his fear. I feel it, too, a surge of
pure emotion through our bond. "Gods, Rhya, for once, would
you just listen to me without fighting every step of the—"

I never hear the rest of what he says. The sky rattles as another blast of dark maegic collides with the wards. They give one
final, faded pulse of resistance, flickering the faintest shade of
red, then dissipating in a cloud of useless vapor.

The wards are down.

For a moment, there is only stillness. The entire city holds its
breath, waiting to see what will happen. Penn and I stare into
each other's eyes. No longer fighting, no longer saying anything
at all. His free hand lifts to my neck and he jerks me close. Our
foreheads collide with a jarring thunk.

"Stay safe," he whispers fervently. "For me."

Then his mouth is on mine in a hard, brutal kiss. It lasts no
longer than a heartbeat. It tastes like goodbye. Before I can even
think of returning it, he is gone—racing toward the front gates
without a word.

Soren shoots me a brief, unreadable look and then he takes
off, running after Penn so fast he is no more than a smear of dark
navy fabric to my eyes. Though the tears glossing over their surfaces may have something to do with my blurred vision.

"Ace," Farley says. He sounds as shaky as I feel. When I drag
my watering eyes to him, I see he looks even worse. "We should
get inside."

Despite his words, neither of us moves. All around, people are running for shelter; soldiers are scrambling for weapons. Everyone seems to have a purpose, a destination, a plan. Except us. We are a point of stillness in the chaos, unmoored and uncertain.

We both glance briefly toward the keep. Toward the promise of shelter. Then, in unspoken unison, our gazes swing around in the opposite direction, down the straight stretch of roadway that separates us from the fortified tunnel on the far side of the crater, where, even now, our friends are readying themselves for whatever evils might burst through those heavy stone doors.

I know Farley is no more enthused than I am at the prospect of hiding out while others fight and bleed and die. But I have no skills in battle and no weapons to speak of—besides the dagger strapped to my thigh. Thank the gods Carys agreed to add the slit so I can access it easily.

Carys.

Realization blazes through me. "Farley. Carys is all alone."

His light-green eyes flood with purpose. He immediately begins hobbling in the direction of High Street, his cane moving at a steady clip.

"What the hell are we waiting around for, Ace? Let's go!"

SINCE MY ARRIVAL in the Northlands, I have heard many stories of the Reavers' brutality. I have seen the hatred that fuels their quest to wipe my kind from the face of the earth with my own eyes, in that bloody clearing atop the Cimmerians where a whole unit of soldiers lay butchered in the snow. But whatever tales I have heard, whatever horrors I have seen, cannot compare to the things I witness the night of Fyremas.

Farley and I are halfway down High Street when the tunnel

falls. There's a telltale explosion—much like the ones that rained down upon the wards, only closer, louder, and infinitely more terrifying.

It would take a troll to breach them, Penn had said of the stone doors that seal the tunnel. *You are safe.*

But I am not.

No one is.

We are nowhere near the explosion, yet the impact still shakes the ground beneath our feet. The resulting boom has me covering my ears and ducking for cover, certain I am about to be blown to bits. A cloud of dust and ash fills the air, spreading outward in a fog.

From here, we cannot see whatever is blasting its way into the city. A maze of streets separates us from King's Avenue and the gates beyond. But when my senses stop ringing, my ears pick up the unmistakable roar of battle on the wind. And I know, without a doubt, the stronghold of Caeldera has been shattered.

"Fuck," Farley curses, hobbling faster. He nearly loses his footing on an uneven sidewalk in his haste.

"Careful," I mutter. "We're nearly there."

We pass the apothecary, who is frantically pounding wooden boards over his shop windows. I want to tell him not to waste his energy, to get to safety, but merely nod in greeting as we rush past. The chocolatier is long gone, his door ajar. He left in a hurry. The cobbler and her wife peer out at us from behind their half-closed shutters, fear etched plainly across their features.

Carys's whole building is dark, but the door swings inward the moment we come to a stop on the street outside, as though she's been waiting for us. She urges us into the dim shop without a word. Baby Nevin is swaddled tightly against her chest. As soon as we clear the threshold, she bolts the door once more.

"What's happening?" she whispers, staring from me to Farley. "We heard the alarms. Uther took off to see what was going on. He said not to leave until he came back, but I just heard an explosion . . ."

"Reavers," we say in unison. "They've breached the tunnel."

"But the wards!"

"The wards are down. We have to go, Carys."

Carys grips her baby tighter. Her face is ghostly pale. "We will be safe enough here."

"Not as safe as the inner keep—"

"I'm not going to the keep. My husband told me to stay here until he returns. That's what I plan to do."

I swallow a gulp of frustration as she collapses stubbornly onto a straight-backed chair she's turned to face the door. I notice a slender, lethally sharp saber sitting on the end table beside it. When she sees me looking, Carys shrugs. Her lips curl up at one side and a ghost of humor drifts through her eyes.

"I'm no Ember Guild member, but Uther taught me well enough to stop anything that comes through that door."

"I'm relieved I have you two fearsome ladies to protect me," Farley says with only the slightest edge of mockery in his tone. Grinning, he slips the bow and quiver off his back and passes them to me. "Take this, Ace. You're a better shot than I am."

"But—"

"I'm covered." He gestures down to the short sword at his hip. "Just take it, would you? We both know I can't aim worth a damn when I'm leaning on a cane for support."

"Thanks," I murmur, fingers closing around the quiver. I feel instantly safer with a weapon in my hands.

Discussion stalls as we sit in the dark shop, flinching each time an explosion sounds in the distance. None of us has the heart to keep up the charade of normal conversation. Physically, we are in the room, and yet our hearts and minds are far beyond the confines of these four walls, caught up in the battle that rages on in the streets, coming closer and closer as the minutes tick by.

Certainly, there is horror in the fight; however, there is a different sort of horror in the wait for that fight to end. In sitting idly by, counting minutes, counting heartbeats, praying that the news, when at last it comes, will be good.

I have never before felt so useless. A pathetic girl in a pretty dress, sitting in the shadows, hiding out instead of helping.

What have you spent these past weeks teaching her?

I am a failure. I have no aptitude for maegic, no ability to keep anyone safe. Would that this gift had passed to someone else. Someone worthy of it. Someone who could actually be of some consequence in a war zone, instead of hiding out like the worst sort of coward.

One haunting thought chases another across my mind, a dark circle that snakes through me and coils at the center of my chest. My Remnant burns, a constant reminder of my own stagnation.

"*Carys . . .*" I try again when a blast hits so close, the chandelier rattles over our heads and several bolts of fabric tumble to the floor. "We should really—"

"I'm not leaving," she repeats for the umpteenth time, digging in her heels. "Uther said—"

"Uther did not know the severity of this situation!" I cast a desperate look at Farley, but he merely grimaces, at a loss for what to do. We can't exactly drag her, kicking and screaming, into a battlefield with a baby in her arms. No sooner can we leave her here alone.

We are stuck.

"At least take the baby and get out of sight," I plead with my pigheaded friend. "If the fighting reaches us . . ."

Carys heaves an annoyed sigh but ultimately does as I bid, moving toward the rear sitting area. She drags her saber with her.

Farley blows out a tense breath. "Stubborn as an ox, that one."

"She's scared. She doesn't want to leave her home."

"She may not have a choice, Ace."

The sounds of battle edge closer, increasing in decibel as the bloodshed spills outward from the breached tunnel down King's Avenue, into surrounding neighborhood squares and side alleyways, and, eventually, onto the quaint cobblestones of High Street. I listen to its approach, a melody unique to wartime—the heartrending peal of screams, the piercing clash of blades, harmonizing into an anguishing din that grates at both the ears and the heart.

All too soon, the fight rages right outside our door. I tuck a high-backed chair beneath the knob, but I know the barricade is flimsy at best. Scurrying up into the window display, I squeeze between two mannequins and press my face against the glass pane to get a look outside.

"Rhya—"

I silence Farley with a terse hand gesture. People are running down the street, their faces streaked with dust and grime and blood. Not soldiers but civilians, many of them still clad in their fanciest Fyremas attire. My heart lurches when I see a mother dragging two children in her wake, desperation contorting her face as their tiny feet stumble.

"To the keep!" a Dyvedi soldier is shouting as he runs in the opposite direction, pointing wildly over his shoulder. "Take shelter in the keep!"

The door of the shop directly across the lane cracks open. I watch two cloaked female figures dart out, not even pausing long enough to turn the locks. The cobbler and her wife join the fray of fleeing Caelderans and disappear. One shop down, the apothecary's hammer and planks lie abandoned in front of his half-boarded windows.

The fleeing crowd thins, then tapers off until only a handful of stragglers streak past the window, heading in the direction of the marketplace and the palace beyond. When a shadow lurches to a stop at the front door, my heart seizes in panic. I realize it is not an enemy as desperate fists pound and a familiar voice calls out.

"Carys! Gods, Carys, are you in there?"

Hopping down from the window display, I tear away my makeshift barricade, pull back the bolt, and yank open the door as quickly as my shaking hands allow.

"*Keda?*"

"Rhya!" She gapes at me, eyes wild. Her slim face is coated in grime except for twin trails down each cheek, where tears stream in a steady torrent. Her dress hem is in tatters. Her arms reach out for me, like I might pull her physically to safety. "Thank the gods! Please, let me in! I tried to make it to the palace, but they're coming, they're *here*, and I—"

She never finishes her sentence.

Her hands are still reaching out for me when the tip of a blade plunges through her heart.

CHAPTER
THIRTY-TWO

Keda's body hits the ground at my feet.

The Reaver who killed her jerks his weapon free, grunts, and spits—a gob of saliva flying from his iron-pierced lips to the sidewalk. His eyes are completely devoid of emotion as they lift to mine. His head cocks to one side, regarding me like a quarrelsome pest to be exterminated.

He raises his sword once more.

I do not think. I merely react, the coiled snake of power in my chest striking out before I can second-guess it. My palm comes up and shoots a stream of pure, focused air directly at the Reaver's chest. He flies backward like a puppet on invisible strings, sailing clear across the street and smashing through the window of the cobbler's shop. I stare at the jagged hole his body leaves behind for a fleeting moment, hoping he will not come back through it.

Hoping he is dead.

When he does not reappear, I drop to my knees on the sidewalk. Keda is already gone. A pool of blood surrounds her prone form, seeping into the fabric of her pretty yellow dress. She'd been embroidering it for weeks, stitching tiny, perfect daffodil blooms along the sleeves and hemline. For spring, she insisted, there was nothing like daffodils.

She will never see them bloom again.

She will never see anything again.

Her eyes, always so bright before, are sightless as they stare upward at the midnight sky. I swipe my hand across her face to close them, then get shakily to my feet. The street is abandoned. Everyone has fled or been killed trying. My gaze follows the sound of glass shattering to the end of the block, where three more Reavers are bashing out windows with their axe handles. They move methodically down the row of shops, thorough in their destruction. I do not take my eyes off them as I reach into the quiver across my back and pull an arrow free.

If I could feel anything but numb in this moment, I might be afraid. They are a fearsome sight—clad in leather and fur pelts, tattoos snaking across their pale skin in otherworldly patterns that make them, even as mortals, appear more maegical than any fae I have ever met. Their hair is twisted into braids, their cheeks streaked with black war paint. Discs of dark iron wrap their wrists and pierce their brows, thread through their lobes and bolt their nipples. Around their necks, displayed on lengths of rope, lumpy bits of flesh hang like jewelry.

Fae ears.

"Another damned point! Over there!"

They've spotted me. They roar as they charge, their guttural war cries ringing in my ears. I step carefully around my dead friend to meet them head-on, casting out a prayer that Carys and Farley are wise enough to bolt the door. I do not glance back to check as I lift my bow.

The first Reaver catches an arrow between the eyes. The second through the heart. The third makes it too close for me to fire. With a flick of my wrist, I send him flying across the street, a stream of air blasting from me like a cracking whip. He hits the stone wall of the apothecary's shop headfirst. I hear the snap of his neck and a grim sort of satisfaction bubbles beneath the icy well of detachment within my chest.

Four men dead at my hands. Five, including Gower. Five tally marks on my soul. Five cracks in the foundation of my once-pristine morality.

And I cannot bring myself to care.

I feel cold as ice. Cold as my Remnant mark. Cold as Keda's body will grow, lying in the rubble as the city comes apart around her.

"Rhya!" Farley is shaking me. "Rhya, are you all right?"

I blink, startled by the sight of him. I had not heard him leave the shop, but here he is—standing on the street, his red hair shining in the firelight that still burns all around us in merry torches, the only remaining vestige of a ruined celebration.

Carys stands beside him, baby Nevin bound against her chest to free up her hands. She clutches the saber in a white-knuckled grip.

"Keda is dead," I tell her, barely recognizing my own voice. It is empty. Eerily empty. As though all my emotions have been cleaved out.

"I know," Carys whispers. Her eyes are full of tears as they flicker behind me, to where the Reavers lie dead. "Rhya, love . . ."

I shake my head. "More will come. We cannot stay here."

There is no more argument from Carys. Not this time. We move in silence, picking a path through the streets to the palace—a walk I have made nearly every day since I first arrived in this city. A walk I have done so many times, I could probably find my way back blindfolded. It typically takes me no more than a half hour, if I am in a hurry.

Tonight, the journey lasts far longer. Our progress is excruciatingly slow. Carys has the babe to carry, and Farley, gods bless him, is only able to move so fast with his cane. My feet itch to run. My body crackles with unexpended power as I creep around corners, checking for threats before waving my friends forward. We pass the bank, its stately windows smashed, and hurry by the blacksmith, his forge gone cold.

At the start, we see no one. No one save the dead, left to lie on the streets where they have fallen. Some are missing their ears—taken as trophies by the Reavers who cut them down. I swallow hard and avert my gaze.

As we near the lakeshore, the very air grows perfused with an apprehension that makes all the hair on the back of my neck stand on end. The sounds of battle rise from an undercurrent to a crushing riptide, washing over us without relent. Carys's and Farley's faces are the picture of trepidation as we reach the perimeter of the marketplace.

We all draw up short, stunned into stillness.

Tonight, there are no happy vendors selling spices, stirring wine, roasting chestnuts; no patrons wandering the stalls with fat coin purses, bartering for the freshest produce. No. Tonight, it is a graveyard. A pile of dead, Reaver and Caelderan alike, tangle together like partners in a macabre dance that will outlast any fiddler's tune. The ancient apothecary is slumped by my favorite fountain, his wizened hands clutching the belly wound that killed him. None of the powerful elixirs he stocks in his orderly shop can call him back.

"Gods help us," Farley mutters, tracing a three-fingered sigil in the air, the meaning of which I can only guess. "Gods help us all."

Under her breath, Carys chants the words of a prayer. I catch snippets as we move across the marketplace. ". . . may their souls journey safely from shadow into flame, from flame into aether . . ."

I say nothing, gripping my bow tighter. Trying not to look too closely at the carnage. We are halfway across the square when a woman starts screaming for help—a sound of such suffering, we all glance at one another in alarm. I jolt into motion only to pull up short, remembering my companions.

"For gods' sake, *go!*" Carys cries, pushing at my back. "We'll only slow you down. We can make it the rest of the way without you."

"But—"

"Rhya." Farley grips his sword tightly. "There are people who need your protection far more than we do tonight. We are well armed and well trained. We know the way. *Go.*"

The woman shrieks again, a bloodcurdling wail.

"Just . . . get to the keep!" I bark at Farley and Carys, blinking back tears. "I'll catch up as soon as I can!"

"Be careful!" Carys calls after me.

But I am already running. The woman's screams are fainter now. I follow them down a short alleyway that splits in two, picking the leftward fork at random. Hoping it might lead me to her. In my head, I see that mother with her two tiny children, running for their lives. I see more bodies being added to that pile in the marketplace.

I run faster, bounding on currents of wind. Practically *flying*. Barreling from the mouth of the empty alley, I suddenly find myself on King's Avenue. Battle rages on all sides. Guild members and common foot soldiers swing broadswords and shields against the Reavers' double-bit battle-axes. There is no sign of the woman whose cries drew me into the fray, nor is there any chance to find her. The moment my foot hits the street, I am ducking blows and spinning beyond the reach of blades.

My hands move without executive command, firing on autopilot. I let my arrows fly, one after another, taking down more Reavers than I can count. When I spot a fallen Dyvedi archer with a near-full quiver on his back, I snatch it up without thinking twice.

He will not need it anymore.

In the distance, I spot Cadogan leading a charge of troops toward the tunnel, sword held aloft as they drive the enemy back from whence it came. Jac is by his side, matching his strikes, his axe swinging like a windmill above his head. A bit of the ice encasing my heart cracks open when I see them.

Still alive.

Still fighting.

I waste several precious seconds looking for Penn but cannot find him anywhere. He is likely by the tunnel where the fighting appears thickest, taking on half the invaders singlehandedly—even exhausted nearly to his limits. I can sense only the faintest pulse of his maegic through the bond. It lets me know he is still alive.

For now, that is enough.

I move in the direction of the lake, slipping through pockets of combat like a ghost. My arrows find their marks. I lose track of how many lives I take, how many Reavers I bring down. I no longer care to tally them, even if I know that later, when all this is over, I will carry the weight of their deaths on my heart for the rest of my life.

I have nearly reached the bridge when a shadowy figure appears in my peripheral vision without warning. I whirl around, bow aloft, arrow nocked, string taught. My hands still as I recognize the set of crystalline-blue eyes looking back at me.

"Hello, skylark," Soren practically purrs. Maegic hums in the air around him, thick as syrup. His irises are liquid with it, churning like the deepest ocean currents, the blue striated with silver. He wears no weapons that I can see and seems not at all ruffled by the absolute chaos unfolding to every side.

"Soren," I say dumbly, staring at him.

"Behind you."

"What?"

His eyes flash with annoyance as he sidesteps me. I pivot to see a Reaver not five paces away, his battle-axe lifting for what will surely be a death blow. Or what would have been.

The warrior's face, contorted in battle fury, shifts to something akin to panic. His weapon clatters to the ground and he grabs at his throat, clawing with increasing zeal, as though his airway is blocked. Red mottles his cheeks. His eyes go blood-shot, then glaze over. He seems to be suffocating. Suffocating on nothing, so far as I can tell. Yet, when he collapses in a heap at my feet, going limp as death claims him, water floods from the corner of his slackened mouth.

"Drowning on dry land . . ." Soren tsk-tsks from beside me. "A shame he didn't have gills . . ."

"You—" I gape at him. "How did you do that?"

But Soren has no answer for me. He is already turning to face another string of attackers. I stand there, paralyzed, watching as he conjures a stream of water from the nearby fountain with no more than the flick of two fingers, then sends tendrils of it toward the trio of incoming Reavers.

He showed me this same trick once, the day we met—a dance of globules around a goblet. I remember thinking it was beautiful.

There is nothing beautiful about this.

The clansmen do not even have a chance to steel themselves as the water invades their mouths, their noses. Fills their throats, surges into their lungs. They drown where they stand, falling lifeless to our feet when their strength gives out.

"Gods," I whisper.

"Godlike though I may appear, I assure you I am not one."

Soren's eyes swim with so much maegic, it nearly overflows. Silver flashes in aqueous blue. "And you would not be so impressed by my power if you had learned to wield your own."

"You . . . you . . . you suffocated them."

"No, I drowned them. But if you desire, *you* could suffocate them. You could snatch the air from their lungs in a blink, wind weaver."

I start to shake my head, but another tattooed behemoth is running from the fray, eyes locked on us with deadly intent. I send an arrow flying through his heart before Soren has time to turn around.

"Thanks," he says drolly, blasting more tendrils of water at a group of nearby Reavers who have gained the upper hand over a contingent of foot soldiers.

"No problem," I mutter, firing two more arrows.

We fall into a natural attack rhythm, battling back to back as we make our way toward the lakeshore. He covers my blind side, I shield his. Together, we take down a fair number of the Reavers who are chasing terrified civilians as they flee onto the bridge—me with my bow, Soren with less conventional methods. He does not just favor water as a weapon; he fights like water. There is a fluid strength to his every action, a fathomless power fueling his every move and countermove.

"I'm almost out of arrows," I call over my shoulder to him. "If you happen to see a quiver—"

"You don't need arrows."

He declares this as he hurls a massive ball of lake water at a group of six charging warriors. It sweeps them backward across the sand, into the shallows. They swing their axes and brandish their fists, but there is no fighting this sort of enemy. Their heads vanish beneath the teal surface, never to reappear.

I glance at Soren. He isn't even winded. "A handy trick, that."

"Mmm."

"But I do need arrows," I say stiffly, reaching into my near-empty quiver. "If I'm going to be of any use."

He turns to face me. The perfect symmetry of his chiseled features is marred by the quirk of one dark brow. "You have a far better weapon at your disposal. You need only use it."

"I can't."

"Why?"

"I can't control my power like you do. It surges out in a blast, all at once, and . . . sweeps me away."

"Sweeps you away?"

"I lose control. Lose *consciousness*. And I don't favor my odds of survival if I spend the rest of the night asleep, at the mercy of anyone who stumbles across my body."

Soren's mouth is a flat line of disapproval. "Has Pendefyre taught you nothing at all?"

"He taught me to keep the storm inside contained!" I nock another arrow. It is one of my last. "To shut the gate within, so it does not rip off the hinges and kill me in the process."

He shakes his head and growls, "Godsdamned Pendefyre and his godsdamned need for control."

"Can we focus?" I fire an arrow at a particularly large Reaver who has cornered a family by the foot of the bridge. "There are more important things tonight than my inability to weave the wind."

"No, there aren't," he snaps, an uncharacteristic bolt of temper. His hand finds my arm and he jerks me to a stop. Beneath the maegic, his eyes are full of tightly leashed frustration. "Listen to me."

"Soren—"

"Pendefyre wants you to lock down your power because that's how he manages to coexist with his own. Like an alcoholic at the bottle, he consumes in extremes. All or nothing. Feast or famine. It is simpler for him to abstain when the alternative is annihilation." Soren leans in so his face is a hairsbreadth from mine. "But you do not share his vices. You do not possess the same issues with control. You simply need to learn to drink in moderation—and from someone who knows how."

I jolt back an inch. "I don't think—"

"Deep down, you know I am right. Think of the times your maegic has come to you naturally. Not when you've forced it out, not when you've coerced it with brute strength. When it flowed without thought, easy as a breath in your lungs."

I see my arrows sailing, always finding their marks. I see my feet flying over cobblestones, wings of air beneath me. I see my palms lifting, a pure blast of power sending Keda's killer through a windowpane.

All those times, I had not forced the maegic. I had not even thought about it. It had come to me just as Soren said—like a natural extension of self.

"Your power is not the problem," he murmurs. "Your teacher is."

I jolt. "But—"

"You are not like him, skylark. You are like *me*." Soren's liquid eyes are a roving tide, shifting over my face. His hand rises for the briefest moment to where my bodice plunges, coming to rest on the exposed whorls of my Remnant.

I nearly leap out of my skin. No one else has ever touched my bare mark before. It is excruciatingly sensitive under his fingers, the skin tingling in a way that makes it impossible to breathe, let alone speak.

"You said there is a storm inside you—one that needs taming. I'm going to let you in on a little secret," he tells me softly. The tingling intensifies, a flood of pure sensation, as he sends a pulse of maegic directly into my skin. "It is not a monster to be shoved into a cage, nor a daemon to be subdued. There is no storm to tame. *You* are the storm, Rhya Fleetwood."

We jerk apart as another group of Reavers run at us, shattering the moment. But as I reach for another arrow in my quiver, I cannot stop thinking of Soren's words and what they will mean for my future . . . assuming any of us lives through this night.

You are not like him, skylark.

You are like me.

My quiver is empty when I catch sight of a familiar face racing toward the bridge. Racing toward me. His gray hair streaks back from his face as he runs to my side. In his eyes, worry wars with steadfast composure.

"Uther!"

"Have you seen Carys?" He is winded and sweaty but otherwise appears unharmed. "I went to the shop; there's no sign—"

"She and Farley were making their way to the keep, last I knew. I was with them until we hit the marketplace, but I got drawn into the battle and lost track of them."

His worried gaze sweeps the lakeshore. My own follows, widening in surprise at what I see. The fighting is dying down. The sand is littered with dead—mostly Reavers, I note with no small amount of satisfaction. The few who remain alive are being driven back down King's Avenue. Some are fleeing outright toward the tunnel. However impossible, it seems that we might actually win this fight.

"I'm sure Carys and Nevin are safe inside the keep," I assure Uther, grabbing his hand and giving it a reassuring squeeze. "She did not want to leave the shop. She wanted to wait for you there. But when the fighting hit High Street, I gave her no choice."

"You did the right thing. Thank you, Rhya. For going to her, and for forcing her to head for safety. I know how stubborn my wife can be."

"Oh, she would've been just fine without me. She has her saber, after all."

He smiles. "I'm relieved to hear it. Still, I'll feel better when I confirm it with my own eyes. We have seen heavy losses—soldier and civilian."

"But the worst of the fighting seems to be over."

"For now," he agrees. "Pendefyre and Mabon have sealed the tunnel again. For how long, we cannot say. Whatever enemies remain in the city are being executed by Cadogan's and Jac's units as we speak. But the clans are only a precursor. Efnysien's army awaits outside the city perimeter. Five thousand men in red, prepared to crush us if the Reavers do not succeed."

I inhale sharply. "So many."

"Take heart, Rhya. All is not yet lost." He clasps me lightly on the arm. "Not while we still have breath left to do battle. No matter how dark the night, dawn always arrives eventually."

"And with it, a full battalion of Llŷrian reinforcements," I say, as much for his benefit as my own.

"Never thought I'd see the day King Soren fought shoulder to shoulder with the soldiers of Dyved." He looks past me to the sandy shore. I follow his gaze to the Water Remnant, who is simultaneously drowning two iron-studded warriors in the shallows. Even from this distance, I can see the ultra-bright flash of his grin.

"Can't say he hasn't been useful," Uther murmurs. "He's nearly cleared the whole shoreline. Should make it easier to get folks into the keep, where it's safe."

"I'll help direct them."

"Thanks, Rhya," he says, but his eyes are on the bridge, where a steady stream of people are still making their way toward the proffered sanctuary of the palace. I know he is looking for

Carys and Nevin in the crowd. Just as I know he will not be able to think of anything else until he knows they are safe.

"Go on," I urge gently. "Go see if you can find them."

"There's no time."

"Uther. This may be the *only* time." I grab his hand again. "The red army may wait until dawn to unleash fresh hell upon us. Or they may not. We may survive the night. We may not. Either way . . . you'll fight better knowing your family is behind those thick stone walls."

Uther hesitates for a moment, weighing personal desire against his unshakable sense of responsibility.

"Penn would want you to take care of your family," I add softly. "He would not fault you for this."

I see the moment he makes his decision; his steady gray eyes light with pure, unadulterated relief. He shoots me a fleeting smile as he takes off toward the bridge. His words carry back to me as he melds into the crowd.

"I'll be right back!"

I lose sight of him almost instantly. He must be no more than a fourth of the way across when an earsplitting clatter draws my attention sharply upward. I can scarcely believe what I am seeing at first.

Rocks are plummeting down the cliffs to either side of the waterfalls, a great avalanche of stone. Boulders big as wagons roll from the upper reaches, shattering houses into splinters as they tumble toward the ground. At first, I think it must be a rockslide— that perhaps the foundations of the city shook loose as the wards fell, destabilizing the petrified lava flows that encircle us. But the origins of this avalanche soon become alarmingly apparent.

All the blood leaves my face at the sight of the mammoth forms climbing over the rim of the crater. They are vaguely human-shaped, but that is where the similarities end. At least five times the height of the average man, their skin is the grayish-white hue of a frozen lake, their clothing a cobbled mess of hides from dozens of animals. Hanks of dirty hair hang down around wide-set eyes in blunt-featured faces. They have no weapons. They do not need them.

I know, even before I hear it confirmed by the screaming soldier ten paces from me on the shore, what they are.

"ICE GIANTS!"

They scale the walls like I might shimmy down a tree, their colossal feet crashing through the copper rooftops of homes that cling to the highest reaches of the cliffs. I hope like hell that those who live there have already evacuated.

Horse-sized hands close around rocks and pieces of shattered foundation. There is no time to prepare as the giants begin hurling debris onto the city. It rains down, smashing through buildings and splashing into the lake. Ants beneath a hailstorm, we scatter in every conceivable direction along the shore, seeking cover wherever it can be found. I find myself completely alone, dodging and weaving, one eye fixed on the sky for incoming projectiles, the other trying to chart a safe course through the panicked crush. Helplessness crackles in my veins.

Only moments ago, I thought we had the upper hand, that the battle might be over. Now, as I watch the ice giants making their way down the cliffs, my throat tightens so much I can no longer pull in breath.

"Watch out!"

The cry comes a split second before what looks like the foundation of a house hurtles through the air, toward the stretch of shore where I, along with about a dozen soldiers, am seeking shelter. Their battle-weary faces contort in terror as they catch sight of the death heading straight for us.

My hand shoots up without thought, rising high over my head, my fingers flexed straight. I call the wind and, in a blink, it comes—unfurling from my chest in a thick coil. I take a breath and give it shape, envisioning a solid wall of air dense enough to stop just about anything, large enough to shield everyone around me.

I stumble backward as the heavy chunk of foundation slams into my air shield, feeling like I've been socked in the gut. But I merely grit my teeth and, with a grunt of exertion, shove with all my might. The foundation lurches backward, then lands in the lake with a massive splash. The soldiers shoot me looks of gratitude before they bolt off the sand, out of range of whatever the giants choose to toss next.

Luckily for those of us on the ground, most of their attention is focused on the palace. For every boulder that hits the city, three pelt the keep's stone walls, where so many Caelderans have gone to seek shelter.

Where Carys, Nevin, and Farley have gone to seek shelter.

My eyes widen as I watch the spire where I sleep smashed to bits. The tower shakes beneath the onslaught. In increasing horror, I realize this was always their plan. A first wave to herd us like cattle into one convenient location. And just when we begin to lower our guard, a second wave to carry out the slaughter.

Distracted by dark thoughts, I bleat in undeniable terror as a boulder the size of a barrel hits the sand not six paces from me. Leaping backward, I collide with a warm, firm chest.

"You're okay," Penn rasps. "I've got you."

I whip around to look at him, drinking in the sight of his face—streaked with blood from a wound at his temple, covered in dust, dotted with sweat. The shadows under his eyes look like bruises. The sword in his hand is caked in gore and glowing red. I have less than a heartbeat to appreciate the fact that he is still breathing before his hand envelops mine and he starts tugging me along.

"Penn, they're attacking the palace—"

"I know." He sounds grim. "I need to get you clear, then I'll go back and help."

"Carys and Farley are in there!"

"No, they aren't." He pulls me up three wooden steps, onto the pier that runs the length of the lake. "There's a root cellar beneath the barracks. I brought them there myself."

"They're safe?"

"They're safe."

The warmth that floods me at this news is snatched away before it can take proper form. I dig in my heels, dragging Penn to a stop.

"Rhya, we can't stop here—"

"Uther."

His dark eyes narrow. "What?"

"Uther!" I dart a glance back at the palace. Thousands who fled there are now reversing course, streaming into the blood-stained ruins of their city as fast as their feet can carry them. I search in vain for a head of gray hair among them. "He's on the bridge. He went to find Carys in the keep. *I* sent him in there, Penn. We have to—"

My words splutter into useless silence. Because, as I watch, the tallest tower gives one last shudder as a boulder clips it in the middle, and it topples sideways. It collides with the middle tower, the crack of stone so loud it cleaves the atmosphere like thunder. Both turrets wobble for a moment, then fall as one from that impossible height all the way down onto the palace below. They crack the domed roof of the Great Hall like the shell of an egg, cave in the outer wall of the courtyard, then pitch forward onto the lake.

Onto the bridge.

Time seems to slow in the seconds before impact. From the safety of the shore, I watch as those stuck halfway across look up and see the sky falling down upon them. There is no time to move. No time to even scream. There is no escaping it. No out-running it. No air shield to save them from their fate. The impact shakes the whole city, a bone-rattling reverberation that echoes throughout the crater.

Hundreds of Caelderans are still on the bridge when it is bur-ied under tons of rock and stone. Nearly all of them innocent civilians.

At least one of them a soldier.

A decorated lieutenant of the Ember Guild.

A man of stalwart spirit and fierce loyalty and unflagging kindness.

A leader of men.

A loving husband.

A new father.

A friend.

My friend.

I'll be right back, he said to me.

The last words he spoke.

The last words he would ever speak.

In the silence that follows the fall, watching the teal waters of the lake swallow the mangled mess of stone, I feel my heart shat-ter into irreparable pieces.

"I sent him in there," I whisper brokenly. In the distance, screams rise to a crescendo. *"I sent him in there."*

There is no time to wonder about Uther, no time to mourn the unfathomable loss of so many all at once. With the palace brought down, the ice giants bellow guttural cries of victory that pierce my eardrums and chill my heart.

Then they begin to climb down into the city.

"Form ranks!" Penn yells. "Jac, Cadogan, Mabon—gather your men! Take position at the shoreline!"

I cannot move. I cannot breathe. I can only watch as my friends fire orders at their units, swords at the ready as they prepare to face this new threat. Dyvedi foot soldiers form orderly lines along King's Avenue, preparing for a second bombardment. Soren, shoulders tense, fixes his eyes on the fallen palace and the giants who brought it down.

There are ten of them, by my count, each as tall as a building and nearly as wide. They wade across the lake, waist-deep in the teal water, their sights fixed on us with lethal promise.

They will kill us all, I think, watching them come closer. *Stomp our city flat beneath their feet. Devour us whole and use our bones as toothpicks when they are finished . . .*

"Crossbows!" Mabon bellows from the left flank. "On my signal!"

A volley of bolts sails across the lake. Many find their marks, striking the giants in their arms, their legs, their fleshy abdomens.

Still, they keep coming.

"Archers, hold steady!" Jac commands from the right flank. A line of men with longbows draw back their bowstrings. *"Fire!"*

The arrows, too, hit home. But the giants pause for no longer than a breath—momentarily annoyed by the barrage of pointy sticks ricocheting off their skin, but not deterred. Their anemic faces are set in masks of rage as they continue to wade our way. The lake steams around them as they move through it, their flesh so cold it instantly turns the surrounding water to frozen pulp.

I understand now why they are called ice giants. It is not so much their hoarfrost skin, nor their inclination to make their homes in the coldest reaches of the world. It is the utter lack of warmth in their eyes. Their stares are cold as death, unfeeling as the snow of the Cimmerians. I have never felt so sure of my own impending death as I do in that moment, standing on the shoreline, watching them approach. The soldiers around me shuffle nervously. Someone is praying under his breath, a plea on the wind.

". . . may ever the gods shield those who are faithful and true . . ."

The giants cross the midway point.

"Swords at the ready!" Cadogan is yelling at his contingent of soldiers. "Shields aloft!"

But I am no longer paying much attention to the soldiers. I am, instead, fixated on the sight of the two men standing side by side at the water's edge. Both broad of shoulder, their stances a mirror of sheer fortitude. Through the bond, I feel a surge of power unlike any I have experienced before.

As one, their arms lift. In Penn's hands, twin balls of flame; in Soren's, two massive globes of water. Like a dance they choreographed so long ago the steps are ingrained in the marrow of their bones, their maegic blasts out across the lake in a coordinated attack. Fire engulfs two of the ice giants, burning their frosted skin and catching their hair. They roar in pain and fury, clutching their melting faces and stumbling backward.

Soren brings two others down. Water invades their gaping mouths, just as it had the Reavers in the streets. They choke and gag, their mammoth hands grabbing uselessly at their throats as they slip beneath the surface. The water is quick to close over their heads, a current under Soren's command.

Mabon's and Jac's voices ring out, calling volley after volley of arrows and bolts. Penn's immolating giants lose their battle. They, too, are swallowed by the lake.

Four down.

Six remaining.

They march on, water surging around their waists. Three-quarters of the way across now and gaining speed. If Soren and Penn can take them down, perhaps we are not done for after all. Perhaps we will not perish. Perhaps—

I feel the moment Penn's maegic splutters to an end, his fire extinguishing. He has pushed himself beyond the pale this night, has given all of himself. Both muscle and maegic. His knees hit the sand, his shoulders concave as he gasps for breath, then collapses forward in a heap. Panic sluices through me as I see him fall. Through our bond, he is no more than a faint flicker. A brittle heartbeat, only half breathing.

I come unglued from my spot behind the contingent of swordsmen—the city's last line of defense. Penn told me, in a tone of granite, that under no circumstances was I to leave their ranks. I agreed, then. But that was before. Before I watched him burn out. Before I saw Soren grappling with the six remaining giants at once, his face a portrait of strain.

I run down the shore on winged feet, crossing the divide in three great strides. My heart is a battering ram, slamming against my rib cage as I sail to a halt between the two men. Soren, to my left, still battling; Penn, to my right, barely breathing.

In the distance, soldiers are shouting orders, sending volleys across the sky. Their voices are snatched away beneath the growing roar of wind that sweeps across the lake, churning still water into froth. Their arrows are yanked off course as the air through which they fly begins to whip round and round, a torrent gathering strength, growing faster and faster with each passing second. Sand kicks up around me, forming a funnel cloud. I allow my arms to extend at my sides, the golden sleeves of my dress flapping wildly as the sheer force of the tornado I have unleashed lifts me off my feet.

Soren's eyes flicker to me—just once, just for a second. Long enough for me to see the surprise in their depths as he beholds me rising into the sky. Higher and higher. I am nearly at eye level with the ice giants now. They stare at me, not twenty paces away, their vacuous gazes struggling to comprehend what they are seeing. Their steps falter, a moment of uncertainty.

I close my eyes.

You are the storm, Rhya Fleetwood.

And I am. I feel it there, inside me, not so very deep beneath the surface. A hurricane, a tempest. Dark clouds swirl, spurred by destructive winds. I do not attempt to tame them. Instead, I pull them close—invite them out to play like old friends, long overdue for a visit.

For so many years, I feared the darkness inside. All my life, afraid of what I was. Of who I was. I'd been running long before I ever left Seahaven. Holding back those clouds for fear of what would happen if I allowed them to close in.

I am not running anymore.

I let the darkness fold over me. Surge through me. Under my skin, into my marrow. I let it take me in its arms and waltz me, slowly, toward the end. And it is not half so dark as I had feared. For inside those clouds, there is light. Not the sun shining through, nor the heat of flame . . . but the white-hot flash of an electrical current, striking across my storm.

I taste copper on my lips and know my eyes are leaking blood. Electricity sparks down my spine, tiny volts of pain. Every hair on my body stands on end as the air inside my tornado turns to pure static. My chest aches like one of the ice giants has closed a fist around it and is gradually squeezing the life from me. But I cling to my last remaining shreds of cognizance, letting the maegic gather strength, letting the charge build within me until I cannot hold it any longer.

My eyes slit open at the moment of release. The bolts race through me, shooting from the mark at my breast, then down my arms and out my fingertips.

Lightning.

It branches out in beautiful arcs, hitting the ice giants squarely at the center of their chests, piercing the surface of the water. The lake absorbs the charge, then amplifies it a thousandfold, the water conducting the electricity in an outburst that illuminates the night sky to daylight.

The giants writhe as they are electrocuted. Eyes rolling white, toothless mouths gaping, spines arching as convulsions splice their bones. Their bodies are no more than steaming husks when the lighting storm finally dissipates.

I smile at the sight as my own body, pushed past the point of all endurance, loses hold of the vortex keeping me aloft. I plummet back to earth in a tangle of gold skirts. I do not even have the strength to try to catch myself.

Thankfully, Soren is there to do it for me.

He lets out a low grunt as his arms close around my body. I can do no more than blink up at his face as he cradles me to his chest.

"A handy trick, that," he says, eyes swirling with maegic and something else. Something like wonderment.

My lips part to respond, but I cannot quite manage it. My strength is flagging, my consciousness hanging by a thread. As Soren's gaze roves over my face, reading the exhaustion etched across my features, he sends a sudden pulse of pure power straight into my chest, lending me a bit of his seemingly bottomless reserves. It crashes through me like a tsunami and coils around my aching Remnant. It feels different from Penn's—not a heated scorch, but a soothing swell. Shoring me up from the inside out, until my very soul feels saturated with his mercurial brand of maegic.

Still, it is not enough to keep me from fading.

A dark sea of exhaustion is beckoning me into the depths.

My lids flutter shut.

And I slip under.

WHEN I AWAKEN, I am lying on a simple pallet in an unfamiliar room. The flaming mountain of Dyved is painted over the door. A rack of weaponry rests against the wall. It takes me a moment to realize I must be in the soldiers' barracks.

Every muscle in my body protests as I push to my feet. My head spins so much, I have to catch myself with one hand on the wall before I collapse. I wait until the waves of dizziness subside before I leave the room.

Outside, it is chaos. The communal dining room has been turned into a makeshift field hospital. Injured Caelderans are everywhere, draped over tables, slung across stacks of chairs, being treated by anyone with a free set of hands. Before I've made it three feet, I find myself assisting an old woman who is attempting to wrench a soldier's dislocated shoulder joint back into place. When the deed is done, she meets my eyes—the first time she's truly looked at me since I stopped to help—and gapes.

"Wind weaver." Her whisper is reverent. She makes the sign of the tetrad in the air. "Gods bless you."

I do not know how to respond to that, so I merely nod and continue on my way. There are more survivors than I'd dared hope for, with all manner of battle wounds. I've stopped again to help—this time aiding a set of distressed parents who are stitching up a rather nasty gash in their daughter's leg—when I feel the warmth of Penn's presence.

He waits until I am done bandaging the wound before he claims me. He says nothing as he comes to a stop by my side, merely intertwines my fingers with his and leads me slowly out of the sickbay, into the early light of day. The sparring pits outside house more survivors. I spot the old chestnut roaster moving among them, passing out parcels of steaming nuts to bleary-eyed Caelderans. His wrinkled face is streaked with blood and etched with sorrow, but he manages a small, gap-toothed smile when our gazes catch.

Penn leads me down toward the lake. There are still bodies littering the shore, blood staining the sand. His jaw is tight with tension. The air is heavy with unspoken words.

Dawn has broken while I slept. I look around the ashen pallor of morning, stunned silent by the devastation. The palace has been reduced to a pile of rubble. The lake steams faintly, still far too hot to risk wading in. The surface is dotted with thousands of dead fish—unintentional casualties of my electrical storm.

I look for a long moment at the submerged remains of the bridge, buried beneath the fallen turrets. I know the answer to my question before I voice it. Still, I have to ask. Have to hear it spoken aloud before I can convince myself to believe it.

"Uther?" My voice cracks.

Penn shakes his head.

"Damn it." Tears—long held back during the endless night—fill my eyes. "*Gods damn it.*"

Penn says nothing at all. There is nothing to say. His friend is dead, his city in ruins. And yet, we are still here. Still alive. So he pulls me into his arms and lets me weep against the hollow of his throat. His chin comes down to rest upon the top of my head as he holds me close, his hands gripping me so firmly I can hardly draw breath.

"Carys is asking for you," he says when I've quelled my tears. "She's at her shop. She's . . . not doing very well."

I jerk my head back to meet his eyes. They are infinitely grave. "Does she know? That I was the one who sent him into the palace?"

"Rhya—"

"She will hate me." Another wave of tears threatens to overtake me. "And I cannot blame her for it. It's my fault."

"It is not your fault."

"I'm responsible. I practically killed him myself."

"You did not kill Uther." He shakes me lightly. "You saved countless lives during the battle. You saved us all, Rhya. Without you, we would be naught but pulp in the giants' hands. Carys knows that. Everyone knows it. One day, they will write songs of this battle, and sing of the wind weaver who cast a light in the darkest of moments."

My lips twist. I am not entirely sure I like the sound of that. Glancing around, I trace the lines of wreckage. It will take a long time to rebuild the fractured buildings and splintered homes. It will take even longer to heal the scars of all we have lost.

"Efnysien was already hesitant to enter the city when he heard Soren had joined the fight. But he turned tail and fled as soon as he saw your lightning," Penn tells me. "He realized, without the Reavers or the ice giants, he had little chance of taking the city. His army was already fleeing south by the time the Llŷrian troops arrived. Soren is chasing them from our borders as we speak. He wants nothing more than to tear his stepbrother limb from limb."

"He's not alone in that regard."

"We will have our chance at retribution, Rhya."

"You don't think Soren will catch him, then?"

Penn shakes his head. "Efnysien is a coward above all. He values his own life much more highly than those of his men or his allies in battle. He fears our maegic almost as much as he covets it. So, for now, he will flee back to his dark kingdom of sand and shadow to reevaluate his next plan of attack."

I swallow hard. "He will come back."

"He will come back," Penn agrees. His tone hardens into a vow. "And if he does not, it matters little. For I will hunt him down and eradicate him from this earth, even if it is the last thing I do. He will pay—in blood—for all that he has taken from us."

I shiver at the ferocity of his words. There is no doubting the truth in them. Efnysien has started a war. One we will finish.

For Keda.

For Uther.

For the hundreds lost.

For the futures stolen.

"Will Vanora sanction a war?"

Penn stills. "Vanora is dead, along with half the courtiers in the throne room. Crushed when the towers came down. The Ember Guild is still working to dig out any survivors."

"Gods."

He nods.

"Penn, I'm sorry." The words feel woefully inadequate in the wake of such sweeping loss. "I know your relationship was . . . *complicated*. But she was still your family."

"Vanora has never been my family. Not really." He looks at me again. His eyes burn like embers, smoldering even beneath the crushing sadness that presses down on us. "The only family I care for is the one of my own choosing. My horse. My men." He pauses. "You."

My heart flips inside my chest. I want very much to stretch up onto my tiptoes and press my mouth to his, but a thought occurs to me before I can act on the urge.

"Wait a minute—you're the king!"

"I suppose."

My eyes bug out of my head. "You *suppose*?"

"It doesn't change anything." He heaves an indifferent shrug. "I will continue on as I have for many years. I will rebuild my city, secure my borders, and see my people restored. And, when that is done . . ."

"War," I whisper.

"War," he confirms.

We stand there for quite some time, arms wrapped around each other's waists, staring at the shattered skeleton of the keep. Saying nothing. Eventually, I close my eyes, slipping into the calm center of my mind. I feel Penn—the thread that tethers us together. Flame and heat, a furl of warmth in the lapping waves.

But . . .

There is something else beneath the surface.

Another tether, wrapping around my soul. The same, and yet altogether different. Cool and crisp, fluid as water as it falls over the smoothest rocks of a riverbed. It stretches out beyond the crushed city. Beyond, even, the confines of the crater. And I know, in the depths of my soul, if I were but to follow it . . .

I would find myself face-to-face with King Soren of Llŷr.

Penn's arm tightens on my waist.

I open my eyes to meet his.

"Come," he whispers, brushing his lips against mine—light as a feather, but heavy with promise. "There's a world to remake."

GLOSSARY OF TERMS

Anwyvn—A land shared by mortals and fae.

Aurea Tree—A mythical golden tree at the heart of Seahaven's Starlight Wood.

Avian Strait—A narrow pass through the Cimmerian Mountains, the only known route into the Northlands and the site of many bloody battles.

cyntroedi—A variety of giant centipede, white in color with toxic green venom, found in dark underground climates.

Caeldera—The capital of Dyved, a city contained entirely within a dormant volcanic crater.

Cull—The uprising of mortal men against the fae race two hundred years ago.

culling priest—Holy men who hate the fae and preach on the need for blood purification in Anwyvn. Many claim to be descendants of the original priests who slew the emperor and his family.

Dyved—A Northlands kingdom occupying the plateau in the northwestern corner of Anwyvn, beyond the Cimmerian Mountains.

Ember Guild—A unit of highly trained warriors who answer directly to Prince Pendefyre of Dyved.

fyre priestess—A sect of holy women pledged to honor the God of Flame.

Fyremas—A Dyvedi holiday widely celebrated to mark the start of spring.

fyrewisps—A low class of fae, also known as will-o'-the-wisps or ghost lights, often seen floating in bogs or forests by travelers at night.

halfling—A human-fae hybrid from both bloodlines, typically powerless, only discernible from humankind by their pointed ears.

Hylios—The capital city of Llŷr.

ice giant—A legendary hoarfrost monster found mainly in the Frostlands and the Cimmerian Mountains.

leylines—A network of maegical threads deep in the earth that knit together the fabric of the realm.

Llŷr—A Northlands kingdom spanning the northeastern corner of Anwyvn, notoriously ruled by the bloodthirsty King Soren.

nymph—Slang for a fae with water powers.

Paexyri—Mythical mounts once ridden by fae riders in the time of maegic, said to run with twice the speed and stamina of a normal horse.

point—A derogatory term for fae kind.

portal—A maegical gateway in a place of power, allowing for instantaneous travel across the leylines of the land.

Remnant—One of four reincarnated vestiges of element power.

Red Chasm—A deep deposit of iron ore running through the Midlands.

Starlight Wood—A forest of ancient trees on the western shore of Seahaven, long rumored to be a place of great fae power.

sylph—Slang for a fae with air powers.

tetrad—The four Remnants.

Thawe Bridge—A rope suspension bridge at the southern foot of the Cimmerian Mountains, connecting the Northlands to the Midlands.

twyllo—A game of cards and wagers popular in the Northlands.

ACKNOWLEDGMENTS

Thank you, first and foremost, to you.

My readers.

When I stumbled backward onto this career path ten years ago, I was a broke college student armed with nothing but a handful of high hopes and a small mountain of student loans. I had no idea what I was doing or what to expect when my first novel entered the stratosphere. It so easily could've been a disaster.

But you—all of you—turned the most far-flung wishes into reality. You spun a spontaneous side-quest into the wildest ride of my life. I will never be able to express my gratitude to everyone with a JJ book on their e-reader or bookshelf. Your reviews, your fanart, your messages . . . your sheer enthusiasm for my words and characters . . . they are what keep me going day after day, when things get fuzzy around the edges and imposter syndrome inevitably creeps in.

You changed my life.

You made my life.

I must also express my dearest thanks to my agents at Bookcase Literary Agency, Flavia Viotti and Meire Dias, who did not laugh in my face when I told them I wanted to abruptly shift genres and explore the wide, wide world of fantasy. Thank you for coming along with me to Anwyvn, and for trusting me when I told you that this was a story my heart needed to tell. None of this would be possible without you.

To Sarah Blumenstock at Berkley, thank you for taking a chance on me (and Rhya). Your insights have been invaluable in turning this book into its best possible version.

To all the many sets of hands that touched this manuscript, from its initial draft form to the final version that appears on shelves, from designers to copyeditors to formatters to printers to cover artists to marketers to foreign language translators . . . I am in awe of your talents and perpetually amazed by your efforts. I couldn't ask for a better team at my back.

To my cat, Atticus, for screaming at inopportune times, chewing on every available piece of paper, ruining my writing flow, interrupting my sleep schedule, and, overall, being a nuisance . . . I cannot thank you, but I do still enjoy your presence. (Usually.)

Last, but never least, I must mention my family. Most especially, my parents, David and Christine. There is no "thank you" that can make up for your steadfast support during my moody stretches, your silent coffee deliveries when I am deep in the writing cave, your subtle prompts to perhaps take a walk because I've been at my desk for six straight days and have not seen sunlight or breathed fresh air. You are my eternal anchor, always keeping me grounded, and somehow simultaneously my springboard, setting me up to soar. I love you.

JULIE JOHNSON is a New England native and internationally bestselling author. When she's not writing, Julie can most often be found adding stamps to her passport, drinking too much coffee, and avoiding reality by disappearing between the pages of a book. She published her debut novel on a lark, just before her senior year of college, and she's never looked back. Since, she has published twenty other novels, which have been translated into more than a dozen different languages and appeared on bestseller lists all over the world, including *Der Spiegel*, *AdWeek*, *Publishers Weekly*, *USA Today*, and more.

VISIT JULIE JOHNSON ONLINE
JulieJohnsonBooks.com
Author_Julie
AuthorJulie
JulieJohnsonBooks

Ready to find
your next great read?

Let us help.

Visit prh.com/nextread

Penguin
Random
House